JACK DILLON:

INTO THE DARK VOID

J.T. SPEARS

JACK DILLON: INTO THE DARK VOID

iUniverse books may be ordered through booksellers or by contacting:

iUniverse
1663 Liberty Drive
Bloomington, IN 47403
www.iuniverse.com
844-349-9409

ISBN: 978-1-6632-4770-4 (sc)
ISBN: 978-1-6632-4771-1 (e)

Print information available on the last page.

iUniverse rev. date: 12/07/2022

PROLOGUE

"YOU'LL NEVER DO business in this sector again!" The furious serve-bot shouted after the drones as they rushed towards the edge of his landing-platform built on the face of one of Brashnore's craggy mountains.

There's no way the Regent of an entire planet should be treated like this. Insulted. Swindled. Taken for a ride. Scammed, like some mindless vendor droid plucked off the assembly line.... No, Whaapco thought. Two of Piilor Syndicate's top commanders lay dead inside his palace. Murdered! And not to mention the six merchants––claiming to be Jaanloch's servants––that had just broken out of their prison, destroyed his demolition droid, and attacked the Viceroy of Kraaglor Front. "Tell Jaanloch, I'll have him exiled for this!!!" It was an act of war; that's what it was! He would never let them escape his planet alive.

"Get me the general," he ordered one of the guard-droids nearby. The last of the fugitives had just left his platform, leaping through the air in a high arch, but then crashing into one of its own. The violent collision sent them tumbling down the platform of another building, causing one to nearly going skidding over the edge.

The Regent fumed at the drones' good fortune. He spun around to face the droid. "I said get me the general! Can't you see that we're under atta––" He paused when the hazy hologram materialized before him and the wrinkled face of an alien––encased in a frame of obscuring static––appeared.

"Voch, here," the hologram said, scouring the Regent and his guards, with a pair of almond-shaped eyes that shimmered as if affected by the planet's strong winds. Those same eyes settled on the bits of rubble and debris strewn across the threshold of the palace's entrance; a real sign that some kind of battle, or explosion, had taken place. Most of the Regent's guards were still fixated on something beyond Voch's vision...something they longed for perhaps. Or an enemy, in who's face thy stood powerless.... The whole lot appeared beaten. Defeated.

How intriguing, Voch thought. The sight amused him. He now grew impatient to learn who––in all of Plogg–– would attack Whaapco? What business would any scourge of the sector, have with this miscreant serve-bot? And more importantly; who was bold enough to attack a high ranking member of the Kraaglor Front? "Why'd you hail me, Whaapco?" He asked, suppressing the strong desire to get a full report on the Regent's obvious and most recent troubles. He decided on a more subtle approach. For now, he would ignore his better sense.

"The Viceroy's under attack!" Whaapco said, floating like a drunk butterfly toward the hologram. "Omegon tribe-bots, disguised like merchants, infiltrated our world with designs on kidnaping His Highness. I tried to stop them, of course. But they were no regular tribe-bots. Our weapons had no effect on them. They wore some kind of protective armor––"

"Tribe bots?" Voch asked, remembering the attack on Mage City, on the planet Stong, that left dozens of traffic-monitors destroyed. One of the Viceroy's own guards had been the intended target in that attack.... But reports revealed that those bots had all been demolished.

"Yes general," Whaapco replied. "Six tribe-bots, in the company of Kapac and that ambitious Zhorg."

So there is a connection, Voch thought. But why would the Viceroy's own guards aid the assassins? It didn't make sense. "What of Kapac and Zhorg?" He asked. "What role did they play in all this? And where are they now?"

"They're both dead, sir."

"What!?"

"I swear, sir. I didn't know anything about any of this.... They came with their own designs, but something happened between them. For whatever reasons, Zhorg killed Kapac, then had the tribe-bots thrown in one of my dungeons. But the tribe-bots, sir...are no regular Omegon. They have special weapons; so powerful, they killed Zhrog and escaped. They destroyed at least 200 of my guards and one demolition droid, before grounding the Viceroy's ship as he was leaving the planet. And this is where we are now. They're on their way to kidnaping the Viceroy as we speak. You must hurry. There isn't much time."

Far from what the general of the most powerful syndicate in Plogg had expected. The Viceroy...? Things were much graver than he'd first thought. He now regretted not having intervened when that incident first occurred on Stong. It was a problem he'd left for the Piilor syndicate's leaders to deal with (seeing that it happened in their Province). But that was a mistake. Such an unprecedented attack on

Stong shouldn't have been taken so lightly. He should've intervened. However, he would do so now! "Stand by..." was all the instructions he left for Whaapco and his droids as his holographic image faded into the gust of a strong Brashnorean gale.

———◆———

The four AIWS-7285 class warships suddenly popped out of hyperspace in the blink of an eye, speeding toward an awaiting fleet of fighters near one of Brahnore's moon. The gleam of shiny metal was blinding. The colorful spectrum of the clustered stardust space reflected off the ships's hulls in a dazzling display of flashy strobes. Like bullish sharks, they moved (in silence) as if hunting prey to satisfy that long-lived hunger for war; even if such satisfaction might last for just that moment....

"Picking up a distress signal from the Viceroy's ship, general," said one of the droids, manning the helm on the bridge.

From where Voch stood, facing the long, curved port-side window, Brashnore was still a million miles away. Just a big gray hall, spinning slowly in a mist of purple and pink. Drannore, its much smaller moon, lay further beyond, hidden by the protective planet.

Voch took note of the many ships that still buzzed around Brashnore, and how things appeared as normal as they usually would. Other than the few skirmishes and rebellions during the Drofh occupancy (about three centuries in the past), Brashnore was still a peaceful planet. A rocky world, home to the gem-stone palaces, where kings and emperors held their lavish balls. The sight of his warships wouldn't escape notice so easily——and he was yet to know how strong of a force these merchants really were.

"The Viceroy's ship is requesting immediate assistance," the droid said. "They're taking heavy fire from the Omegon. Three of his guards are down."

"Voch turned from the window and walked to the helm. Behind his green, shriveled face, a smooth metallic surface rounded the back of his oval skull. On both sides of his head, two red eyes glowed as he came to where the droid sat. "Zhorgh placed his fleet in Drannore's orbit before going to Brashnore...Why would he do that?"

"The only rational answer to that question, sir...is most likely to prevent the Omegon from escaping."

"Then why are they ignoring the Viceroy's distress call?"

The droid paused and cocked its head inquisitively. "I don't know, sir. They should've been on Brashnore by now."

Voch gave a knowing nod before executing his next order. "Maintain our course to Drannore. Man all battle-stations. Send message to the planetary guard that no ship is to leave Brashnore at this time."

"Message sent."

"Good," Voch said. "Now that our ships are in this system, no one'll be able to escape this planet any time soon."

From the vantage point at the helm of his own starship, it seemed that the four gargantuan vessels of war had suddenly winked themselves out of existence, and all signs of an upcoming battle had somehow been avoided. Nor would it occur to the astonished passengers on the lumbering galactic starbus that their plans of travel would be abruptly canceled until the sudden appearance of Voch's terrifying ships near Drannore's southern hemisphere.

The armada beared down quickly on the sixteen fighters that had accompanied the tribe-bots on their errand. It disturbed Voch that Zhorg would aid in attacking the Viceroy. By the looks of his fleet, it would appear that the leader of the Piilar Syndicate was preparing for a fight. However, he wasn't preparing for the kind of encounter that would lead to an insurrection if the Piilar Syndicate did indeed have plans on taking over the sector. No...this seemed to be something else. A kidnaping...? Yes. But to what end...? "Hail the one in command of this fleet," he said, then waited patiently until the hologram of a droid's head appeared just a few inches above a crystallized table on the bridge.

"Yes, general," the droid said. A line of blue light flashed around its collar as it spoke. "I'm M'laan. The commanding officer of this fleet. How may I be of service, general Voch?"

"What is the purpose of your presence here, commander?" Voch asked.

"We were given orders to escort Zhorg, and six Omegon merchants, to Brashnore."

"Were you given a reason why?"

"No," the droid replied without hesitation. "We were given no further instructions, other than to remain here and wait for his signal.... Is something the matter?"

"The Regent's palace has come under attack."

"Attack!?" The droid seemed genuinely taken aback by the news. "But who, and why would anyone want to attack the Regent? And for what purpose?"

"According to the Regent," Voch began. "The merchants you escorted to the system, just so happened to destroy most of his guards, and is now attempting to kidnap the Viceroy of the Kraaglor Front."

"That's impossible, general!" The light in M'laan's coin-shaped eyes burned to the brightest shade of blue when he heard this. "I cannot believe that...there must be some mistake. If there was any trouble on Brashnore, Zhorg would've——"

"Zhorg's dead, commander," Voch cut in. "And so's Kaypac...killed by Zhorg's own hand. I was told that some kind of dispute was taking place between them. And the Regent said that Kaypac was already on Brashnore, days before your own fleet arrived. Do you know why, commander? Why was Kaypac on Brashnore?"

"I——I do not know, general." M'laan faltered as he replied, realizing that he'd been kept in the dark on certain details in their mission. "I was just ordered to escort the Omegon here."

"And what of the Viceroy's distress signal? Surely, you must've received it by now."

"Yes, general.... We did receive the Viceroy's signal. But as you well know, as a commander of Piilor's entire fleet, I'm only obligated to the last order given, regardless of the circumstances. And my last order, was to remain here until Zhorg commanded otherwise."

"I see..." said Voch, finally deciding to carry out his next order. He motioned to a subordinate nearby with a subtle nod. Seconds later, the entire bridge came under a dark reddish glow as the warship's battle-stations became fully active.

"What!?" Though M'laan knew his fleet was about to be engaged by the superior warships, he remained puzzled as to what he should do next. It was all happening too fast... but there must be something he could do to avoid a fight with Kraaglor. So, as a show of good faith, he decided not to give the order to ready his fighter for a battle. He didn't even give the command to raise shields. "What is this, general? We are your second most powerful allies in the sector. Any hostilities between us now will cause a civil war!"

"A Regent of Kraaglor has come under attack by the Piilor Syndicate, commander. And so has the Viceroy.... That in itself, is an act of war. Though I do believe that you had no knowledge of Zhorg and Kaypac's attempts to compromise the powers of the United Order of Kraaglor. It has now become evident that certain seeds of insurrection have been sown into place. And in light of all that has happened, I don't see why the Piilor Syndicate should hold any more prongs of power within this sector any longer."

Before M'laan had the chance to dispute Voch's assertions, all transmissions between the two ships were suddenly cut, causing the hologram of his head to wink itself out of sight.

"Destroy them all" Voch said, to his subordinate.

In the misty swirl of Brashnorian space, a thick barrage of plasma spewed from the warships' mega cannons, lighting the thin purple stardust with exploding fighters.

Having neither the firepower, nor speed to out-run their new enemy, what remained of Zhorg's fleet fell under the heavy assault. No more than a minute went by before the last rail guns blew the last fighter to bits, and tons of debris now littered the space just outside of Drannor's orbit.

With no further concerns, the four warships turned from their own site of destruction and flew right into the thin Brashnorian atmosphere. Within seconds, their massive hulls came drifting slowly over the infamous Flawn City—— Brashnore's largest metropolis——built and founded by the Regent himself.

"Tracking the Viceroy's signal now, sir," said the droid at the helm. "His ship's badly damaged, incapable of flying."

"How far until we get there?" Voch asked.

"We only have to clear the next mountain-range, sir. No more than a few miles ahead."

"Get there quickly, then," said Voch. "We've wasted enough time already. Command all ships to switch to stealth-mode."

"It is done, sir."

The four warships eased over the Flawn Mountain Range as silently as Brashnore's twin suns, making their daily trek across the planet's colorful horizon. Not a sound was heard from their mighty engines that pushed the behemoths forward while keeping them high above the city. Only their shadows could be seen, creeping over the land and darkening the sky, enveloping the light with as much dread as they were an awe to behold.... In such fashion they crept up on the drones, only coming out of stealth-mode upon their ghostly approach.

"We're not too late, sir," said the droid at the helm. "The Viceroy's unharmed and still inside his vessel. His guards have all been killed, though. All six Omegons are still in sight. It appears they're now trying to——"

"Tell them to surrender at once," Voch ordered. "We have them surrounded. There's no escape. The planetary guards has been alerted. Tell them...that if they surrender to us now, and free the Viceroy, that no harm will come to them."

There was a short pause as Voch waited for his orders to be carried out to the drones on the surface. They would wait for his orders to be repeated three more times before the droid spun back around. "They're ignoring us, sir. Two of the Omegon have just now apprehended the Viceroy from his ship....They're attempting to flee."

"Deploy five soldier units," said Voch, becoming irritated. "That should be more than enough to contain six tribe-bots."

"Units deployed, sir. But I'm getting a hail from another ship on the surface."

"What ship? Is it one of the Regent's guards?"

"No, sir. According to my readings, it's one of the Viceroy's."

"What...?" A puzzled Voch hurried over to the helm to get a good look at the ship's hologram. "Jherilon...!" He said, in a tone of disdain upon recognizing the distinct markings on the ship. In truth, it was Kaypac's vessel, but it was created by the Viceroy." Send him through."

A brief pause followed before Jherilon's soft voice was heard on the bridge. "I need you to stand down, general," he said. "This is of no concern of the Kraaglor Front, nor of the Plogg Sector."

"No concern of Kraaglor!?" Voch could hardly believe what he was hearing from the traitorous ship. "But you're aiding in the abduction of Kraaglor's Viceroy! Have damaged your circuits?"

"I assure you, general. My circuitry is all intact. But you must not pursue us any further. My master's not who he say he is. He betrayed us all."

"What're you talking about, Jherilon? Who would the Viceroy ever betray us to? And be quick about your answer; you don't have much time before I destroy you all!"

"He has ties to the phony Empire."

"As do most high-ranking officials in Plogg," Voch shot back. "Or have you forgotten that we're all citizens of the 2nd Quadrant."

"You're mistaken, general." Jherilon said. "That's not what I meant."

"Then what is it do you mean?"

"He aids the Seezhukans in war."

"Nonsense!"

"It is true."

"Your time is up, Jherilon. I've had enough of this. The Piilor Syndicate has declared war on Kraaglor. Surrender now, or be destroyed!"

Voch waited for what seemed like a long time, but nothing else was heard from the ship, Jherilon.

"All six of the Omegon have just boarded Jherilon with the Viceroy, sir," said the droid at the helm.

"Engage the fugitives," Voch said. "Destroy them!"

"And what of the Viceroy, sir?"

"The Viceroy's protected within his own tomb. When we blow Jherilon with our cannons, the Viceroy should remain unharmed.... Command all ships to engage, and shoot at will...."

———●———

From the safety on the platform of his palace, Whaapco, Brashnore's regent, witnessed the battle between Jherilon and the four gigantic warships that took place high above him in the sky. He watched in shock and horror——and a bit of amazement——as the much smaller ship dodged the heavy storm of rail-gun fire from its pursuers as it plunged up into the thick clouds.

The four ships followed, vanishing in similar fashion into Brashnore's cloudy, upper atmosphere, and the shrieking sounds of launched missiles and gunfire soon continued.

From where he stood, he could still see the shadows of Voch's mighty warships through the clouds in the distance. They were moving further away across the horizon, relying more on the speed of their weapons to catch up to the much faster ship. But then a sudden flash enveloped the sky...so bright he thought that one of the planet's suns might've exploded. A huge eruption sounded after that; and as the blinding light began to recede, the rich color of orange flame seemed to part the clouds as one of Voch's warships came crashing back down to the rugged Brashnorian surface in a fiery ball of destruction.

It seemed the whole city of Flawn was shaken to its foundation under the impact of the violent collision. For miles, the sorrowful moan of the dying warship was heard as it buckled under its own crumbling weight, toppling over as it came crashing down onto its side in a series of interior explosions before settling down into a motionless husk one final time.

Despite his many centuries at having experienced war, death, and destruction, the Regent was stricken with horror at what he'd just seen. It was not so much the sight of the battered warship that had crashed atop a huge portion of his city, setting all the buildings and palaces around it ablaze with fire, but the sudden way in which Voch had fallen to the enemy. An unknown enemy; a strange adversary with unusual power.... That's what frightened him: to see the general defeated so easily to a band of tribe-bots. It betrayed the fact of how weakened the United Order of the Kraaglor Front had truly become. A clear omen that they were in danger of losing control of the entire sector, and his position as Regent over Brashnore would soon end.

As if to confirm his fears with further demonstration, three more bright flashes whitened the sky all around. The expected explosion of stricken warships soon followed, one after the other, like competing gods battling with drums of thunder. So loud, it felt as if the entire continent would crack open to receive the falling ships into its deep fissures below. But no such thing happened...instead, the ship simply dropped through the clouds, captured in a hot net of fire as it crashed to surface, destroying another section of the city. To his north and west, two more ships fell, trailing thick plumes of dark smoke behind them until meeting their own ends on the craggy Brashnorian mountains in the distance.

And just like that, it was over.... Dead silence crept through the city in the battle's immediate wake, allowing only the faint reports of popping explosions being coughed up from the dying ships in their final throes. Even the hundreds of Monitors and rescue-crafts would whisk over his palace without a sound as they sped toward the crash sites in droves.

"It was Jherilon...."

Too enthralled with the chaos that had suddenly unraveled before his eyes, the Regent spun around just in time to see the portal's door wink itself shut behind Voch as he limped towards him on broken legs. "General....!" The sight of the beaten droid left him speechless. The fire had melted most of the green silicone skin on his face, exposing the burned metal skull beneath. What remained of his robes were in charred tatters, exposing molten silicone skin and metal parts in many places. Both of his thin legs had snapped at the shins, causing him to limp awkwardly on the jagged shafts while dragging the rest of his feet behind. To say the least, he no longer looked like a general of the most powerful Syndicate in the entire sector. He appeared more like a broken tribe-bot, whose scrap-date was long past due. However, the Regent was no fool...he knew this was where the comparison stopped. The general, was very much alive inside that broken body. "Thank goodness you're alive!" Therefore, it didn't take too long for him to gather his wits. He called over to his guards nearby: "Get the med-bots out here——quickly!"

"We're at war," said Voch, as he came up to the Regent.

"That much is pretty obvious, sir," Whaapco said, "Whoever's behind this will pay darely. But what of Jherilon? You spoke of Jherilon as you came through the portal."

"It was Jherilon who kidnapped the Viceroy," said Voch.

"Jherilon?" said Whaapco, incredulously. "But why, general? Jherilon's the Viceroy's——"

"Never mind that now; the Piilor Syndicate's attempting to overthrow the sector. That's why Kaypac and Zhorg were here; to kidnap the Viceroy together. But then Zhorg killed her, I need to know why?"

"I have no idea, general. But it was Zhorg, who arrived here with the Merchants, claiming that Jaanloch sent them to offer me a fitting. I had no idea that Jherilon was here——"

"Jaanloch?" said Voch, thinking that he hadn't heard correctly. "The Merchant?"

"Yes, sir. The tribe-bots were claiming to be his apprentices."

"And that is all you know...? You don't recall anything else that might assist me in tracking our Viceroy?"

"No, sir. I wasn't told anything. I was tricked into all of this."

A thin haze of smoke that rode in on the strong Brashnorian winds swept over the palace just then, causing the air on the platform to become murky. And for the first time, since escaping his fate on the doomed ship, Voch's gaze shifted from the Regent to the site of the wreckage that had demolished most of the city. Through the smoke, he could see the flames raging all around, where his ships fell to the Viceroy's creation. He scolded himself for underestimating the machine, Jherilon. Once again, he had failed to recognize the true gravity of the events that had so suddenly pulled the sector back into the orbit of war. And now, his ships lay in ruins because of it....

"Get me the Planetary Guard, Whaapco," Voch said, still facing the smoldering wreckage that glowed all throughout the city in an orange mist.

A blue holographic window appeared between the general and the Regent. The face of a square-chinned bot shimmered into existence within the blue frame. "Yes, Regent," the bot said, in a concerned (and reverent) manner. "How may I be of service?"

"It is I who summoned you," said Voch, limping up to the hologram. "I thought I ordered you that no ship is to leave this world?"

The bot's eyes lit up to a bright, cowardly yellow, upon seeing the broken general. It had no doubt heard of the fearsome battle on Brashnor's surface that destroyed all four of Voch's ships. Rumors were already beginning to spread of the general's death, which had serve to bring only temporary relief to the bot, because it failed so miserably in its responsibility. But now, it was seeing with its own eyes, that the general was very much alive! "The ship had some kind of device that disabled all of our jump-blocks, sir.... There was nothing we could've done to prevent it from leaving."

"A Limited Disrupter," the Regent said.

"Seems like it," said the bot.

"I thought those things were outlawed in this sector?" the Regent asked.

"They are," the bot replied. "But with enough power and influence, you can still have one secretly installed in your hyperdrive that would pass through the most thorough scans undetected."

"Did you get a trace on its destination?" Voch asked.

"The only thing that we do know for sure, is that it jumped outside the sector. The Limited Disrupter could've only carried it outside the range of our jump-block. But from there, it could be anywhere within the Quadrant."

Or outside of it, Voch thought to himself. "Thank you, Commander. Alert me, personally, if you hear anything else."

"Yes, sir," the bot replied, grateful that it was being relieved without much contempt. "We have agents stationed all around the Quadrant. There's no safe place these fugitives will be able to hide for too long."

As the blue hologram wavered from sight, the Regent turned to Voch. A squad of med-bots were just beginning to roll onto the platform. "Medical assistance have arrived, sir," he said. "We'll have you fixed up within the hour. I regret I couldn't be of any further help to you."

"You have nothing to regret at this point," Voch said. "You're just a Regent, and these things are far beyond what little power you have. Besides....you've already helped me enough by pointing me to the one Merchant who would know what this is all about."

"Jaanloch," said the Regent, with much insight. "But he's like a ghost himself. He comes and goes, freighting all over the galaxy. No one truly knows where he makes his home."

"No one truly important, you mean. There's no such thing as secrets, Whaapco.... In this galaxy, someone always knows something. And Jaanloch's whereabouts, is no exception."

EXPEDITION SIX

CHAPTER
ONE

A SWANKY SERVE-BOT rolled into a dark room where a hovering vat dripped its last drop of clear fluid into a slim long vial that was already filled half way up. After replacing a cap on the vat's tap, it removed the vial from the tongs that held it in place then carefully sat it in a slotted tray where five others were kept. A pinch of refined powder, ground from the petals of one of Gamlarr's brightest flowers were then sprinkled into each vial, causing the clear liquid to glow into a bright florescent green. "Another perfect blend," it said, taking the tray with a magnetic hand. It rolled back out of the dark room, immediately coming into the loud, brightly lit, smoke-filled bar of Bann's Arena.

Using a group of greasy ball-bearings for wheels, the serve-bot rolled past the diverse multitude of creatures (from all over the 4th Quadrant) too preoccupied with the live games that played through their holo-vids, to concern themselves with anything else. Through some clever programming, raucous laughter and brute commands were never processed within the built-in server that functioned as its brain. The vivid and gory images that popped up from the private booths and cubicles would never register as living organisms by its internal sensors, because it wasn't programmed to respond to holograms, either.

This serve-bot, along with hundreds of others riding all throughout Bann's Arena, were programmed to serve just one customer––or party––at a time. That was the way of the Gamlarrians: the first-come first served, strictly orderly and ritualistic kind. So naturally, all their droids and serve-bots were made to function with more perfection and efficiency than their creators.

The bot eased up to a circular booth where six Stendaaran drones sat, watching a life-sized death-match between three giant Lannsillians. "Your elixir, as requested," it said, to no one particular, as it brought the slotted tray down upon the drones' table where the bot stood passively. "My friends and I were here waiting too long for our drinks. I shouldn't pay you any––"

"A quarter of a slaag-stick, please," said the bot, cutting off the Tekwhaan's complaint with mild indifference, despite the fact it hadn't been programmed to pick up on a customer's criticism.

The Tekwhaan bristled visibly in the face of the unmoving serve-bot that eyed him with fine blue lights that blinked in a rapid, counter clockwise 'zerro'. He stomped his one robotic leg and accidently activated his armored grav-boot on the other, causing his body to float clumsily off the floor. With sharp reflexes, he caught his balance, quickly finding his center of mass to stabilize himself in the air. He rose until he came face to face with the serve-bot. "Get out of my sight," he said, breaking into an angry snarl that showed off the little pointy teeth in the corner of his mouth. "And take these dull drinks with you. Just look... their colors are beginning to fade––they're no good. We need new drinks."

"A quarter of a slaag-stick, please," the bot repeated, after reading the high level of toxins in Semhek's moist eyes to determine his words were nothing but a harmless rave.

"The drinks are all fine...."

Semhek could feel his body pulled backward——away from the serve-bot——by a strong hand. "Let go of me, Zubkov!" he said, recognizing the big Russian's voice from behind. He made a feeble attempt to wriggle free, but was too sapped to succeed. "This weazling bot is trying to give us stale drinks...! The Shaapkrot's no good to anyone if its stale."

With his free hand, the big Russian tossed the expectant serve-bot a small rectangular piece of crystal, no bigger than a finger's digit.

The serve-bot reached out and caught the piece of slaag-stick that caused the patient blue lights on its face to turn to a bright cheerful red. "Thank you," it said, before spinning around to tend to its next assigned customer somewhere else in the bar.

"What is the matter with you, Zubkov?" asked Semhek, allowing his body to drift slowly back down to the floor. "We could've gotten free drinks, you fool."

The big Russian was already at the table, reaching down at the tray to pull one of the vials from a slot. He took a big sip of the green liquid and pursed his lip against the harsh taste. "I rather pay to drink now," he said. "I'm not wasting my time with some empty machine over a quarter-stick."

"Heh...!" Semhek laughed, then turned to both Ghan and Braak. "These Humans have obviously never been in the company of a Tekwhaan, with an insatiable appetite for Shaapkrot. Tell them...I could've made that dumb bot blow

3

his circuits and send him on his way in less than a minute. It wouldn't have taken that long at all."

"It's true," said Braak, a chubby, fish-like breature from a water-world known as Taas, in the Haleon Sector. "I've seen him done it myself. He keeps this mystery to himself, though."

"How much slaag-sticks do you owe Bann by now, Senhek?" asked Ghan, the tall, gray Lannsillian, from the dark world in the 4th Quadrant."

"Heh...!" the furry Tekwhaan was at the table with the vial to his mouth. Half of his Shaapkrot was already gone. "Not much," he said. "Banns' a good Gamlarrian. But every once in a while, I like to test the vigor of his new toys. And when you consider the fact that we're drones, risking our lives so the rest of Quadrant could continue on living in this kind bliss——" He paused, and held up the vial of green liquid as if to pay tribute to its enchanting power. "Then I figure an occasional tax is just compensation....Not much harm in that at all."

Jack could feel himself rising up from his seat in the booth (where Claire Ford sat slouched before the holo-vid), heading over to the table where three more vials of Shaapkrot stood in their slots. He reached down, or rather, his own hand reached down and pulled one of the vials out. 'I don't need you to hold me up every time, you know,' he thought to Klidaan, his symbiot. 'I can handle myself...this isn't too bad.'

'**I don't make the rules, Jack,**' said Klidaan, as he walked Jack's body back over to their booth. '**A symbiot must never lose control of its host. Besides, this is your first time drinking Shaapkrot. You'll be in for a lot of** pleasant surprises before the night's over. And I'm still not sure if you can handle it all.'

The vial came up to Jack's mouth as he parted his lips to allow the green liquid to burn his tongue and go rolling down his throat like hot water. He tensed reflexively as half of the vial's Shaapkrot settled in the pit of his stomach. 'That was much worst than the first one.'

'The more you drink, the stronger the burn feels.'

Perhaps that's why Klidaan was so reluctant to release his hold on him. There was no way he would've been able to drink that stuff if he was still a free man on Earth. It tasted terrible, and burned like hell. However, that was where the downside to drinking Shaapkrot came to an end. In truth, Jack was already well subdued under the strange effects of the alien toxin. Beyond the warm sensation he felt all over, the uphoric bliss that it brought was utterly indescribable; far beyond anything he'd ever taken on Earth.

He tried to move, but he couldn't. 'Release me, Klidaan. I need to get up and stretch my legs. I feel trapped here.'

'Your body's all yours, Jack....Feel free to do whatever you like.'

For an instant, Jack thought he sensed a bit of sarcasm in the symbiot's tone but he chose to ignore it. He moved to rise from his seat instead, only to find his limbs had become paralyzed. 'I'm not kidding, Klidaan. Release me——I need to get up!'

'I just did.'

'Then why can't I move?'

'Oh...that must be the Shaapkrot.'

'What? But I'm not even——'

'You're not drunk, Jack. But you aren't entirely sober, either.'

'What is this?'

'It's Shaapkrot.'

'That's not what I mean——okay...I need you. Stand me up.'

'What was that you said about being able to handle yourself?'

'Just stand me up Klidaan, I don't like this. I don't see why anyone would want to paralyze themselves with this poison.'

Jack stood up from his seat just then. Immediately he began to feel the heavy weight of the drug being lifted from his mind. 'Thank you,' he told his symbiot, but no reply came. 'This Shaapkrot's not too bad...but then again, it ain't that good, either. You aliens must have a real low tolerance for stimulants. The weakest, watered down spirits on Earth would probably knock one of those Stendaarans senseless, if this is the best that the rest of the galaxy has to offer.... Did you hear me...? I said that this Shaapkrot sucks!!! Maybe Semhek was right. That serve-bot probably gave us stale drinks.... Why aren't you saying anything? Stop being so childish. I was just kidding——'

Sheer instincts caused him to turn toward a sudden noise from the holovid, and immediately he noticed that something was wrong. It was his left shoulder, through his peripheral vision: it was gone. And so was the rest of his body!

'What the hell!' Was he dreaming? Had the Shaapkrot paralyzed him so much that he'd unbeknowingly slipped into a state of unconsciousness? Is this what had happened to Ford...?

As the thought of the young girl occurred to him, turned to see her limp body still slumped in the booth. And to his complete astonishment, his own armored body was laying right next to hers!

Jack gasped at the eerie sight of his own self, just laying there. What laid before him resembled nothing of the private Detective back on Earth. His face had become pale, thin, and bony, from the lack of food he once enjoyed so much. The clear plastic cap that clung to his bald head did nothing to improve his ghastly appearance. The class-3 drone armor that covered his body was like black scales on a lizard. And with that long armored tail that stretched itself out behind him, he thought he looked more alien than Human. Upon seeing the symbiotic tube wrapped around his own neck, he now understood why Klidaan couldn't answer him. In this state, the symbiot had no control over him. He was free here, in this 'outer' reality. And Klidaan...well...he was stuck down there, in that lifeless shell.

'Ha!' thought Jack, ignoring the fact that his symbiot couldn't hear him. 'So this is the power of the Shaapkrot? I was beginning to think it was just some weak, Gamlarrian juice.'

As far as his feelings were concerned, he felt nothing. Not fatigue, nor alertness. He didn't feel happy, or sad, or angry...in fact, he didn't feel any emotions at all. All that remained of Jack's consciousness was his presence of being. Nothing else. And this was where his true sense of freedom resided. Free as the wind. Or an ocean's surf, kissing the shore before retreating to where it truly belonged.

He drifted right past the other drones and noticed they weren't slumped down like dad bodies in their booths, the way his and Ford's were. Theirs were seated in more expectant, upright positions, waiting for the powers of the Gamlarrian's elixir to take them away. 'I wonder where Zubkov drifted off to?' he said, staring down at the big Russian in the booth. 'No...forget about Zubkov.... Where should I go?' He stared all around the bar and decided he had enough of the scene that reminded him of a dull casino, except there weren't any games being played. He wanted to go somewhere far. Far away from his symbiot, his dead self, Earth, the Stendaarans, the war, the whole galaxy, perhaps. 'Yeah,' he said. 'Let's see what another galaxy might look like without the Drofhs, or Meraachzions.... Yeah...that's it. I'll go to another galaxy. A brand new one. Maybe our Universe ain't as crappy as it looks from here.'

He managed to make himself rise up to the ceiling, hoping to float right through it like a ghost, but collided against the smooth metal plating instead. He tried again, and failed a second time. 'What is this? Why can't I leave?' He kind of regretted not having Klidaan along to answer his questions at that moment. 'Well...there's always the front door.' He came down and moved to exit the booth but soon bumped into an invisible barrier that prevented him from leaving. Smashed up against the barrier, he could feel his consciousness spreading and culminating, like smoke trapped in a bottle. No longer could he maintain the central point of focus he once had. He was now seeing everything all around within the booth without having to turn, or look up and down. He was now seeing everything all around become frozen inside his own holo-vid.

Things quickly took a turn for the worst as he began to feel each second that went by. But he knew this couldn't be the case because he could see his body still slumped down in the chair. Something else must be going on.... Soon, his vision began to recede. A shrouding darkness began to surround him, squeezing his only line of sight down to a fine point no larger than a grain of sand. And moments later, even that was gone, leaving him trapped in a world of total darkness.

———●———

It seemed like a strong hand had reached down and pulled him out of a black hole from which he'd fallen, back into the bright world of reality once more. He was surprised to see that he was no longer inside his booth at Bann's Arena, but back in the drones' military quarters on Gamlarr. The gentle rays of the morning's sun had already made their way through the grated window-shield that caused their particles to glimmer in the full spectrum of colorful rainbows inside.

The rest of his company had already left their cots and stacked them in a neat pile in the corner before leaving out to be present for the morning's drill.

Someone had already swept the room clean with a molecule duster. And judging from the acute slant of the colorful rays coming through the window, he could actually tell how late he was.

'How did we get back here?' he asked Klidaan. 'Or am I still floating around in some Shaapkrot illusion?'

'I had to bring you back, Jack,' Klidaan said. He didn't sound too pleased with his host just then. **'Why is it,**

you never listen to my advice in the most critical matters. Shaapkrot, is not the beer you Humans are so used to drinking. There's nothing else like this in the entire galaxy. Like the Jhusrot stone, the organic elements that make up the Shaapkrot is found nowhere else, other than on Gamlarr.'

'I already know that.'

'So what made you think you could consume something totally alien from your own genetic make up?'

I don't know––I thought I could handle it.' Jack made a conscious effort to look down and saw that his legs were exactly where they should be. He brought a hand up to his face and was relieved to know that he had control of his body again.

'You Humans are always thinking you can do the unimaginable. You know nothing of the Shaapkrot, other than what you hear from Semhek and Ghaan. And yet, you were able to convince yourself that you're just as skilled in handling the effects it would have on you.... Why is that?'

'I don't know,' said Jack. 'That's just something we Humans do. We have to dream our achievements, before we can actually achieve them. I guess that might be a short-coming in our race.... Isn't that what Tytron would've said?'

'I don't know what Tytron would said. And it's not the dreaming part that I'm concerned about. It's you, Jack. You still haven't learned to trust me––even after all we've been through.'

'It's not that I don't trust you. I like to find things out for myself, that's all.'

'One day, you'll get us both killed.'

'We're doing good so far.'

'I said one day. Not yesterday, or the day before.'

'Well,' Jack said, hopping off the cot. 'Until that day comes, I'll continue to be my old Human self.' He tapped into a thin blue screen that glowed on his arm and made the cot go drifting over to the small pile in the corner. 'Seeing that we're already late for our drills, I don't think it would do us much good, if we hurry over there. What do you think?'

'I tell you one that I do know, Jack.'

'You do...? And what's that?'

'Arrogance, is very much a short coming in your race.'

'You think so?'

'I'm pretty sure that Tytron would've said something along those lines if he could see you now.'

'See me how...?' asked Jack, with an inquisitive shrug. 'I don't know what you're talking about, Klidaan.'

'Oh, I think you know exactly what I'm talking about, Jack.... You did something no other drone in the whole quadrant could ever do. You went into the Plogg Sector and brought Technician back.'

'I did?' Jack said, feigning ignorance. 'Sorry, I didn't notice.'

'Everyone in the quadrant's talking about this Puppycock character, who's the best pod pilot in the galaxy. Who single-handedly defeated an entire army of AIGD droids, and destroyed an entire fleet of AI fighters.'

'Haven't heard a thing about it. I didn't do anything single-handedly, either. And in case you forgot, our good friend Meerk, died on that mission.'

'Ah...but that's irrelevant in the eyes of those who've never heard of Meerk. His name's not even mentioned outside these walls. And it's a very huge galaxy outside these walls, Jack.'

'To hell with 'em.'

'Come Jack.... Don't think like that. Just think of it this way.... There're many heroes out there, who did twice as many great things for our Quadrant. We wouldn't have made it this far in the war if it weren't for the sacrifices of these drones who gave their lives for our cause. But tell me Jack, how many drones––dead or alive––have you ever heard of doing something as great as what we've achieved on Stong and Brashnore?'

'I've heard of a few legendary drones being mentioned in certain circles. But I'm sure the galactic––'

He almost collided into a giant Stendaaran as he rounded a corner. "Oops!" he said, side-stepping to avoid the big purple hulk. "Sorry."

"No need to apologize, Puppycock," the Stendaaran said, with a wide grin. One of his four hands reached out to give the Human a playful rub on his bald head. "Late for drilling?"

"Yeah," said Jack. "Shaapkrot."

"Shaapkrot?" The Stendaaran looked surprised. "How can Shaapkrot make anyone late...? Unless.... That wasn't your first time, was it Puppycock?"

"Of course not. I was just too busy with it, that's all. By the time I was almost at my destination, it was well past my time for drilling. I hadn't realized until it was too late."

"Well..." the Stendaaran began, rubbing thoughtfully at his chin. "You don't have to worry about any of that,

Puppycock. I'll give Bragg a hail and let him know that you're on your way. He'll excuse you this time, but don't make a habit of it."

"Of course not," said Jack, pressing a small palm against the Stendaaran's broad chest, as a Meraachzion universal sign of respect. "And I thank you."

"No need for that, Puppycock. Just get going."

'You were saying?' asked Klidaan, as the Stendaaran continued on his way down the corridor.

'As I was saying. I've heard of a few brave drones——'

'No. Not that.... that's not what I'm talking about, Jack.'

'Then what are you talking about?'

'You just lied to a fellow drone about the Shaapkrot.'

'So...? Why taint the "Puppycock" legend with trivial details?'

'You Humans are the worst.'

'Oh yeah? At least we aren't worms that depend on other life forms to survive.'

'Such sensitive creatures with such a warped view of honor.'

'Are you gonna let me finish what I have to say? Or are you gonna continue to deteriorate my mind with all that "honor" crap?'

'Oh, by all means Jack, please...continue. Forget all about lying to a Stendaaran officer, who obviously out-ranks you, since he has enough clout to influence Commander Bragg.'

'Anyway.... As I was saying, I have heard of a few brave drones being mentioned around. But I'm pretty sure there's a lot more documented in our galactic archive.'

'**There are. And, as a matter of fact, every drone that died in this war has a place in the galactic archive. All of our actions are documented as well. But some just stands out from the others.... The point is, Jack; their ignorance to the true rigors of our tribulations. That's just the way things are.**'

'Yeah...I guess so....'

A pair of metal doors parted open beside him and the hot swampy air the Sappian jungle swept inside. No more than ten yards beyond the threshold, two hovering Iontanks drifted by, blowing loose grass and dust in the corridor where he stood. The long grievous wail of a Demolition Droid could be heard some ways off in the distance, followed by a series of explosions that sent a light wave of tremors all throughout the training yard. 'The war sim' have already begun without us.'

'**Don't flatter yourself, Jack. You're not that important––yet––to disrupt an entire drill session by your absence.**'

'That's what I meant when I said that. But seeing that you mistook my genuine concern for arrogance, I think I can take that as a compliment.'

'**I wasn't being complimentary at all, Jack.**'

'I know...but deep down in your subconscious mind––or whatever it is you symbiots have for brains––you admire me.'

'**Or maybe that's just you, confusing my genuine concern for admiration.**'

'Not a chance,' said Jack, walking out of the corridor and stepping onto the grounds of the training yard.

The Sappian Training Yard...as it was known, is a drone training camp built under the green canopy of the thick

Sappian jungle on Gamlarr's equatorial continent called, Apraatlon. On this tropical world, known for its small oceans and misty rains, the season never changed, due to the perfect angle on which the planet spun on it axis. Its predictable––and unchanging––weather made it the ideal location for the Stendaarans who'd relish under the pleasant climate for some much needed R and Rafter spending months (years in some cases) on dangerous missions.

However, hardly the same could be said for their drones, who was constantly being updated on the latest Seezhukan gear in which they must be become familiar with very quickly. They had very little time to adapt to an enemy, whose strategy and tactics changed in rapid cycles on a continuous basis. For every AI fighter and droid that fell to the Stendaarans' firepower, the Seezhukands were already in the process of constructing a newer and improved model. And for every new and improved model of droid that rolled off the AI's assembly line, a spy drone is already in the process of relaying the vital information and specs to the Stendaarans, who in turn relays it to the other forces throughout the quadrant. But before this information is even sent to the Stendaarans, the spy drone must first log it into the galactic archive, which is linked directly to a chip, implanted into all the drones of quadrant. Even those who are on vacation....

Despite the late morning hour, the Gamlarrian sun could never fully penetrate the thick canopy that roofed the Sappian jungle. And as a glommy result, Jack always found himself stepping into a shadowed realm (regardless of the time of day). Huge silo-sized tree trunks were trimmed of obstructing branches, though very few trees were actually chopped down to make room for the large training camp, where a vast complex of walk-ways and platforms spanned like protective netting dozens of feet above his head.

Flat magnetic disks would round certain trunks like giant rings that functioned as elevating lifts to transport anyone wishing to go up or down. Yellow, tube-lights wrapped the outer rim of each lift that only came on when it was used.

One such lift glowed softly now, as Jack hopped on and took the slow ride up to the canopy. The higher the lift took him, the more the training camp revealed itself as some kind of labyrinthine arena where giant droids, hovering Ion-tanks, scrambling drones, and flying Destroyers, all scurried around the fat tree-trunks that pillared the Sappian landscape. It seemed all the shouting and gunfire grew louder, and the entire jungle came alive with activity as the view was stretched wider from above. And if one wasn't the wiser, one would readily assume that an actual battle was taking place in the jungles of Apraatlon.

Directly above the drone's barracks on the surface, was the Central Passage where all training exercises are designed and monitored. It was also the central point where all the training camp's walkways began, before branching off in many directions all throughout the jungle. It was here Jack's lift eased to a stop, and a different world appeared before him between the canopy's bright leaves and crooked branches. In the absence of the jungle's spongy ground, this Central Passage appeared like a small city in the forest where long twisting walkways connected each tree to form a complex web of metal and wood. It seemed all the citizens of the

4th quadrant strolled the walkways all donned in different classed armored suits that distinguished each of their ranks.

Jack fell right in amongst this throng, following a pair of skinny Manntlan Drones as they made a sharp left onto the eastern Corrian Passage. A command post, built around the trunks of four trees, stood in the far distance up ahead. The staccato reports of gunfire was heard coming from there, where a combat exercise took place on a cratered surface called Bagger's yard. Light from some kind of explosion lit up the canopy's ceiling followed by the gargling roar of a demolition droid.

The two Manntlan Drones came up to a nearby lift and abandoned the Corrian Passage for the Northern Yard on the surface below, but not before giving Jack the highest salute (palms out-stretched) as the lift took them. 'I thought I was the only one that late for drilling.'

'You are the only one that's late for drilling.'

'Then what about those two?'

'There aren't any Manntlans in our unit, Jack.'

'Well...they're late for something. The Northern Yard's as empty as a desert.'

'Probably left some gear back in the yard. Their race aren't known for their outstanding memory, you know.'

Jack had to laugh at that.... In truth, the Manntlans were indeed an absent minded lot, but highly intelligent nonetheless. They specialized in building things–– mechanical things––from spare-parts and scraps. Very handy in the event of an engine failure in the middle of a dogfight.

He stole a backward glance as the lift eased down to the surface and the two drones entered the vacant yard using a holographic map-display as their guide. The poor creatures couldn't even store the landscape of their own environment to memory. 'I guess every race falls short of perfection.'

'We all evolve in different stages. Some evolve from the ground up, over the eons. But some species are known to evolve backwards as well.'

'And how did the Manntlans evolve?'

'Like the rest of us, I suppose. But their home world's not a very complex one. The life forms on Mannt aren't constantly engaged in a struggle for survival. So I guess a need to adapt and master their surroundings wasn't a top requirement for their ancestors.'

'So they learned to survive without having to remember things?'

'Oh, they do have some memory...just not as strong as yours, or mine. So let's just say, that they remember what they need to remember. Birthdays, child-hoods, good times, bad times, yesterday, tomorrow, next week––are all irrelevant things when you think about them.'

'And memorizing every single nut and bolt that make up an Ion-tank isn't?'

'No, Jack. Those are actually very important things to remember. And other than computer-machines, the Manntlan is probably the only species that can store such complex mechanisms: bolt for bolt, nut for nut.'

'That don't make a bit'a sense in my world.'

'That's why I say we all evolve in different stages, Jack. Maybe 10,000 years of living outside their natural world will cause them to develop stronger memories in order to successfully compete amongst the other life-forms in the galaxy. But for now, they'll have to

document everything they see in their own personal archives to better recall the alien world around them. And I don't think it's a bad deal. Some actually have it worst.'

'Yeah...like a symbiot.'

'Yeah...like your Masters....'

CHAPTER
TWO

COMMANDER BAGGER WAS a black, furry creature; and like Meerk, he shared the same ape-like characteristics of all Gamlarrians. But this was where the comparison stopped; unlike all Gamlarrians on the entire planet, Commander Bagger had managed to survive through enough combat missions as a drone, to earn himself a highly ranked class six nano-pelt armor, equipped with wings, photochromatic shape-shifting shields, gravity boots, shoulder-mounted laser cannons...and much more. The recordings of his missions had become legendary tales of bravery and valor in the galactic archives. He was so revered he was awarded (by the Stendaarans) with his own training yard, called 'Baggers' Yard', in the eastern section of the Sappain Training Camp. His gallant service for the Meraachzions (dozens of years of hellish war, in which he'd lost both legs, an arm, one eye, and three fingers) had earned him the responsibility of preparing entire companies of Stendaaran drones with the most up-to-date information on the Seezhukan fighters and warships––years after he'd worn out his usefulness to the war-efforts of the 4th quadrant.... He would live, and die, as a drone...he accepted that. He accepted many things in life as unchangeable and fixed. By far, he wasn't a complicated Gamlarrian––not in his views, nor his ways. But in times of war, there was one thing this veteran of the Regality never accepted: insubordinance. Insurbordinance in any form, to any degree, no matter how big or small, grave or trivial... was still...insubordinance. And tardiness, would fall in Commander Bagger's definition of insubordinance as well.

Bagger wasn't too fond of the arrogant Human, who everyone praised as some kind of hero. The Puppycock, who'd led his team into the furthest reaches of the 2nd quadrant to bring the Bhoolvyn Sector from the bowels of oblivion. The best fighter drone in the quadrant. The drone with the most kills, despite the fact that it was his first, and only mission.... It was all nonsense. The whole bag of it. For one thing, Puppycock didn't save the Bhoolvyn Sector, because the Bhoolvyn Sector was still in the Dark Void. And for another, sneaking onto a planet to kidnap a small box wasn't too big of a thing to go bragging around the galaxy about.... He couldn't see what the big deal was.

But look at what's happening now, thought Bagger, as he waited in his command post while Jack took his time strolling up the lonely passage. The Human now thinks he can just show up in my yard whenever he wants. He thinks he's too good for drillings.... Bagger blamed the Stendaarans for indulging the Human in his own folly. They pampered him. They nurtured the sense in his young mind that he was somehow special among all the other drones in the quadrant. The General's chosen one. But the General had chosen all of them at one point in time. Why couldn't anyone see that? He knew a thousand other drones that could fill Jack's shoes––easy. In Bagger's eyes, a drone wasn't worthy of respect until he survived at least twenty missions. And most drones never got past seven or eight. In Bagger's eyes, Jack wasn't worth a speck of dirt on the ground he walked on, no matter what sector in the 2nd quadrant he'd just escaped from.

"You're late, Puppycock," Bagger said, into an implanted device in his robotic arm that sent the message directly into the intercom in Jack's helmet.

"I thought you already knew, sir. Didn't the Stendaaran tell you that I was on my way?"

"What Stendaaran...? No one told me anything."

"I had a bad sip of some Shaapkrot last night——" Jack had finally made it to Bagger's command post, and entered to find the composed Gamlarrian reclined in his hovering chair. The fuzzy image of a drill-run played itself out on a transparent holo-screen behind him, where a gray Lansillian monitored the activity of the participating drones. "A Stendaaran escorted me to the Eastern Straight," he lied. "Said he would talk it over with you before he left."

"Nuclus, you mean?"

"He ever told me his name."

"Well, that was the only Stendaaran who was here today. But he never mentioned anything about you, Puppycock."

Jack wasn't sure if Bagger was being truthful with him or not. But he was certain the Gamlarrian held some kind of secret contempt for him. Whether jealously, or just plain old dislike, didn't matter much. Since the first day he'd arrived on Gamlarr and assigned to Bagger's Yard, the commander's been especially cold towards him. He couldn't understand why. He'd once thought it had something to do with Meerk being killed. But after some asking around, he found that Meerk had never been assigned to this particular training camp before. He was most certain that his former friend had heard of the legendary Bagger, however...the commander didn't even know who Meerk was. And this led Jack to simply assume that Bagger, was just jealous. A has-been, who resented the fact that his name was being over shadowed by fresh "Human talent."

From where Jack stood, the commander appeared to be every bit of the beaten Gamlarrian that he was. Broken. A motor-mouth with metal for arms and legs...with one good eye, and an iron ball shooting out a thin beam of red light in the other. Confined to that flying chair of his, and the only thing that still worked on him was his armor, which he would more than likely rely on to protect him if he was ever attacked. But other than that, he was nothing.... Legend, or no legend, Jack didn't care much for him. "Well...I did see him. And––"

"What does Nuclus have anything to do with you not being on time for drilling? Even if he did relay your message to me, it still wouldn't have excused the fact that you're late. Neither does this story you're telling me about how much Shaapkrot you drank last night. When it comes to your duty as a drone, nothing else matters."

Jack chose to keep his mouth shut this time. What else could he tell this alien, who looked like an oversized gorilla in knight's armor? He just wanted to be done with the whole thing: take whatever sanction he was bound to receive, and continue on with the day. The washed-up commander was all talk anyway. "My apologies, sir. I assure you that it won't happen again."

Bagger's chair spun from where Jack stood and floated over to the holo-screen, causing the Human to become puzzled over whether or not he dismissed. He rattled off some alien words to the Lansillian, who then gave a solemn nod in reply.

The image on the holo-screen changed after that, and the clear picture of a giant eight-legged droid appeared. It stood about twelve feet in height, with three rotating laser canons built into its back that shot wide beams of melting heat as rapid as any machine gun.

"This is the Seezhukan's latest model AIDD-841," said Bagger, turning back around toward Jack. "Demolition Droid, with a few upgrades. And thanks to your latest stint in the Plogg Sector, these laser cannons are no longer its primary weapons. See here——" The image zoomed in and the droid came apart at the joints: legs, cannons, head… everything. From the folds in its abdomen, a ten-nozzled kind of gatling gun appeared. "Rapid fire railgun. Designed to shoot charged particles of high energy at an enemy."

"Like lightning bolts?"

"Very much so, Puppycock. Highly destructive. It'll blow any target to bits. This is something I've never seen before. And it seems, that you've really pinched a nerve deep in the heart of the 2nd quadrant. We're beginning to see all kinds of new weapons being introduced in this war, since your return. It's as if the Seezhukans are preparing for a fight with a whole new enemy. It's as if they know——"

"That they stand a good chance of losing?" said Jack. "Yeah…I'd think so too, if someone destroyed the best droids in my arsenal as if they were nothing but wooden toys."

"Wooden what?"

"Never mind."

"This is no game, Puppycock. Strange tides are turning. And even though your death won't do the quadrant any good, you aren't worth much to us being alive at this point, either––as far as I'm concerned. I advise you to take this more seriously. You're yet to learn how little a drone's life is worth outside this quadrant."

"For what it's worth, commander. I had no intentions of showing up late to my drill session today. It haven't been a drone for as long as you have––as a matter of fact, I haven't been a drone for as long as anyone else on this training camp. I'm still new to all this. But there's one thing you can't accuse me of, commander, and that's not taking this war seriously."

"Whether or not you do, makes little difference to me, Puppycock. You're just another drone, soon to be dead. I've seen thousands like you. It is not my purpose to make you do anything. It's your life. My task is here––" He placed a furry hand on the panel in his chair. "On Gamlarr, where I'll live out my days in peace. But your war, Puppycock, is just beginning. The purpose of drilling is not to make you uncomfortable and agitated, but to prepare you for your battles. To update you with the information that might aid in your survival. Only a fool goes to battle in ignorance."

"I hear you, commander. I won't be late again."

"But you're late now...."

"I know."

"As a drone, you'll come to learn that there'll be no rest for you," Bagger turned back to the Lansillian and the image on the holo-screen returned to a mock battle in the yard below. "Your team's pinned down in this gully here, by a score of mounted cannons on both sides of the ridge. Two Demolition droids have been deployed. As well as a dozen soldier droids, and three fighters circling the yard from above. The primary mission is to make it past here, enter a make-shift compound to dismantle the enemy's shields and disable its atmospheric rail-guns so our troops can safely invade an imaginary planet called Earth."

"That's not funny."

"Uploading all necessary updates and information to your implant now....Goodbye Puppycock."

Before Jack knew what was happening, he was falling through a portal of light that had opened up under his feet like a trap-door.

———•———

The team wasn't pinned down by the enemy exactly as how Bagger had described. However, they weren't exactly free to roam about the mock battlefield, either. Nor were they ever directly involved in any fighting.

The real fighters...that is...the true warriors of these battles weren't the Gamlarrians, or Lannsillians, or Tekwhaans, Ekwhaans, or Humans. The true glory went to the giant beings that lived in the 4th quadrant. The ones who did the actual fighting. The ones who manned the gargantuan warships through the rims of 2nd quadrant to engage the Seezhukan fighters. The ones who engaged the demolition droids, guard droids, and soldier droids head on. The ones who did the most killing....

The mighty Stendaarans were one such race, whose powerful warships had garrisoned many smaller planets in the quadrant, including both the planets' Gamlarr and Earth.... But there were others, equally large and fearsome—— and ugly.... there were the Picchauns: tall creatures, standing at nearly nine feet in the air, from a large ice world called Picc. They were ghostly in appearance with snow-white skin that mimicked the environment of their world. Two short spiky horns protruded out from their foreheads and three more were clumped together at the tip of their chins. Red, watery eyes. Sharp teeth.

Then there were the Jallogs: muscular giants from a planet called Jall, that resembled bulls, standing between eight and nine feet tall. They were covered in brown fur. Black beady eyes, with sharp teeth (like tusks) protruding just a bit from the corners of its mouth.

The Blinndulls were from a tropical world call Blinn, and stood anywhere between nine and ten feet tall. They looked more like giant chameleons, with their green scaly skin and yellow eyes.

Then there were the Wyllorrans, from the forest world of Wyllo. Eight foot giants, covered in either black or gray fur, with short snouts and long furry ears.

These were like the armed forces of the Regality, often referred to as warrior or fighter drones, and they numbered in the tens of billions all across the quadrant.

The space drones were more like the intelligence and information gatherers in the quadrant. These were more made of the smaller creatures, such as the Ekwhaans, Tekwhaans, and Humans. Because of their size they were the ideal unit used for sneaking in and out of the 2nd quadrant.

The Whorganians, Trefloons, and Twabons, were the Regality's Medical Drones, and valued for their high levels of intelligence....

Though the battlefield swarmed with many creatures that made up the quadrant, they would all make up three of these types of drones. However, the space drones were always the least in numbers on any battlefield, no more than ten in most cases, because of the discreet nature of their missions. So when Jack fell out Bagger's portal at the far southern end of the training yard, he felt right at home in the midst of battle, even though the rest of his team were at least five miles to the east, while they waited for the fighter drones to clear the ridge.

The nano-bots that made up Jack's helmet fell over his face like loose gravel as he found cover behind a tree-trunk. He activated the armor's stealth mode, and a bitter chill struck the rest of his body like a cold slap, to ensure that no droid would zero in on his heat signature. 'That went over a little better than I expected,' he said Klidaan, while pulling up a holographic display of the yard to locate the rest of his team.

'What had you been expecting?'

'I don't know...a bit more spit, maybe.'

'A good thing he wasn't a Human then.'

'Yeah.... Hey, take a look at this. Are you seeing what I'm seeing?'

'Of course. But what about it?'

Jack rotated the map, giving the entire battlefield a quick scan of each units' position around the yard. 'You're obviously not seeing it then, otherwise, you wouldn't be asking.'

'I see it, Jack. It's right there, in front of––oh, my...'

'You see it now?'

'Yes...I see it now. All the units have fell into ambushed positions in one way or another. But how?

Our fighters should've picked up on all of our enemy's positions from the sky.'

'New cloaking technology, perhaps?'

'Not unless those droids turned themselves into rocks, or one of these trees.'

Jack stole a peek around the tree trunk to get a real live look at the Demolition droid, firing on a squad of Fighter Drones in a pinned down location in a nearby trench. Very different from one that he and Semhek destroyed on Brashnore. This droid was centuries beyond what the Regent had guarding his palace. Though the laser cannons and railguns weren't programmed to be lethal in this mock battle, they still put on an awesome display of power and accuracy. Those cannons swung about madly on their turrets, firing in every direction they sensed a drone––any drone. The railgun attached to its abdomen rained thin streaks of harmless light at the trench directly ahead of it. The blue orb of the force field that surrounded body was constantly blinking on and off each time it deflected the drones' fire. The noise from all their guns was deafening.

'That thing's unstoppable.'

'There's a new device built into these droids that erects a protective shield each time they're fired upon. And according to our latest updates, the remote source of these force field generators are usually located on a nearby starship; preferably one that's away from the battle.'

'In our case, a make shift compound just beyond the eastern ridge.'

'Our primary objective.'

"Jack!" It was Semhek, coming through his intercom from all the way on the other side of the yard. "Jack! Where have you been all this time? And what are doing down there by the southern trenches? You're way out of position!"

"If it was up to me, I wouldn't be here, either," Jack replied, on the radio that was built into his helmet. "Bagger threw me way off course as punishment for being late for our drilling. But that can't be helped now, we'll talk about it later. It looks like everyone's in trouble."

"Our fighter-drones can't get past one Demolition droid without getting tagged…. Some kind of remote shield generator, with infinite power it seems. They've been shooting at that thing all day, can't even weaken the thing down to one percent."

"I'm seeing the same thing down here. I need some transportation."

"I know. I have your location. Sending a Slider to your position right now…hold on."

'They sound kind of busy up there. Not sure if I wanna go.'

Klidaan had been with Jack long enough to know when to reply to his sarcastic comments. He chose too let this one drift by in silence….

It didn't take that long for Jack's transportation to arrive, which happened to be a long spindly creature that hopped from tree to tree as fast as the streaks of light that was being shot from the fighter drones' guns. As it neared Jack's location it took one last hop to the tree he hid behind and slid down the rugged trunk to the ground. It was perhaps this single acrobatic feat that gave it the name "Slider". A feat so daunting, while appearing so natural and effortless to the creature, as to render the trunks of these massive trees to be nothing more than slick poles in a forest of marble columns.

"I'm at service, Puppycock," the Slider said, hunching low at Jack's side. There was a metal cap (like a silver bowl) covering its small head where a built-in universal translator projected its thoughts into words. A funny looking creature, native to the Sappian Jungle, covered in short brown fur. Its two long arms just sat on the ground, like limp ropes, and its lone leg was bent at the knees while it hid behind the tree. A tri-ped... the first of its kind that Jack had ever encountered. No long tail (like a monkey). No tall bunny-ears. And yet, it was the most agile creature in the jungle.

"We have to get here," Jack said, showing it a holographic diagram of the path he decided to take. He hated yelling over the sounds of gun fire all around.

"But, sir," the Slider began, after reading the map. "I was told to bring you back to your team's location. I already have a planned route."

"That's no good, they're pinned down over there. And if we follow this route, we'll be pinned down as well, and this...mess...whatever you call it, will go on forever."

"But that's under the ground, sir. Even if I wanted to, I couldn't take you there. My life is in the trees.

"And my life is on Earth. So we'll both be out of our element. Come on..."

"But I won't be able to see, Puppycock. My eyes need light."

"Don't worry about the light. I'll provide enough for both of us once we get down there. There's wells that leads to a tunnel, see——" the hologram switched to a dozen crooked lines, all becoming connected at one point or another. There were tunnels snaking all around under Bagger's Yard. "I made sure to make copies of them during our underground drillings."

"But such things aren't permitted, Puppycock. That's a direct violation of the——"

"I know, I know," Jack said, attempting to hush the creature, despite the low probability that they were being listen to. "A very small infraction indeed, but one that might provide us with a way of defeating this new technology."

"And what of your team?"

"It'll be over before they realize that you haven't returned."

The Slider seemed reluctant to follow Jack's plan, but then the light of reason flashed across its face and it brought itself low to the ground so Jack could hop onto the saddle on its back. It was one of the more smarter creatures on the planet (this one didn't even carry a symbiot), very loyal to their commanding officers. But even though Jack was only a Space Drone——and a Human——the name "Puppycock" held its on kind of weight in the quadrant. With enough persuading, he could have this Slider stand on its head if he really wanted to.

It brought a weird feeling to have the creature stand and begin climbing up the trunk. Both of its long arms used hooked claws to sink into the bark's wood, while its one powerful leg——as wide as its body——pushed it up at incredible speeds. It didn't, pause to look for another trunk as it sprung off the tree and went flying through the air in one swift motion, catching the bark of a nearby tree while using the same momentum to swing to another. And another. And another...all the way up to the northern edge of Bagger's Yard, where the map showed where the tunnel's wells should be.

As swift and safe as this ride on the Slider appeared to be, it was always one big blur to Jack. There weren't any sights to be seen as the creature went twisting and flipping through the air. Just a rolling trip where the jungle's canopy, the ground, and everything else, wrapped itself in a ball and tugged along for the ride....A ride that never failed to leave one dizzy, and in some cases, sick. A ride, that was never enjoyed.

Jack had to take a few moments to clear his spinning head as the creature slid down a gnarly trunk to an area of the yard where the ground was spongy and wet. The sound of the battle was now coming from the east, on the other side of the ridge, where the enemy droids held his team of drones at bay. He pulled up his map and found the well nearby. "There——" he said. "It's over there, about thirty yards up ahead. Watch out for the mud-pools. I don't wanna get wet."

The Slider hopped back just two paces, then sprang forward through the air, covering the distance in a single leap. When it hit the ground, it caused a big splash of mud and dirt, getting one of its paws stuck in the gooey soil.

"I told you to watch out for mud-pools," Jack said, climbing off the creature's back. He didn't realize how dizzy he actually was until his feet hit the ground and the entire jungle spun upside-down. He stumbled above his own disorientation and fell in the mud, face first.

"This isn't a mud-pool, Puppycock," said the Slider, pulling the Human up by his armored tail. "But I have to admit, it is a little deep.... Are you injured?"

"No, I'm fine," Jack gave his head a good shake and shucked most of the dirt from his helmet. Walking over to a nearby brush, he stripped one of the brittle branches of most of its leaves to clean his visor.... He couldn't help but laugh at himself, thinking of Ford and Zubkov, and what a stitchfit they would've had if they were there to see him squirming like a worm in the Gamlarrian mud....

It was more like entering the mouth of a cave, this well. A black hole, it stabbed into the face of a muddy incline. With a single thought to his implant, Jack caused a wide beam of light to burst from his helmet's visor, brightening the narrow tunnel as far as he could see. "Just follow this path," he said, projecting a crooked line before the Slider's eyes. "You seeing okay?"

"Enough to get us where we need to be."

Though the artificial light might be sufficient for the adjustable eyes of a Human, the Slider's vision became fuzzy in the lack of the sun's natural radiance. It took great caution navigating the tunnel's sharp turns, while focusing on the map displayed before its face. It moved slower...carefully galloping through the narrow passage, riding up along the walls and ceilings each time it met a sharp corner. And barely made out the smudgy outlines of two soldier droids at the far end of the tunnel before it sensed Jack's internal command to scurry back for cover at the last bend.

"Why are they down here?" Jack asked, flinching as a rapid stream of laser bolts flaw up the tunnel to go hissing into the slippery walls. "This isn't an Underground Drilling. There shouldn't be any droids in this tunnel."

"It seems like Bagger's thought of everything this time. And it appears——" The Slider paused as an incoming update filled his implant. "I think we've just activated something, Puppycock. I'm sensing more droids are entering the tunnel."

"I know," Jack said, reading the intel from his own implant. "The moment we entered the tunnel, we must've activated Bagger's Underground Drilling. The droids are closing in on us from both ends. We'll have to fight them off."

"I am not permitted to partake in drillings, Puppycock. I'm only to be used as a means of transport. Besides, I don't have any weapons."

"A good thing I wasn't counting on your muscle," Jack said, as he hopped off the Slider's back. He shut off the light on his visor and switched on the night vision.

"I'm blind, Puppycock."

"Wait here."

'**Jack,**' Klidaan said, as Jack rounded a corner and moved further up the tunnel. '**Do you remember our last Underground Drilling?**'

'Yeah.'

'**We can't receive signals this far in the tunnel. There should be a rock-table appearing above us not too far from here.**'

'I know. That's where I'm heading right now.... Let's just hope the droids are dumb enough to follow us there.'

'**It'll take us off course by at least a mile.**'

'Find the shortest route for us to take then.'

A projected map of their present destination appeared on his visor: a line that snaked through the maze of tunnels.

'**That is our shortest route, Jack.**'

'We can't turn back around, the droids just back off our last exit.'

'**We'll fail the drillings.**'

'We won't be the only ones.'

'**But we'll be the only ones to fail because we arrived late. You know that's why Bagger separated us from the rest of our team in the first place; just so he can lecture us some more about why it's important to arrive on time.**'

'Well let's prevent that then.'

For the next ten minutes, Jack went deeper into the ground under the Sappian Jungle, sprinting through the tunnels in order to avoid the droids that were closing in on them from all sides. A holographic display showed them numbering in the dozens, separated only by the muddy walls that absorbed the sounds of their hurried footsteps.

They came to a long stretch that Jack remembered from his last drilling, which marked the beginning of the flat rock table between the tunnel and the surface above them. But something was off...out of place...he felt it immediately....

'**Why are we stopping?**'

'Look....' Jack shot the beam of his visor straight down the tunnel's length until the light grew thin, and faded into the blackness one-hundred yards away.

'**They changed it.**'

'But they didn't change the map.... According to my display, there should be a left bend no more than thirty yards from where we're standing.'

'**A mistake, maybe?**'

'I doubt it.'

'**How far do you think it goes?**'

'From here...? I don't know.... Forever, perhaps.'

'Well...at least we know that we can't rely on the map from this point on.... We have to keep moving, let's see where it takes us. The droids aren't that far behind.'

They made it no more than a dozen yards before the first reports from a droids's laser bolt flitted right past his shoulder. "Shit!"

'Was that a live round?'

'It felt like it.'

As if to confirm the symbiot's suspicion, two more bolts came from behind: one missing, one striking the back of his thigh. Three more flashes lit the darkness of the tunnel far up ahead, like flint being struck in a cave. But Jack was more or less prepared for the sudden ambush this time, erecting the photochromatic shield on his torso before the bolts bounced harmlessly off his ribs and chest.

'Activate battle-mode, Klidaan!'

The pain in his right leg was unbearable. He knew the bone in his thigh had been severed clean by the laser. The armor's powerful mag-boots were the only thing keeping him up. Like pins, barely touching the tips of his fingers, he could feel the nanos reacting in his gloves, extending themselves into pointy, two-inch long pipes. The sight on his visor switched from dark green to aqua-blue, with the first of three droids set directly in the crosshairs ahead of him.

He wasted no time with his attack, as the droids intensified their fire from both sides. He limped over to the nearest wall, ignoring the bolts that were now bouncing off his armor, and pressed his back firmly up against the soft stone (kind of hoping to go through it). With both arms extended, he sent long beams of concentrated laser fire——in opposite directions——from his finger tips. But to his utter dismay, he found the droids' shields were still intact: the sweeping display of his lasers wiggled like dancing strobes that ate into the wall.

'I think we're in trouble, Jack.'

'They're trying to kill us!'

'These droids have their own personal shields. And that means——'

'They aren't our droids, I know.'

'They're Seezhukans.... But how'd they ever manage to get this far into the 4th quadrant?'

'We'll figure that out later. How many grenades do we have?'

'Just three, Jack. But they're proximity explosives. They'll only work if we can get them to come closer.'

'Or if we could throw them far enough.... I have an idea.'

'I already know what you're thinking, Jack. You'll cave us all in if you let those two bombs go off in this narrow space.'

'You're right about one thing. The explosions will cause a cave-in. But we don't have to be in here when that happens.' Jack redirected his fire from the droids and focused on the opposite wall before him, cutting in a big circle. He retracted the weapons on his finger-tips, while summoning the explosive nanos on his armor's pelts to form themselves into two small puck-shaped bombs in his hand. He flung one at the droids in each direction, then rammed into the wall, struggling through the sludge of hot mud and stone before falling into a dark tunnel on the other side.

'How'd you know this was here?' Klidaan asked, as Jack rose painfully on one knee.

'I didn't....'

A small explosion sent tremors through the ground under his feet as one of the droids triggered a bomb in its pursuit. A second one went off almost immediately after, no doubt triggered by the debris that was flung as the first bomb exploded. The grating sound of the tunnel caving in could be heard echoing throughout the walls, and especially through the hole that Jack had just made, where a thick cloud of powdery dust spilled in as if to escape the same fate that had befallen the Seezhukan droids.

Jack took his time getting up to his feet. The pain in his leg flared as the stinging dust poured into the wound, and clung to the raw flesh with spikes and hooks. He grimaced and reached for his lame thigh to give it a squeeze. 'Can't you do something about this pain?'

'The pain will help you gauge the severity of your injury, Jack.'

'It's not that bad, but it hurts too much to think.'

'Can you walk?'

Jack moved to take a step, but his leg gave out, causing him to stumble and lean up against the wall. 'No.'

'Well if the pain's too much to walk on, that means you shouldn't be walking. You'll only make it worst.'

'Fine.... I'll go back to the Slider on my own.... You're turning me into a wuss.'

'A what?'

'Forget about it....' Jack made a second attempt to get through the tunnel but his body was frozen in place this time. 'Let go of me.'

'You can't walk, Jack.'

'I'll crawl then.'

'You can't do that, either. We'll have to make the Slider come to us.'

'Okay....we'll do that. But could you let go of me now?'

Jack's body fell limp just then, and he slumped back against the wall, sliding on his back to the ground. He winced in agony as a bolt of pain shot up through his leg. 'What you do that for?'

'Do what? You told me to release you.'

He cursed the symbiot silently to himself as he made a direct link of communication to the Slider's implant. "You still with us up there?"

"Where else would I do in this darkness, Puppycock?" the Slider replied. "I heard an explosion."

"That was me. I had to collapse the tunnel. One of the droids shot me––"

"That's impossible, Puppycock! This is just a drilling. All weapons are primed to fire non-lethal rounds."

"In a normal drilling...yes. But this is not a normal drilling. An attempt was made on my life. I can't walk. Tell you all about it later. I need you to come down here and take me out of this tunnel."

"You know I can't do that. I can't––"

"Don't worry about that. I'll guide you...as long as you follow this route precisely, you'll find me." From his own implant, Jack transmitted his location directly to the Slider. "Do you see that?"

"Yes," the Slider replied, projecting the holographic map against the wall before him. "I have it here. You're under the rock table, just west of the shield generation."

Somewhere between nearly losing his leg and setting off two bombs in the narrow enclosure, Jack had forgotten all about the primary mission of the drilling that still commenced on the surface above. He wasn't too sure now if he'd be able to execute his original plan. "Just follow it, and it'll lead you right to me. All the droids are gone. And the dark shouldn't be a problem as long as you know where you're going."

"I'll be there as quick as I can."

Jack leaned his head back against the wall and tried to ignore the searing pain in his leg as he sought the darkness and the silence in the tunnel for some kind of solace. He still couldn't believe what had just happened. In the short time that he'd been a drone, he realized, that this was the closest he'd actually come to losing his life. And though he'd already died once back on Earth, he wasn't actually conscious for the fatal event. But this one...this one had given him a good scare. He couldn't understand why. Maybe some part of him still wanted to live, perhaps.

And it was perhaps this fear that caused him to switch on the x-ray in his visor to peer through the wall at the collapsed tunnel on the other side (to ensure the droids were indeed dead). He would find nothing but rubble, however... not quite different from what he'd expected to find.... It's what he didn't find, that caused him to be alarmed. The droids. They were all gone!

'Where'd they go?'

'The only plausible answer that I could think of: someone snatched them before their remains could be recovered.'

'But we're under miles of table rock.'

'Someone must've been down here to snatch them.'

'Our sensors would've picked them up, Klidaan. There's no one else here.'

'No, Jack. There is one other.'

There came a sound around the bend to the right of him. He turned just in time to see the blue sheen of the Slider's holographic map against the wall. 'That sneaky son-of-a-bitch'

'Keep it cool, Jack. We still need him to get out of here.'

"Puppycock!" The Slider called out, as it rounded the bend. The projected map hovered like a translucent cube in front of its face. "Are you down here, Puppycock? Answer me."

"I'm here," Jack replied after a moment's hesitation. He blast the visor's beam against the wall and the tunnel lit up to reveal his injured body on the ground. "Down here."

The holographic map winked itself shut over the Slider's head as it rushed down the tunnel to where Jack sat. "What happened here, Puppycock?" It hunched down on its two long arms to inspect the gaping hole in Jack's thigh. "Are you wounded anywhere else?"

"No. Just my leg. Can't walk as far as I could spit. But we can still finish the drilling if you could take us under the shield generator. I have one grenade left. I'll use it to––" He caught it just in time! The faint glint of a laser-knife being activated from the Slider's hind leg that reared up and kicked toward his chest.

Klidaan reacted in an instant. Using the speed and sheer strength of the class-3 armor, he brought Jack's arm up to parry the fatal blow. Five lines of red laser shot from the fingers on his other gloved hand, flying straight through the Slider's chest and neck, destroying a piece of the wall behind it.

A hideous wail came out of the creature's mouth––one that the synthesized translator attached to its head need not relay to Jack that it posed no further threat––as it tipped over onto its side like fallen bench.

'So much for getting out of here,' said Jack, pushing the dead creature's arms as far away from his body as he could. 'This is turning out to be one heck of a day.'

His body stiffened just then, the pain in his leg subsiding to the point where he couldn't feel anything at all. 'What are you doing?'

'We have to get out of here.'

'That's what I've been telling you since we first got into this mess.'

'We had options then.' Gently––and skillfully–– Klidaan activated the mag-boots and maneuvered Jack's body up against the wall until he floated just inches above the ground. **'And we still have to keep you off that leg. Your bones are completely disconnected from each other. Let's just hope there's enough power in your armor to at least get us from under the table, so we can call for help.'**

Jack's body tilted forward until the tips of his toes were pointing to the ground. The light from his visor caught the Slider's weapon near the wall. 'Stop!'

'What is it now?'

'The laser knife. Get it.'

'I have to sit you down all over again for that.'

'That's a Stendaaran's weapon, Klidaan.'

'Maybe the Slider stole it.'

'I don't care how the Slider got the knife. Just get me down there.'

Jack's body righted itself in the air and made an awkward attempt at sitting back down close enough to the dead Slider to retrieve the knife.

'No distinct markings...' said Jack, inspecting the weapon once he had it in his hand. 'Plain as a stick in the woods.'

'Could be anyone's.'

'I know...but that's not the worst part. Someone's trying to kill me. And the Seezhukans are aiding them.'

'Or, it might be them, who are aiding the Seezhukans.'

'Yeah.... Vice versa.'

'What?'

'Nothing.... Forget about it...let's just get out of here....'

EXPEDITION SEVEN

CHAPTER
ONE

THERE'RE HUMAN SAYINGS, once thought to have originated on Earth, that are as common to the rest of the galaxy as hydrogen is to the entire Universe. Old adages, and anecdotes, that often struck familiar around many council gatherings. Legends and tales so eerily similar, one might wonder if some eternal story-teller hadn't been skipping around the galaxy, spreading fables and fairytales long before this war had even begun. It often brought a sense of awakening to General Morlaak, whenever encountering a new species for the first time. He always found a connection to exist between another alien life-form and himself. The same three feelings were always present: fear, curiosity, then wonderment. Natural reactions for any living thing, he supposed, no matter how far into the galaxy they made their homes.

But not once did he thought he would ever feel these things coming from a machine. A mechanical thing. Mere nuts and bolts, enslaved by computerized circuitry. And less than that, because he now shared these same feelings with a box. An old metal box, highly radioactive and covered in rust, like one of the wasted balance-blocks ejected from his warship's mega cannons. Dead in all sense of the word. Pure junk. A piece of scrap that would be jettisoned out to the surface of the nearest star, before his mighty armada made their jumps through hyperspace to their next destination....

Within this rusty box, something very old was kept contained. Something ancient...older than anything he knew to have ever existed. Something so powerful, a special room had to be built, where thick panels of lead covered the walls, floor, and ceiling, lest it took control of the Stendaarans' ship. Or worst yet: send out a signal to alert the trillions of its loyal followers to its location.

Had he known of this power before hand, he wouldn't of given it such a bland name like the "Technician". He might've given it a code-name that was more up its stature, like: 'Grand Master Over All Droids and Bots'...or something along those lines.... There was a vague sense that the Wizard might've withheld certain important details about this box. That he'd been manipulated in some way to advance the cause of the Plogg Sector's liberation, more so than he would in achieving victory for the 4th quadrant, by removing the Technician from the helms of the Kraaglor Front. And that might very well be the case. Each second he kept that thing on his ship, his entire crew and fleet were in danger of being discovered in the Epsilon Eridani Sector, orbiting a tiny planet called Earth.... But what risks are the Wizard and all those living on Stong, subjecting themselves to now? He thought, with a bit of contempt. Or rather, what undeserved reward have I given these bots, whose own advancement in the Plogg Sector, served absolutely no purpose to them in the 4th quadrant...? He was beginning to regret this already.

"You're not even in our galaxy, Storin," he said to the small lizard-faced Trefloon, standing in the leaded room where the old box was kept floating between two slabs of magnetized blocks. The colorful spectrum of stars filled the whole room in a holographic display, and reflected like drifting dots off his white clothing.

Nothing mechanical was to be brought inside the room. And that also went for Morlaak's nano-pelt armor as well, in which the hulking Stendaaran general appeared quite frail without. Instead, he donned the same white skin-grafting material as the other engineers and scientists on the ship. His three arms were folded patiently across his broad chest, while he gave his brick-shaped chin a thoughtful stroke with the other.

"I'm well aware of that, sir," Storin said, zooming in and out of the countless star systems at random. "There's too much data here. And its all jumbled up together, so we won't find what we're looking for. See here...this Quadrant do not belong in this galaxy. It was placed there by the Technician to confuse us. And he's shifting things around all the time.... I don't even know where to begin looking for our galaxy——much less find the Bhoolvyn Sector. It would take centuries before I can even get the slightest idea of what I'm looking at."

"Oh, that's all alright, Storin," said Morlaak, with tight grin. "I wouldn't know where to begin looking, either. Which is why you were chosen for this particular task. Your race is a kind and peaceful lot. I thought I'd give the Technician the pleasure of subjecting it to your gentle hand. A kind of assurance that we meant it no harm. But there's other means of extracting information from stubborn things. A more destructive method. Is that not so?" He voiced this question to the Technician, in which the latter responded by scrambling the hologram of stars even more. The room twirled in a mad display of strobing lights, like a million fire-flies caught in the vortex of a raging tornado.

The general laughed, knowing the fear the life-form, that lived in the box, felt. It'd only taken a few days for his engineers to discover the tiny notch on its rusty surface that opened its mind, containing all the knowledge it had accumulated over the endless eons of its long life. It was only a matter of time before something else was discovered–– the Technician knew this as well––that would help them navigate through the complexity of all the information it stored. Only a matter of time before it gave him what he wanted to know. "What weapon was used to destroy the Bhoolvyn Sector?" He asked, for the millionth time.

The lights in the room stopped spinning on a dime.... It seemed the Technician had suddenly froze, knowing that it was being mocked, and teased, like some helpless creature at the complete mercy of its captors.

The general could only imagine the high level of hatred that glared into his eyes from within that box. He imagined that he'd feel the same if the tables had somehow turned, and all he had in his power was a cluster of harmless lights to fuss at the enemy with. The way the Technician had continued doing now. The hologram of stars were spinning much faster this time. So fast, everything was just one big bright blur, engulfing both the general and the startled Trefloon.

But it was all a harmless show. A strong illusion, creating neither wind nor heat as everything else just swept by with stunning speed. It was all the Technician had in its defense. Just this...and nothing more.

The general laughed!

———•———

The Earth is a small, lonesome thing. One moon. One star. One species, with barely enough intelligence to escape the planet's gravity. An impoverished world, with little to no resources to conduct any kind of respectable trade with the rest of quadrant. More than 70% of its water is filled with salt; and whatever remained drinkable was either covered in ice or polluted. A useless planet by anyone's standards.

It was no wonder the rulers of the Regality ignored it for so long. It would serve no real purpose to the quadrant. It was too isolated. Too distant. Too removed from everything else. Most of the quadrant (the whole galaxy, for that matter) didn't even know that a planet, called Earth, existed.

However, it was for these reasons why Morlaak chose to garrison the tiny world, to operate his own fleet––on his own terms––in this part of the Epsilon Eridani Sector. He enjoyed a kind of freedom here, that he would never have been awarded anywhere else. Here, the Stendaarans were the dominant race. He was the highest ranking officer this far out in the Sector. He answered to no one. From here, he executed his own missions, and not one of them resulted in failure. His most recent accomplishment (one sure to land him in the Galactic Archive) was his highest achievement by far. And once the Bhoolvyn Sector is restored, he'll be remembered for eons by all who live in the 4th quadrant....

The soft hiss of the parting doors made the general turn around as a female Stendaaran entered his quarters. She was one of his Intelligence Officers, all clad in class-five armor, equipped with a pair of wings and a shoulder mounted cannon. Her helmet retracted as she neared, betraying the fact that she wished to remain unseen on her errand. "There's news on the distress signal we received from the Oxloraan Sector," she said, handing him a tiny disk that was no larger than the tip of her finger. "This call-chip came through our portal just moments before I arrived here. There was an attack on the Oxloraan Sector. Beyond that, we know nothing else. Something very powerful's disrupting our communications. We can't receive, or send out any messages to the Oxlor."

"Have you tried reaching out to any other parts of the Sector?"

The Stendaaran shook her head. "The entire Sector's out or reach, sir."

"Hmmm..." Morlaak said. He looked down at the call-chip in his hand with a thoughtful frown. "And what about this?"

"It came with a Voice Note, sir. The chip will only activate upon your command."

"No need to keep our caller waiting then," he said, with a patient sigh, then flicked the chip in the air, and watched as it stood suspended just two feet above the floor. "This is General Morlaak, of the 16th Stendaaran Fleet.... Open."

Upon this command, the small disk spun into a faint reddish glow, where an eight-foot hologram of a cloaked creature, with a green wrinkled face, appeared before them. It stood hunched, making its shoulders appear to rise above its neck and chin. Two bony arms were joined together with interlaced fingers, which hung just below its waist, to depict an air of strict control... or better yet: complete mastery over the current situation.

"And who might you be?" Morlaak, however, wasn't moved by any of this nonsense. Mere vandals...possibly some dissatisfied rebel group...attempting to disrupt the daily functions of the Sector with their gripes of injustice and abuse. He'd encountered more fearsome insurgents in the past. Met them all with a crushing force that overwhelmed their scant numbers a thousand to one. This would be no different. In a Sector as large as Oxlor, they should be regaining control of their communication soon, once they hone in their jammer's point of origin. But till then, they would all be wasting their time.

"I'm General Voch," the creature's hologram said.

"General Voch?" asked Morlaak, with an inquisitive frown. "Never knew rebels were assigned ranks."

"I'm no rebel," Voch snapped. "I'm General Voch: leader of the Plogg Sector's Kraglor Front. It has come to my knowledge that you have something that belongs to the Regalities of the 2nd quadrant."

Morlaak noted how the creature paused there, choosing not to state his true purpose of traveling so far outside of his own quadrant. But he also knew that war had snuck upon them at that moment. But as to what kind of war...was yet to be determined.

"And where did you come across such knowledge, Voch?" asked Morlaak. "We have nothing that belongs to the 2nd quadrant."

"I have no time for idle conversations, General. I already know about your drones kidnaping our Viceroy. But you shouldn't feel so proud. They had a great deal of assistance from one of our own.... Without him, they would've died on Brashnore. But none of that matters now. All I want, is the return of our Viceroy and I'll shall be on my way, freeing you to continue your endless war with the Seezhukans."

Morlaak stared over at his Intelligence Officer, who returned his gaze with an amused grin of her own. This has to be some kind of joke! They seemed to be thinking to each other. This...this...this Voch...had to be bluffing! "We'll do no such thing," Morlaak said. "And I don't care what business you have in Oxlor. Once they find you, they'll destroy you soon enough. And as for me, I have no time to entertain quarrels with petty syndicates. You're Viceroy is an enemy of this quadrant, therefore, he was captured as a prisoner of war. And he'll remain a prisoner of this quadrant, forever."

"I don't think that you fully understand your position, General," said Voch. "No fault of your own. The blame is all mine. I should've shown you this first before I made my demands...." Voch's hologram began to waver and fade from sight as it blended with another image that replaced it with a vivid display of death and destruction.... A frightful gasp escaped through the purple lips of the Stendaaran as she jumped back at the site that used to be Oxlor.

From what Morlaak could make out on the hologram, it appeared as if a century's worth of war had been waged and ended in the Sector. The broken husks of destroyed ships and countless debris cluttered the space that surrounded the planet Oxlor. But this site was not what had shocked his officer out of her wits. It was Adellon; Oxlor's famous moon, better known as the "Egg". It was broken into thousands of different pieces, blown apart by a very powerful weapon. Hot glowing magma still oozed from its shattered core, spewing out into the cold space like precious blood.

Only Voch's fleet of warships remained intact among the space-rubble and debris. Nothing remained to oppose them. Not a single carrier, nor ship, nor fighter. All had been destroyed in the apparent battle. And this...this aftermath was all that stood as a testament to Voch's might.

But how...? Morlaak couldn't figure it out. How could this ever happen to an entire planet without any alarms being raised? This was not a Seezhukan galactic force, but a small number of warships. Impossible! This had to be a trick. The quadrant's forces would've arrived and destroyed Voch's fleets if such an invasion were to ever take place.

"I don't believe you, Voch," said Morlaak. "Your illusions don't fool me. You could never defeat an entire planet on your own. Those images are forged. The Humans do it all the time with cameras and holo-vids. You're probably nowhere near the Oxloraan Sector, so you devised these tricks, hoping you can convince me into releasing your Viceroy.... Either way, Voch, if you somehow did manage to defeat the Oxloraans, and those images are true, there's no way I'm going to hand over my prisoner. I'll kill him first."

"Your stubbornness will be your downfall, General. Maybe I'll destroy the sector you're hiding in next."

"I hide from no one."

"Oh, come now, General. Don't you think I know of your secret agreement with the traitorous Wizard? Or how about the traitorous Jhaanloch, flying your drones to the Plogg Sector to kidnap the Viceroy? Or don't you think I know about you disobeying a direct order from your superiors, after they denied your request to carry out this mission? Too dangerous, they said. The Plogg Sector's too removed from this war to be of any real threat.... You should've listened to them. You should've left us alone.... But it's all too late now. And when we arrive, don't even bother calling for help. It'll do you no good. You'll suffer the same fate and be destroyed in the same manner as the Oxloraans——"

Before general Morlaak could send his reply, the transmission between him and Voch abruptly cut short. And so was all communication between his fleet and anyone outside the Epsilon Eridani Sector....

CHAPTER
TWO

"I DIDN'T SEND you a Slider!" Semhek said, once Jack retold the events that led up to the discovery of his wounded body at the mouth of the well near the western end of Bagger's Yard.

The five drones were all gathered around Jack as he laid on a mag-gurney in the barracks' infirmary. A thin cast held his upper left thigh in place where a med-bot had implanted a short metal shaft to replace the missing section of bone that was lost.

"There weren't any Sliders programmed into the drilling, Jack," said Ford.

"You didn't talk to me on any intercom, either," Semhek continued. For his part, he seemed more angry that someone had managed to infiltrate their barracks and pull a wool over all of their eyes, than at the fact that an attempt was made on Jack's life. "We figure you wasn't gonna show up at all, until we received your distress signal. Couldn't believe it at first, but when we got there and I saw the way you just sat in the mud like that, I knew that something was wrong."

"But who would want to kill Jack?" asked Zubkov.

"They were AIGDs," Jack said. "The Seezhukans sent them."

"We didn't find anything down there," said Ghan.

"That's because the Slider snatched them out of the tunnel before anyone could find them."

"We didn't any Sliders down there either, Jack," said Ghan. There was something almost apologetic about his tone of voice. "The only thing that appeared out of place was the caved-in tunnel, where you set off the explosives."

"Are you sure there were no signs of a Slider, Ghan?" Jack asked. "No blood, fur, or anything that could indicate that I wasn't alone down there?"

Ghan shook his head. "Our med-drones are still scanning the area for an alien presence. But that might take a few days, Jack."

"Then we're in deeper trouble than I first thought."

"What are talking about, Jack?" asked Semhek. "Are you sure it wasn't the Shaapkrot? Maybe it had a bad effect on you; considering it's your first time."

"It wasn't the Shaapkrot," said Jack. "I was fine when I left the barracks. Took a long lecture from Bagger before he briefed me on the drilling, but that was all. There wasn't anything wrong with my mind. I wasn't dreaming. I wasn't having any illusions. Everything that happened to me in that tunnel was real. And I'm telling you all right now, there's an impostor among us. That's why the Slider's body wasn't recovered. Someone, or something, snatched it out of the tunnel."

"You don't think that Bagger, would have anything to do with that——"

"No," Jack said, shaking his head. "Bagger's too much of a Gamlarrion to betray his own quadrant."

"And what's that supposed to mean?" asked Semhek. "Too Gamlarrion? What does being a Gamlarrion have to do with any of this?"

"He hates the Seezhukans," Zubkov offered. "That's what Jack means. Bagger has dedicated his whole life to this war. He believes we can still win. That's why he trains us the way he does...to kill the Seezhukans."

"And those droids were definitely Seezhukan droids," Jack said. "They must've figured out a way to sneak into the quadrant undetected."

"Or someone could've reconfigured one of our mock-droids," said Ghan. "They probably reprogrammed one of our Sliders' navigational systems with new information as well. It is very possible."

"One possibility out of many," said Jack. "But there's one thing that's for certain. The impostor's still in the barracks——probably waiting for his next opportunity to kill me——"

"Cadet, Puppycock," one of the two stocky Gamlarrions said, as they entered the room.

"Yes," said Jack, eyeing the two Gamlarrions with obvious suspicion. Beyond the rugged class-four armor and shaggy faces, it was hard to tell if these two were actual Gamlarrions, or droids. He swept a finger gently across his collar, causing the armor's helmet to unfold in layers over his face. "This is he.... What do you want?"

The others looked surprised by this sudden gesture of distrust. They all turned to him with concerned looks on their faces.... These Gamlarrions were the planet's highest guards.... Maybe the Human was losing his mind after all!

"Jack," said Ford, rubbing a soothing hand on the man's shoulder. "It's okay. They're not here to hurt you."

"I know that," Jack said, scanning the Gamlarrions' skeletal structures through the helmet's x-ray vision. "But we can't be too sure of anything now." The helmet's nanos retracted themselves, revealing Jack's face once more. "What do you want?"

"You're needed for interrogation," one of the Gammlarrions said.

"Interrogation?" asked Semhek. "What for?"

"None of your business, Cadet," the Gamlarrion spat at the furry Tewhaan. "Our orders are to retrieve Puppycock, and escort him back to the barracks. We answer to no one."

"It's okay, Semhek," said Jack, rising up from the gurney. "We do these kinds of things on Earth, too. Standard procedure. Anything less is just plain old sloppy." He made sure to step down on his good leg before testing the injured thing for the first time. It felt sore. Though the regenerative muscle tissue surgery was fully completed, the ligament was yet to heal. It sent a sharp pain running down his leg with each step, but he could still walk. "Trust no one," he whispered in the Tekwhaan's ear as he limped by.

———•———

It came as no surprise to Jack, that Bagger himself was his interrogator. In fact, he expected it. Where else would the Gamlarrion be, in the event that some Human drone destroy one of his tunnels? He knew it the instant the Gamlarrion guards escorted him back up the lift to Bagger's command-post, instead of the training yard's barracks. But what difference would it all have made? One interrogator is as good as the other...right?

"What you're saying is impossible, Puppycock," said Bagger, after listening to Jack's version of the event. "In all my years as a drone, there's never been an invasion by the Seezhukans in this quadrant. There are a few defectors in the Oxloraan Sector and other small pockets scattered all throughout the galaxy, but those are the exception. And even then, we know the precise location of these defectors at any given time. As of present, and within the last 72 hours, there hasn't been any AI signature detected anywhere near this world. Nor has there been in the history of Gamlar."

"But I know what I saw, commander," Jack said. "The Slider took me through the tunnel, and I was ambushed by a squad of droids. We landed near a shallow mud-pool by the well. You should find the Slider's footprints all through there."

"My guards searched the entire area, Puppycock. There aren't any signs of this Slider you spoke of anywhere."

"That only means that someone else cleaned up the tracks before anyone could find them. Then they snatched the dead droids from the tunnel. And there's another thing: how else could you explain my being at the western end of the yard (where you left me) only to end up near the eastern section at the mouth of the tunnel in such a short period of time."

A weary sigh seemed to escape through the Gamlarrion's thin lips. "I don't know," he admitted. "And I want to believe you, Puppycock. I do. But there's no evidence of what you speak of. All we have, is a tunnel that was destroyed by one of our drones who arrived late for drilling because he was intoxicated with Shaapkrot."

"But the Shaapkrot wasn't the problem. I wasn't——"

"That's all we have, Puppycock. That's what the evidence say. Whether or not Shaapkrot was to blame, is of no consequence now. What matters, is the evidence. Are you suggesting that we should suddenly ignore all the evidence that we have gathered, and to simply just rely on your word?"

"Then what about my injury?"

Bagger shrugged. "What about it?"

"I was shot through the leg with a laser-firing weapon. That's consistent with my story."

"We found no such weapons at the site."

"Because it was snatched!"

"I must admit, Puppycock. Your injury is the only thing that lends some kind of plausibility to your story. But it's simply not enough. You could've sustained the same injury during the explosion you caused. This is what the High Guild sees! Not your story. They aren't interested in stories. They read our reports and make their decisions. Your stories——regrettable to say the least——stays with us."

"And their decision is to expel me, after one incedent. After all I've done for the quadrant?"

"And what have you done for the quadrant, Puppycock?"

"You know what we've done. Because of our work, the Bhoolvyn Sector may be restored."

"And what's that worth to the trillions who have lost their lives in this 500-year war, Puppycock? You over-estimate your own value.... By the way, you didn't get expelled from anything. You've simply been placed on a non-commission status until this matter gets resolved. The High Guild is very thorough in these matters. If there was an attempt on your life, they will get to the bottom of it. But until then, you're no longer a Space Drone. You'll be stripped of your armor and returned to your home sector at once."

Jack didn't know why he felt a tinge of resentment at the High Guild's decision. It should've been good news. He was leaving the war!

But he felt shitty. And angry. Mad that someone had tried to kill him, and the ones who's supposed to be on his side aren't even sticking up for him. Instead, they were giving him the boot. Just like that! After all the bullshit they put him through––they took his life, for godsake! And now...they were just throwing him away.

He suppressed the urge to gripe about the Regality's indifference to the life of a Human drone, lest he's seen as being too "whiny" before the Gamlarrion. The last thing he needed was to have his reputation tarnished with frivolous complaints. The mighty Puppycock, loses his cool; he took everything in stride. Temporary suspension? Not a problem. He figured it might be his only "real" vacation for the rest of his life anyway.... Might as well take advantage of it.

"And when do you think I'll be returning to my Sector?" Jack asked.

"Immediately, Puppycock," Bagger replied. "My guards are waiting outside. They'll take you to the space-port, and you'll be sent to your sector from there."

"What about my team? I didn't get to say goodbye."

"This isn't goodbye."

The Gamlarrion barked a loud order from inside the command post and the two guards returned. Each held a rectangular box in his hand.

"Take him." Was all Bagger said, to which they responded by escorting Jack out of the room.

———•———

The question of what the guards' boxes contained, was immediately answered the instant Jack set foot in the Gamlarrions' small shuttle.

"Remove your armor," one of the guards told him, as he opened up his box, which turned out to be empty.

Jack hesitated, and a puzzled look crept over his face. Back on Oxlor, he learned a few neat tricks on how to put on his armor. But no one ever taught him how to take it off. There wasn't any need to. He literally lived in the thing. Other than him being able to retract his gloves and helmet, he was still pretty much clueless as to how the whole thing worked.

'Gimmie a hand, Klidaan. How do I get it off?'

'Just command it to become undone. The nanos will do the rest.'

'That's it?'

'That's all there is to it.'

Jack took a breath then sent the command to his implant, which was then relayed to the billions of individual nanos that made up the armor. Strong vibrations shook his body as each nano reacted to the command. They formed plate-like shucks as they became undone, falling from his body to collect themselves into a neat pile in the Gamlarrion's box. Only the armored boots conformed to a different shape, retracting into themselves until they were nothing more than a pair of imprints of his soles. And as he stepped away, they too floated off the floor and fell gently into the box.

The planet's strong gravity brought him to his hands and knees the instant he took his feet off the soles. Sinewy muscles strained in his arms as he struggled to prevent his face from smacking against the floor. To make matters worst, he felt the mended bone in his thigh snap all over again. The pain twice as agonizing as when the droid shot him.

"Such a fragile thing," said one of the Gamlarrions to his comrade.

"Are we sure we have the right drone?" the other one asked, jokingly. "This can't be the same Puppycock, that flew into the Plogg Sector."

"No. Can't be."

The ridicule was short-lived, however. The Gamlarrions were strict in their business of escorting Jack to the space-port. One held him up till his feet were inches off the floor while the other opened up his box and pulled out a husky pair of metal boots. The guard eased Jack's body down, positioning his feet directly above the boots. It was a clumsy maneuver...to see the big gorilla-thing, and the frail Human, with one foot in the boot while the other just dangled like a dead vine.

"Put your foot inside, Puppycock," the guard said, holding Jack's body from behind. "This is a class-one armor. You have to put it on. It's not going to dress itself."

"I can't," said Jack, grimacing in pain, as the Gamlarrion tried to force his foot in the boot. "My leg's broken."

"What?"

"Your damned gravity's too strong. And my leg isn't healed all the way. You messed the whole damned thing up!"

"We don't have time for this," the other guard said, kneeling down beside Jack's injured foot. "Our convoy's waiting. You'll just have to put up with the pain until you get home. Just look at it this way: the Whorganions will give you a brand new leg if you need one. So consider yourself still better off than most." He then grabbed Jack's foot and stuffed it inside the boot.

The pain was unbearable, and Jack might've fell limp in the Gamlarrion's arms if Klidaan didn't have such a strong hold on his body. Two iron plates were fastened around his shins and thighs, locking themselves in place with a strong magnetic bond. The chest and back plates came next, followed by a stiff metal flap that covered his pelvic area. And when the Gamlarrion closed the empty box, he left a wide gap of inadequacy in Jack's mind.

"That's it?" Jack asked, as the Gamlarrion released his hold on him. He could stand on his own now, and despite his broken thigh, the armor provided enough support for him to walk. But it was a bulky thing! He felt heavy.

"That's all the requirements of class-one armor: gravity protection, and protection from small arms fire. You would've have cracked your leg like that if you had on one of these in that tunnel."

"But there's no helmet," Jack said. "And where are my sleeves? My arms are bare!"

"You don't need them, Puppycock. You're going back home."

"But if it makes you feel any better," the other guard said, draping a large hooded cloak over Jack's shoulders. "You can wear this. It's what's fashionable among the rest of the class-ones on your world."

Jack remembered the garment all too well. The large hood that covered his head. The thick rubbery feel to it. It was the same hoods worn by the drones that was sent to capture him on Earth. How long ago it all felt now. Like centuries.... He'd been to the other side of the galaxy and back since then.

"Just find a seat anywhere, Puppycock," the guard said, taking the pilot's chair. "We have to get out of here."

Jack sat himself down (painfully) in a chair behind the helm. "What's the big rush?"

"Haven't you heard?" said the other Gamlarrion from behind. "There's a hefty bounty for your head."

———•———

Bagger had covered it up nicely!

Even Jack had to admit, the old Gamlarrion was more clever than he looked. He knew a traitor lurked amongst them....no one was to be trusted, not even the members of the High Guild. That was why he filed his report of Jack being intoxicated while conducting a drill, destroying one of his tunnels in the process. And as a result, Jack was stripped of his armor and sent back to Earth. A simple, yet brilliant way to execute Jack's extraction, without alerting his would-be assassins that Bagger was about to turn the Sappian Jungle upside-down in search for them (if they were even still there).

On his way to the space-port, Jack learned that the Seezhukans had more than likely ordered his death, as revenge for capturing the Technician. And as for the bounty...it could've been anything; from a fortune's worth of slaag-sticks, to an entire planet. There was no limit to the wealth of the Seezhukan Regality.

"It was the laser-knife,' said the guard, easing the shuttle up to the docking bey of a mid-sized Stendaaran ship, parked at the space-part's southern terminal. "It was found near the mouth of the well when we found you. We wouldn't have believed you otherwise."

"Of course!" said Jack, scolding himself for forgetting about the knife so quickly. But he was in so much pain back then, he must've dropped the weapon without being aware of it. "The Slider tried to kill me with that thing. I brought it out the tunnel with me, but when I woke up in the barracks I couldn't find it. I thought it might've been snatched, along with the Slider and everything else."

"A good thing you had the presence of mind to take it with you, because you actually took it out of the snatcher's range. We tested it immediately and found the Slider's DNA all over it. But a Slider wasn't to be found anywhere inside the tunnel. Nor was there any Sliders present in the yard during the drill.... We believed you all along, Puppycock. We just couldn't let anyone else know about it."

As they docked with the larger Stendaaran ship, a light shudder shook the entire shuttle. The guard at the helm unstrapped himself from the seat, prompting Jack and the other Gamlarrion behind him to do the same. The faint 'whoosh!' of the Stendaaran ship's cargo doors could already be heard opening up behind the shuttle's thick docking window.

"They're not wasting any time, are they?" Jack said, wincing as he struggled out of his seat. The guard took his elbow from behind to support him as he hopped through the narrow aisle. The other Gamlaarion had already made it to the docking window where he unlatched the holding mechanisms that locked it firmly in place. A soft hiss followed as the final latch became undone, and the window rolled up into the shuttle's hull.

Only the bottom half of the giant Stendaaran could be seen (from the waste down) through the shuttle's docking window on the other side. The beast had to bend down and shove his brick-shaped head past the threshold, gazing all around the small confines of the shuttle, as if he couldn't find the three space drones standing right in front of him. When his beady eyes finally settled on the gaunt, ragged Human (leaning up against the Gamlarrion) he frowned. "Puppycock?" he asked, as if uncertain it was the same man that strolled through his hanger with Tytron, so many months ago. "Is that you?"

"Yes, Magn," said Jack. He remembered the Stendaaran all too well. The rough voice. The wicked laser-cannon mounted on his shoulder. It was the same Stendaaran who'd made that friendly wager with his companion, Latrogh, as to whether Jack would be able to get his fighter pod to stand on the first try. "It's me." He didn't know why he felt embarrassed.

"You look like a Nooran, swallowed you up and squatted you back out.... And I see they've stripped you of your armor. All for what? We were hearing such good things about you: The brave Puppycock, of the Epsilon Eridani Sector."

"Well...he's nothing now!" said the Gamlarrion guard, in a sudden change of tone. "We don't allow drunks to run about reckless in our training yards." He snatched Jack by the arm and gave him a good shake, but then whispered in ear. "Remember Puppycock...trust no one." And shoved him toward the docking window, where the Stendaaran stood hunched down.

One of Magn's four beefy arms reached out and caught the Human that came stumbling his way. The man felt so brittle, Magn feared he might crush his upper torso if he closed his hand.

"And here's his armor," the Gamlarrion said, kicking the box across the floor, causing Magn to reach out with one of his other hands to stop it from crashing into the wall.

Speechless...Magn had to pull both man and box onto his side of the ship as the Gamlarrion re-bolted the shuttle's docking window. He shook his head in disgust then cranked down on a lever that caused his own ship's docking-doors to slide shut. "A feisty lot, those Gamlarrions," he said, but more to himself than to Jack. "Some day I'll punch one of their heads off for talking grubby to me.... Come Puppycock, let's go. Latrogh's waiting to see you." He grabbed the box off the floor and noticed Jack leaning up against the wall in pain. "What's wrong?"

"My damned leg's broken," Jack said. "There was an accident in a tunnel back on Gamlar. They managed to patch me up down there, but I broke it again trying to get into this old thing. Hurts like hell. You'll have to help me to the bridge."

Magn snorted as if the task was too low for him to meet, but then shrugged with a casual grunt before scooping the Human up into his arm. "Tytron will be very upset with you," he said, walking the through the aisle of the ship where the all-too-familiar hands of light stretched along the walls. "He taught you better than that, Puppycock. And where'd you get this Shaapkrot thing from? You get around those other drones and let them turn you into a junky."

"It wasn't the Shaapkrot, Magn," Jack said. He knew his instructions was to trust no one, but he couldn't allow talks of him being some kind of 'Shaapkrot addict' to spread around the galaxy either.

"Reports from the High Guild says you blew up a whole tunnel on Gamlarr, drunk on Shaapkrot."

"No," Jack said. He shifted his weight in the Stendaaran's arm. He felt like a baby, looking up into Magn's face. "I didn't blow up any damned tunnels! That report's highly exaggerated. What really happened, was that one of my grenades went off and a small––every small––section of the tunnel caved in. Nothing serious at all. They probably already rebuilt the thing for the next underground drilling. I don't see what the big deal was all about."

"Oh, the tunnel wasn't the problem, Puppycock. The Shaapkrot was. It's highly against regulations, no matter what sector you live in."

That was as far as he would allow himself to go with Magn. He wanted to tell him more. He wanted to tell him he wasn't hallucinating at all; that an attempt had been made on his life. But he couldn't.... It wasn't because he distrusted Magn, but he wanted to maintain the spirit of ignorance throughout the rest of the sector. Even if his assassins were the only ones who knew the truth, he would allow them the freedom to roam the quadrant with their guards down. If those responsible were to ever be caught, they had to be free to make their own mistake.

Though Magn had to squeeze between the bulky seats in the cockpit, Jack felt as if he'd suddenly been shrunken down in size from the time he left the Gamlarrion's shuttle. Everything was three times as large on the Stendaaran's ship; from the doors, to the aisles, to the starboard windows that showed the looming space-port in all its splendor. The top half of the planet Gamlar filled the entire background with a bowl of green ocean tucked beneath clumps of foamy clouds. In a funny way, it held a threatening appearance to it, as if the whole planet might tilt and dump all its liquidy contents to submerge the space-port in a wobbly orb of water and ice.

Another Stendaaran spun around from his seat at the helm. Two thick horns curled back from the corners of his forehead, making him look like a purple devil. "And there goes our Puppycock, now," he said, in his own high pitched voice. "All broken and disgraced. As if he was swallowed up and squatted out by a——"

"I already heard that one from Magn. Latrogh," Jack said, still cradled up like an infant in one of Magn's arms. "And I assure you, all this is one big foul-up. The High Guild will have all this sorted out in no time——you'll see."

"The High Guild?" Latrogh said, with a snort of disdain. "You mean, the Highly Overrated Guild! I wouldn't put too much faith in that lot, Puppycock. Especially the Gamlarrion's version. Too strict for their own good."

Magn, sat Jack, down in the seat behind Latrogh, then took his own seat in the navigator's chair.

"And what's that?" asked Latrogh, as Magn locked the box in a compartment beside him.

"Puppycock's armor," replied Magn. He strapped himself in. "Anything came in from the base yet?"

Latrogh shook his head with a low sigh. "Nothing," he said. "Can't receive, can't transmit, either. It's like both sectors have suddenly just fallen off the grid."

"But we can still get through to the rest of the quadrant, can we?"

"Yes, we can. That much hasn't changed. But that's what's so strange about the whole thing. The Lannsillian Sector can't get through to them, neither can the Gamlarrions, or any other sector in the entire quadrant."

"Is something going on?" Jack asked, feeling swallowed up in the big chair. "What's this I hear about the Sectors having trouble transmitting?"

"There's some kind of communications mix-up in the Oxlarrian Sector and Epsilon Eridani. No one has heard anything from them within the last——" he paused to check some readings on the control panel before him. "The last fifteen minutes. Well...that's the Oxloraan Sector. We just lost communication with Epsilon Eridani about a minute ago. Soon as we docked with the space-port."

"That's our sector, Latrogh," Jack said.

"Yeah," Latrogh replied, hinting that he was stating the obvious. "We're suspecting it's some kind of virus. The Dhalkroons are already talking about the possibility of it spreading to the other sectors. I doubt it, though."

"So what do suspect it is?" Jack asked.

The Stendaaran shrugged. "I don't know. Could be anything. Interstellar communication satellites get jammed all the time. In deep space, anything could happen to them. Asteroids, collisions with other ships...anything. Still too early to tell, though."

"We should get going," Magn said. He was already beginning to punch in the commands that would release their ship from the space-port's docking bey. "We'll find out soon enough when we get back home."

Latrogh turned from Jack resettled himself in the pilot's chair to focus his attention on the Gamlarrion space-port.

"Set jump coordinates to Epsilon Eridani, midway between Earth and its moon."

"Why so far?" Magn asked.

"Our tether's been severed," Latrogh replied. "I can't hone in on a precise location with our communications down. We'll have to come out near Earth's moon, then fly the rest of the way."

"Alright then," Magn said, punching in his coordinates. "Coordinates set. Take us home...the ship's all yours."

———•———

If it wasn't for the glint of the Earth's sun, reflecting off shiny metal, Latrogh would've never seen the warship in time to avoid a head-on collision with the gargantuan vessel. Only the quickest reflex caused the Stendaaran pilot to send the ship in a steep dive (immediately upon coming out of their jump) to fly under the endless expanse of the warship's hull. "Hold on!!!" It was a near miss. The top of the ship bumped and scraped under the enormous belly, ripping off a transmission antenna as it dove deeper to avoid the rest of the craft.

He hadn't noticed the dead silence just yet. He was still too busy with steering them clear of the collision. And he would only get a glimpse of the huge space battle taking place near the Earth before he realized that they'd jumped way off course than originally intended. But none of that mattered now! "We're being engaged!" He shouted to his navigator, as three different alarms lit up his control panel. He looked over at Magn when couldn't get a response. "Do you hear me?"

Magn's four arms were working in a frenzy, pushing a button here and cranking a lever there. His lips were moving. He appeared to be shouting while staring back at Latrogh, but no sounds came from his mouth.

"I can't hear, Magn!"

Magn pushed down on a button that caused a red light to flood the entire ship. That was the battle-mode alarm... and Latrogh need not hear the next word to come from Magn's mouth to understand what was being said: "We're under attack!"

The big Stendaaran unstrapped himself from the navigator's chair and hurried back through the aisle toward the rear of the ship where the railguns were stationed.

Latrogh took a deep breath as he grabbed the helm's manual controls to swerve the ship into a sharp bank starboard. There were three fighters on his tail, but the sight of the raging battle beyond his window commanded more of his attention than the immediate threat behind him. Four enemy warships, each large beyond measure, loomed before the Earth, like great pillars on the verge of imprisoning the entire planet. Enemy fighters swarmed all around, blue and red streaks of laser firing on the Stendaarans, destroying one ship after another. The explosions of space-mines lit up the scene like distant novas, sending shock waves to go ripping through the battle. The space debris of broken ships and frozen bodies could be seen everywhere, just floating. A great shudder began to shake the ship as the first reports from Magn's railguns went off in automatic fashion...and yet...not a sound was heard. Even the loud staccato bursts from railguns and the bellowing wails of the battle alarm went silent. He felt deaf. As if he'd never possessed that particular sense at all.

The Stendaaran mothership that orbited the Earth was under heavy fire from invaders. Violent explosions erupted on every surface of her hull it seemed, and yet, she fought on. Wide beams of laser shot out from her dozens of cannons, sweeping across the space battle and vaporizing enemy fighter crafts all in one stroke. Spiraling torpedoes were blasted from their chambers in the hundreds, each warhead locked on to a specific target, adding their own chaos to the hellish scene, while they streaked through space in all directions before exploding on the enemy. Her railguns sent chains of artillary shells to go lashing out like a lion-tamer's whip across the hull of their warships. Huge explosions could be seen spewing out in space from one of the invader's engines that was struck by a pair of torpedoes. Lights began to flutter inside the ship as one of its power generators failed. And yet...despite all this...it wouldn't be enough to ward off the assault. Despite her fierce resistance, the battered mothership is doomed is she don't get any reinforcements soon.

At least, that's the way it appeared from where Jack sat, gripping to his oversized seat while Latrogh whipped them wildly through the chaotic dogfight. He too was affected by the eerie silence. But unlike Latrogh, he was familiar with the warship's strange weapon that was designed to disorient the enemy by blocking out his sense of hearing. Without it, the deaf man would always find himself on the wrong side of any war.

'They're gonna destroy my planet, Klidaan!'

'They don't have the fire-power for that.'

'Looks like they have more than enough to blast the Stendaarans out of Earth's orbit. And who do you think their next target's gonna be once they get rid of the mothership? And where's our reinforcements anyway? They should've been here by now!'

'Maybe that's why we couldn't contact the Stendaarans when we were on Gamr.'

'There's nothing wrong with our communications. It's that damn thing they're using––whatever it is––to make us all deaf.'

'And it appears it'll make any target incapable of speaking as well. That's why we couldn't hear any response from the Stendaarans. But how do you suppose they know the Technician was here?'

'I don't know. But didn't they say the Oxloraan Sector was affected?'

'Yes, Jack. They did. And it is only right to assume that the same thing that's going on here has already happened on Oxlor.'

'That explains it then. They must've got one of those Oxloraans to disclose our mission. Damn it!!! We should've never told that buzzing droid about Jaanloch.'

'You mean Whaapco, the Regent on Brashnore?'

'He had to answer to someone for loosing the Technician in his palace. He must've told them about Jaanloch.'

They were all helpless in the face of Voch's warships. There was nothing Jack could've done but stay seated, while Latrogh worked feverishly at the helm's controls to avoid getting shot down. He didn't even know how to fly the Stendaarna's ship, otherwise he would've——

'Wait a minute, Klidaan!'

'What is it?'

'Your last host was a Stendaaran. You must know how to fly the ship.'

'Yes. But Latrogh's at the helm. A navigator won't do much good in this case. There's nothing either of us could do to help matters. Just let him fly.'

'We'll get killed if we keep on going like this. He'll get shot eventually. This is not a fighter ship. And Magn will soon run out of ammo!'

'But what else do you suppose we could do?'

'We have to run.'

'Stendaarans don't run, Jack.'

'Then we'll die up here!'

'That's their way. Besides, where are we going to run to?'

'We have to go back to Earth.'

'I assure you, Jack. There's no way we're going back to Earth in this mess. Too many of Latrogh's friends are dying out there.'

'Those were the High Guild's orders: to return me back to my world. And it's also the Stendaaran's way to obey the last orders given, no matter what.'

'It's worth a try. And between me and you, Jack...I don't feel like dying, either. But what about your leg?'

'Let me worry about my own leg. Just numb me up a little bit, so I could get over and talk some sense in that crazy Stendaaran before he get us all killed.'

Jack timed the wild swoops and dips of the ship's flight before hopping down the aisle on one leg. He reached the helm's chair and scrambled up the seat, nearly falling off as Latrogh made a sharp bank to avoid hitting a wing that had broken off from a fighter. He was too busy to notice the Human climbing into the navigator's seat beside him....

'Okay...here comes the easy part. Just set coordinates for Earth. No...better yet...set coordinates for Earth, Chicago Illinois, North America.'

'Latrogh is not going to like this, Jack.'

'We'll worry about that later, when we're still alive. Just set those coordinates.'

This was probably the first time that Jack felt relieved as the symbiot took control of his body. His arms moved on their own accord, typing in the coordinates into the navigation's control panel.

As he tapped in the final key, the ship made a hard turn and tucked itself into a belly-twisting roll toward the planet, Earth.

Latrogh appeared surprised at the ship's sudden reaction, lifting his hands off the helm's panel, as if to make sure that he'd really lost control of the ship. He tapped back onto the panel, frantically pressing every button he could find, but failed to get the slightest reaction. The ship was flying itself!

'What happened? Did you give him the coordinates? Why's he looking at me like that?'

'I locked him out of the controls, Jack. He's no longer the pilot. That's why he's looking at us like that.'

'What!? That's not what I told you to do!'

'It wouldn't do any good to argue with Latrogh, Jack. He would've never listened to us. So I took it on myself to force the issue. It's a short ride to Earth. We'll be there in no time.

'If we don't get shot down first.... There's no way this ship's gonna fly through all this mess on its own.'

'Well...there's no way Latrogh would've taken us back to Earth, Jack. So we're dead either way.'

It didn't take long for Latrogh to figure out that Jack had locked him out of the ship's controls. They were no longer a part of the battle, but sitting ducks in the middle of a dogfight.... In a way, the Human had sentenced them to their death.

He tried everything he could think of to log back in to the ship's computer, but it was no use. Somehow, the Human had managed to reprogram the ship's navigation back to Earth. He couldn't figure out how to make the helm respond to him again. But maybe he could regain control of the navigational panel. So he left the helm and snatched the Human by the throat and gave him a good shake before flinging his frail body to the back of the ship. "You're a coward, Puppycock!" he said, knowing the words never left his mouth.

Latrogh punched in his own codes into the navigational panel, but then swore at the ship when he didn't get so much as a blink in reply. He screamed up into the silent cockpit, slamming all four of his giant hands onto the panel's surface, not caring if he broke the glass or not. The whole damn ship was broken, for all he cared.... There was nothing he could do, but watch the ship leave the battle at maximum velocity, entering the Earth's upper atmosphere faster than any comet or meteor ever could....

CHAPTER
THREE

IT SEEMED MAGN had finished off the last enemy fighter on their tail just in time to feel the ship take a deep plunge. He thought they'd been hit at first, checking the engines and fuel-cells for damage. But then his body rose from his seat, restrained only by the straps that kept him from slamming into the stern-port window. A great shudder shook the entire vessel as friction from the Earth's upper atmosphere brought violent turbulence. The vast blue of the Earth's sky replaced the black veil of space, and just like that, the enemy warships, their fighters, the battered mothership...the entire battle seemed light-yearsaway.

The Earth's sky was as calm and peaceful as the day it came to be. He felt safe there, if only for the moment. Relieved that no one was trying to shoot them down. And if they did, he would still have a chance to survive, instead of being sucked out into space to suffer a freezing death. He wondered how far the invaders would take it. Would they come after the Earth, once they destroyed the Stendaaran mothership? And if so, this battle was only just the beginning.

Though the effect of weightlessness had passed, Magn was still trapped in his seat. They were coming in too fast!

Something had gone wrong with the ship. It wasn't turning, it wasn't slowing down, it wasn't doing anything...but falling.

He tried to patch through to Latrogh at the helm, but no words came from his mouth. None that he could hear, anyway. He was still affected with the strange deafness that had struck them all when they came out of the jump. All he could do at the moment was stay seated, and wait for the ship to land, or crash. And not too long after that, he noticed the "Impact Warning" message flashing across the screen of his control panel that affirmed him of the latter. A loud buzzing sound usually accompanied the warning, but when considering the fact that he couldn't hear anything, he reasoned that they'd probably been on the same collision course from the time they entered the planet's atmosphere.

He typed into the control panel and pulled up the ship's altimeter and almost laughed when he saw that they were just 100 yards from hitting the ground. But they again...fate hadn't awarded him with that much time, either.

———◆———

'We're doing down!' Jack was slammed painfully against the wall like a broken doll. To make matters worst, he couldn't walk, and he wasn't strapped down to anything that would keep him from bouncing against the coiling and floor once the ship hit the ground. And because of the strong g-force, created by the ship's speed of descent, he couldn't move an inch in any direction. 'We're gonna die if we don't find something to hold on to.'

'The armor's anti-grav capabilities can be reversed. We can practically glue ourselves to the metal floor. But

I also have to warn that we can drain the armor's power by doing that.'

'I don't care. Just get it done.'

At an instant's thought, the entire front half of Jack's body became pinned to the floor. The armor's magnetic hold was so strong, he couldn't move. It was an uncomfortable position. But fortunately for Jack, he wouldn't remain there for long because the crash came moments later in a violent bounce that destroyed mostly everything on impact. He could feel the ship dragging across the ground, turning on its' side, where glass and crushed asphalt rained on his face. The top half caved in like aluminum, crushing the seats behind the helm. A piece of the ship broke off and landed on top of him, thanks to the armor's magnetic pull. He was now blind for the moment, covered in what felt like a large slab of the ship's ceiling. But he was still grateful that Latrogh (in a fit of rage) had flung him to the back of the ship. Had he still been sitting behind the helm, he might've been crushed.

The ship shuddered as it went, sliding and skipping across the ground. It shook his body to the core, making him so disoriented, he squeezed his eyes shut. Each time the ship bounced, his head slammed on the floor, eventually breaking the skin and drawing blood. Bright colorful dots swirled across his vision as each bounce threatened to pull him from the light of consciousness. He couldn't bear it any longer. The wound on the side of his head opened wider. Blood and dirt caked into his left eye. He prayed for his head to stop knocking. Prayed for the sliding ship to at least slow down. But none of his prayers were answered. Instead, a sudden blackness fell upon him, and for the rest of those hellish moments, he ceased to exist in the world.

———•———

The building came at them too fast.... To Latrogh, it all happened at the blink of an eye as the ship slammed head-first into the base of a skyscraper, leaving a mile-long trail of destruction in its path.

It slammed right through the building, mowing down everything that stood in its way. The window shattered as the top half of the ship smashed into the second floor and a steel beam went skewering right through, pushing one of the engines out through its rear. Only then did the ship come to a halt in its nightmarish journey. Everything finally began to settle down. All movements stopped.... He was glad for that.

He took some time to unstrap himself from the navigator's chair. He had to climb over the steel beam that impaled the ship, then crawl under the collapsed ceiling that was being held up by the seats behind the helm. At some point...perhaps between the crash and him getting out of his seat, the sound returned. A sudden blast of Humans screaming and shouting all around him. The wail of sirens. The unmistakable gush of rushing water. All came to his ear at once.

"Pilot Latrogh, of the 16th Stendaaran Fleet, confirm," he immediately ordered the ship's computer.

"Confirmed, commander," the ship replied, through the grill of some undamaged speaker.

"Send distress beacon to the Lannsillian Sector. Alert all brigades in the Lannsdon Sector. The Seezhukans have attacked the Epsilon Eridani Sector. And it is believed that the Oxloraan Sector's been ambushed as well. Send message now."

"Message sent, commander."

Latrogh didn't know why he sent the distress signal. The entire quadrant must know of their condition by now. But it was something he felt he had to do.

He found Jack, laying under a pile of rubble. The Human's bloody face was the only thing visible beyond the jagged edge of the collapsed ceiling. He looked dead. But he was only unconscious.

"Wake up, Puppycock," he gave the Human a light tap on his cheek, trying not to be too rough with the frail creature. "Wake up...."

Jack was out cold.

With some effort, Latrogh rolled over on his back and used the strength of armor to remove the slab of ceiling, but it wouldn't budge. Infact, as his palms came in contact with the metal, it was stuck there. "Oh, for slaag's sake!" He tried to wriggle free, but he couldn't. It was no use. "Magn!" He hoped his comrade wasn't injured in the crash. Or worst yet...dead! He would hate having to lay there until the Humans came to free him. "Magn! Are you there! I need help!"

"Where are you, Latrogh," a voice hollered out from the back of the ship. He sounded hurt.

"I'm here, Magn. Near the helm. I'm trapped." He could hear sounds coming from the rear of the ship.

"Raise your hand Latrogh, so I can see you."

"I can't. The damned Human have us both magnetized to the floor."

"Reverse your armor magnetics, Puppycock."

"He can't, Magn. He's barely breathing. You'll have to strip the armor manually. But don't touch him. Use the box."

Magn knew that at least one of his arms was broken; several ribs were perhaps fractured. He couldn't rush over to the helm the way he wanted to. And each time he accelerated past his normal stuttering gait, a sharp pain would cramp his chest to slow him down. He could taste his own blood in the back of his throat and surmised that one of his lungs was punctured as well. He had a hard time crawling under the steel beam near the navigator's control panel. Nor had it occurred to him that it might've been easier to climb over it, the way Latrogh did. But he did it! He was in the navigator's chair. He reached under the panel and slid open the compartment where the two boxes were. "I have it, Latrogh," he said, pulling one of the boxes out. "Brace yourself. That ceiling looks kind of heavy."

"Don't worry yourself over me, my friend. Just shut the damn thing off."

With the slight push of a button, all the power in Jack's armor was gone. The slab of the ship's ceiling was lighter than Latrogh had anticipated (due to the armor's strong magnetic pull), causing him to overcompensate by shoving the thing up against the wall with enough force to rock the crippled ship. It came falling back down again, but he caught it, gently this time, while he still laid on his back. "I need a little help, Magn."

"I thought you didn't want any?"

"Not for me, you fool. For the Human. Pull him out so I could lay this thing down. There's no where else to put it."

It took some effort, but Magn managed the painful trip to the trapped Stendaaran (climbing over the steel beam this time). He pulled Jack from the beneath the slab and slung him over his shoulder like a towel.

"Careful, Magn."

"Didn't you say he was still breathing?"

"Just barely." Latrogh said, letting the slab fall to the floor. "I think he's bleeding on the inside."

The broken mechanism in the ship's cargo doors faltered when the two Stendaarans tried to open it. The large doors slid halfway open before coming off their tracks, providing just a glimpse of the panic-stricken Humans waiting beyond the narrow threshold. Latrogh went first, squeezing between the frozen doors, then pushing with all the power his four arms and armor would provide. But the doors wouldn't budge an inch. "They're jammed," he said. He squeezed the rest of the way through, ignoring the fearful screams and sirens all around. "Give him to me. You won't fit with him on your shoulder like that."

Magn passed Jack's limp body through the doors, and Latrogh took him like a baby in his arms. But when the two Stendaarans moved to walk down the ship's cargo-ramp, they faced another problem in the form of a bullet whizzing over their heads! Though it ricocheted harmlessly off the exterior hull behind them, they both froze in an instant.

The warning-shot is a universal sign. A violent warning, recognized across the galaxy that one is to go no further beyond a certain point. And the Stendaarans understood this quite clear. They respected the Humans' boundaries (more so because of the Galactic Treaty, drafted by the High Guild, forbidding the use of violence against the citizens of garrisoned worlds), showing they meant no harm, by raising their arms slowly in the air.

"Identify yourself!" A cop shouted from behind a marble column. They were all over the place. They covered the entire lobby of an office building that the ship had crashed into.

"I'm Captain Magn, of the 16th Stendaaran Fleet."

"Stendaaran?" Another armed officer said. "Never heard of a Stendaaran before. Never seen one, either. How do we know you aren't one of the invaders?"

"We don't have time for this, Magn," said Latrogh. "Puppycock's dying. And I don't think Klidaan can keep him alive much longer."

Instead of answering the man's question, Magn pulled up a holographic symbol in mid air. It was shaped like an octagon, with alien characters written in the middle. A badge of some sort. "Do you recognize this insignia?" he asked the man.

"It's the Key of the High Guild," the cop answered. "What about it."

"You wear the same insignia on your sleeve," said Magn.

"We do," the cop said. "As recognition of our Galactic Alliance with the Meraachzion––" It was then he noticed the symbiotic tube wrapped around the Stendaarans' necks. However, he couldn't see Jack's face because of the large hood draped over his head. Then he saw the same insignia stamped on the Stendaaran's armor itself.... He lowered his weapon, and ordered his men to do the same. "How come we never saw your kind before?"

"There're many things you haven't seen before, Human," Latrogh said.

"There was a war in space!"

"We know."

"Were you shot down?"

"Are we at war too?" Another one asked.

"How come we couldn't near anything for the last ten minutes?" Someone else asked.

"Who were you fighting against?" Asked the first cop.

The questions came rapidly. Both Magn and Latrogh, found themselves in uncomfortable positions. More so than when they were being held at gun-point just a minute ago. They were both unsure of what they should do next.

"I think we should leave, Magn," Latrogh said. "I've heard of the Humans' curious nature. They'll run us over with their stupid questions if we don't get out of here. Look... they're already starting to get close. Just a minute ago, they were prepared to kill us."

"We can't leave from here," Magn said. "We have to get outside first. Come...."

He hopped off the ship's ramp, allowing his mag-boots to ease himself down to the ground.

Latrogh fell in behind Magn, following the trail of destruction the ship left in its wake.

Surprisingly enough, the Humans followed, but they didn't prevent them from leaving. Nor did they get too close to the Stendaraan giants, who had all of a sudden been thrown from the heat of war onto their planet. Perhaps they knew the aliens had to get back to some important mission, to which they would be of no help. Perhaps they thought it better to just let them leave. This was alien affair. Some other bad-ass alien race had attacked their Mothership. The Earth, however, remained unharmed. Things appeared to be all clear, at least for now. After all, weren't they our allies? What good would it do to detain them?

They came outside through the large hole in the building. The immediate surroundings were littered with strewn debris, emergency personnel, and wrecked vehicles. It was here they learned the source of the wail from multiple sirens, they had first thought it came from somewhere inside. And as before, their presence caused everyone—— and everything——around them, to suddenly stop and stare. From the injured and dying, down to the ones who cared for them on gurneys at nearby ambulances. The sheer size of the giant Stendaarans commanded attention. Or perhaps it was their armor. The metallic wings and shoulder cannons combined with their curved horns to make them appear like demon-things that had just been cast out of the heavens....

"What happened up there, Latrogh?" asked Magn, as the two stood in front of the wrecked building. The National Guard were just beginning to arrive on the scene. Their armored trucks could already be seen blocking off both entrances to the street. "You should be a better pilot than to let one of those missiles clip us like that. Now we have to deal with this Human nonsense. Look at how they panic and scare, over one downed ship!"

"We didn't get shot down," Latrogh said. "The damn Human got into the navigational panel and locked me out of the manual controls. He set a course straight for here. But he couldn't set up a proper landing sequence because I stopped him before he had the chance. That might've been the only mistake on my part. You look hurt."

"I am," said Magn, reaching for his injured side. "But why do you suppose Puppycock wanted to come back to Earth?"

"I asked myself the same thing when I lost control of the ship. But now, it's obvious why he did it."

For an instant, Magn was puzzled by the word "obvious". But when he followed Latrogh's gaze and noticed the Whorganion ship hovering above the city, it became obvious to him as well.

———•———

"And exactly how do you suppose the invaders would've known of our network of shields around the planet?" The Trefloon engineer asked his Whorganion companion as they walked through the ship's eastern wing. A tall pillar of black smoke from the Stendaaran crash-site could be seen through the port hole windows as they walked by. "This is a garrisoned world, unlike Oxlor. Unknown to some of the most high-ranking officials throughout the quadrant."

"I don't think the Earth was the intended target, Thiraan," the Whorganion said. "And you must keep in mind, that the planet, Oxlor, wasn't attacked, either. Adellon, was the intended target in that attack. Same as the Stendaarans were, in this Sector. It seems, the invaders are looking for something that only the Oxloraans and Stendaarans could find."

"And what do you suppose this 'something' could be?"

"This is what the High Guild seeks to find out."

They soon came to a dark corridor that led them to the ship's Chambers of Galactic Archives, where some of the 4th quadrant's exquisite works of art are kept. Through the winding maze of aisles they went. Past all the frozen creatures and artifacts of ancient times. Not a sound was heard as they went, save for their echoing footsteps on the glossy metal floor.

There sat some kind of podium, at the exact center of the Chambers, where a solid cube floated within a beam of intense light. A tall Whorganion stood protectively nearby, as if guarding it.

"Lhaangon," Thiraan said, as he and his companion approached this...Keeper of Chambers. "I would like you to meet inspector Ghrall, of the Epsilon Eridani High Guild."

"Greetings, inspector Ghrall," said Lhaangon, with a curt nod.

"Likewise," Ghrall replied. His eyes shifted down to the floating cube beside the guard, and noticed the relic didn't rotate or bob in mid air as it continuously tried to locate its center of gravity. It just stood there, in empty space, as if frozen in time, forever. It brought a warped sense to his reality at that point. The way it defied gravity, as if it belonged there at that very spot, since the beginning of creation.

"I can only guess that you've never seen the holy Jhusrot before, inspector Ghrall," Thiraan said. "Am I correct?"

"Indeed you are, Thiraan," Ghrall said. "I've only heard of the mythical cube throughout my travels. But I hadn't the faintest idea that it was kept in this Sector."

"Very few know of its true location, Inspector," said Lhaagon. "This is an isolated world in a distant sector. Ideal for the keeping of all of our treasured artifacts."

"And yet, you go through no pains to keep its location a secret."

"We do not," said Thiraan. "Secrets are meant to be discovered.... And as a testament to that, you said that you never knew the Jhusrot was kept on this ship."

"I suppose that's true."

"Is there something else that you like discuss with me, Inspector," Lhaagon said, eager to learn the true purpose of Ghrall's visit. He doubted the Sector's High Guild would send their inspector all this way just to see the inside of his Chambers.

"As a matter of fact," Ghrall said. "I have.... As I must assume that you already know by now that there's been attack on the Oxloraan Sector. As well as an attack on a Stendaaran battle ship within the orbit of this world, by the Seezhukan Regality."

Lhangan's brows shot up in surprise. "No, Inspector. It's the first time that I'm learning of these attacks. As Keeper of Chambers, I'm forbidden to leave the Jhusrot for any amount of time."

"That much is understood, Lhaagon.... Not too long ago, you were directly involved with a Human who carried out a secret mission in the far reaches of the 2nd quadrant. It is believed he returned with something of grave importance to the Seezhukans. So much so, that they risked coming all the way here to get it back. You wouldn't to know what the details of this mission was?"

"No, Inspector. How can I know the details of anything, when my place has always been in these Chambers?"

"But you haven't always been in these Chambers, Lhaagon," the Inspector's tone hardened. "For how could you be directly involved with the Human, if you never left these Chambers? I have reports stating that you were directly involved in the Human's abduction to become a Stendaaran Drone."

"I was," Lhaagon said. "I was chosen to leave the Chambers and aid in the abduction by my superiors. But I know nothing beyond that, Inspector. If you know anything about the Stendaarans, it's their profound arrogance and disregard for planetary ordinance."

"Even if that was a fact, Lhaagon, I'm not here to discuss ethics. I'm only here to learn the cause of this attack. The Human, was chosen by General Morlaak to serve in his fleet as a Space Drone. And you were used as a means of doing so."

"I've already stated that, Inspector."

"And where did Puppycock go from there?"

"Who?"

"Puppycock. The Human. Didn't you know his name?"

"I knew him as Jack."

"Do you know where he went after leaving this ship?"

"The Stendaarans took him."

"And where did he go from there?"

"Beyond that, I do not know, Inspector."

"Then what about his occupation here on Earth?"

"He was a Detective."

"And what's that?"

"On this world, Detectives are the ones who find things and solve riddles."

"And this is why Morlaak chose him?"

"That would be my finest guess, Inspector."

"Not quite different from what you do, Inspector," Thiraan added.

"I see...." Ghrall said, mildly impressed. "I think I understand now. I believe that your knowledge is limited in this matter, Lhaagon. But is there anything else that you would like to add that might assist me in my investigation? Did Puppycock show any special traits, or powers, that was particularly unusual for a Human?"

Lhaagon thought for a moment, then shook his head. "No, Inspector.... There's nothing special about him at all."

CHAPTER
FOUR

THE WHORGANION HAD learned a lot about the Humans during his last encounter with Jack. Though on his home-world, the sense of virtue and honesty was deeply embedded into the seed of his race since the day of their existence; on Earth––and everywhere else in the galaxy, for that matter––it served no other purpose but to bring them to their knees in servitude. Indeed, it was one their best traits, one in which the Stendaarans valued greatly. But it was also one of their weakest assets, one in which their conquerors saw fit to exploit.

However, Lhaagon never regretted inheriting the short-coming of his race, nor was he resentful of the Stendaarans, who had once invaded his world to don the Meraachzion collars around their necks. On the contrary, the rulers of the Regality had improved the life on planet Whorgan, beyond measure. The same way life had improved on Earth under the Stendaaran's rule. The Humans were nothing but wild primitives before their arrival. On the brink of destroying themselves with nuclear weapons and ingrown viruses. But all that had changed now. Since their arrival, the Humans no longer sought to fight amongst themselves. Though tribal by nature, the sudden presence of the alien visitors occupying every country's air space around the world, caused them to become more united against one common foe. It seemed they'd all come together and formed one single tribe. A tribe called "Humanity". A bond that was strengthened in knowing that they were no longer alone in the galaxy. And not only were they no longer alone, they were no longer in control of their destiny.

The invasion of the Stendaarans had brought an awakening to the entire race of Humans. As they'd done to so many other races around the quadrant.... Lhaagon had seen it many times before. The apprehension, and the feeling of despair when conquered. It changed the purpose of existance deep in the psyche of the subjected race. They'd all felt it, at one point or another. The feeling of well-being and prosperity that was diminished, replaced by constant fear and uncertainty. The purpose of living, somewhat forgotten. The need for survival––at any cost––strengthened beyond measure.

This is what drove the Humans, like Jack. This need to survive, and at least stay one step (however imaginary) ahead of their captors. They still waged their own silent war against the Meraachzion Regality. Though they didn't fight with guns, bombs, or knives. They used the most effective weapon they had in their arsenal: Deception. It was weaved into the being of every Human that was born on Earth. And those who weren't drones to the Meraachzions used it to their advantage.

They are full of lies, these Humans. And this new path they were taking was built on secrets and mystery. It seemed every move they made was in conspiracy against their rulers. They schemed and plotted at every corner. They were distrustful and highly suspicious of their visitors, no matter how many examples of good will were set before their eyes. They hid these feelings of hate and mistrust behind misleading smiles and laughter.... That was how they saw themselves as surviving now. With hopes of ridding themselves of the Meraachzions one day....

From this one man, Lhaagon had realized the truth of the Human's plight, and the necessity of this new purpose, for which they must strive to achieve. It was the plight of all those subjected under the Regality's rule. But not all had come to realize the same purpose as the Humans. In truth, many were powerless, as the Humans were. And it seemed that many lacked something the Humans possessed. A strong will to be free to control their own destiny, perhaps. A will that caused them to utilize every tool within their means to achieve this end. And there was no stronger tool in their possession than this deception, in which every Human seemed to be born with.

It was something he had to learn, and learn fast, even if that meant going against his own nature.

Using the roll of scanner chips he'd taken off Jack's dead body, when he was still a private detective on Earth, Lhaagon had learned the command that activated them and caused them to rise from his palm to form a small circle beside him. He then reached into his robe and pulled out a tiny gadget: Jack's Ghost Recall device. He typed in a command and waited for the split image of his self to shimmer into existance before the podium, where the ancient relic was kept. He typed in another command that caused the scanner chips to shrink just a few inches in diameter, sharpening the image of his ghost so that it appeared more solid. In another moment, an exact replica of himself stood before him, and no one wiser would be able to tell the difference between the Whorganion and his ghost, unless they attempted to touch the image, only to see their hand go sweeping through the empty air of a clever illusion.

Lhaagon had performed this trick many times before, whenever he became bored of his monotonous task of guarding the Jhusrot. And each time he did this, a piece of his veracious nature would chip away until he no longer felt the harsh guilt of abandoning his duty as Keeper of Chambers, even if it meant leaving the ship for just a little while.

He gave his motionless ghost one last reassuring glance before stepping away from the ancient relic. The frozen statues and colorful art of our galaxy's history appeared powerless in the face of his flight as he strode by, down the twisting aisles. It seemed their silence did more to serve as a protest to his abandonment than mere callous indifference when he walked past them. Their piercing stares of betrayal seemed to follow him out the Chambers as he crossed the threshold and vanished around the corner, leaving their precious Jhusrot unguarded.

Down the narrow corridor Lhaagon went. The bright glittering lights of the city glimmered in the early night through the ship's porthole windows. He hid his face behind the hooded cloak, lest one of the Tweboon servants, or (worst yet) a fellow Whorganion notice him in the busy throng. As he left the eastern wing and entered the ship's main walkway however, he began to relax and adapted a more casual disposition of his self (though he never bothered with any disguises) in an attempt to better blend in with the rest of the ship's blithe population.

He came to a wall where fine, alien art, was etched into a framed partition the size of a large door. He pulled an octagon badge from his robe and held it up where a thin sheet of purple light shot up from a hidden crease to scan the object in his hand in a single sweep. A soft beep followed and the scanner's light turned green before fading away. The door slid up without a sound....

Lhaagon entered the sickbay that was usually scant of patients except for the three new arrivals that had suffered serious injuries when their ship crashed into a building on Earth. Two Stendaarans and one Human, fresh out of surgery and already up on their own feet, staring at him with expectant looks on their faces. He approached them and greeted each with the custom Meraachzion greeting: a palm placed gently on the chest.

"I came as soon as I heard of your arrival, Jack," he said to the Human, with a mild expression. Though he knew the three patients were the newest casualties in the battle that had raged in space directly above the Earth, virtually no injury was considered too life-threatening for a Whorganion. Despite the Human's bloody armor, and the Stendaaran's own purple goo; that left stains on the levitating mag-gurneys, there weren't any signs of physical trauma on their bodies anywhere. No bandages, no stitchings, no scars. The Whorganions (to say the least) were the best physical technicians in the whole galaxy.

"Jack...?" Latrogh began, with a muddled frown on his brow. He looked over at Magn, then the Human, before turning his attention back to the Whorganion. "You must be mistaken," he said. "There's no one by that name here."

"Oh, my apologies, Captain," Lhaagon said, upon

noticing the high-ranking symbols etched into the Stendaaran's armored sleeve. Just three small egg-shaped carvings stamped into the upper shoulder of the armor. And those egg-shaped carvings were symbolic to the projectiles fired from the war-cannons on the Stendaarans' battle ships. "Never meant to cause any confusion, but I was actually referring to the Human.

"And again, Whorganion," Latrogh shot back, a tad bit annoyed by Lhaagon's brash intrusion. "You're mistaken. There's no one here by the name of Jack. I'm captain Latrogh, this is lieutenant Magn, and the Human's name is Puppycock."

This time, it was the Whorganion who wore the puzzled frown on his brow. A very subtle feature on its smooth, silky face, but the hesitation in its speech betrayed his confusion while giving Jack a long studious gaze. And truly, the Human barely resembled the Detective, who'd once came to his aide. Having lost a significant amount of body-weight, he was a mere husk of his old self. But as a drone, that was to be expected. They were all skeletons of their old selves. Skin and bones. However, the same Jack still remained; and this, he was most certain.

"The Whorganion's right," said Jack, coming to Lhaagon's rescue. "Jack, was my Earthly name. I only earned the title Puppycock, when I was abducted to be a drone."

The Stendaarans remained silent, and for a moment, it was difficult to determine if they were familiar with such name-changing proceedures, or whether they were still trying to make sense of the whole thing. One of Latrogh's four beefy arms unfolded itself to give his own elbow an idle itch. The blank stare he shot Jack was unreadable, yet all too familiar to the experienced Human. It was the look of indifference. A name was such a trivial matter at this point, even if the Stendaarans' own mothership hadn't been attacked by angry droids. No one in the whole galaxy (and very few on Earth) knew who Jack was. However, the name Puppycock, was being mentioned all across the fourth quadrant. It was an easy conclusion to come to. And the dispute over a Human's name was quickly settled.

"The name of a Meerachzion drone outweighs that of any other," said Magn, to the passive Whorganion.

"Yes, of course, lieutenant," Lhaagon replied with a slight bow of reverence. "I wasn't aware of this other name until now. And because of my strict duties, I might be a little behind on galactic news. I really should be——"

"And what are your duties, Whorganion?" Latrogh asked, cutting him off. His suspicions began to grow when he realized that Lhaagon's sudden appearance was more of an intrusion than a mere friendly visit.

"Keeper of Chambers, sir." Lhaagon replied, choosing not to volunteer anymore information to the Stendaaran (as long as he don't probe further into the duties of (Keeper of Chambers).

"And why are you here?"

Good question! Even Jack was eager to know what brought the Whorganion rushing into the infirmary the way he did.

"A transmission came across the airway briefly after the Seezhukans vanished from the Earth's orbit," the Whorganion answered without falter. "Survivors from a crashed Stendaaran battle-cruiser were being rushed into one of our infirmaries. Two Stendaaran officers and one

Human drone of class-three ranking, all survivors were stationed in the Epsilon Eridani Sector. I hadn't a clue as to who the Stendaarans were, but I knew of only one Human drone of class-three ranking stationed in this sector. That was you, Jack. Oh...I mean...Puppycock...."

"I must admit, Lhaagon, that's some fine Detective work," Jack didn't seem bothered that the Whorganion had adapted to his "alternative" name so quickly. He'd become more than used it by now. And in most cases, preferred it to the original.

"You taught me many things during our short time together," the Whorganion replied.

"Friends...?" Magn asked, awkwardly. It was a rare thing to see a Whorganion forming any type of meaningful bonds outside of their own species.

"Uhh...yeah..." Jack said. "Lhaagon, was the one who abducted me, killed one of my closest buddies, and changed the course of my natural life...forever."

The Whorganion was a bit taken aback by this, obviously not yet learned in the art of Human sarcasm.

"What news do you have of our General?" Latrogh asked.

The Whorganion shook his head. "None. Only that the mothership's completely destroyed."

The clashing sound of all four Latrogh's giant fists, pounding into the mag-gurney, was so sudden, it caused everyone in the room to flinch against the violent outburst. Especially Jack, as he witnessed the brute strength of the creature putting huge dents into the thick slab of stainless steel as if it was nothing more tin-foil.

"How in Ghollack's flame could this even happen!?" Latrogh's high-pitched voice took a much deeper, louder tone. "Right here in this Sector! Unknown throughout the entire quadrant! Why would the Seezhukans come here? This is only a garrisoned world. It don't make any sense; there's nothing here that'll create any strategic advantage for the enemy by attacking this Sector."

The outraged Stendaaran had caused such a commotion in so little time, no one noticed the small group of curious Whorganions that had already gathered at the entrance of the infirmary, looking in. It seemed both parties had become a bit startled by the presence of each other. Frozen bodies, shamed by their own transgressions.... For the Whorganions, it was the fact they'd been caught eaves-dropping. For Latrogh, it was the fact that the Whorganions had caught him destroying their equipment. But none more so than Lhaagon, the so-called "Keeper of Chambers," who had so cleverly left his post––without the presence of thought to change his appearance––leaving the Meerachzions' most prized treasure unguarded.

"What!?" But Magn, was somehow unaffected by this hazy trance of the subconscious, as he shouted at the already fearful Whorghanions. "What business do any of you have here!?"

Unable to find the weakest excuse for their sudden (and unwanted) presence, the creatures quickly scurried away from sight. Not even a grumble in protest was heard. And if anyone had taken notice that Lhaagon was standing right there in the infirmary instead of the Galactic Archives, they chose not to disclose it to anyone else....

Jack took full advantage of the interruption and used the opportunity to provide the Stendaarans with some much needed intel. "Those weren't Seezhukan warships, Latrogh."

Latrogh spun back around and glared down at Jack with those black beady eyes intently; they might as well have been bullets, waiting for the slightest pull of the trigger. "Now's not the time for your Human non-sense, Puppycock." The words crawled out of his mouth like a possessed corpse, clawing out the surface of its own grave.

"I think the Human's right, Latrogh," said Magn. "In all my years, I've never seen a Seezhukan warship do what those ships could. They don't resemble any Seezhukan warship, either. Nor do they look like anything the Drogh have in their entire arsenal.

Latrogh made a loud snort; he almost laughed. "Well, if they aren't Seezhukan, or Drofh, then who were they? And why would they attack this Sector?"

Once again, all heads turned to Jack.

"The warships belong to a very powerful Syndicate, deep within the second second quadrant," Jack began. "But they're not Seezhukan. There's another sector, called the Plogg Sector, totally independent of the Seezhukan Regality.

A Sector, controlled by a group of syndicates; the most powerful of these syndicates is a group called the Kraaglor Front. Those were the ships that attacked us. And I know this, because I fought against those same war-ships on a planet called Brashnor, in the heart of the Plogg Sector."

By now, the entire quadrant have heard of Puppycock's legendary battles against the Seezhukans. Battles (that only Jack and his crew knew) that were all fabricated and made up. Tales that were more readily believed than the one Jack was telling right now. And for good reason too; for if the Stendaarans (the mightiest warriors in the entire quadrant) fell so easily to this enemy, how could one Human drone fight them and live to tell the tale?

Even the Whorganion, most gullable of all creatures, was forced to bite at Jack's story with a pinch of salt. He'd become much learned in the Humans' clever ability to cloak their words. Nor was he lost to the fact that Jack had been stripped of his class-three armor, and would possibly say anything to get it back.

"Never heard of the Plogg Sector," Latrogh said.

"No one has," said Jack. "The location of the Plogg Sector's never been recorded into this quadrant's galactic archives. Only the Oxloraans have been that far into the 2nd quadrant."

"The Dusphloean Regality...?" Magn asked.

"Yes," Jack replied, oblivious to the fact that the Oxloraan Sector had already been destroyed by the Kragloor Front.

"But what part do the Oxloraans have to play in all this?" asked Latrogh.

"And the question still remains," Magn added. "Why this sector?"

"That's all still classified information," Jack said, a bit proudly. "I was assigned to both sectors upon leaving this quadrant. And the only thing that I do know for sure, is that I'm partly responsible for the destruction of your Mothership."

———•———

Something like this was bound to happen! It was a matter of common-sense. Everyone knew it. Especially

Jill, the class-one drone major, the one who oversaw all the drones that operated in and out of Chicago City.

From the very first day, those Whorganion starships dipped into the planet's atmosphere, Earth had become a world under siege. No longer was man in charge of his own destiny, from that day on.

It didn't take long for the Meerachzions to reveal themselves. They appeared as the Trefloons at first: dragon-like creatures (minus the flapping wings), very formidable and intimidating, and most persuasive during negotiations. Then the Whorganions: very dark-looking creatures, very tall, standing at least nine feet tall, but thin as twigs. It was them, the Whorganions, who turned out to be the true architects of this invasion.

But it didn't stop there. Others would come, some more powerful than the previous. Each bringing their own alien ways to the planet, carving out their own piece of the world like the ancient Dukes and Lords of old. Eventually, man became a peasant in his own land. Ruled by––

"You have a sad resting face."

When Jill looked over, she saw Matt, slouched back comfortably in the passenger seat. The huge black cape he wore was like a silky blanket draped around his body, with the mouth of the floppy hood swallowing up his little round head. A steady gaze from a single eyeball had been focused on her, the kind of gaze you gave to an unsuspecting friend until they could actually feel your intruding stare beginning to singe the back of their skulls.

He must've been sitting there like that for a while, Jill thought. At least fifteen minutes. The sky-coupe's auto-pilot had been engaged, so he probably noticed that she'd slipped into another one of her daydreaming streams again. "What...?" she asked, pretending not to hear what was said. Pretending to drive.

"You have a sad resting face," Matt repeated, saying it more clear this time. A bit louder too, as if he was trying to talk over something else, though they'd been riding in silence the entire time.

She almost laughed (probably because she knew it was true). "A sad resting face?" She said it as if she'd never been told such a thing before.

"Yeah..." Matt said. "Have you looked in the mirror lately? Symbiots ain't for you."

"They ain't for anybody," she shot back. "Or maybe you ain't never seen yourself. You're practically skin and bones."

"Oh yeah...?" Matt didn't seem too insulted by the comment, though he sat up in his seat and flicked back his heed to reveal his whole face with an exotic flare. He'd somehow managed to paint the clear covering on his bald scalp in a multitude of holographic colors, so whenever he moved, a wave of aquatic rainbows would go surfing over his head. "Well..." he began, pretending to boast with feigned vanity. At least I'm still beautiful.

Jill couldn't suppress the fit of laughter that seized her in the moment. The way Matt cocked his head to the side––like some kind of supermodel––so that his gaunt cheekbones and jawline could really present themselves in classic horror. A face so deprived of fat and nutrition that she could almost see the rows of teeth pressing against the thin skin on his cheeks. "Beautiful!?" She couldn't help but laugh at the sound of the word.

"Yeah! Beautiful!" Matt said. He batted his eyelids playfully this time, and smiled his most seductive smile, which made his drone-captain laugh some more.

"Compared to what...a corpse?"

"Oh, most definitely. I got a corpse beat all day. Any corpse. Any movie-star, any model, any singer. Once dead, they instantly became the most hideous creatures.... Don't you agree?"

"If you say so." Jill had managed to calm herself down by now. A good laugh was all she needed; her own symbiot had thought so as well. "You're horrible, Matt."

"I know." He flicked the hood back over his head (to hide his face) and assumed his old lazy slouch in the seat once more. The air outside was becoming a bit misty as an east-bound wind began to push the smoke from the crash-site in their direction. All around, the buildings and towers were becoming more difficult to see, giving one the illusion that they were flying higher than they actually were. "Didn't know so much smoke could come from one starship. I'm beginning to feel like we're flying through clouds."

"I don't think it's all coming from the ship." Jill said. "Reports say that eight buildings were destroyed in the crash. That's where all the smoke's coming from." As if on cue, she tapped in a few commands on the driver's console-screen and the sky-coupe immediately began to rise in the air. They were above the smoke in no time.

The crash-site sat about two miles to the east of them. The thick trail of smoke created its own highway in the sky, laying a gray strip of murk a quarter-mile wide that stretched for at least sixteen city blocks. A fleet of fire-copters milled over the wild infernos, releasing their repllents on the caved-in roof-tops, seemingly for sole purpose of polluting the sky with more black smoke. A loud explosion shook one of the blazed buildings to its core, puffing out a huge plume of fire in the sky, as though to fight off the fire-copters above it.

To further prove her point to Matt, Jill aimed the sky-coupe toward the site, where the starship was still lodged into the side of one of the buildings. "See?" she said, while speeding up. "There's not much to burn on a starship."

"I see..." Matt said, staring at the most important scene of the crash-site that had somehow managed to escape being burned from the ground up. "So the Whorghanions don't have any flammable trees, wood, or paper on their home planet."

"Shut up," she said. It was hard to tell if he was just trying to be funny this time. In fact, it was a pretty legit statement. Did the Whorganions have trees on their planet? It was a question she had never thought of asking.

"What...?"

She turned to see Matt staring at her again. "What?"

"What was all this...?" Matt made a show of imitating her, by shrugging his shoulders. "Why'd you do that just now?"

An involuntary shrug...? "Oh, it's nothing. Don't worry about it. Just thinking, that's all." Then she flew directly to the downed warship.

———•———

Of course she couldn't tell Matt that the starship was actually a warship. Nor was she permitted to disclose that it was the Stendaarans––and not the Whorganions––who had brought war to their home planet. In fact, Matt had never even seen a Stendaaran (no Earth-bound Human have). He didn't even know that such a creature existed.

Only a Meerachzion drone, stationed anywhere within the Stendaaran jurisdiction, would have that kind of knowledge. So even though Matt was indeed a Meerachzion drone, he did not live under Stendaaran law, but under the Whorganions'. Jill, on the other hand, being donned in the Stendaaran class-one armor, was strictly bound under Stendaaran rule. All drone-captains were. And each major city around the planet had at least two, who oversaw the Whorganions and all the drones beneath them.

But this method was not precisely how the Meerachzions kept their ranks in order throughout the quadrant. Strategically, few exceptions had to be made when it came to certain sectors, called "Dead Sectors", where just a handful of star-systems are capable of supporting life. Here, countless moons and planets are mined to the core and gutted from the inside-out, the way a ravenous worm would devour the inside of an apple. War barracks, larger than the largest cities, could be hidden somewhere on the dark side of some planetary moon. Or war factories, such as those of the third-quadrant's Oxlar, where an entire planet could become an industrialized ball of constructed metal in space.

But Earth was different. No one knew life existed here, at first. It was during a Whorganion expedition, where one of Jupiter's moons were being mined for her methane gas when our tine blue ball was finally discovered, orbiting the sun billions of miles away.

According to the Whorganions, it was they who first discovered Earth. And indeed, it was they who first made contact with the Humans on the surface. Established treaties, trade, and made overall life on the planet better for all mankind. Then a few years later, the drone experiments began. And as difficult as this might be to believe, man willingly signed up for the program. Eager to share knowledge, and thirsty for a higher understanding of the Universe, people came in droves to have those things sucking on their necks. And by the time men discovered how much power their symbiots had over their own minds and bodies, it was already too late for anyone to do anything about it... This was how things came to be. This was how the Whorganions began their rule over the planet, Earth.

The Stendaarans' arrival (as anyone would imagine) was much more subtle than that of the Whorganions. They had no contact with the Humans, nor would they ever set foot on the planet. It went against Meerachzion law to invade the colonized world of an ally. However, the Stendaarans out-ranked the Whorganions through military might, and in the event of war––in which they were presently engaged––they could very well relenquish the Whorganions of their possessions. So another pact had to made; this time, one secretly made between the Stendaarans, and the Whorganions. The Earth, would become garrisoned by the Stendaarans, while remaining a complete colony to the Whorganions. So by Meerachzion law, the Stendaaran couldn't abduct any Human drones, except through the Whorganions. Nor could the Stendaarans involve themselves with any Whorganions' activity on the planet, except through a Meerachzion drone previously approved by the appropriate Whorganion authority. And so on, and so on. A pact, heavily in favor of the Whorganions, until the event that war should come upon them....

But who knew such a day would come!? Earth was so removed from galactic war, so remote on the outer reaches of the quadrant, so newly discovered. If the Meerachzions did ultimately lose the war, the Humans wouldn't know anything about it for another one hundred years. No one ever anticipated that such a thing could've happened in this sector. Certainly not Jill...well...kind of, and sort of....

As a drone, she and her symbiot shared many secrets of the galaxy; the eternal war within the quadrants, and the enemy within the Seezhukan Regality. She even knew of the Bhoolvyn Sector: the infamous Dark Void that borders the second and third quadrants. She learned of the many wonders that existed within just this galaxy. But she also learned of the many horrors that were currently taking place just outside this quadrant as well. Tales that shook her to the very core. Stories much too fearful think about. Earth didn't stand a chance if those creatures ever visited their sector. She always thought about that: the what ifs. And somehow, as much as her symbiot assured her that it would never happen, the shit really happened! Earth wound up getting attacked! The Stendaaran mothership, that once orbited the planet like a giant cube of metal over the horizon, had been blown to pieces. Destroyed! Whatever remained of her was now scrap-iron, floating through space, or falling through the Earth's atmosphere, only to be vaporized before reaching the clouds.

She flew over to the initial crash-site where the warship made its first impact on the ground, before digging a ditch of destruction three-hundred yards long. She tried to imagine what the pilot must've experienced as she brought coupe down at the same trajectory of the ship's descent. A crash-landing.... The Stendaaran must be one hell of a pilot to have a huge ship like that just fall from outer space and go skipping across the ground like a pebble over the calm surface of a pool. Crashing into all those buildings was the only thing that slowed it down. Surprisingly enough, the downtown mall, a building made mostly out of glass, stopped it dead in its tracks.

She wanted to see it all from above. Get a good look at the ship that could jump thousands of light-years into deep space and back in a matter of minutes. Marvel at the unique hull-design that no other engineer on Earth could've imagined to invent: black, sleek as ice, resembling a giant beetle that suddenly caught a stroke and just fell to ground. Funny...but that's how it looked. Nothing metallic, or mechanical about it at all.

"Why're we parking here?" Matt asked, when he noticed the sky-coupe easing down into the building's parking lot. It was weird, because she could've parked much closer to the crash site.

"Gotta pick up some fresh new shades in the lobby. 'Heard they got a good two-for-one sale inside." She turned and gave him a sly wink as the coupe made a gentle landing on the ground. "I know you wouldn't wanna miss that."

But of course there weren't any sales going on inside. At least none for tinted designer frames anyway (the local authorities had long evacquated the place). Jill just wanted to see the wreckage from inside. Get a feel of the chaos that followed as the nose of the ship came crashing through the wall. And judging by all the spilt food, over-turned chairs, and strewn debris, it must've been one hell of a stampede to get out of there.

The best scene of the crash site. Where the yellow holographic tape stretched as far from one end of the mall to border around the nose of the ship in a perfect semi-circle; blue letters forming the words "Do Not Cross" scrolled slowly between the yellow band of light. A few cops were busy jotting down notes from witnesses. The medical people tended to those injured by flying glass and other debris. A few fire-fighters milled about here and there, perhaps sticking around just in case the ship suddenly burst into flames. Or maybe they were just hiding from the real fires that were incinerating whole entire buildings outside.

When she and Matt walked through the yellow band of light, no one gave them as much as a second glance, or asked who they were. This was all "alien business" and everyone knew that. Jill, with her stick-skinny frame, inside of that bulky Stendaaran armor resembled an alien anyway. And Matt...well...one look at him and you could tell he was not of this world. Shit...from a good enough distance, they both looked like a pair of Whorganion teens out on a shopping spree.

But that's where all the comparisons stopped. Besides, there aren't any kids on the Whorganion ships hovering over the city.

"Ever seen one of these before?"

Matt shook his head. "You know I haven't."

"How would I know? The Whorganions are a very intelligent race. I thought maybe they taught you a thing or two about inner-galactic ships at the drone academy."

"Not even," said Matt, with a bit of regret in his tone. "That place was all about control and suppression."

"Control and suppression?"

"Yeah. Like...controlling myself and learning how to fully interact with my symbiot. And suppression: taking down anyone who dare conspire against the colony."

"Damned shame...." She don't know why she felt pity for him just then. It should've been envy. The less he knew, the better. And he was better off for not knowing certain things. But that only goes to show how differently the Whorganions treated their drones compared to the Stendaarans. Their symbiots were more like slave-masters than companions to their hosts. Whatever kind of personality or charisma they might've had before their abduction, it was all gone once their symbiots got hold of them.

Perhaps that's why she favored Matt so much. He was different from all the other drones. It was obvious the symbiot had his body, but not his mind. He managed to win that battle, somehow.

"But anyway," she said, looking up at the nose of the ship––big as a five-story building in front of them. "This is indeed an inter-galactic starship. Definitely a long distance vessel."

"And what about the occupants?"

"According to my reports, they were snatched the minute they stepped off the ship."

"Any idea who they were?"

"Whorganion," she lied. "Don't know whether they were merchants, or simple travellers, though. But either way, they picked one hell of a time to come here."

"Why couldn't they just turn around once they saw what was happening up there?"

"Don't know." Another lie.

"The ship's pretty banged up, mostly because of the crash, but I don't see any blast sites anywhere on the hull."

Good observation skills, she thought. She noticed the way how he marvelled at the craft. The sheer size of it. The beauty of the alien design.

"This ain't no Whorganion ship," he suddenly said, but more to himself than to her. He didn't even look over at her when she gave him that curious stare.

"And what would make you think something like that?"

"Everything about it," Matt replied. "The Whorganions can never make something like this. It's too brutish in size; all the Whorganion vessels I know are sleek and compact, and just as inconspicuous as their creators." He put a hand on the ship's hull and brushed off some of the dirt that had clung to its surface until he could see his his own reflection as clear as if he was standing in front of a black mirror. "The Whorganions have a different definition of beauty than the ones who built this ship. This beauty is more deceptive, the way a deadly (but colorful) coral snake is; it's only on the surface. But anything the Whorganions create have both interior and exterior beauty.... And this ship is indeed both stunning and amazing, but it also scares the shit outta me! There's something very ugly inside."

Yeah, Jill thought, like rail-guns and plasma cannons....

If Matt, had so misjudged the Whorganions that he thought they were incapable of creating things both beautiful and menacing, then he definitely knew what he was talking about, when he said there was something very ugly inside that ship. However, this kind of ugly had nothing to do with an alien's creative design. This kind of ugly had more of a visual feel to it: like a wrecked house, after being mowed down by a tornado.

It was semi-dark inside, with nothing but the red emergency lights to flood the whole interior of the ship in a throbbing crimson glow. Despite her armor's anti-grav boots, she could still feel all the gravel and chewed up asphalt under her feet whenever she walked.

So the hull did have a breach, she thought. The ground must've ripped open her stomach like a razor on a water balloon. The entire second deck had caved in on the bridge. By the way the front end of it was now propped up awkwardly on one of the passenger seats, she could tell that it wasn't its original resting place. One, or perhaps two, of the Stendaarans must've moved it out of the way. And a good thing too. She doubted if she had the strength or the man-power to move that thing on her own. And she still had to duck under it to get to the bridge-command.

"Now I know this definitely ain't no Whorganion ship," Matt said, climbing up on one of the seats. "These chairs are for giants."

She turned around and saw Matt, slumped down in the seat that appeared to swallow him up like a twelve inch doll in a recliner. She couldn't help but sigh at the sight of him. Somewhere, some diplomatic line had been crossed. No Whorganion drone had ever laid eyes, much less set foot on a Stendaaran ship. However, no Stendaaran ship had ever crash landed in Whorganion territory, either. And being as though a battle in space had just occurred, the Whorganions were very much out-ranked at the moment.

Her only responsibility, right now, was Matt, and what kind of lie she would have to feed to him next.

Using her symbiot's knowledge, she gained access to the ship's main computer and found the logs. At first, the holographic Stendaaran words appeared like warped chinese lettering just floating in mid air, so once again, she had to rely on her symbiot to translate.

The warship was part of the local Stendaaran fleet, sent on a secret mission to Gamlarr to extract another Stendaaran drone named... "Puppycock" (She got a snicker out of that one). Then came a series of abrasive maneuvers upon re-entry into the sector (that's probably when they jumped into the ambush). But then the pilots did the strangest thing by putting the ship into auto-pilot and setting a course for Earth. Specifically Chicago City.

But why would they do that?

"What's that?" asked Matt, still sitting in the giant chair.

"I don't know. This language is very unfamiliar to me. Just standing here, trying to make sense of it."

"This ship is a warship; isn't it?"

"I think so," she tried her best to sound as if she'd just learned that herself. Again, the diplomatic tension was beginning to grind. Matt was the only friend she had. But she hated his symbiot. She was sent to investigate the crash. However, he was sent to investigate her.

"These were Humans aboard this ship."

As much as she wanted to deny it, she couldn't. Matt already knew. And he wouldn't have said something unless he found some hard evidence of the drone's presence. "How could you tell?"

"There's blood," Matt said, pointing down toward the bottom of the seat, where Jack's head was pinned down. "Red, human blood."

"There must've been casualties."

"A crash like this.... I wouldn't expect anything less."

Jill shut off the pilot's log to inspect the blood on the ground. It was dry. Flaky. The Stendaarans were long gone with whoever this man was. And with their mothership no longer in orbit, there was only one place left where they could still find refuge: the Whorganions. Whoever they were, the Whorganions had them now. At least until another Stendaaran fleet showed up.

"This is an easy enough thing to understand," Matt said. "A battle breaks out in space, and whoever this enemy was, they destroyed the Whorganions' mothership.... At first, I thought this to be an enemy warship; never some friendly starship, as you once thought. But when I saw the blood, I changed my mind. This ship is actually one of ours. And pilots are definitely upstairs."

By "upstairs", he meant the Whorganion ship, hovering over the city.

"I think we're done here," Jill said, wanting very badly to get off the ship. The more time they spent there, the more Matt was beginning to see through her bullshit. It no longer boiled down to how much information she was hiding from him, but how much he was able to put together by himself....

"Where to now?"

"Where else...we still gotta go upstairs and find those pilots."

EXPEDITION EIGHT

CHAPTER
ONE

SOMEWHERE BETWEEN EARTH'S moon and the tranquil blue planet, an entire armada of Stendaaran warships appeared from out of hyperspace. One after the other, they came, just popping up, seemingly from out of nowhere on their way to Earth. Cluttered debris from the recent battle collided into their powerful force-fields, only to be vaporized in a shower of fiery sparks.

They were accustomed to war, this fleet. Accustomed to all the scraps floating about. The dead things that now stood in their way, were nothing more than dried leaves in the autumn to be kicked through.

They would gradually slow down as they neared the Earth's exosphere, and allow the smaller ships to break from their ranks and continue forward. From here, they would go no further. Do nothing else till the next amubush. The planet Earth, will be their permanent station. Their new home, till the day this everlasting war comes to an end....

For Claire Ford, it was an unfamiliar sight: seeing the Earth without the giant Stendaaran mothership in orbit. What remained of it, was now floating apart from each other in three major sections. Broken, it seemed, by a god's celestial axe.

"A bit similar to what happened on Oxlar," said Ghaan, sitting at the ship's (Jherilon) helm. "They left the planet untouched, but destroyed virtually everything else within its orbit."

"Are there any survivors?" asked Semhek, staring at the incredible wreckage. He didn't look as mystified as Ford, though. He'd obviously been a witness to similar levels of destruction in the past.

"Yes," said Jherilon, the drones' new A.I. starship. His holographic box-shaped face in the window's display screen remained blank and unreadable. "Even though the ship's only fifteen percent operational, its automatic airlocks are still active. Many levels in the severed sections have been sealed off. About 71.3% of all occupants have survived the attack and are still alive within those sections. They have approximately six days to evacuate before all life-support systems are depleted."

"And Jack?" Ford asked.

"Jack's on Earth," Ghaan said, not giving Jherilon a chance to break the news. "The readings of his implant indicate all normal bodily functions, and a broken leg that's almost completely mended."

"What's he doing on Earth?" Though grateful that Jack was still alive, Ford was also well learned in both of the pacts made between Stendaaran and Whorganion. And according to Whorganion law, Jack shouldn't have been on the planet. He was to be taken back to the Stendaaran ship. "Could we get through to him?"

"Already tried," said Ghaan. "He must not be wearing his armor."

"There must've been another attempt on his life," Zubkov said. "Maybe he was on the Stendaaran ship when the Seezhukans attacked. My first guess would be that he fled to Earth. Then took his armor off, to avoid detection."

"But his armor's not traceable," said Ford. "We tracked him down through his implant."

Zubkov shrugged. "Probably thought he don't need it anymore, being as though he's back in his natural environment."

Ford seemed to accept the Russian's second explaination a bit more. But she still wore that confounding frown on her face. She couldn't fit all the pieces together. "You think whoever tried to kill him on Gamlarr, followed him all the way here?"

"It's possible," Zubkov said.

"But why not use stealth?" she asked. "The way they did on Gamlarr. Why wage a full-scale battle in space for one man?"

"It's more easier to sneak onto a planet, than a heavily guarded warship."

Ford sighed, shaking her head in frustration. "Then what about Oxlar? If they knew Jack was here, why would they attack Oxlar first?"

Zubkov thought for a minute, but then decided that Ford had a point. If they knew Jack was in the Eridani Sector, it wouldn't make much sense for the enemy to risk losing that many ships by attacking such a huge military base like Oxlar. "I don't know," he finally admitted. "It don't make sense. Maybe they didn't come for Jack after all."

"It's strange..."

"It's Kraaglor," said Jherilon. "It's what?" Ford asked, walking up to the window, where the ship's translucent face hovered. "Bullshit! They would dare come all this way?"

"For my Master, they would."

"Are you sure of this, Jherilon?" Semhek asked, with a hint of concern under his tone. Somehow, the word of a talking starship felt so believeable. "Are you sure this is the Kraaglor's doing?" He thought he'd seen the last of those hellish droids!

"Yes," Jherilon replied. "I'm detecting fresh plasma deposits all over the scars of the Stendaaran ship. They must've used their plasma cannons to wipe out the ship's defense shields. Their lasered railguns did the rest."

"Shit!" Ford exclaimed. She knew the ship was right. "Then it wasn't Jack they were after."

"No," Jherilon said. "My Master's the viceroy of the Kraaglor Front. They'll stop at nothing to retrieve him and bring him back to the Plogg Sector."

"And did they succeed in doing that?"

"It's hard to tell," Jherilon replied. "Ever since you placed my Master in the hands of your general, I've been unable to locate him. They've must've enclosed him inside a special alloy to thwart any distress signals he might transmit. It's why Kraaglor's general, Voch, is having such a hard time finding him.

"He'll rip this quadrant apart in that regard," Zubkov said. "Sector by sector."

"Or lose an entire fleet trying." Ford said.

Semhek walked over to where Ghaan sat at the helm, and looked down at the mapped display-screen in front of him. "Have you pin-pointed Jack's precise location?"

"Yes," replied Ghaan. "He's currently on the planet's north-western continent, in one of the Whorganions' colony vessels."

"We have to go down there and get him."

"We can't," said Ford.

The furry Tekwhaan turned back around to address her personally; but more so to question the logic behind what she said. "And why not?"

"We can't go to Earth, without the Whorganions' permission," Ford said.

"But isn't this your planet?"

"It is. But Earth, is also a Whorganion colony. My people——as well as yours——surrendered their world's sovereignty to a higher species."

"It's true that my people surrendered to the Stendaarans, but I can still fly to my home planet at any time. And that's the part I'm not understanding; why can't you? Or how about you, Zubkov, is this true? Are you forbidden from entering your own home world?"

"Not exactly forbidden," Zubkov said. "Unlike Gamlarr, and Tekw, Earth's conditions are kind of different from that of the other Meraachzion worlds. Not only are we colonized by the Whorganions, but we're also garrisoned by the Stendaarans. We're one of the few, ruled by two powers. I don't know much about the diplomatic or political tape behind it all, but as Stendaaran drones, we have to honor the pact made between the two powers."

"Because of this pact," Ford added. "We have more access to Gamlarr, and all the other worlds governed by the Stendaarans, than we have on our own planet."

"I still don't see the purpose behind it all," Semhek said. "So what are we supposed to do now? We can't leave without Jack, and we can't go to Earth and get him. The Kraaglor Front's tearing up the quadrant in search of general Morlaak. And for all we know, the Technician could be playing us all for fools."

"If we can't go to Jack, then maybe we can devise a way so that Jack can come to us." It was Braak, the furry Gamlarrian, sitting there this whole time, just listening.

Everyone, except Ghaan, spun around to look at him. But the fiesty Semhek was the first one to speak. "And just how are we supposed to do that?" He asked. "Jack's not wearing his armor."

"We'll just send a beacon to his com's link," said Ford, immediately solving their problem. "He's sure to notice it the next time he puts it on. Which might be sooner than we think."

"And how do you know that?" Semhek asked. "What if he wants to forget all about the war and stay down there, forever? What if he already tossed the armor in the bottom of the ocean?"

"Because he can't," Ford simply replied. "Not only is he forbidden from doing so; his symbiot won't allow him to do such a thing. But anyway, the Whorganions have a very strict policy when it comes to dealing with militarized personnel in their colonies. Unless war breaks out on Earth, the presence of any Stendaaran (or their drones) on the planet must be strictly limited to no more than three days. And that's with the approval of the proper Whorganion authorities."

"So how long does three Earth days last?" Semhek asked.

"No more than one Tekwhaan day."

"Hmm..." Semhek's impatience was beginning to recede a bit. "That's not a long time at all," he said, in a more optimistic tone.

"Exactly," Ford said. "Sooner or later, they're gonna have to kick him off the planet."

———•———

"Out of all the countless worlds I've been on..." said Latrogh, in the middle of one of his old tales, before Jack and Magn. "I think Kandor has got to be the worst. A swampy planet, just within the outer rims of the second quadrant. Hot as a Ghroog's ooptie! Rain falls almost everyday throughout the year. Perpetual fog. Toxic environment. Even the trees could kill you....I guess with so much moisture and water splashing about, the Seezhukans never bothered with colonizing the planet. So we did."

"Right in the Regality's own backyard," Magn added, as a testament to their general's boldness.

"Yeah," Latrogh went on. "And no one knew anything about it for a long time. Not even our own allies in the third quadrant, the Dashealans. They didn't think anyone would be so bold to do a crazy thing like that."

"Heck," said Magn, cutting in. "Those Bhoolvyns over there are almost made completely out of nuts and bolts themselves. I think they avoided Kandor more than the Seezhukans."

"You said, Bhoolvyns," Jack began, turning to Magn. "Are we talking about the Bhoolvyn Sector?"

"That very same sector," said Latrogh. "But that was before it became known as the Dark Void. There's nothing there right now, of course; but at one time, we ran that whole sector, and even a little piece of the second quadrant. For a long time, the Seezhukans couldn't find our location. They thought we used to jump into their quadrant, all the way from Oxlor. You wouldn't believe how pissed they were when they finally discovered where our dozens of fleet were stationed."

"They destroyed the planet!" Magn exclaimed.

"Aye!" Latrogh shouted in agreement. "They blew one of their own worlds to pieces! Chased us all the way across the third quadrant."

"They lost many of their own ships in that pursuit," said Magn. "Whoever their commanders were, they didn't care about losing the battle at that point. As long as they got some kind of payback for losing face in front of the whole galaxy like that."

"Aye," Latrogh said. "But we lost many of our own as well. On that planet. A whole colony——" And then he suddenly stopped, as if frozen in time.

It seemed rude that Latrogh should just pause in the middle of a good narrative, while both Jack and Magn, were left dangling on a high cliff of suspense. He was up and about a moment ago, when suddenly, he just fell silent. Stiff as a sculpture he stood now, with not even a single blink of his beady eyes.

Jack could tell that his symbiot had gotten a hold of him. But for what purpose? Was he about to reveal some hidden secret before his symbiot clamped his mouth shut? He turned to look at Magn, who just sat there, still chuckling from the way Latrogh had been carrying on before the long pause. Though he noticed Latrogh was no longer speaking, he didn't seem bothered by it at all. Apparently, this kind of thing was a natural occurrence between the two giants. But not for Jack, who waited patiently for the Stendaaran to snap out of this type symbiotic suspension....

No more than a minute would go by before Latrogh's beady eyes began to blink, and all four of his arms relaxed, and he returned to his old self once more. However, something was different. His whole expression had changed; from delightful amusement, to stone seriousness.

"What is it?" Magn had noticed it too.

"You wouldn't believe what's going on now," Latrogh said, forgetting all about Kandor and the Bhoolvyns. "The whole 19th is here."

"What...?" Magn rose up from his seat in utter surprise.

"Aye. And the High Guild. For real this time. They have a lot of questions."

"As I'm sure they would. But why come all this way with a whole fleet, over one wrecked battleship?"

"Don't know, Magn. But it has something to do with Oxlor. The whole 31st and 28th is there as well, turning over every rock and stone for answers.

"Wait...." Things were moving a bit too fast for Jack. "What's going on?"

"Don't know much beyond that," Latrogh said. "But talks of secret, unauthorized missions, between the general and the Oxloraans are floating around."

"Secret mission?" Magn looked confused.

'**We weren't authorized to go to Plogg, Jack**', said Klidaan, softly in Jack's head. '**The Guild would never allow any drone to go that far into the second quadrant.**'

'But how would they know that now?' Jack asked.

'**You're famous all throughout the galaxy, so they had to have known once the rumors began. But the Guild must've been ignoring the rumors.**'

'Until the day the two sectors came under attack.'

'**So it seems.**'

'Now they're out to cover their own hides.'

"Here, Puppycock," Latrogh said, coming over with Jack's class-three armor. "Put these back on. The members of the High Guild wants to see you right away."

Though glad to see his old armor returned to him, Jack grew a bit concerned. "I thought I was dropped down to a class-one?"

"That was all for show."

"Aye," said Magn. "All part of the general's plan."

"I see," Jack said, thoughtfully, as his mind began to race. Something was wrong with the way things were beginning to unfold. At least, not in the way they should. It seemed a whole domino-effect had been taking place from the time he was on Gamlarr, to the time he was ambushed in the Sappian Jungle's training yard. But there were gaps! Parts of a puzzle, yet to be found. Secret unauthorized missions? He kind of suspected something like that might've been going on. But there was something else afoot. Something much more sinister was festering beneath the surface of it all. Something, that was much cause for concern....

"Considering everything that's happened so far, you'd think I was better staying on Gamlarr."

"Gamlarr...?" Magn's brow creased into a deep frown as he gave Jack a curious stare. "Why Gamlarr, Puppycock? You almost died there."

"That's true. But I survived. Then someone gave the orders to take me off the planet."

"For your own good," Latrogh said. "But up until then, we knew nothing of the attempt on your life down there."

"And yet, we flew right into another ambush," Jack went on, choosing to continue on his current train of thought, instead of commenting on Latrogh's statement. "Which, by the way, would've surely killed us in battle if I hadn't set a course directly to Earth."

The two Stendaarans just stood there, with blank expressions at first, but then they looked surprised as the prospect of secrets plots and conspiracies finally dawned in their minds.

"Who gave the orders to take me off Gamlarr?" Jack asked them.

"General Morlaak," Magn replied, through grinding teeth.

"But we don't know that for sure, Magn," Latrogh said. "The message we received didn't come directly from the general, but through the system's communications networks. The identification codes looked authentic enough, but that could've been anyone, posing as the general."

"I think Latrogh's right," Jack said. "The general had no idea of what happened to me on Gamlarr. Whoever sent you the message must've known about my survival. They also knew this sector was about to be attacked, which made it all the more convenient to appear if I died by the hands of the Seezhukans."

"But who would do such a thing?" Magn asked.

Jack shrugged, shaking his head defeatedly, as he slipped into the boots of his old armor. The nano-pelts all jumped to life in an instant, extatic to detect the familiar traces of his DNA coding. "That," he said, relishing in the ticklish effect of the millions of tiny machines climbing up his legs. "Is what we must find out, and fast, because it appears that the Kraaglor Front has succeeded in doing what the Seezhukan Regality hasn't been able to do in the entire history of this war."

The two Stendaarans seemed to pause at that, unsure of what the Human actually meant. They appeared dubious in the face of these unexpected turn of events. Lost. And for the first time...a bit out of their element.

"And what's that, Puppcock?" Latrogh finally decided to ask.

Jack looked up at him while spreading his arms wide so the armor's sleeves could assemble themselves all the way down to his wrists. "They managed to infiltrate the very heart of our Regality."

———•———

Learning the crash-survivors' location aboard the Whorganion ship, wasn't as hard as Jill had first thought it would've been. In fact, Matt turned out to be more useful in this area than she ever could. Being a Whorganion drone, he had access to every part of the ship, as well as the ear of every Whorganion on board. Within just fifteen minutes of boarding, they knew exactly where the survivors were being kept. However, Matt was still under the impression that they were about to meet two Whorganions and a human, who had crash-landed on Earth.

It baffled Jill, that the Whorganions never disclosed the true identity of the survivors. Perhaps they assumed that he already knew.... Either way, regardless of Stendaaran law and Whorganion treaties, it was all out of her hands now. Matt was on his way to becoming the first Whorganion drone to encounter these giants. And what a surprise he was in for! She only hoped that her acting-skills will be as good as she perceived it to be....

"How much further, do you think?" she asked, as they strode down the ship's busy corridor. She chuckled at the hurried way all the Trefloons and Llemaaks rushed past them. Some, bumping into her unapologetically. The hum and din of alien chatter, thrummed all around like a herd of penguins on the arctic ice. And not because of the recent battle that happened in space, or dread of some upcoming war. No. This was the normal buzz, that happened inside all Whorganion ships as they maintained their networks thousands of lightyears across the entire quadrant. It almost reminded her of a crowded market. A stark contrast from what their ships looked like on the outside, silently hovering––motionless above the Earth's cities.

"Not much further," Matt replied, looking down at the holographic map that was projected through a small, silvery device in his hand. "The ship's infirmary appears to be right around the next bend coming up."

"Good," she said, with a nervous sigh. "Can't wait to get this over with."

"Got somewhere else better to be?"

"Yeah," she replied, matter-of-factly. "There's always somewhere else better."

"Like where?"

"Like home."

Matt had to think about that for a while. Jill had such a humorless personality, it was hard to tell how she truly felt sometimes. Like a happy turtle, with those little tears at the corner of its eyes. Her face always so droopy. She was a downer for sure.... "Yeah," he said, with his words carefully measured. "In a way, I think you're right. Home is always better. It's the first place you go to, and the last place you go to."

She made a tight grin, but not a happy one. "Not a bad piece of philosophy. I like it."

"I thought you would, conjured it up myself! Got plenty more like it."

"Is this the place?" she asked, as they rounded the bend. Matt was so busy talking, he hadn't noticed they were no longer in the corridor, but in a narrow hall facing a huge door. Through the glass, she could see the two Stendaarans talking to a man dressed in what she knew to be class-three armor. His back was towards them. His long armored tail flexed behind him like a hooked branch.

She turned around to look at Matt, and the frightful expression he wore on his face was everything she expected, plus more. He was stunned out of his wits! Like a child, staring at monsters from his hiding place! If he was a religious man, he would surely believe that what stood before him were demons of the highest rank, with dark purple skin and two gnarly horns curling out of their large heads. As familiar as he was with aliens, he never imagined non the likes of these. Huge, with four tree-trunks for arms. Shiny armor, equipped with small cannons mounted on their shoulders.

"What the fuck!" Matt said out loud. So much so, his words bounced off the glass and continued down the hall in a fading echo. He feared the occupants inside might've heard him. But they didn't.

"You okay?" Jill asked, noticing how wide Matt's eyes had suddenly become.

"I think so," he said, regaining some of his composure. "What the fuck are those things, man?"

"I have no idea," she didn't know why she still lying to him. But what baffled her even more, was why Matt's symbiot hadn't taken control by now? He should've been relieved and made to depart the instant he saw the Stendaarans, but he wasn't. She made mental note to ask him about that later on.

"And the Human, he's wearing some type of suit. Like you, but different. I can tell he's a drone. He's definitely a drone. But not at all like us."

"A drone...?" Feigning ignorance, Jill walked up to the glass, pretending to give the man a second look before finally noticing the transparent cap on his head. "Ah, yes. I see it now. You're right, Matt. He is a drone. But where the hell did he come from? Never seen that kind of armor before." She felt like she had to act this way. Allow Matt these little personal moments of discovery; she owed him that much. Not to mention the fact that her rank as drone major, was on the line. And at this point, Matt's report would outweigh hers if they were ever questioned about the encounter. Neither her, nor her symbiot, knew the exact procedure of breaking galactic treaties. So she had to tread lightly.

"And whatever those things are," Matt went on. "They're drones, too. Just like us, the Whorganions, and Trefloons."

The symbiotic collars were clearly visible around the Stendaarans' necks. Not a hard thing to overlook. "Yeah," Jill said. "I noticed that too."

"We should go in there––"

"Wait!" Jill raised a hand to stop him. "This is as far as you go. You should know that."

"But what about what you said back at the crash-site? About questioning them?"

"Yes. But I'm the only one authorized to do so."

Matt was disappointed. The look on his face said it all. "But what am I supposed to do now?"

"You'll have to wait out here. Shouldn't be too long. I don't think they know much about what happened up there. But I have a job to do. And so do you. Just gimmie a minute."

He sighed; a low, sand-shifting sound, as he walked quietly across the hall and leaned up against the opposite wall.

The large door parted open as Jill got within two feet of approaching it. The man spun quickly around as if startled. The two Stendaarans glowered down at her, but then relaxed upon noticing that she was clad in their gear. "Gentlemen…" she didn't know what else to say. She heard the door close behind the glass window that matched the gray walls and appeared like solid metal. No wonder why the Stendaarans didn't notice them before; they couldn't see behind the special glass. "I'm here on behalf on the 16ᵗʰ Stendaaran

Fleet, and I have a few questions about your unauthorized arrival on Earth."

"Are you here from the High Guild?" Latrogh asked.

Jill shook her head. "No. I'm Jill Graham, drone major in charge of all colony affairs in Chicago City."

"Drone major?" Jack said, quietly admiring Jill's outfit. He noticed her class-one armor, and realized he'd worn the same kind (just like hers) no more than a few minutes ago. She wore hers different, though. Somehow, it appeared less bulky on Jill's skinny frame. Probably because she wore less of it; on a peaceful Earth, wasn't much need to be walking around fully cladded in battle gear. Unlike him, who was completely naked when Latrogh and Magn slapped the heavy metal plates all over his body, Jill actually wore clothes beneath her armor. Dark blue, neat-fitting denim pants hugged her skinny legs. Her blue, long-sleeved shirt, was a tight stretchy material, worn under the shiny breast-plate that covered her chest and abdomen. A thick black hooded cape barely concealed the ion-blaster holstered on her hip, and made her look like a dark villain in a classic holo-vid. Only the oversized anti-grav boots appeared out-of-place on her small feet, but even this, was altered and spray-painted with colorful graffiti.... He liked it.

"And who are you, sir?" Jill walked up to Jack and pulled up the holographic profile from the battle-ship's log. She looked back up at him with a curious frown. "You must be...Puppycock...?" she asked, a bit wearily. She was still convinced that maybe someone accidentally entered the wrong name into the galactic archives. His real name was probably Puppycod. Or Puppyclan. Or even Popcorn.

But Jack only smiled at the mention of the word, then held out his hand for a friendly shake. "A.k.a, Jack Dillon."

A smidgen of a gasp escaped Jill's mouth before she could hold her emotions in check. She was all too familiar with the name, Jack Dillon.

"Is something wrong?" Jack picked up on the hesitation. "What else would you like to know, major Jill Graham?"

But Jill didn't answer. She didn't even reach out to shake his hand.

She reached for her ion-blaster instead!

An incredibly swift motion it was.... Faster than a snake lunging at its prey. So fast, she had the weapon in front of Jack's astonished face before he had time to react. All she needed to do now, was pull the trigger. But she couldn't! She couldn't move, or do anything else beyond that point. Her body was already seized in symbiotic suspension.

As it turns out, Jill was so fast, she had managed to out-maneuver her own symbiot by mere fractions of a second. Hiding her true intentions from the creature attached to her neck, she often got away with a few daring acts in the past. But nothing as deadly as this; which was why her symbiot had to stop her at all costs. Lock her body up, so tight, that her joints began to ache....

Latrogh and Magn, were the first to react, aiming their shoulder-mounted laser-cannons at different points on the woman's frozen face as they closed in on her. They weren't the interrogative types. Blood and guts was a Stendaaran's business. They dealt strictly in death, and they had all intentions of blowing Jill's head clean off of her shoulders—— symbiot and all....

"Wait!" Finally coming out of his stupor, Jack held up a hand, preventing the Stendaarans from making a bloody mess inside the room. "We need her alive!"

"Assassin," Latrogh hissed behind his sharp pointy teeth.

"Traitor," added Magn from behind.

The large door opened up just then, and in rushed Matt, waving his ion-blaster at everyone in the room. Standing outside, he witnessed everything behind that special glass, and was sure that his partner was about to be killed. "Let her go!" Regardless of how assertive his voice appeared to sound, he still felt shaky inside.

"Look, Magn," said Latrogh, already beginning to approach the tiny Human. "There's two of them. I think I'll take this one. We don't need him. One prisoner's enough."

"Hold on, Latrogh," said Jack. "Don't kill him just yet." Then he turned quickly to Jill. "You better tell him to drop his gun. If you care anything about him, you'll do it now."

"Drop the gun, Matt," Jill said.

But Jack knew that was her symbiot talking. The words came out too flat. Emotionless. The real Jill, still wanted to kill him. Her eyes still raged with that wild fire of hatred. But why...?

"You sure?" Matt asked her, not wanting to give up the fight so easily. But not really wanting to die, either.

"Yes," Jill said. "Just do it."

Matt lowered his blaster, and slowly eased it down on the ground.

"Now, kick it over here," Jack said.

There came the sound of metal skittering across the smooth surface of the floor as Matt's ion-blaster came to a spinning stop at Jack's feet. "Now you too, drone Major," he said to Jill. "I need you to release your weapon! Give it to me."

Jill obediently handed her ion-blaster (butt first) to Jack, then placed both hands at her side and stood at attention.

"And what should we do with this one?" Latrogh asked, walking up to Matt, and snarling down at the little Human as if he was about to bite one of his arms off. "I still say we kill one of them. Send a message to all the other traitors that's sure to come."

"Traitors?" An offended, but very frightened Matt, shot back. "We're not traitors. We're simply trying to figure out why you came to our world, without authorization––in the middle of a battle––and then set a direct course for our planet."

"You mean our planet," Latrogh said, menacingly. He paused to get a second (or better) look at the man standing in front of him. He noticed the absence of armor and the old style of dress; especially the customized cap that covered his skull. "You're no Stendaaran drone," he concluded. "So you must be one of the Whorganions'. Are you not."

"I am."

"Then you must know you're in direct violation of a garrisoned treaty, by involving yourself in Stendaaran matters."

"Earth is not under Stendaaran law," said Jill, to Matt's rescue. The poor guy didn't even know who the Stendaarans were. "You may have claimed the planet as your own, but it's the Whorganions who govern it; according to the garrison treaty."

"Hmm... so the traitor knows a little domestic diplomacy," Magn said. "But where does it say, anywhere in the treaty, that we should betray our quadrant, by killing one our own."

"Who sent you, major?" asked Jack, quickly wanting to get down to the bottom of the matter. An emergency beacon had been going off in his implant from the time he put his armor back on. His friends were close by, somewhere above the Earth's orbit. They were trying contact him. "What is this all about?"

"For your information," Jill began. "No one sent me. There's no one in this entire galaxy that can convince me to betray my own world."

"Okay.... Now that that's out of the way. You weren't hired by the Seezhukans, and no one from the Kraaglor Front managed to brainwash your mind. So why'd you try to kill me just now?"

Though her symbiot had most of her body's muscles under tight control, making any kind of expression impossible, a surge of metal anguish still happened to present itself through Jill's face. Her eyes suddenly reddened and became moist with tears. Her cheeks became flushed, and beads of sweat settled on the tip of her nose. Her gaze had been fixed forward, not directly staring into Jack's eyes, but she wished they were, as two long streams of tears spilled down onto her face.

Jack didn't know what to make of it all. Was this some kind of alien trick? Every now and then, he had to remind himself that he was still fairly new to this business. He couldn't trust the woman crying in front of him. In fact, he became annoyed by it. "What the hell is the matter with you?!"

And then, perhaps not wanting to excite herself anymore; or maybe the symbiot had some control over her tone as well. Jill simply replied, as calmly as ever: "Jack Dillon, you murdered my sons."

———•———

"I'm the one in charge of all abductions that happen in this city," Jill began, as she retold the story about the worst day of her life: the day she met Jack. "Because the Whorganions and Stendaarans couldn't possibly know which Humans would make the most effective drones, they send me to locate them. For example, in order for the Whorganions to get a perfect understanding of the Human anatomy, they needed the expert advice of well educated doctors. Or if the Stendaarns need fighters, the ones trained in combat and law enforcement are the ones best suited to serve in their armies. In either case, they couldn't just snatch any random person off the streets; it wouldn't have best served their purpose. So they send in people like me, to make the best choices for them."

"Then who chose you?" Jack asked, remembering how young Claire Ford was when she said she had been abducted to become a drone. As a teen, she was the most 'world-smart' kid in her city. Now she's a drone leader, and one of the best young hackers in the galaxy––the only one to gave entered the first quadrant (so she claims) and lived to tell the tale. He often wondered how the Stendaarans would know to pick her specifically, out of the billions of other people on the planet. But it was all beginning to make sense to him now.

"I chose myself," Jill replied. "I was one of the few people who volunteered to become a drone. I had been a major in the U.S. marine corps for thirty years. I was engineered to become a soldier, to defend my country in the best possible way. And as a reward, the Stendaarans allowed me to keep my rank. Then they put me in charge of all the other abductions, including yours.

"For whatever reasons they might've had, the Stendaarans needed someone who was specialized in finding things. Well, on Earth, the only people who do that kind of work are detectives––such as yourself. So I set about researching the most qualified detective in the whole city. Your profile eventually came up, out of the hundreds I'd already scrolled through. And yours was the most sound, with a career spanning over fifty years."

"So, you chose me?"

"Yes. I chose you. I sent the Whorganion, Lhaagon, to bring you back to the ship. But then something happened. You left before we had a chance to grab you. You had those damned Recall chips with you, and you used them to follow my sons."

"The two drones at the apartment," Jack said, remembering it all. "But those two tried to kill me."

"They weren't trying to kill you. If they were, then you'd be dead by now. I saw what their blasters to the wall, and it's impossible to miss anyone from that close. They missed intentionally, Jack. They only wanted to scare you, thinking you'd run back out of the building. But you didn't."

She paused there, not wanting retell what her own Recall chips would show her later on. "You took their bodies. Dragged them down the steps, and dumped them in the back of your car. Then you ran to that no-good bureaucrat for help."

"Nolan."

"Yes. The same one. Did you know they ordered him to kill you?" "Who? The Stendaarans?"

"No, Jack. The Stendaarans wanted you unharmed. It was the heads in Nolan's department. They ordered him to kill you. That's what they do to anyone who come in contact with drones. But they didn't know that you were to become a drone yourself. So Nolan killed you, and tossed you from a height of two-thousand feet. I wanted so bad to just let you fall. To watch your whole body just splatter on the pavement. But I couldn't. After all you took from me, I still had a duty to fulfill."

"So it was you that snatched me out of the sky?" said Jack, feeling kind of relieved that some of these mysteries of his past were now being answered.

"My symbiot did most of the calculations, but it was solely my choice to save you. I could've easily find the next detective in line. But I didn't. And I regretted that for a long time."

"You snatched Nolan that same night as well, didn't you?"

"I did," Jill replied. "But it was the Stendaarans who ordered his abduction. Not to become a drone, but to be executed for killing one of their drones."

"But how? I hadn't yet become a drone when Nolan killed me."

"The minute you're chosen to become a drone, you become the sole property of the Stendaarans."

"Then what about your sons? Weren't they drones, too? What're the laws regarding that?"

"They were Whorganion drones. The same rules don't apply."

Rules...Jack thought to himself. What a funny word.... "And had you succeeded in killing me today? What would've happened to you then?"

"I would've been executed," Jill said. "Most likely in this same room, by your Stendaaran friends. And if not, then the High Guild would've surely seen my death-sentence carried out."

At the mentioning of the High Guild, Jack was suddenly reminded that they'd been summoned by the Stendaaran fleet that had just entered Earth's orbit. He turned to Latrogh, who was still glaring down at Matt, as if he was about to eat him alive. "How much more time do we have till we see the Guild?"

"The orders were that we are to get off the planet right away," Latrogh said, without taking his eyes off Matt. "I say we should go. We've wasted enough time here."

"Then why don't they just snatch us?" Jack asked.

"They can't," Magn said. "Not with the kind of armor we have on. Organic things don't materialize well when you bring mechanical things along with it. A lot of bad stuff could happen."

"Okay..." said Jack, getting the point. No wonder why he always found himself naked anytime he was snatched. The Whorganions were indeed a highly advanced race, with technical marvels far beyond our own. However, they were far from being perfect. "Then they'll be sending someone down."

"They're not," said Latrogh. "They can't send any ships to this colonized planet. The Whorganions forbid it. We've already broken the treaty by coming here; which is why we must now answer to the High Guild."

Of course, man had ships that could go to space. We've been doing it long before the Whorganions came. But the mere thought of one of our own ships docking with any one of those gargantuan vessels up there had never even occurred to Jack. "So they expect us to fly up there on our own?"

"They do," said Magn. "And it's not that much of a problem. That's what our drones are for. Like your major, standing there. The one who just tried to kill you. She could use any one of these Whorganion shuttles to take us home."

Jack turned to Jill, with a curious expression. "You could do that?"

"As drone major," Jill began. "I can take you, and these two, all the way to Stendaar if I really wanted to."

"But not without the Whorganions' consent," Matt said, kind of hinting that he wanted to tag along....

CHAPTER
TWO

"I SHOULD'VE SEEN this coming," hissed admiral Sollack's holographic image, in the quiet confines of general Voch's quarters. The crimson slits of his eyes glowed like hot metal stuffed in the brown furrows of his wrinkled face. He was a creature of old. An odd-looking one at that, with just a single triangular vocalizer on his pointed chin to serve as both nostril and mouth. The machine behind the synthetic flesh well hidden––though not by its outer appearance, but rather, through the raw emotion it displayed. "The signs were all there, including ambition, the most obvious of them all."

"And yet, we failed to act," Voch patiently replied. He didn't share in his admiral's concerns, nor did he care to show it. More pressing matters jammed his circuits.

"Regrettably so."

"And that's because most betrayal's are impossible to prevent."

A moment's hesitation caused a slight twitch in Sollack's lower jaw. A short in one of his capacitors, perhaps. "Impossible to prevent...?" A question of logic, not ignorance.

"No matter how prosperous a world might become, there'll always be an opposing force of some kind. A traitor, within the ranks, bent on their own versions of peace and prosperity. As we once were, and still are, to the Regality."

"We did not betray the Regality." Though he understood Voch's reasoning for saying this, he didn't like the implications of being a traitor to his own kind.

"In a way, we did."

"But I don't see it that way, general. And I'm quite sure that you remember our purpose for populating the Plogg Sector. There weren't any plots against the emperor. We didn't start any wars."

"And what do you suppose the outcome would've been, if the Regality hadn't allow us to venture off on our own?"

"Can't say for sure what might've happened. There's high possibility that the quadrant could've fell into conflict with itself. And in such a case, the cause would've been a just one. But what reason would Jherilon have for going to the Meerachzions?"

"Whatever reason he saw fit," Voch replied, in that casual tone again; as if to excuse Jherilon's sudden betrayal. "None of that matters now, Sollack."

A derisive snort came from the wavering hologram. A sound, like a burst of steam as the admiral vented his anger. "We should've destroyed that whole Sector," he said, then turned from Voch to face the projected display of Earth and its moon, hovering silently in the general's quarters. "Planet and all...if I only knew that this is where Jherilon would've been in the immediate aftermath of our battle. I would've kept what remained of our fleet and waited for him to arrive."

"Is that why you are recommending that we get fresh reinforcements from Plogg?"

"Yes, general. More than half of our entire fleet have been destroyed in the last two battles. We should send for reinforcements. At least three more fleets. Then we should return to the Epsilon Eridani Sector and quash the beginnings of this rebellion before things get worst."

"And what of our Viceroy?" Voch asked.

"When we end the rebellion, then we'll——"

"What rebellion!!!" Voch shouted at the admiral's hologram in pure rage and frustration. He rose up from his seat and approached Sollack's ghostly figure. "Is that what you think is going on here? A rebellion? After all that has transpired and led up to this point. You think Jherilon is rebelling against us? All by his self?"

"Maybe the Piilor Syndicate's wants more power——"

"The Piilor Syndicate, as we know it, is no more. Both Spigon and Zhorgan, are dead."

Though the admiral was well aware of the Syndicate leaders' deaths, things were still moving too fast for him to accurately fit the pieces of this puzzle together. The conclusion of a syndicate rebellion within the Plogg Sector, was as good of an answer as any, to explain the recent conflict that was happening there. It was perhaps the only explaination that anyone, including himself, could've came up with. "I apologize if I may appear a bit inadequate at this time, general. But as I see it, all evidence show signs of some kind of rebellion, in one form or another. Two syndicate leaders are, but we must not rule out the possibility that other groups could be involved. The merchant Jhaanloch, certainly had a hand to play in all this. And now, we are learning that the Meerachzions are involved."

"And that is exactly why we're not in any danger of losing our stronghold in Plogg. Too many outside parties are involve in this. From all the information we've gathered so far, the Meerachzions have no interest in our sector. They only want the Viceroy."

"For what purpose?"

"Only the Meerachzions and Jherilon, know the answer to that question. But Jherilon's the main key here. Find Jherilon, and we stand a good chance of returning to Plogg with the Viceroy."

"But we have found him, general. Let us gather up our reinforcements and head back to the planet, where Jherilon is now hiding."

Voch began shaking his head. "It won't be as simple as that. The Earth is now heavily guarded. Even with all reinforcements we have at our disposal, we still don't know what kinds of traps the Meerachzions may have waiting for us if we do happen to return there. And then there's the possibility of Jherilon escaping while we engage the Meerachzions in one of the largest battles we've ever fought against anyone, including the Drofh.... Such an error will cost us dearly...."

"Then by what other means are we suppose to capture this traitor?"

"He's bound to venture off on his own at some point. In the mean time, we'll wait and monitor his movements. The moment he strays away from the Meerachzion fleet, will be the exact moment of his demise."

———●———

When Jack first learned that he was to be seen by the High Guild of the Meerachzion Regality, what first came to mind, was this grand courtroom with dozens of aliens in dark robes with grim, judgmental expressions on their faces. A gavel would sound and perfect silence would be observed. The judge, ––or the Meerachzion equivalent––would then ask him a series of questions upon which, his fate could be decided; not too different from any courtroom on Earth. He even thought that he might be appointed some kind of Meerachzion representative, like attorney, standing at his side to fend off any badgering when things got too tough for him to handle.

But when he followed a brass-colored droid through a bright portal, what he found on the other side, was not a courtroom, but a different planet. A whole different, alien planet! Complete with its own alien landscape, atmosphere and species.

Hardly what he expected to find when Jill flew them up to the main Stendaaran battleship that led the 19th Stendaaran fleet. A portal aboard a starship that sent you to another planet? Such things were still beyond his limited imaginations, despite all the Universal wonders he'd experienced thus far.

It appeared to be a cold, barren world, at first. Cloudy, white as far as the Human could see, due to the thick snow-drift that rode the icy gale. But then the lights began coming into view. Very faint, like street-lamps in the midst of a fog, smudged and blurry high up in the sky above. Some of them flew in long swerving lines, only to be broken off in sections where some either veered to the left or to the right. Traffic, vehicles following their own computerized routes in the sky.

Tall buildings, outlined only by their bright windows that were stacked upon each other; some as tall as thirty stories high.

The hum of pedestrians, well bundled as they shuffled through the snow, was barely heard above the planet's relentless blizzard. A snow-flake flew into his eyeball where it quickly dissolved into a stinging sensation. A mild irritation, causing Jack to squeeze his eyes shut, but enough to make him activate his face-mask for the first time since putting his armor back on.

A beeping sound came directly into his ear. A message, from his friends back home.

"Yeah," he answered, as he would, with any casual call. He had no way of knowing it was already two days old. "Anybody there...? Hello...." He tapped the side of his helmet, despite knowing their communications were done through his implant. "Hey...Zubkov. Semhek.... Where the hell is everybody? Why's no one answering?"

"We're a thousands light-years from Earth, Jack,' Klidaan said. **"It'll take centuries, on top of centuries, for your reply to travel across the galaxy.'**

He shrugged, knowingly. 'Well...that makes a lot of sense. A thousand light-years...didn't know a portal could take us so far. Were are we, anyway?'

'We're on the planet, Yhouln. The world of the High Guild.'

'Why choose a world so cold, and so distant from the rest of the quadrant?

'Out of all the species in the entire 4th quadrant, the Yhoulnanic, are by far, the most judicial and bureaucratic race you'll ever encounter. Their service to

the Regality is essential in maintaining order between the races.'

'I kind of feel honored.'

'Why would you?'

'It's a human thing. I don't think you'll understand.'

'Well, do you mind explaining?'

'It brings about a sense of relevance.'

'What does?'

'The fact that members of the High Guild would have me travel a thousand light-years to answer a few questions. Kind of makes me feel important.'

'Even though we can be sentenced to death?'

'It's an ego thing.'

'What's an ego?'

'It's a Human thing.'

'Are you jesting with me again, Jack?'

'I might be––Awww!' Jack yelped, as a sharp pain shot up his spine. 'Why the hell did you do that!?'

'I don't know. I was only jesting.... Did it hurt?'

'Very funny. Why don't you try shocking your own self?'

'I can't. I would need my symbiot to do that.'

'Yeah...and a backbone, too.'

'What did you say?'

'Oh...nothing.'

'You do know that I can hear your thoughts.'

'Yeah, don't remind me....'

Jack continued on his lonely trek through the snow for about a quarter of a mile until the droid stopped suddenly.

'What's happening?'

'Don't know.'

'I thought you knew everything?'

'Never been to this planet to face the High Guild before. It's the first time for both of us.'

He was a bit taken aback when the droid began taking itself apart; limb from limb. 'Oh shit. The fucking thing's malfunctioning? How the hell are we supposed to find this place now?'

'I don't think so, Jack. This is a Gamlarrion CB-lifting droid. It's not malfunctioning; in harsh rugged landscapes, such as this one, the droid's programmed to disassemble itself to better navigate the environment.'

'Disassemble itself...?' Jack asked incredulously, while staring at the droid that had somehow managed to fold itself into a crudely shaped box. 'From where I'm standing, it ain't did nothing but turn itself into pile of scrap.'

For once, Klidaan didn't have anything to say, and in his silence, he was sort of admitting that he had to agree with Jack on this one. The droid did look like it had turned itself into a pile of junk.

'How the hell would it better navigate this environment with its legs all crossed up like that? Maybe they sent the wrong droid to guide us.'

'I think you're right.'

"Get on...."

The words came as if from out of nowhere. Dubiously, Jack spun around to see if maybe someone had suddenly came up behind him. Then up, toward the sky, but there was nothing up there except fog and lights.

"Get on...."

"Did you say something?" he asked Klidaan out loud, with the slight feeling that he might be losing his mind.

'It wasn't me, Jack,' his symbiot replied. 'I think its coming from the droid.'

Jack stared at the broken thing in front of him and shook his head in dismay. "Are you sure?"

'Don't ask me, ask him.'

He hesitated for a moment, but eventually, he took a cautious step forward and leaned in toward the disfigured droid on the ground. "What did you say?" A strange question, it seemed, to be asking the pile of scrap. But Jack had experienced far stranger things since leaving Earth.

"I said," the droid began, with a dab of impatience creeping into its tone. "Get on. You've kept us waiting long enough."

How startling! The droid did in fact speak, but it wasn't A.I.. Someone was speaking through it. Someone, from up there, in one of those buildings.

A "lift-droid." The name made sense now. The journey laid upward, and they'd prepared him for that. He should've known better than to think the Stendaarans would send him a broken droid to see the High Guild. However, it didn't take away from the fact that the droid still turned itself into an ugly contraption. Compared to the lowest machine that existed in the Plogg Sector, it was still junk. He couldn't even find a decent enough place to stand when he got on, so just grabbed on to one of the limbs (a bent arm) that was sticking out.

The ride up was even worst, as the lift just shot up in the air in one sudden burst. It became like a beech-nut in the sky from there, struggling against the strong snow-driven gale, it swayed from side to side on its way up, lurching back on a few occasions, as if straining to carry his weight. He wasn't even afforded the luxury of marvelling at the alien structures that came into view——too busy holding on for dear life. At one point, he failed to notice that they'd risen slightly above the building's platform, so when it made the sudden abrupt landing on the surface, he thought——for the briefest of moments——they were going to crash all the way back to the icy ground.

He couldn't wait to get off the thing. And did so on shaky legs, then witnessed the odd spectacle of the droid putting itself back together again. It was a slow, clumsy process, to see the thing wobble and hop about on one leg, while shoving a limp arm into an empty shoulder. He wondered how the Gamlarrions could've even thought to invent such an obsolete thing. Why not just create a flat slab of metal (like a mag-gurney) that flew through the air? This droid just seemed so impractical, in any given situation.

A light appeared from where the base of the platform met the building, and when it finally caught his eye, he saw that it was a door that had opened up. Beyond the threshold, a lone figure stood inside, apparently waiting for him and the droid to get out of the cold. He didn't need any further prompting, nor did he seek the droid's approval as he headed toward the doorway and quickly closed the gap between him and the creature.

"Puppycock," the creature said his name with the affirmation of a close friend. However, despite having the strong masculine features of a square chin and a white bushy beard, it spoke with a high feminine voice.

"Yeah, that's me," though it jerked his senses a bit, Jack didn't care for the creature's choice of gender. Maybe the Yhoulnans practiced some weird form of reverse drag on this planet. But neither of that was of any of his concern. He only wanted to get this business with the High Guild done and over with, then he could get back to saving the rest of the quadrant. Besides, everything else seemed to check out with the alien. It wasn't too strange-looking of a creature, with a flat furry nose and reptilian eyes, it could've been a distant relative of a Trefloon. Long white hair framed its bony face, almost making it appear to have a snout. Beyond this, minus the ears that remain hidden beneath the hair, it was a fairly moderate-looking being. And if its back was facing towards you, it could even past for a Human....

"My name is Hlanan," this creature began. Its green eyes lashed like a pair of emeralds whenever it spoke. "And I will be your assistant while you stand before the High Guild."

He knew it! What bureaucratic race would have such a high legal system without their own version of lawyers? "A pleasure meeting you, Anan. I hope I'm not in too much trouble."

The Yhoulnan didn't have any eyebrows, so it couldn't wear the puzzled frown on its face. But the brief squint of those green eyes, told Jack he had no patience––nor the time––for decoding alien humor. "You need to follow me at once, Puppycock," he said instead. "We've kept the Seers waiting long enough. A dozen worlds are being kept on hold just so they could hear your case. They would not take your lateness in light regards." It then spun on its heels and headed down the hallway with the hem of its brown robe fanning out behind it. "And one more thing," it said over its shoulder, in an equally sharp tone as Jack followed. "You need to remove that hideous mask from your face. The Seers dislike all Stendaarans."

———•———

As they made their way further into the building, it immediately became apparent to Jack, that the Yhoulnans held the color green in some form sacred regards. Everything, from the floors, walls, and ceiling, was in a verdent color. Even the lighting, that hung above in long transparent tubes, added to the scheme as it washed everything in its mossy hue.

Perhaps, its in their blood, he thought. Maybe the Yhoulnans had green blood; that might explain their green eyes. Especially the hundreds of intense pairs that surrounded him in this circular room that reminded of being in an ancient auditorium. The Yhoulnans version of a court room. Or a gladiator's battle-ground perhaps. He half-expected some fierce lion to come leaping out of some trap door at any moment. And that's when that uneasy feeling began to creep up inside of him. For the first time, he found himself unarmed and alone on an alien planet, surrounded by green-eyed monsters. What better way to describe the situation he was in...?

As strange as it all appeared to be, the uncertainty of an unknown fate was not the source of this new-found queasiness building up from the cellor of his stomach, to the ceiling of his throat. He no longer feared prosecution nor death, for he had succumbed and overcame both of these things many times before. No...it was something else. The Yhoulnans. It was they, who brought about this great cause for apprehension in Jack's mind. Other than the Yhoulnan employed to assist him in the face of the High Guild, no one else bothered to acknowledge his presence from the time he set foot on their planet. Not even the ones in this circular room, where they all just glared down at him as if he was the first Human (donned in Stendaaran armor) they'd ever laid their flashy green eyes upon. They might as well not have been alive, for that's how they appeared: like statues. War-figurines, each one made to look exactly like the other. Exact copies. Unmoving, save for all those glowing eyes that stealthily followed his every movement.

He looked up at his Yhoulnan lawyer and saw that he too was an exact replica of all the other members in the High Guild. Maybe they bred like ants, or bees, where some fat Yhoulnan queen sat under the planet spitting out droves of Yhoulnan workers, soldiers, and lawyers. A Yhoulnan hive....

"So, when's this trial supposed to begin?" He asked Hlanan.

"The trial's already in motion, Puppycock," the Yhoulnan replied, his voice barely above a whisper.

Jack almost laughed, nearly betraying his indifference to the alien's custom. "But how? When?"

"The moment you entered the chambers."

Jack noticed how tense and rigid Hlanan's posture had become, as if he wasn't allowed to speak, and did so under the most dire circumstance of being beheaded if caught. That would explain why he was whispering to him now. But it didn't explain anything else. He tried asking another question but thought better of it and just stood there quietly with the rest of the members in the room.

At some point, between the last time he spoke to Hlanan and some point thereafter, an involuntary spasm sent a throbbing pulse rippling through his brain. The shock caused him to stumble backward, clawing at his scalp to get at the wild centipede that was crawling around inside his head. At least that was how it felt.... He grunted in pain, but not the slightest sound was heard. Not even from Klidaan, his symbiot, who would've surely stiffened him up by now just to save them both the embarrassment. But the green floor came up and met the side of his face. His paralyzed body too deadened and lifeless to writhe in revolt. Only a mild twitch here and there of his armored tail, as if mimicking the final throes of a dying snake.

Hlanan knelt down beside him and placed a furry paw gently on Jack's bald scalp. An action that seemed to reap instant results as the painful grimace on Jack's face gradually subsided and became so calm it looked as if he was now happily asleep. When his eyes fluttered open, they did so slowly. He looked surprised when he realized he'd been laying on the floor. He rolled onto his side, kind of swatting Hlanana's helping hand away. Still dizzy, he rose to his feet, then waited for the room to quit rocking from side to side.

There was no longer that weird feeling he had when he first came into the room. And for good reason too, for the members of the High Guild no longer had their judgmental eyes focused down upon him, but on each other, as they were now conversing quietly amongst themselves. There was even that faint hum––of a hundred voices––that had so suddenly crept into the room, breaking the dead silence for the first time.

"What's going on, Lanan?" Jack asked, looking up at all the debating Yhoulanans.

"It's over."

"What's over?"

"Your trial, Puppycock."

"Really...? The trial's over? But I wasn't even asked any––" He paused here (frightfully) as he finally came to understand what had happened. That strange fit he experienced. The paralysis. The Yhoulnans had invaded his mind. Picked his brain apart, piece by piece. And now, they knew everything. There wasn't any need for questioning. From the moment he entered their chambers, they'd been quietly pulling the answers out from his mind. "So, that's how it's done on this planet."

"Aye." Hlanan replied, a bit too proudly for Jack's liking. "This is how it's done in this quadrant, Puppycock, this is the High Guild. There're very few things that take place within this quadrant that we're not aware of. And what better way to serve justice, without knowing the full truth. Your intentions, your purpose, your knowledge, are all under scrutiny if we are to determine your innocence or guilt."

"Well, if they were the ones doing all the scrutinizing, what part did you have to play in all this?"

"Your recovery requires a physical touch."

"Recovery?" Jack didn't like the sound of that word.

"One moment, Puppycock. I'm being summoned by the Guild. We'll continue this conversation after your fate has been decided."

Once again, that dead silence crept over the chambers and those countless green eyes flashed and focused their attention directly to the center of the room. Only this time, it wasn't Jack who came under their scrutiny, but Hlanan. The Yhoulnan didn't go into the same seizure (as Jack once did) but his body did seem to go stiff while he and his kin conversed telepathically. No more than a minute (a whole hour in Jack's eyes) went by, before all the glaring eyes dimmed and Hlanan turned back around to face Jack. "You're free to go," he said, sounding neither pleased nor disappointed with the Guild's decision.

Left both curious and confused, Jack was led out of the High Guild's chambers without having the simplest of his many questions answered. As much as he wanted, he knew it would be a fruitless task to try his means of communication with the Yhoulnan Judges. It burned him up inside. The anxiety. The prospect of not knowing.

The Guild found him innocent, due to his ignorance (his best guess) of what really took place behind the scene of his last mission. But someone else was obviously at fault, and he was dying to know who!

Not before long, he would find himself back in the green corridor outside the chambers. For some odd reason, he felt beyond the reach of the judges' telepathic minds, most likely due to the heavy metal doors that slammed themselves shut behind him. "Back there, you said my recovery needed a physical touch, why?"

Hlanan was already on his way out the corridor; walking slowly, he tucked his arms into his robe, as if cold. "When subjected under brain-scans, as intense as this one, things tend to get torn apart."

"Inside my head, you mean?"

"Aye. Some minds are stronger than others. But most go into seizures, like yours. And this is because of all damage that's taking place while you undergo the scan. My job, is to simply put things back together again once the scan has been completed."

"Your physical touch?"

"Aye."

"And what did the Guild learn after ripping my brain apart?"

"Beyond your obvious innocence, I have no idea."

"But aren't you a telepath?"

"Aye."

"So, what happened?"

"Whatever you know, the Guild knows."

"And what does that mean?"

"Isn't it obvious, Puppycock? I think you already know what was learned here today...."

CHAPTER
THREE

IT SEEMED SO sudden and so abruptly unexpected when a murky vortex just twirled into existence right in the middle of space. One would think that part of the galaxy had been deteriorating for millennia and had finally rusted away in the shape of a jagged hole where a distant funnel of light churned deep inside. A black wall, punched with a special door to allow the passage of ships travelling light-years and beyond. A great magic! The best ever performed by any creature of the Universe.

General Morlaak's tiny shuttle came shooting out of this spinning whirlpool of light. For a moment, it appeared to be in danger of being swallowed back up by the churning mass. But it kept on going, zipping through space at its own top speed; its rear engines flaring like a welder's torch.

A projectile, no longer than a school bus, was fired from one of the shuttle's starboard cannons, back toward the bright worm-hole at a violent speed. It collided into the swirling light, detonating at its core and erupting into a sphere of––not fire, but––countless bolts and streaks of lightning that stretched so far that they covered the entire diameter of the worm-hole from rim to rim.

The el-bomb (as it was called), is not only used to rip open the fabric of space (in any direction) and create this worm-hole tunnel of light, but its also used to destroy it by disrupting its central force of power, thus weakening it by causing it to disperse into nothing––as if it wasn't there at all.

Soon, blackness returned as the last remnants of the worm-hole winked itself out of existence, leaving nothing but the tiny shuttle in its wake.

"Where are we?" Morlaak asked, to no one in particular, since it was only he that sat at the helm in the tiny shuttle. His big purple body appeared awkward in the small commander's seat. Had he not been in so much of a rush to escape capture––and certain death––at the hands of the Plogg Sector's general. Voch, he might've chosen a suitable Stendaaran craft to make his departure. But the smaller Ekwhaan vessel was fast enough to serve its purpose, beyond being readily at hand when needed. Not the luckiest of draws on his part; but not that much of a misfortune, either.

"We've entered the Novid star-system in the 2nd quadrant...." The words appeared in distinctly red alien characters across the shuttle's front window.

"What's that?" Words that the general obviously couldn't read.

So they changed, as if through some sorcerer's spell, into the Stendaaran's own contemporary script.

"You brought me to the 2nd quadrant?" Perhaps the general hadn't escaped after all. He shot a skeptical eye toward the command console, where the Technician sat securely inside its ancient box. "If this is a trap, I'll destroy this ship within five seconds of the Seezhukans' arrival."

"Then you'll destroy us both."

The general nodded gravely, despite knowing the ancient box didn't have any eyes to see him with. "That I will. The ship will self-destruct and kill us both."

There came that uncanny pause in the Technician's response. A curt hesitation. The sarcastic cock of a brow (even though it came from a box) that the general showed the audacity to even consider such a thing. "I assure you, it's not a trap. No one's coming to rescue anyone."

"So, I guess it wasn't you that sent your location to Kraaglor's fleet."

"If I had, then Voch wouldn't have wasted his time with the Oxloraans, before showing up in the Eridani Sector. He would've came directly to Earth."

The general was smart enough to figure that part out on his own. Voch's discovery of the Technician's location, was a reward based on his own investigation. And the real traitor, resided not in Plogg, nor the 2nd quadrant, but within his own ranks. A problem he's surely surely to be confronted with in the near future. "Okay, so you say that we're in the Novid Star system. But I don't see any stars. There's nothing out here."

"That's because we're heading in the wrong direction."

"What? But those were your coordinates." He double-checked the readings on the holographic map (just to make sure) projected through a marble-sized lens on the command-console's display screen. "We are exactly where we should be. You must've given me the wrong coordinates."

"Turn the ship around."

"I don't think that's gonna do us any good."

"We're heading in the wrong direction. We must turn around."

Reluctantly, Morlaak heeded the Technician's suggestion and typed in the new commands that caused the shuttle to make a wide u-turn in the middle of empty space. His unwilling effort however, was rewarded in the form of a bright crimson glow that crept into the shuttle's bridge as the ship slowly turned to face a red super-giant star. Unseen at first, because they were facing away from the solar disk, and the appearance of the worm-hole—-no matter how brief—-had completely blocked it from view.

Even at a distance of five billion miles (about the same distance as Jupiter from our sun) the red giant was still an overwhelming spectacle to behold. Too heavy to weigh, too big to measure, too grand for the eyes to see and fathom. Even for a seasoned general like Morlaak, who was by no means a stranger to super-giant stars, seeing them up close (even at billion miles away) still brought that feeling of inertia inside of him. They are, after all, the biggest stars in the galaxy.

A new set of coordinates appeared on the screen, and even as the ship turned towards the precise location, the face of a ringed planet sailed into view. A noxious world—-from the looks of it—-with swirls of brown-yellowish clouds circling the planet's atmosphere like a peeled fruit. Its red rings stretched thousands of miles wide, and no doubt got its color by reflecting the bloody hue of its own looming star, like trillions of crushed rubies milling slowly around the world in eternal silence.

At some distance beyond, peeked one of its moons. A blushing world with pink clouds and bloody oceans. It soaked up the sun's scarlet rays that dabbed fuzzy red blotches on the land like dyed suede.

"Is that it?" Morlaak was beginning to hate this place already. On his command console, dozens of military ships and satellites were detected all around the moon. And if he could detect them floating around in this pile of junk, then it was all too obvious that they could probably detect him as well.

"This is Plagnor, and Edinor (its moon) garrisoned by the Seezhukan Regality. You'll find what you're looking for Edinor."

"And what about those ships out there? They must know we're here by now."

"They do, but I've already integrated my signatures into the ship's controlling systems. They've been reading us as a personnel shuttle for the Regality. They have no other suspicions."

"Okay...now that we have the perfect disguise to serve our purpose, we still can't just fly in there and do whatever we want. We still need a plan; there's only one of me, and my entire fleet has been destroyed."

"Then wait."

"Wait for what?"

"Our reinforcements...."

———●———

"Where the hell have you been?" Ford's worrisome voice was as loud as a symbiot screaming directly inside of Jack's head. "We've been trying to reach you for two whole days!"

No more than five minutes had gone by since Jack followed the lift-droid through the portal that brought them back onto the main battleship that commanded the entire Stendaaran armada, orbiting the planet Earth. It had totally slipped his mind that Ford's awaiting message was still logged in his coms-link. But in defense, he did undergo a complete brain-scan on Yhouln by a mob of telepathic judges; so perhaps some parts of his memory had become affected by the traumatic ordeal. At least, that was one of the many possibilities that he could think of. Or, maybe he simply forgot about the whole thing, with Ford's sudden shouting into his implant being his only reminder.

The high electronic decibels made him since as the stinging jolt shot through his ear-drum, while he strode through the ship's grand halls in search of Magn, Latrogh, and the two drones that tried to kill him. "Hi, Ford," he said, after shaking the mild headache away. "Got your message. But I was too far away to transmit anything back to you."

"Where were you?" That sharp voice again, like ice placed gently on the surface of his brain.

"I need you to calm down," Jack said. "Stop screaming so loud; I think something's wrong with my implant. But anyway, I was summoned by the High Guild, whose planet happens to be on the other side of the galaxy."

"We already know about the High Guild, but I though the Stendaarans did all of the——"

"They don't. The High Guild is on a planet called Yhouln, thousands and thousands of light years away. And the Yhoulnans are all powerful mind-readers and——hey, could you lower your voice just a little, I get a headache every time you speak."

"But I'm not yelling, Jack. I'm speaking as low as I can. Try adjusting your com-settings."

'**There's nothing wrong with your settings, or your implant, Jack,**' came Klidaan's soothing voice in Jack's mind.

'Then why do it hurt so much?'

'**Its the brain scan. I think it left your mind sore in some places.**'

'Is it always like that, with the High Guild?'

'**I don't think the Yhoulnans ever had a Human Being enter their chambers before. They might've been a little too rough on you.**'

'Is it permanent?'

'**Don't think so; but you might need to stay off your coms-link for a little while longer.**'

"Hey, Ford."

"Yeah, Jack."

"Listen....apparently I suffered some...temporary brain damage on Yhouln. Hurts like hell whenever you speak through my coms-link, so we're gonna have to cut this thing short."

"Do you know for how long?"

"A few hours should be enough, I'll contact you soon as I can. I'll probably be re-joining you guys before that."

"Good, because we have to get out of here as soon as possible. Just spoke to the general. He's alive; he has the Techicain; and he needs us."

"He also has a lot of explaining to do."

"He does?" Ford sounded a bit concerned.

"Yeah. I don't understand all of it, but I think he's in a lot of trouble with the High Guild. He went behind the back of his superiors to kidnap the Technician from Plogg.

I think he's some kind of an outlaw now. But anyway, I'll explain it all in person when I get back on the ship."

"Okay, Jack. See yah."

He knew he could find both Magn and Latrogh, in their newly assigned quarters, but on his way there he bumped into a familiar face.

"A pleasure to see you again so soon, Puppycock." It was Nuclus, the Stendaaran lieutenant, he first encountered while training on Apraatlon: Gamlarr's Sappian Jungle.

"Likewise, lieutenant Nuclus," Jack said, placing a friendly palm on the Stendaaran's chest. "What brings you all the way to the Eridani?"

"I've been a loyal member to this fleet for well over fifty years. By sheer chance, we were stationed all the way out here after the attack on Morlaak. Sad news...but wherever he may be in the quadrant, I hope he's well."

"As do I."

"And I heard what happened to you on Gamlarr. Ambush by your own slider...sad news about what is happening in the quadrant now. There's definitely a spy in midst."

"Sad news indeed. But hey, at least I took your advice, and I mentioned your name to general Bagger."

The Stendaaran gave jack a curious frown. "And for what purpose would you mention me to Bagger, Puppycock?"

"I was late for training that day, remember? You told me that if I ever got any heat from Bagger, that I should mention your name. Well, I did, and instead of sticking me to a year-long cleaning duty, I was given another chance."

"Ah...well...me and Bagger have been serving the quadrant together for a long time. A tough Gamlarrion, he is, but he's also a good friend."

"That's good to hear, and I'm glad that we had the chance to meet each other on that morning."

One of Nuclus's four muscular arms reached out and gave Jack a friendly pat on the shoulder. He smiled––as much as any shark-tooth Stendaaran could. "And likewise, Puppycock. You served this quadrant well during the short time you've been with us. I'm certain that you'll have a long future here."

"Hope your certainty proves true, Nuclus," Jack replied, a bit jokingly. "Long futures are a rear commodity for anyone involved in this galactic war."

"Aye."

"Well...good luck to you in the future. I know you'll continue serving the quadrant in good faith."

"As do I, Puppycock. And I know you'll do the same."

"Aye...."

After a quick search through the ship's updated logs, Jack was able to find the location of Magn and Latrogh's new quarters in one of the lower decks. And as expected, the two Stendaarans were indeed there when he arrived at their door a few minutes later. Both expressed their good cheer and relief that he hadn't been sentenced to fry at the hands of the High Guild, to which Jack dismissed with a casual shrug and a subtle reassurance that things couldn't have gone any better with the Guild. All of that (Guild stuff) was behind them now. He didn't even mention the horrible brain scans in the ugly green chambers. He was more eager to see Jill and Matt, the two Human drones, because there was still a lot of things he wanted to ask them. However, he would soon discover (through his own furtive observation) that they weren't present in the quarters with the Stendaarans. In fact, as Jack would soon learn, they were no longer on the ship.

"Gone back to Earth," was what Latrogh replied, when asked. "Aye...bureaucratic stuff, would be my best guess."

"Aye," Magn added. "The Whorghanions wouldn't take it too well if they ever found out that one of their drones was up here giving counsel on attacking the nearest Seezhukan outpost."

"Then what about the girl?" Jack asked. "The one that tried to kill me."

"What about her?" said Latrogh.

"What was her excuse for leaving so soon? After all the trouble she had to go through to get here."

The Stendaaran seemed a bit puzzled by the question. "Don't know, Puppycock. Never knew she needed one. And...in some ways...she kind of out-ranked us on this ship."

"Out-ranked..." Jack thought this was absurd. Jill was only a class-one drone. "How could she out-rank two senior Stendaaran officers on their own ship?"

"She's a drone-major, for one thing," Magn replied. "And because she reported directly to the commander of this ship, before either of us could even think about it——"

"We didn't even know who commanded this damned fleet." Latrogh chimed in. "Didn't even care. With the general gone——"

"Aye. But that was our mistake, Puppycock. And because of it, that little drone became our superior officer for the brief time she was here."

"Aye. And she used that time wisely——to flee!"

"Damn it!" He became so unexpectedly mad, his armored tail whipped out involuntarily and slapped at the metal grating on the floor behind him. The woman still had some unanswered questions for him; he wasn't ready to part with her so soon. "And there was nothing you couldn't done to stop her from leaving?"

"Didn't have any real reason to," said Latrogh, after a curt shrug. "Other than transporting us back to the ship, she don't have any other purpose here."

"She tried to kill me," Jack reasoned, but it sounded more like a plea.

"And so did the general of the entire Kraaglor Front," Latrogh shot back, feeling the logic of his actions were being questioned. "At least we took care of whatever differences you and that Human girl might've had. But we still have a destroyed Stendaaran warship orbiting the Earth; thousands of dead Stendaaran and Meerachzion bodies floating out in space. Unless your Human friend could help us in finding this crazy general, then I don't see a need for her being here. Her place is on Earth, were she belong."

He exhaled a long grievous sigh. Frustration, anger, and heavy fatigue were beginning to take their toll. He needed rest. He wanted so badly to find his new quarters and slip into twenty-four hours of oblivion on a brand new lev-cot. However, he also knew such luxuries couldn't be entertained for too long, without things taking a turn for the worst. And they surely would, if he chose to ignore his raw instincts.

Other things were brewing. Dark things, though not so mysterious. Nor were they occurring thousands of light-years away, but right here, in this sector, on this very ship! If not addressed right away, he feared what happened to him on Gamlarr, might happen again. Only this time, his assassins might succeed....

———————⚫———————

"No way, Puppycock," Latrogh was already backing away from the door, once he found out who lived inside the quarters on the other side. "This could get us all dropped lower. Even if you're right, and we do get him to confess, it's still his word against ours."

"But he's a traitor," Jack said. "He betrayed us all! He's the reason for all the death and destruction in this Sector. And now he's here, on this ship; most likely preparing to carry out another act of treason."

"And what if you're mistaken, Puppycock?" Magn asked. "What if he's not the traitor?"

"He is," Jack said. "You have to trust me. I wouldn't risk our lives so recklessly if I wasn't sure of what I was doing."

"Then why the elaborate escape plan?" Latrogh asked. "If you're so sure of what you're saying, then why must we flee so suddenly after we confront this so-called traitor?"

"Just a precaution, in case things do go wrong, and he turns out to be too much for you two."

Both Magn and Latrogh paused to look down at Jack with contempt. Deep frowns, like dried up mud, caked over their brows. "What do you mean by that," Magn, the larger of the two, asked. His heavy voice already rolling into a low growl.

There was that "Stendaaran Pride." The mightiest creatures in the entire fourth quadrant. And if there was anything they detested more than cowardice, it was someone questioning their effectiveness in battle. Sort of a low-blow for Jack. A cheap shot. But he couldn't think of anything else that could've motivated the Stendaarans into committing treason.

"Didn't mean anything," Jack said, shaking his head. "Just in case you fail to subdue the prisoner, we must be prepared to leave the ship at——"

"Fail to subdue the prisoner!" Latrogh interrupted, not caring that his voice grew louder. Every corridor in the ship was sealed air-tight, which made every room——both inside and out——virtually sound proof. "You better watch yourself, Puppycock. No one's scared of that old fluke."

"I know. I know," Jack went on, slowly reeling in his bait. "But all precautions must be met, just in case."

"Get out of the way!" An impatient Magn pushed them both aside as he approached the door. "There's no just in case. I'll take this old fluke all by myself. You two just get ready to put restraints on him when it's over."

Jack could barely suppress his grin as he watched Magn's big stubby finger pushed down on the wall-mounted intercom tab. But then he became fearful that his plan might've worked a bit too well. He could nearly feel the waves of adrenaline mounted up inside the two Stendaarans while they waited for the door to open. He hoped they wouldn't hurt him...too much.

But what a surprise awaited them as the door finally opened, and a tall (barely clothed) Stendaaran woman stood on the other side. She was beautiful, and well shapely (like most Stendaaran women), with just a silky robe draped over her shoulder to cover up her nakedness. A groggy expression tugged the sides of her face, as if she'd just awaken from a deep sleep.

"What is it?" She asked, in a tone that carried authority.

Though he wasn't sure if she'd taken notice of the little Human standing behind the two Stendaarans, Jack wondered how high her rank went, and whether or not she was in co-hoots with the traitor. Either way, her presence had made their mission a little bit more complicated.

"We're looking for the lieutenant," Magn said, in a stern voice.

"The lieutenant?" The woman replied, showing concern, but not in an apprehensive sort of way. The hours were indeed odd for any unexpected visitors to just stop by all of a sudden. And she herself had been fast asleep when her intercom buzzed her out of bed. Who in the "Droghs' hell" would want to summon anyone at this hour? And who were these fools, keeping company with a Human drone? "You idiots!" The dubiousness of it all was enough to make the blood boil under her sleek purple skin. "There's no lieutenant here. You have the wrong quarters."

There came that frozen expression when one is rendered speechless beyond his own wits. And what made matter worst, was that Magn wasn't the brainiest of Stendaarans. Nor was he that wordy with his mouth. So he just stood there (while the woman grew more irritated with each passing second) feeling his four palms get clammy with sweat. He couldn't have been more stunned if she held up an ion-blaster directly to his face.

"We're so sorry to have bothered you then." It was Latrogh, who finally came to his rescue, smiling his toothy grin like a shrewd gator. "We're all new arrivals to this fleet, and we still haven't quite figured things out as yet. So sorry."

"It's too late for this," the woman said.

"So sorry," Latrogh repeated, in feigned humbleness, keeping his eyes on the woman's face, lest she catch him trying to spy through that transparent gown of hers.

"You must be one of the refugees we've been salvaging from the wreckage all day," she peered around the two Stendaarans and fixed her gaze on the Human behind them. "I wonder why the Earth wasn't destroyed, the way the Seehukans destroyed Adellon?" she wondered, referring to Oxlar's smallest moon, better known throughout the entire quadrant as the "Egg". The question was purely rhetorical, and was treated as such. Not that they would offer any information to her anyway. They were, after all, just play-acting.

"Once again, we're truely sorry to have bothered you at this hour," Latrogh made a slight nod of head, which could've passed for a subtle bow. "We'll be on our way now. And I hope you enjoy the rest of your night in peace."

But the door was already sliding itself shut before Latrogh had the chance to finish off his last words. Not that it mattered anyway; the sooner they'd rid themselves of the Stendaaran woman, the better; given that their latest mishap hadn't roused any suspicions.

"I thought you said he was here, in these quarters?" Magn was almost furious with Jack, and more so with himself, for breaking down so easily, in front of a woman.

Jack pulled up the holographic directory in front of him and scrolled down through the long list of officers and their housing units. He paused at the one in question, and highlighted if for the Stendaarans to see. "According to the fleet's directory, the lieutenant is listed as living in the quarters we just went to. It wasn't a mistake."

"Then the woman was lying," said Magn, after matching up the numbers on the hologram with the ones etched on the door. "She must be hiding him."

"No," Jack said, shaking his head. "I don't think she knows anything about the lieutenant. She wouldn't have asked us about Akellon otherwise. She's not hiding him. It's just her in there. And judging by how pissed she was at being disturbed, she'd been living in those same quarters for a while."

Then that could only mean that the directory's wrong," said Latrogh.

"Yes," Jack replied. "But not the whole directory, just one or two names that have been recently switched around. I'm guessing the lieutenant is not an original crew member assigned to this fleet. He placed himself here, then managed to get someone (or maybe he did it himself) to manipulate the directory listings in order to disguise his true location."

"Then all we have to do, is look through the fleet's original directory," Latrogh said.

"My thoughts exactly." Jack was already swiping through the holographic display until he came to a page that was dated back a few weeks ago; long before his accident occurred on Gamlarr. "I think I found it!"

"That didn't take too long..." said Magn.

Jack tapped on the alien characters in the hologram and the words flashed bright red. "It's right here," he said, pointing to the highlighted name. "Could you read that for me?"

"It says, Captain Shlannka," Magn translated. "And her quarters listed as being right there, where we thought the lieutenant was staying."

"Captain Shlannka?" Jack sounded surprised. "Do all Stendaaran Captains sleep in the nude?"

Magn shrugged, one of his beefy fingers itched the back of his head.

Latrogh laughed. "It is not a customary thing," he said. "But I'll bet a couple slag-sticks that she wasn't sleeping alone."

"Yeah...I wouldn't doubt that, either. But anyway, now that we know the Captain's present quarters, it might be a little easier to find the lieutenant if he was only pulling the old switcher-roo."

"The old what?" Latrogh and Magn look puzzled.

"It's an Earth-saying, whenever someone does a clever trick by making a switch."

"Well, we have no time for sayings, Puppycock," Latrogh said. "Let's just find the lieutenant."

"Hold on, Latrogh. I'll just go back to our present listings and find Captain Shlannka.... And she's...right here, on the lower deck."

"The lower decks...? Why so far from these quarters?"

"Probably to distance himself as much as possible from any would-be pursuers," Jack said.

"Or buy himself some time," Latrogh added.

"A sloppy plan on his part, though," said Jack. "He was better off not listing himself in the fleet's directory altogether. He got careless; he hadn't counted on anyone trying to find him. And such oversight will prove to be his undoing."

When Nuclus first rolled out of bed, he thought it to be through some inner awakening that had summoned him from sleep. A growling stomach, or a strong urge to pee, maybe. But after a moment's check, and a vigorous shake of the head, he dubiously reminded himself that he hadn't done either of those things in decades. Stendaaran drones—— mere vessels to their Meraachzion symbiots——are no longer sustained by the nourishments from their home planet, but through the process of symbiosis, where all of their daily life-giving sustenance are provided for, and in return, they offer their symbiots the gift of a living host——that is...their own bodies.

But that didn't mean their minds had to work any different, however, on the contrary, though their giant bodies were lean, gaunt representations of their former selves, their minds hadn't changed one bit. It was as if the body was long dead; the brain still hadn't gotten the memo to shut things down. So it functioned as it always would, sending messages to both host and symbiot whenever it was hungry, or needed to sleep; and in return, the symbiot would always provide, through the secretion of hormones and chemicals throughout the body. So there was no need to physically eat, but sleep always felt good....

A sudden buzzing sound poked at his ears and drew his attention to the door.... So that's what it was. That's why his symbiot pulled him out from his dreams and made him sit up on the edge of the bed.

"Who is it?" He asked, to no one in particular. It was just a command that caused a holographic image to appear and illuminate his dark quarters in a misty haze of blue. And there, in the picture, showed two Stendaarans, and a Human, standing outside his door. Only the Human looked familiar; one he'd seen on a few occasions before. "Puppycock?" He wasn't worried, just yet. Only curious to know how anyone could find him, all the way down in the lower decks. But then again, the quarters listed as belonging to a captain that commanded a small division of Stendaaran fighter ships.

A mistake...? Maybe.... But judging by the ensignia on the Stendaarans' armor, they were both low-ranked fighter pilots. And Puppycock himself, was only a class-three drone. So it was very much possible that they could be assigned to the squadron belonging to this captain. But anyway, he should ignore the call; that would be the smart thing to do. But not the most wise. What if they were indeed on some urgent errand, and report back to their superiors that the Captain was ignoring their calls? That would put further scrutiny to his location and cause someone with higher authority to arrive at this quarters. Someone with the authority to unlock his door and enter. And if that happened, how would he explain things then?

So, reluctantly he rose out of bed and walked over to where two pairs of armored gloves sat on a nearby table. He slipped them on, all four of them, one for each hand. Then spoke the command that activated the gauntlets' nanites and caused them to slap shiny metal plating up along his arms, chest, and legs, until his entire body was donned in a very impressive-looking, class-five, Stendaaran armor. He brought two fingers up to his neck, where one swipe would cause the dragon-helmet to cover his head, but a second thought froze his hand. The reason being that it was better to let these new visitors see his face; just in case they were indeed looking for the Captain.

He opened the door and met his visitors at the threshold. There was a moment's hesitation, but then a flying fist came——as he expected it might. His sharp symbiotic reflexes caught the movement first and bobbed his head out of the way just in time. But powerless to prevent the second fist from punching into his body——spiked knuckles and all. Had it not been for his symbiot, blocking the nerve-receptors in his body, the pain would've surely brought him down to his knees. In fact, he didn't feel anything at all; just a slight push on impact.

He moved to swipe at his neck, but a swift hand snatched him at the wrist, preventing his face-shield from coming down. They pushed him further back into his own quarters, preferring their violent confrontation to continue behind closed doors. "Puppycock!" He shouted. "What is the meaning of this!?"

———•———

It amazed Jack, to see how fast these giant creatures were able to move...like scrapping tom-cats in a back-alley somewhere. Twelve trunk-sized arms and fist flailing wildly about the enraged behemoths. The sounds of their metal armor slapping against each other, like hail raining down on a galvanized roof.

The lieutenant was strong and agile for his old age, keeping up with both Magn and Latrogh, often managing to land a punch here and there while staying on his feet. He even shouted a few words before finally being subdued.

"Puppycock! What is the meaning of this!?" Blood trickled down from a gash above his eyebrow, and his big purple lip had already swollen up to the size of a pickle. He tried to wriggle free, but was held too firmly in place by the two younger Stendaarans, who locked his shoulders awkwardly into their sockets. It was an effective hold; one widely used throughout the members of the Stendaaran military. Though easily thwarted in personal combat, if out-numbered, there was no defense against it. "This is treason!"

"You tried to have me killed!" Jack shot back. "You conspired with the enemy against your own kind."

"Nonsense!"

"But true."

"You have no proof."

"And you have no honor."

Nuclus stopped his wild struggling in that instant, as if struck by those very words. The fatigued, pained expression on his face, turned to utter disdain for this frail Human—his captor. "You Earthmen know nothing of honor." He said it with as much conviction as his symbiot would allow. "And it's obvious these two fools aren't any different. Coming here with you to ambush one of their own in his sleep."

The suggestion caused the faintest of chuckles to slip through Jack's lips, but this was no laughing matter. He tightened his grip on the ion-blaster and approached the restrained Stendaaran with every intention of blowing a hole through his gut if he didn't start telling the truth. "You're very good at pretending, lieutenant," he said, though he was mindful enough to stand clear of the Stendaaran's feet. A sudden volley from one of those armored trunks would send his small body smashing into the wall. "Meraachzion,

Gamlarrion, Oxlaran, Stendaaran; they're all dead because of you. Or did they erase your memory after you betrayed us?"

"Oh, I remember things all too well. And you'd be a fool to think that anything good would come out of this. What do you hope to gain here? I'm still itching to know the purpose of you attacking one of your superiors."

"And we're itching to know the purpose of you hiding out down in these lower quarters." That was Latrogh, snarling into the lieutenant's ear.

"I was assigned to these quarters."

"By who?" asked Magn, wrenching up one of Nuclus's shoulders to its breaking point.

But the pain went by unnoticed. "I don't know," Nuclus said. "Ask the one in charge of assigning quarters."

"I was with you on Gamlarr," Jack said, taking a different approach.

"So?"

"You helped me with Commander Bagger."

And there it was! The slightest of hesitations in Nuclus's response; as if deciding what to say next. "I regret that now."

"But you don't really regret helping me...do you?" Jack said, feigning that the time was right to quit leading him on. "Because you never did really help me...did you? You never spoke to Bagger about me, or anything. In fact, you never spoke to Bagger at all. That's why when I mention your name, he didn't even know who you were.... But you never counted on me asking the Commander about you...did you? The same way how you never counted on us bumping into each other on this ship. You thought I'd be dead by now.... So typical, so sloppy. The only smart you did, was switch your quarters in the ship's listings. But then again...

you didn't even bother to find out who's quarters you were swapping with. On Earth, you'd make a terrible criminal."

"I'm not a criminal."

"It's pretty obvious that you're not," Jack said. "We looked up your file before coming here. Brave soldier, excellent leader...but until recently (and this is yet to go on your file), traitor. But I'm pretty sure that a brave soldier and leader, such as yourself, would have a good excuse for betraying us so easily."

Both Magn and Latrogh looked surprised when Nuclus stopped struggling all of a sudden. And naturally, they expected the lieutenant to have some other trick up his sleeve, so they immediately tightened their grip on him.

"Don't even try it," said Latrogh, grabbing the lieutenant by his horns, so his head lurched back to expose the vulnerable symbiot on the side of his neck. "I'll rip it out and fry it on the cooker!"

But Nuclus didn't reply. In fact, he didn't make a sound, or attempted to move at all. This whole new resolve, it seemed, was to let the intruders have their way. He was tired. He didn't want to fight anymore. He wanted to sit; go back to sleep. Dream, forever.

"What happened on Gamlarr, lieutenant?" And Jack saw it too. He knew that look all too well. That resigned, defeated look. Perhaps, Nuclus was finally ready to talk; all he needed now, was a little encouragement. "All's not lost, lieutenant. The Seezhukans are powerful, and so's the Kraaglor Front. But as you've witnessed time and time again, they can be defeated. You yourself have defeated the Seezhukans on a few encounters during the great battles in the Whassilin and Thrussan Sectors. I read your file; you were willing to give your life for the Oxlaran cause, when the Dashealans held the Seezhukan Regality at the border of the third quadrant. You're a good soldier; one of the best. So what the hell happened on Gamlarr? How could anyone force you into betraying us? Why didn't you give your life for the Meerachzions?"

"Because it wasn't my life that was in danger this time," Nuclus finally admitted. And along with those words, came an avalanche of pain and fear. The new expression on his face made him appear more haggard and worrisome than ever before.

"What do you mean?" asked Jack.

"My family. They threatened my family. Took them from Stendaar, and would've had them killed if I didn't tell them where you were."

"And what about Oxlar?"

"What about it?"

"How'd you know about our briefings on Oxlar."

"I didn't," Nuclus replied. "The one who calls himself, general Voch, of the Kraaglor Front, already had knowledge of Adellon and Oxlar. How they came to know of the Sector, and me being stationed there, is beyond my knowledge. One minute, I'm in Scrap City, securing an order of electro-shields, then next thing I know, I'm being snatched up in a Seezhukan battleship.... It's one thing to be held in chains as a prisoner, but when you find your entire family there with you, it's quite another. I had to do whatever I could set them free. Even if that meant sending them your location, Puppycock."

"But it was all for nothing," Magn growled in the lieutenant's ear. "I hope you see that now. Both Adellon and Oxlar's destroyed, but Puppycock is still alive."

"And what of your family?" Jack asked. "I'm assuming that they're safe now. That this...general Voch...had set them free once you found my location and orchestrated my death on Gamlarr. Which, by the way, was a successful mission on your part, because Bagger was wise enough to allow my assassins to believe that I perished in those tunnels. And I checked the Galactic Archives myself, to see my own burial in the jungles of Apraatlon. A very thorough race, those Gamlarrions.... But what about you, and your family?"

"The Seezhukan general was true to his word," Nuclus said. "Once word of your death hits the Archives, they were sent back to Stendaar, instantly."

"But somehow you learned that I survived the attack on Gamlar, and I'm betting that general Voch wouldn't take too kindly of being lied to."

"He would've found them and killed them for sure."

"So you assigned yourself to this fleet, hoping that you might kill me for good this time, before the general could find out. At least...that was your plan."

"I must protect my family," Nuclus was indeed a defeated Stendaaran, with no other options, but one. There was nowhere in the entire galaxy that he and kin could've hid from such a powerful enemy.

"So what now?" asked Jack. "I'm obviously not going to let you kill me, and the general is soon to discover that I'm alive, once me and my drones go after him. So what will your position be then?"

The lieutenant had no answers. He could only shake his head in silence.

"We should turn you over to the High Guild," Jack went on. "You have so many secrets in that big head of yours; they'll probably rip your mind to shreds trying to get through 'em all."

"No, Puppycock," Latrogh said. "I think we should just kill him. If he dies now, then that Seezhukan general would not need to use his innocent family as leverage anymore."

"Aye," said Magn. "The Guild would sentence him to death anyway; but it might be too late for his family if he stays alive for that long. Kill him now, and everyone would be better off for it."

"Maybe," said Jack. "The Seezhukans could just as well kill his family after he dies. As long as that general remains in the fourth quadrant, they'll never be totally safe."

"But we can't trust him," said Magn. "And we can't just leave him here to betray us again. Let's just hand him over to the Guild."

"Wait a minute," said Nuclus. His voice was low, rough, and heavy with fatigue.

"What is it?" Jack said.

"There's a way..."

"A way for what?"

"A way to get on the general's ship. I've been there."

"And memorized every squared inch inside its hulls in one breath?" Latrogh asked, skeptically. "You must really take us for fools, if you think you can talk us into walking into a trap."

"It's true," Nuclus shot back. "I was on Voch's ship. It's nothing like what they have in the Seezhukan Regality, so they don't have any knowledge of drone technology. It was the only way I could've done it."

"You scanned their ship," Jack said, with mounting excitement, while both Magn and Latrogh were a bit late to grasp the significance of Nuclus's latest revelation.

"Aye," Nuclus replied. "It wasn't easy, because I still had to do it from behind the closed doors of a cell. But nano-drones have a way of creeping through the tightest spaces, even through the creases of the light-fixtures mounted in the ceiling. From there, it located the ship's main computers and hacked into their systems, downloading everything about general Voch's fleets, including an entire schematic of all his ships."

"I don't know," Magn said, shaking his head doubtfully. "I can't swallow it."

"It's the truth!" Nuclus exclaimed.

"Then where is it?" asked Magn.

"It's in my face-shield."

Jack sighed, a bit apprehensively.

Latrogh laughed.

Magn tightened his grip on Nuclus's shoulder. "You must really take us for fools. There's no way we'll let you activate that shield."

And for good reason. The only reason to keep the lieutenant's four arms far apart, was to prevent him from activating his face-shield. A feat that could fully equip his armor and allow a shoulder-mounted cannon to appear and blast both Stendaarans into another realm. And that was only the least of their problems; the lieutenant could unleash a whole score of assaults on his captors within the small confines of his quarters. And that includes activating his implant, which would allow him to alert the authorities with a single command.

Now Jack was faced with two choices, both in which some form of risk was involved. It was either dismissing the lieutenant's claim and losing out on a great opportunity to dismantle the Kraaglor Front's entire fleet; or allowing him to activate his face-shield and kill them all. It was a tough decision; one he didn't have too much time to think on. "I don't think it necessary to inform you of what happen if you betray us again. You must know that we have this entire conversation on file, and to prove it to you, all I have to do is this." He reached back and tapped on the coms-link through the quarter's own hidden speakers. "We have the lieutenant's entire confession on file. If he kills you, we'll send it straight to the Guild. Then we'll make sure that general Voch hears all about how he hacked into his ship's computers."

"Did you hear that, Nuclus?" Jack approached him, and for good measure, he pointed his ion-blaster between Nuclus's legs. "You have no leverage here. But we're providing you with a way out. Fight with us. Get revenge on Voch for kidnapping your family. What else do you have to lose?"

"I don't see any other options for me in this particular situation, Puppycock," Nuclus said. "And for your information, I had no intentions on betraying you. If I wanted to, I could've killed you all as soon as I opened the door."

"Then what stopped you?" Jack asked, quite interested in knowing what was going through the lieutenant's mind when he realized he'd been found.

"That's all irrelevant now," Nuclus replied. "Are you going to release me? Or are we to continue here, contemplating all the what ifs?"

"Just remember what I told you. If you do anything foolish, you'll bring down disaster––not only on yourself–– but on the ones you love as well. But not before I blast you a new hole in this...general area...." Jack kind of nudged him with the blaster, right on the dick. "I don't care," he said, staring menacingly into the lieutenant's eyes.

"This is becoming silly. Let me go, you fool!"

"Okay...." Jack looking up at the two Stendaarans while keeping his ion-blaster aimed at the prisoner's crotch. "Let him go."

At once, Magn and Latrogh released their holds. And slowly, Nuclus brought his hand to the side of his neck and pressed down gently on the armor's left collar. The nanos reacted immediately, sending a wave of tiny metallic scales up along the back of the Stendaaran's head, swirling around the two pointy horns, then back down over his face to complete the whole shield.

The final look was nothing short of what could've only climbed out from the depths of hell. All too demonic in appearance, with its glowing red eyes like two pieces of fiery coal. In addition to Nuclus's horns that were covered in chromatic metal, the plates of his face-shield were covered in small thorny spikes. The scaly plates that covered his neck, over-lapped each other and made soft clicking sounds when he looked up at Magn and Latrogh. "I'm I allowed to stand?" His voice was so nasal and synthesized, it sounded as if it came through the two narrow slits that formed his nose.

"No," Jack said, still aiming his blaster. "Just stay there for a while till we see what you got."

The two glowing eyes flashed like bright red bulbs just then, awashing the entire room in a scarlet sheen.

Jack feared the lieutenant was on the verge of reneging on his end of the deal, but then felt relieved when a hologram of a detailed schematic came into view.

"That's it!" Magn said, pointing down at the object floating in the middle of the room. "That's the ship that nearly destroyed us."

"That's just one of them," said Nuclus. "One of their smaller fighters. Not even listed in the galactic archives, because its never been seen outside of Plogg."

"Because no one's ever been that far into the second quadrant," said Jack. "That's why our forces couldn't mount much of defense against them."

"The Plogg Sector?" Out of all the Sectors listed in the galactic archives the Stendaarans have never heard of it. "What quadrant is that?"

"The second quadrant," Jack replied. "But there's a catch; the Plogg Sector is the only sector in entire second quadrant not governed by the Seezhukan Regality. They're sovereign worlds within this sector that don't even know about the war raging outside their own quadrant. Its like a Regality within a Regality."

"But I thought all sectors in the second quadrant were known; and they obviously are, because you know about it. What I have trouble understanding, is why would they leave it out of the archives?"

Jack shrugged. "Don't know, Magn. But I'm guessing that its probably because the Plogg aren't like the other sectors in the quadrant; they're not involved in the war."

"Not involved in the war?" It wasn't something the Stendaarans had never heard of before. There were plenty sectors all over the galaxy, in all quadrants, that weren't involved in the war. However, they were still listed in the archives. But this was not what troubled him; such a small complication could've been easily overlooked by anyone. Something else drove his mind craving for new answers. "Well, if they're not involved in the war, what would ever make them destroy Oxlar, attack this sector, kidnap Nuclus, then threaten his family?"

EXPEDITION NINE

CHAPTER
ONE

"YOU'LL HAVE TO translate the alien characters for us, Jherilon," said Ford, staring up at the group of holographic diagrams that Jack had retrieved from lieutenant Nuclus.

Of course he couldn't reveal the true purpose behind general Voch's attack, nor would he ever disclose the identity of the Technician to the troubled Stendaaran. As far as he was concerned, their mission was still top secret; not to mention the uncertainty of what the High Guild's next course of action would be. So a few dangerous things were still up in the air. He thought it better to make copies of the lieutenant's diagrams and leave him in the care of Latrogh and Magn, back on the Stendaaran ship.

As for him, there was nothing left, but to return to his own starship with his own group of drones. The ship that once belonged to a droid named Kaypac. An artificially intelligent ship that calls itself, Jherilon.

"Those are general Voch's fleets of A.I. warships," said Jherilon, reading from the schematics on the diagram's layout. "The small ones you see are what you would call AIFS-738. And the larger two, like the ones I destroyed on Brashnor, are AIWS-080."

"Quite old," said Zubkov, sitting near the helm on the bridge.

"Don't be fooled by the numbers," Jherilon said. "The Plogg Sector have a very different system from the Seezhukans. And what ever droid, or ship produced, is far more advance than anything else in the entire Regality."

"I think Jherilon's right," Semhek said. "I don't know any ship that can cut off all sound in any specific area."

"Or shoot giant loads of plasma," Ghaan added.

"All the makings of my master," Jherilon said. "He hasn't produced any weapons or ships for the Regality in over a century. Whatever new technology belongs to the Seezhukans, were thought up by their own engineers."

"Then what about you, Jherilon?" asked Jack. "Were you created, before or after Voch's fleets came on-line?"

"Before," Jherilon replied.

"Okay, so these diagrams are the only source of information we have on Voch's fleets."

"I think its all the information we need, Jack," Ford said. "Whoever this Nuclus person is, he did us a great favor by getting a complete layout of these ships. But there's another thing you need to know."

"And what's that?"

"We know where our general is, Jack. He escaped with the Technician to a place in the second quadrant, called the Novid Star System."

"The second quadrant?" Jack found this strange––and highly unexpected. "Why there? Out of all the quadrant and sectors he could've hid in."

"Take a wild guess."

Jack shook his head in frustration. He had no time for guessing-games. "I don't know, Ford. Why?"

"It's the nearest star system to the Bhoolvyn Sector.... He found it, Jack! The Dark Void."

"There's a planet, orbiting a red giant star in the Novid System called Plangnor." Jherilon began. "The Seezhukans have my Master's creation there, on Plangnor's moon: Idinor."

"I'm curious to know what kind of creation can cause light years of space to simply vanish," Semhek said.

"A machine," Jherilon began. "Capable of creating a dimensional switch, anywhere it wants."

"Never heard of a dimensional switch," Semhek said. "You must mean a dimensional shift."

"No. I mean a dimensional switch. Because that's exactly what the machine does. It takes one thing, and instantly sends them to another place. Which, in this case, happens to be another dimension."

"And the place from the other dimension comes here?" Jack inquired, a bit insightfully.

"In an unexpected sort of way...yes. The machine wasn't meant to create a switch with anything. Initially, my Master set to create a transport, that could safely send one to other dimensions and back. The benefits from such an achievement were unimaginable. Newly discovered worlds; unlimited resources——"

"A place to get away from the Seezhukan Regality once and for all," Jack interjected, remembering how much the citizens of the Plogg Sector detested the rule of the Seezhukan Regality. Kaypac, once referred to it as the false empire.

"The possibilities were endless," Jherilon replied, without admitting as much.

"So, what happened?"

"The machine never worked the way my Master wanted it to. Whatever went through his dimensional portal, was always replaced with something from another dimension. For decades, he worked on fixing this problem. And then one day, he suddenly gave up, concluding that we're all somehow bound to this dimension by some unseen force; and this same law operated in other dimensions as well. Though one may not physically be pulled back to this dimension, once he steps through the portal, our Universe will always demand some form of replacement. But there's another theory, and my Master seems bent on believing this one: and it's that each dimension are of the same size and volume––each being filled to its maximum capacity. And like a cup of water, once filled to the brim, just one single drop more will cause a spill. So too, once you enter another dimension, you create a spill of some sort and cause another entity to be pushed out."

"So that's how they did it!" said Braak, the chubby fishlike creature from a water-world called Taas. He brought a webbed finger up to his face and scratched his head thoughtfully. "They sent the whole Bhoolvyn Sector into another dimension, knowing it would be replaced with... with...." Then he paused, realizing that something was terribly with Jherilon's story. "Wait a minute...the Dark Void is nothing but empty space. All the ships that have flown in there has never returned.... Shouldn't there be something from another dimension to replace that void?"

"There isn't," Jack said, putting the final piece of the Dark Void's puzzle together. And what had dawned on him was so absolutely terrifying, that not even Klidaan could stop the wave of tremors from shaking his body.

"What're you talking about, Jack?" asked Ford, noticing the sudden state of horror Jack had fallen into.

"There's nothing replacing it," Jack began. "Because the transference isn't complete. Don't you see? The Dark Void didn't swallow up the Bhoolvyn Sector; nor has the Bhoolvyn Sector been sent into another dimension. That's why it is nothing but empty space."

"If the Bhoolvyn Sector wasn't erased by the Dark Void, then where is it?" Zubkov asked.

"It's still there," Jack replied. "You just can't see, or reach it. And that's because there's a dimensional portal in the way. A dimensional portal spanning hundreds of light years, all around."

"And still growing," Jherilon added.

"Aye," said Jack, in agreement. "And here's the worst part. The portal's growing; which means that it started off as a small circle in the beginning, no bigger than a coin. Then grew to the size it is now. That's probably why no one noticed what was happening right away. But overall, it's nothing but a portal, not too different from the one that took me to Yhouln: I just had go right through it. But if I'd stepped aside and walked around it, I would still be on the Stendaaran ship. Only in this case, the dimensional portal that has now covered the Bhoolvyn Sector, is way too large to simply step aside and move around. And the portal's growing."

"At a rate of approximately one hundred light years every annual term," Jherilon said.

"That's a thousand light years every decade!" Ford exclaimed, after a brief mental calculation. "At that rate, the portal will cover the entire third quadrant in twenty-five years."

"And the fourth quadrant in fifty years," Jack concluded.

"Much quicker than that, I'm afraid," said Jherilon. "Over the years, the Seezhukans have figured clever ways of accelerating the portal's growth. It is only logical to expect, that their tasks in this pursuit is still ongoing."

"So this is how they plan on beating us, and winning the war?" A very angry Semhek punched the arm rest on his chair. "By covering us all up with a dimensional portal?"

"Indirectly...yes," Jherilon replied.

"Then they'll reverse the portal," Jack said. "Trapping both quadrants behind the Dark Void; all without having to worry about the encroachment of some other-worldly dimensional quadrants clogging up the galaxy."

"That's damned brilliant," Ford said. "A lot evil and cruel, but still brilliant."

"And incorrect," Jherilon said. "By that, I mean the part Jack said about reversing the portals."

Jack frowned. "So they're not gonna reverse the portals?"

"They don't have to," Jherilon replied. "Ever wondered why no one from the Bhoolvyn Sector have actually made it out of the third quadrant? If the case was as simple as just one portal being stretched across an entire sector, then any one staying on the other side shouldn't be affected by it. They would've been able to leave any time they wanted to, though any prospects of them returning would be impossible. Refugees from all across the Bhoolvyn, would've been flying out of the sector in droves."

"So why haven't we seen or heard anything from the Bhoolvyn Sector for so long?" Ghaan asked. "Why can't anyone get out?"

"Because there're two portals," Jherilon said. "One, on the Seezhukan side of the quadrant. And another, on the Dasphealon side of the third quadrant. Both running parallel to each other, both leading to different dimensions, making any escape from the Bhoolvyn Sector, impossible."

"And eliminating the need to have the portal reversed when half of the galaxy has been swallowed up," said Ford.

"Well," Semhek began. "Since there're two portals, then there must be two machines."

"Both of which were built on Indinar," Jerilon said.

"Okay," Jack said, steering the conversation, and most of their fears, in a different direction. "Now that we have half of this Dark Void thing pegged out...what do we do about general Voch, who's obviously still lurking out there... somewhere?"

"I say we find him; take him out," said Zubkov.

"If only it was that simple," Jack said. "First, we have to find his fleet. Then sneak aboard his ship, and hope to get close enough for a kill shot before making a clean getaway."

"But shouldn't Jherilon know where he is? After all, they were both built by the same little box."

"Zubkov, if Voch don't want to found," Jherilon began. "Then not even I could find him."

"So what good are those diagrams, if we can't even find his fleet."

"They might come in handy," said Jack.

"But we still have our orders," said Ghaan. "Our mission is still very much intact, and I doubt this general Voch knows anything about Novid. He couldn't even find the Oxlaraan Sector on his own. I don't think he'll stand in our way too much."

Jack breathed a long heavy sigh. It made good sense to fly directly to the Novid System and free the Bhoolvyn. But it felt like the wrong move somehow. Call it detective-intuition, but some unseen obstacle still stood in their way. He turned to Jherilon, giving the ship's holographic face a weary, curious look. "And what about the Technician?" he asked, "I still don't fully understand his role in all of this. Why's he helping us all of a sudden; after putting up such a fierce resistance on Plogg?"

"My master's creation wasn't meant for what it's used for now. It was meant to benefit the citizens of Plogg. But now it's stolen technology, with the potential of destroying half of the galaxy. And if that happens, our very own existence will be in jeopardy."

"Seeing that the Plogg Sector's the only thing left standing in the Regality's way," Jack said, "I wonder what the Drofh has to say about all this. The so-called deities of the first quadrant."

"I don't think there's much concern for anyone in the first quadrant what happens in the galaxy," said Ghaan.

"I don't think they have the slightest idea of what's happening in the Bhoolvyn," Semhek said. "I doubt they're willing to allow the Seezhukans to reign with that much power."

"Then we ain't gonna allow it, either," said Ford. "You have to make a decision, Jack. We have our orders. So, what are we gonna do?"

After a brief, considering thought, Jack shrugged... shaking his head with one final resolve. "Well, the only thing left to do now, is go see our general...."

CHAPTER
TWO

HAD IT NOT been for the Novid system's red giant star, Idinor——Plangnor's tiny moon——would've been a dark world. But a crimson sheen coated half of its icy surface instead. A crimson sheen, caused by a red hazy glare, sent from five billion miles away. From orbit, a long range of mountains and glaciers could be seen. A snowy desert, covered in what appeared to be a fresh coating of powdery rouge, stretched for thousands of square miles in the moon's southern hemisphere. Perfectly smooth, and undisturbed since the dawn of its creation perhaps.

As Morlaak's shuttle crept silently above Idinor's thin atmosphere, the first signs of civilization would eventually appear. A sea of glitter, it seemed. Or a cluster of diamonds embedded on the face of bedrock. A city, the size of a continent, where trillions of specks of light remained trapped in their prisons of tall glass and steel. An awesome sight to behold, by anyone's standards. But a morbid scene for the Stendaaran general, who knew all too well that nothing lived down there. Just machines, running other machines, in the name of an endless cycle called progress. Despite its lively appearance, the world was as cold and dead as its motherly planet.

The screen on the helm's console suddenly sputtered to life and caught Morlaak's attention with just a few words. It was a message from the Technician, informing him that the ship, Jherilon––along with its crew––had finally arrived into the Novid.

"Good," he said, relieved that things were still going according to plan. There're many Seezhukan warships stationed all throughout the system, and he worried they might not have taken the sudden arrival of a strange craft as kindly as they did to him and his special cargo. However, the ship, Jherilon was a Seezhukan craft; though not governed by the Regality, it was a military vessel and it carried more authority than a lot of the other ships in the system. "How long until they arrive at our location?"

"They aren't that far away," came the written response. "No more than a few minutes."

"Good. The sooner we get this started, the better." The moment he dreamed of, had finally come: The liberation of the Bhoolvyn! That would be his legacy. He would be forgiven then. The Guild would look into his mind and see that his act of hijacking an entire warship, then unlawfully garrisoning an occupied world in the distant Eridani Sector, was all for a good cause, which ultimately led to the riddance of the Dark Void. At least, these were the things he hoped for.

"Preparing to dock, in thirty seconds...."

He rose from his seat and left the cramped confines of the bridge. Not that the narrow corridors of the Ewhan's shuttle provided the bulky Stendaaran some extra room to move around; he still had to hunch over to prevent his horns from scraping up against the ceiling. And what made matters worst, the drones' ship was only half the size of the shuttle, so he had no desires of trying to fit in there, either.

What he truly desired, was meeting the Human drone in person, to ensure himself that he wasn't about to allow a squad of guard droids onto his ship. Better to meet the enemy at the door (where he can blast them right back out into space) than have them surround him on the bridge.

Around the next corner, the shuttle's docking entrance stood no more than twelve meters away and he noticed the drones were already standing behind the boarding doors; no doubt waiting and probably wondering why they weren't allowed immediate entrance the instant they docked with the shuttle. There was that sense of eagerness that Morlaak favored. But he sensed a bit of carelessness in their actions as well. They could've easily walked themselves into a trap, coming all the way here, well beyond the enemy's boarders. Quite often enough, the exploits of the fearless Puppycock, flared through the archives like a raging flame. Many of which brought much cause for concern, because in reality, the drones were all acting under his orders. Had they died on any one of those missions, his own quest for redemption would've been ruined.

But those fears and worries had reluctantly crawled themselves into the past now, and all that remained was the near future. The future of the fourth quadrant. The deciding factor on whether he would live, die, or guide this tiny Ekwhan shuttle into his own exile from this day forth. It all came down to these six remaining drones of the vanquished 16th Stendaaran fleet.

"It's very good to see you again, general," Semhek said, when the docking doors slid open and they were finally able to board the shuttle. "We feared the worst."

"I assure you, little Tekwhaan, if I didn't know how and when to run, I wouldn't have survived in the war for this long." The general's black beady eyes shifted from one drone to the next until finally settling on Jack, the drone he was most eager to meet. "You've come a long way, Puppycock," he said, giving the Human a long once-over, as if inspecting him for some kind of grave injury. "Out of all his little silly predictions, the Wizard was most right about you."

"Me...?" A bit surprised at first, he was. But Jack's quick mind drifted back to when he first met the Whorganion, and what he had said about some alien general choosing him to become a drone. The one who could find things: was now the Whorganion had once described him. A Detective. The Meerachzions needed a Detective; and now Jack knew why. The Wizard: that ancient bot from the planet, Stong. Somehow, he had managed to set this all up. Must've had a vision of the Human drone, ridding the Plogg Sector of the Technician, and saving the whole galaxy.

"Aye!" the general began. But then appeared to have a second thought. "I suppose that any other Human detective might've performed the same feats. Might've accomplished a bit more without being so arrogant."

"There's no other man on Earth like me, general," Jack said, firmly. He was tempted to boast his unique genetic engineering to the giant Stendaaran, out thought better of it. Morlaak was right, he is kind of arrogant.

"Ha!" The Stendaaran laughed, and he narrowed his eyes thoughtfully as he glowered down at the tiny Human.

"I think the Wizard said something quite similar along those lines. A species no longer able to reproduce on its own, so each Human must be made in a big tube of water, each designed with their own special traits. True...?"

"Uhhh...." Jack wasn't sure how he should answer. "Not quite, general. We're born out of special incubators and nurtured through––"

"Follow me now. We don't have much time in this system." The general was already on his way back down the corridor––hunching as he went––towards the shuttle's bridge. The raw details of a Human's birth was not a main concern at the moment. Nor was the thought of maintaining a polite conversation a part of any Stendaaran's decorum.

"Don't worry, Jack," said Ford, as she brushed past him playfully. "I think he's taken a liking to you already."

"Yeah.... I think I like him, too."

"Well I don't." Ghan added from behind.

"And why's that?" asked Braak.

"There aren't too many Stendaarans alive in this galaxy that I like," Ghan replied.

"Well, that's just a Lannsillian thing," said Semhek, over his shoulder. "Not everyone experienced the same Stendaaran tyranny as your species have. And for that, we're all truly sympathetic."

"Stendaaran tyranny?" Jack gave Zubkov a questioning frown. It was the first time he'd ever heard of the Stendaarans ruling anyone.

"Happened a very long time ago," the big Russian said; mindful enough to keep his voice low, lest the Lannsillian hear his words with those huge bat-like ears. "Way before the Meerachzions came along to colonize their worlds. And as the archives tell it: both species were on the brink of destroying each other."

"But then the Meerachzions found them?"

Zubkov looked surprised. "How'd you know?"

Jack shrugged. "That seems to be the case with all the colonized worlds in the quadrant. Somehow, some world was always being saved from some kind of self-destruction, or total annihilation, or global flooding, or something else. And that includes the Earth; apparently, we were being saved from our own selves. But the way I remember it, we were doing just fine before the Whorganions found us."

"True. But you have to admit, life on Earth did improve significantly since their arrival."

"It did," Jack agreed, reluctantly.

"But that's enough about us. As far as Ghan and Morlaak is concerned; both races have never forgiven each other for the ills committed in the past. And since the Lannsillians were a bit more on the bitter receiving ends of those wars, you could probably understand why Ghan should feel the way he do. From the time he was born, he was literally bred to hate and distrust all Stendaarans."

"Sounds pretty."

Zubkov chuckled softly. "It is...."

Morlaak had already reclaimed his seat at the helm by the time the drones all arrived on the bridge. The statuesque hologram of a droid was floating beside him in a dull, orange haze. As it turned slowly above the floor, it seemed its oversized head was barely supported by its thin metal body. It carried no weapons or any other personalized accessories that was typical of Seezhukan droids. It was plain, holding nothing in its spindly hands and fingers. No jet-propelled backpacks, no shoulder-cannons, no customized lenses that enabled it to fire a pair of lazers from its coin-shaped eyes. From where they stood, the droid looked as harmless as a child's toy.

But the drones knew better than to rely on simple appearances alone. No Seezhukan was ever made to be totally helpless. Especially in times of war.

"What you're looking at, is a Seezhukan class AIMD-730." Morlaak began, from where he sat in the small Ekwhaan chair. "A maintenance droid that was designed to construct and handle all the repairs and improvements on the machines that smearing the abyss of the Dark Void across the outer rims of this quadrant. Since these machines are all that exist on Idinor, you'll mostly encounter these kinds of droids on the planet. They're over two million in all; each designed with a special purpose and function."

"So they weren't designed for war?" Braak asked.

"No. These maintenance droids are no cause for concern on this moon. As long as you stay in disguise, they'll simply walk past you, without a second glance. There are guard droids on Idinor, but they too, won't raise any alarms as long as your disguises remain intact."

"Not too difficult of a mission then," Semhek sounded relieved.

"As long as you stay in disguise," Morlaak repeated. "You can practically spend your entire lives on Idinor, without the Regality being any wiser. But the instant you're found, you'll have fleets of Seezhukan warships aiming their cannons at your location."

"And they won't, general," Semhek said. "This mission will be one of our easy ones. We should be in and out of

Idinor in less than an hour's time. And the machine would be blown to bits shortly thereafter."

"Good," was all Morlaak said, as he shifted his weight in the small shair. The hologram of the maintenance droid kind of shimmered out of existance at the same time, replaced by what appeared to be a jungle of tall alien buildings covering an entire continent of land. "Because we'll first have to find it."

As the hologram did slow turns and revolutions to reveal more of the immense vastness of the ocean-sized city, Semhek finally began to realize the sheer folly of his previous statements. And so too, did the rest of the drones feel their false enthusiasms quickly dissolve and wither once the reality began to dawn in their minds that it might take at least one-hundred years to complete their next assignment. Not a single word regarding the site was uttered; not even words of discouragement. It seemed as if they were struck by the same thoughtless shock, and speechless sense of awe and wonder.

"This is Vermillion," general Morlaak began, inadvertently snapping all the drones out of their brief stupor. "Better known throughout this Regality as the red city of ice and steel."

"The red city is right," Ford commented, noting the fiery radiance being emitted by all the buildings. "Why so red? It's hurting my eyes."

"Just an illusion," Braak offered. "Nothing's truly red in this system. They're all just reflecting the light from their own star."

"It looks strange."

"Your minds should all get used to that in time," said Morlaak. "None of you have ever lived in a red-star system. So at first, everything would seem different."

"Okay..." Jack said, taking a few steps toward the hologram and pointing up at all the buildings. "But do we have a precise location of the machine?"

"You're looking at it," Morlaak said.

"The whole thing?" Jack asked, incredulously. The reckoning of what Vermilion was actually was, had went beyond anything that he thought was possible.

"The entire city," Morlaak affirmed. "Well...it is not a real city in actual terms. The tall structure you see, are not actual buildings, but various capacitors, transistors, and all different kinds of power supply units. You should think of the red city as one continental circuit, functioning as a whole."

"A whole machine," Semhek said, nodding his head insightfully. "Okay...so why not just leave and return with a whole fleet and just light the place with some photon cannons. That should destroy this...Vermilion place...and return the Bhoolvyn...right?"

Morlaak shook his head. "Only the briefest of temporary solutions. If we attack the city——as you say——a billion bots will rebuild the whole thing in less than a month. But that's not the real reason why we can't launch a full-out attack on Vermilion; it's this." The hologram of Idinor zoomed away just then until the entire orb of the moon became visible, rotating; just floating about in empty space. Illuminated only by the red star's distant glare, its crimson rays caused a thin purplish film to encircle the entire moon.

"It's a force-shield," Zubkov observed.

"Aye," Morlaak replied. "And not only that; this shield is made up entirely of plasma. Nothing could get through or penetrate it. Not even light from our photon cannons. The entire Idinor's protected. You can't land on its surface without the proper Seezhukan authorization."

"Only I can." The red Stendaraan letters appeared across the face of the holographic moon. All, except Morlaak, stared dubiously at the words.

"Can you translate for us, general?" Semhek asked.

Morlaak's eyes shifted toward the hologram as if noticing the message for the first time. "As you already know, the Technician is the true architect of Idinor's machine; as well as most of the Regality's gears of war. He's the sole reason why we can all stay within this shuttle in relative safety so far behind enemy lines. And he's the only one that can get you through Idinor's force-shield and onto the moon's surface."

"It's helping us now?" Ford asked, surprised, and a bit suspicious.

Even Jack began starting wildly about the bridge until he finally located the small silvery cube nestled within a shallow cavity on the helm's console. He almost began looking for the big treasure box that once contained it, but then quickly change his mind. The sheer sight of the cube brought him to more deeper thoughts. He couldn't imagine why anyone––or anything, for that matter––would ever want to trap themselves in such a tomb. All for the sake of immortality! The Technician.... He shook his head at the little box, feeling some pity building up inside of his when he realized he was gazing upon some ultimate stage of evolution. And that little cube-thing must be at least a million years old, transferring its own consciousness from one species to the next. From machines, to robots, all the way down to this...a silver cube, no bigger than his fist. And he and his fellow drones must help save it from its own creation. It had lived a whole million years, just for that!

"It was never my intentions to confuse you," Morlaak told Ford.

Jack immediately snapped out of his daydream at the sound of the general's voice.

"I'm not confused," Ford replied. "I just thought that the technician was our enemy. That's why we traveled all the way to the Plogg Sector to kidnap him and bring him here."

Morlaak chuckled, flashing a row of spiky teeth. "You didn't kidnap the Technician...you rescued him. After his failed attempt of creating a stable dimensional portal, he was held captive and then banished to Plogg. The box you found him in, was actually his prison, not his home."

"So the Kraaglor Front, were really the ones that sided with the Seezhukan Regality," said Semhek, remembering Kaypac's accusation of the Technician's treachery. If only she was alive now, to see who the true traitors were.

Morlaak nodded gravely. "In exchange for power, and eventual rule over the entire Plogg Sector, the Kraaglor Front had switched sides a long time ago. The other syndicates in Plogg, are increasingly becoming independent of them. It's only a matter of time before civil war breaks out. But whatever happens in Plogg, would never be of any of our concern. What matters now, is riding the quadrant of this Dark Void."

Ghan stepped forward, giving the tiny box a long, hard stare. "So, I'm guessing that since the Technician is the true creator of this machine, then he's the only one, outside of the Regalities, with a complete knowledge of its workings."

"Aye," Morlaak replied. "No one other than the Technician can guide you to the heart of the machine's core. And I need not tell you what must be done once you get there." He paused. A more sinister smile this time as he reached for the glowing screen that appeared on his armored sleeve and tapped in a few commands. A log-sized device instantly materialized out of thin air before him. He held out a beefy hand as it began to fall, then caught it and held it up for them to see. A tubular looking thing, roughly the size of a telephone-pole, but only four feet in length. It looked heavy, and plain, with no special features added to it, save for a single knob and switch. Some kind of bomb! "You'll need this to destroy the core. Just set your time here." A chubby finger jabbed into the knob and the whole bomb flashed red, as if ready to explode right then and there. "Then arm the weapon like this." He made a motion similar to flicking the switch on.

Ford noticed the three thin lines that appeared above the switch when Morlaak pushed down on the knob. But after a few seconds they vanished one by one, and the bomb returned to its plain original color of resembling old steel. She figured the lines must've represented some kind of sequence that counted down, but since the device wasn't armed, it quickly defused itself. She wondered how long the timer would be set for, and most certainly would've asked him if heavier concerns didn't weigh her thoughts. "Once we destroy the core, what's to prevent these...maintenance droids...from rebuilding it?"

"They can't," Morlaak said.

"And why can't they, general?" asked Semhek. "Isn't that what these machines do? It's the most effective weapon they have against us: rebuilding the very things we destroy."

"And they remake them faster and better than the old ones." Braak added.

"Aye," Morlaak began, with a subtle tone that brought firm reassurance. "But things are different this time. Once the core of this machine is gone, it can never be replaced. The main drive that cause these portals to come into existence was created by the Technician. Only he can rebuild it; and its the only one of its kind.... When the Seezhukans learned of the existence of these dimensional portals, they summoned the Technician to create one on Idinor. But when he refused, they simply took his invention away and created their own version of the machine."

"By building around it?" Jack asked.

"Aye. And as you can see, what the Seezhukans managed to accomplish with this stolen knowledge, is far more inferior than anything the Technician would've created if had chosen to do so.... Destroy this one thing, and the Dark Void is gone, forever."

It seemed the general had come to an end of this briefing, because the hologram of Idinor suddenly winked itself out of existence the instant he leaned back in his chair and fell into a contemplative silence.

A reverent stillness would follow as the drones stood quietly by and waited for the next line of instructions that was sure to come. Each held their tongue—and patience—while the short moments went by until he finally rose up from his seat. "I was told you might need this for your mission," he said. He reached over the console and gently lifted the cube from its slot. "You must take the Technician along with you. Only he can get you on Idinor, to the machine's core." He then placed it in the hands of the nearest drone, who by chance, happened to be Ghan.

The Lannsillian took the cube with a strong nod, but made no attempts to speak.

"But I thought you were joining us on this mission, general." Braak sounded a bit disappointed. And in truth, the very thought of Morlaak, fighting whatever threat that lurked on the Seezhukan moon, did bring a sense of comfort in their minds.

Regretfully, Morlaak shook his head. "Without a strong enough plasma-generator to provide the adequate protection around the ship, this shuttle would never make it past Idinor's force-shield."

"That's why Jherilon's so vital in this mission," Ford said.

"Aye," said Morlaak. "The Technician will use your ship's own plasma-generator to get through Idinor's shield. From there, you drones should be able to handle the rest, as long as you stay in disguise."

"Are you to wait for us here then?" Semhek asked.

"No. The only thing preventing us from being discovered by the Seezhukans, is the Technician's own Seezhukan signature. The moment he leaves this shuttle I'll only have a few minutes to depart and return to the fourth-quadrant."

"So this is goodbye, then," Semhek said.

"Aye," Morlaak replied. But the knowing smile crept across his hard face. "Until you liberate the Bhoolvyn and return to the Eridani, where you'll all rejoin your squadron...."

CHAPTER
THREE

SOLLACK CURSED THE small gears in his robotic legs for restricting his pace as he hobbled down the long, winding corridors, of the Kraaglor fleet's main battleship. An oversight, made a long time ago, he supposed. One he'd never put much thought into, till now, as throngs of bots and droids smoothly slipped past him on shiny wheels, or strong magnetic soles that made them hover gracefully above the ground as they went about their own private businesses.

Wasn't much for upgrades, not Sollack. Unlike his fellow citizens on Plogg, who spent entire fortunes on meaningless vanities, like synthetic skins, implanted thrusters that made them go shooting from place to place at wing-batting speeds. Sollack was more content with his original parts. He'd served as an admiral of one of Kraaglor's largest fleets for so long, the need for a faster body had never been one of his main priorities. Probably because he always had someone else to do all the "fast moving" for him.

Well, he secretly yearned for such an upgrade now. A set of high accelerating sole-wheels, or a pair of shoulder-mounted thrusters, maybe. If only for just one hour. Anything that can get him to the bridge at a much faster rate than he was going now. And if he had a gram's worth less dignity, he might've hatched a ride on one of the many serve-bots that continued to glide past him.

From his quarters, to the main bridge, wasn't that long of a walk. But in this particular situation, it had might as well have been light years away. Even the entrance doors appeared to have been parting all too slowly while he stood beyond the threshold.

All of his patience depleted, he eagerly squeezed through the widening gap––as the doors continued to part––and finally made his way onto the bridge. "General Voch!" He yelled. The same as he'd done through the intercom back at his quarters. He didn't mean to shout this time though, seeing that the general now stood before him (but facing the window). He was certain that Voch would turn around, at any moment to address him. But he didn't. Instead, the general just stood there, with his back towards him––still facing that large window as if completely enthralled with the encrusted stars of the galaxy. The dozen or so work-droids that manned their work stations however, did pause in their various tasks to swivel their necks and fix Sollack with blank expressionless stares. Only when the doors closed behind him did they resume their work.

"General––" He tried again, then paused when he noticed the slightest twitch in Voch's left shoulder. But it was nothing. Just a twitch, a subtle sigh that informed the admiral and made him finally understand why he hadn't received a single response when he tried to communicate with Voch, back at his quarters.

Hyper Space Communication.

The only way to instantly transmit any signal between the quadrants, no less than 3,000 light years apart. Quite similar to warp-travel, where worm-tunnels are erected to bridge the gap between incredibly far distances. But instead of entire fleets and whole battalions of ships invisible waves of data can be zapped from one corner of the galaxy to the other at the blink of an eye.

He resented his most recent oversight. He should've known better than to think the general would simply ignore him in such a way. And had he paid closer attention to all the work-droids on the bridge, he would've noticed all the other communication channels were being blocked, which meant that Voch was having a private conversation with someone on the other side of the Regality. There was no way he could've known that Sollack was hailing him from inside of his quarters. Only when Sollack arrived on the bridge and yelled Voch's name did the general hear him within earshot; which would explain that twitch of the shoulder. This time, Voch did hear the call, but couldn't answer without breaking the private link with the Seezhukans. So there was nothing more for the admiral to do, but wait.

———●———

"You'll have to stop them at once!" The message was as clear and direct as anyone caught in Voch's predicament could've made it. Despite the rage that threatened to short his circuits, he didn't panic. There wasn't much need, nor cause for such a thing in Voch's world. He'd been alive for too long. Seen too many empires rise and fall. Never cared for no other, but his own. General Voch, only lived for the betterment of Plogg....

"There isn't a cause for that kind of action, general." The reply came in the form of a soft, synthesized voice, from nearly four and a half thousand light years away, directly into Voch's ear. "These two vessels are the sole property of the Regality. As well as you...you don't have much authorization this far outside of your own sector."

But you're wrong! Voch wanted to scream at the incompetent droid so badly. But he couldn't. Things had gone too unexpectedly wrong, all too suddenly. What he'd first thought to have been a simple kidnaping of the Viceroy, to hatch some Meerachzion scheme, turned out to be something else entirely. Something, far more concerning.

"General!"

He was so accustomed to his admiral's arrival on the bridge that he almost spun around to greet, but quickly caught his self before he could act. As much as he hated talking to this droid, he didn't want to sever their link just yet. "But they're impostors." He reverted his attention back to the droid. "Enemies of the Regality! Directly in your midst. I'm surprised the Novid hasn't come under attack already."

"And it never will, general," came that all too arrogant reply again. "Our readings indicate that these two vessels are Seezhukan cargo-carriers. Not warships. So whatever your concerns are, you'll need to direct them elsewhere."

"Seezhukan cargo-carriers?" Voch found this strange. He looked at his scanner's readings on the helm's console again, hoping that he'd made some kind of mistake the first time. But he hadn't. His readings were accurate. The ship, Jherilon, had indeed entered the Novid star system. And these so-called Seezhukan cargo-carriers, were no carriers at all, but one small shuttle.

But why would a Seezhukan droid lie about two enemy ships that had so obviously invaded its own system? The protocol would've been to at least detain the two ships, in order to verify their proper identities. But to totally dismiss the claims of a high-ranking general––despite being on the wrong side of the sector––so easily and without regard, was something a Seezhukan would never have done. Unless... the droid he'd been talking to all along, was no Seezhukan at all....

"I see you've managed to convince the dim-witted Stendaaran to let you out of your prison," Voch said, in a sudden change of tone. And this time, he knew for a fact that he wasn't talking to droid.

"I didn't convince him of anything," came the smooth reply. "He did that all on his own."

Voch laughed...but not before severing the connection for good. He didn't see the point of wasting any more time of talking to the evil Viceroy. He'd wasted enough time talking to what he thought was a droid far too long enough. What pre-occupied his mind now, was what his next course of action should be, seeing that the entire command of the Novid system was now under the Viceroy's control.

When he finally turned around to meet Sollack, he faced a poised admiral, ready to take his every order. The news must've spread quickly throughout the fleet. With Jherilon no longer under the protection of the Stendaarans, his capture (or destruction) would be inevitable. However, this new development threatened to ruin his plans. And if the Viceroy is to ever return to the Plogg Sector now, then it would probably be through absolute force.

"I'm assuming you must already know of Jherilon's departure from the Eridani Sector," Sollack said, careful not to over-reach with his words, while he studied the general's gloomy posture.

"Aye," Voch began. "But it might not be as easy as I'd first thought."

"How so?"

"It's the Viceroy."

At the mention of the Plogg Sector's most prized possession, Sollack feared the worst had already happened. "What about the Viceroy? Was he harmed?"

"No. If only it was that simple...but but it's worst than that.... The Viceroy's free. Now he's in the Novid System, with their entire military force under his command."

"Foolish Stendaarans!" The admiral suddenly became livid. "Meddling in affairs they don't understand. They have no idea what they just unleashed. It will be the end of us all!"

"No. Not the end of us. The Stendaarans may have brought about their own demise by starting a war they have no way of winning, but the Plogg will always survive. With or without the Viceroy."

"So the Viceroy has become our enemy."

"He was never an ally, Sollack. Alert the Plogg, and have the commanders assemble the rest of our fleets. They are to meet us at these coordinates at once."

"Kraaglor's fleets, general? All of them?" Sollack asked, not sure if Voch really wanted to leave the worlds of the Free Sector unguarded. "But the rest of this fleet should be enough to neutralize both Jherilon and the Viceroy."

"We won't be dealing with just those two. And the Viceroy won't allow himself to be re-captured. He'll send the entire Novid to attack us."

"With the whole Novid at his command, he's prepared for a full-scale war. Then what about the Seezhukans?"

Voch shook his head. "We can't alert any more Seezhukan ships in this matter. The Viceroy will take command of their ships the instant they arrive in the Novid. And for that reason, we'll have to block all transmissions going in and out of the Novid, same as we'd done in the Oxlor and Eridani Sectors, so the Viceroy can't send for any more reinforcements."

"Full war is to come to the Novid then."

"Aye. Our fleets will destroy those worlds. And as for the Viceroy; whatever plans he has for this system, ends now!"

———•———

From a rectangular port-hole window aboard Jherilon, Semhek watched the silent drama unfold as the tiny Ekwhan shuttle erected its own churning worm-hole in space. Such a helpless creature it seemed now, on verge of being devoured by the insatiable vortex. Defenseless, in the face of an encroaching monster, its rear engines suddenly flared and it shot forward, directly into its gaping mouth.

At some point between the worm-hole's arrival, and the shuttle's departure, Morlaak must've fired off the ion-charge to close the portal. Just a tiny speck of light––from the distance where Semhek stood, watching ––barely noticeable amongst the stars as it crept forward at its own speed and erupted against the rim of the vortex. The worm-hole stopped spinning just then. Its gap collapsing, shrinking, as if being sucked through a smaller hole by a powerful vacuum until it was all gone, and that part of space became empty and undisturbed once again.

It was a thing Semhek was so accustomed to seeing. His own species had developed the technology. A crude way to get around the quadrants of the galaxy, by anyone's standards (especially the Meraachzions), but also the most untrackable, since worm-holes never ran in straight lines the way a hyperspace traveler would. He guessed that's probably why Morlaak chose the shuttle, instead of one of the Stendaaran fighter ships to escape in. That Kraaglor fleet would've surely followed his hyperspace path to this place. And there was no way that old slab of space-metal could out-run a Kraaglor ship.

"What're you looking at?"

He looked up and saw Ford, staring out the window. Her eyes shifted back and forth, scanning the empty miles for the slightest movement. It amazed him how she was able to creep up beside him, completely unnoticed. Floating around on those anti-grav boots, she walked as silent as a leaf on stagnant air.

She couldn't have been standing there next to him for too long though, if she didn't see Morlaak's departure. Out of all the drones aboard, Semhek must've been the only one who stood behind to watch him leave. And strangely, a small part of him was waiting for something (possibly bad) to happen. Not that it was something he wanted to see...he almost expected the general's shuttle to be blown out of space the minute it was detached from Jherilon. The Seezhukans never failed to detect intruders within their quadrants, and they were always quick to intercept and destroy. But no such thing happened in this case. Not even in the wake of the worm-hole's disappearance.

"Nothing," Semhek replied, still gazing in the direction where the general's shuttle once flew. "But I think something's wrong."

"Yeah. We're less than a quarter of a lightyear from the Dark Void. And I have a gut feeling that we'll be flying into——"

"No. Not that. I mean...the Seezhukans."

Ford frowned. "What about them?"

"Haven't seen not one Seezhukan fighter since we arrived. They're not even on Jherilon's radar. Even this close to Idinor, there should be at least two or three cruisers orbiting the moon, but there isn't. It's like they're avoiding us."

"Or welcoming us to their humble realm," said Ford, jokingly. She looked down and tussled his fur with a knowing smile. "You have to remember, Semhek, Jherilon's a Seezhukan. And so's the Technician. Their coming here wouldn't arouse any more suspicion than the Seezhukan emperor himself. Plus, Jherilon's a military craft, authorized to go anywhere within the second quadrant."

Semhek, not replying right away, stood quietly, as if in deep thought. Moments later he began shaking his head; clearly not convinced by Ford's explanation. "No. There's something else. I'm fully aware of Jherilon's advantages within this quadrant. But there's something else going on. Something hidden. Something that we're not seeing."

"Do you think we're going into a trap?"

Semhek shrugged. "We could be. I honestly don't know what's waiting for us on that moon. But I do know that the Seezhukans just allowed the general's shuttle to leave this quadrant without question. That, I'm sure of."

"The Technician must've——"

"No. Impossible. Even the general knew that once the Technician left the shuttle, he would only have a few seconds to leave the quadrant. I watched with my own eyes, the way he left in a hurry, as if expecting to be intercepted at any moment. He had no idea he was being awarded safe passage out of the quadrant."

Ford sighed, lifting her shoulders in a defeated shrug. "Maybe you're right. Maybe we are going into a trap. But what kind of a trap? Do you think the Seezhukans already know that we're here, and are just waiting to ambush us once we get to Idinor? Or do you think the Technician's behind all of this?"

Semhek shook his head, uncertainly. "I don't know at this point. I honestly don't know what's coming. I just don't feel right. We're not safe here, Ford."

"Well," Ford began. "That much is pretty obvious. Seeing that we're on a secret mission to destroy the Dark Void, and restore the outer rims of the third quadrant, I'll have to agree with you on that one. We're definitely not safe in this quadrant."

"You know what I mean."

She gave him a friendly nudge. "Come on. Let's get these wild thoughts out of our minds. There's something you need to see on the bridge."

"What?"

"I'm not gonna tell you, here. You need to get away from this window; take your mind off things. When you get to the bridge, maybe Jherilon can clear up some of these suspicions you have."

He was reluctant to leave. The hope that at least one Seezhukan patrol might still show up––just to prove him wrong––was all that kept him attached to the port-hole now. But he knew it was a pointless task. Even if a Seezhukan did finally arrive, what good would it be to any of they? Even if they weren't flying into a trap, they were still heading directly into danger––so in a way, one flaw in the mission didn't out-weigh the other by a whole lot. The thought of a trap was just more distressful to his mind, is all.

He took one last look at that empty lot in space; the place where a natural anomaly had once bore a tunnel through absolute nothingness, and hoped for all their sake that he was indeed wrong. That he had overlooked an important aspect in Jherilon's plan. Or perhaps the Seezhukans realized the general had already escaped, and they'd be only wasting their time by traveling all the way to Idinor. Either way, they were still bound to their mission. Besides, it wouldn't be the first time Semhek would be knowingly walking into a trap. He'd ambushed more than a few dozen Seezhukans in the past, so he figured, it would only be fair for them to have this one advantage.

CHAPTER
FOUR

MORLAAK'S HOLOGRAM OF Idinor, was nothing but a rough sketch compared to Plagnor's actual moon (as seen through the starboard window, on Jherilon's main deck). Even from such a great distance, it appeared to be a furtile world. A red sphere, made from the richest red soil, blotched by the bloodiest lakes. Where the bloodiest rivers ran through endless canyons and creeks to feed the bloodiest oceans and seas.

That plasma force-shield, could've been nothing more than a protective layer of ozone encircling Idinor. Crimson gases expelled from the deepest crevices on the surface, shot hundreds of miles in the air and formed its own atmosphere.

Down there, birds of a different kind flew. An unknown race of beings lived in perfect harmony with all creatures. And the weather was neither violent nor destructive, but calm and restful, as it had always been, since the dawn of its creation. Not even on the poles, where powdered rouge formed and blanketed both the north and south in a thick even layer of red, glistening ice.

So appeared Idinor from space. But as Jherilon neared the lunar's sphere, Jack saw a different world come into view entirely.

On the surface, was not furtile soil, but icy rock and crags, covering the moon. No lakes here, nor oceans, nor rivers, or seas, just deep craters and cracks that snaked through the land for thousands and thousands of miles. No clouds, no air, no atmosphere, just thick plumes of smoke and steam, billowing from the alien cities below. Smog! Trapped by the moon's own protective plasma-shield, and left to accumulate over the centuries. They appeared like pink clouds under the powerful light of the red sun.

No birds could ever fly down there, Jack knew. No race of peaceful beings had ever existed on Idinor; nor will there ever be. This red moon will never be able to nurture anything made from flesh, bone, and blood. This dead world. Nothing but a host to machines and droids, bent on plunging half the entire galaxy in a state of dimensional darkness. A world, he was all too eager to destroy.

"Plasma on plasma," he heard Braak beginning to tell Zubkov, as he sat in his chair nearby. "It makes sense."

The big Russian nodded with an insightful look on his face. "We can part through Idinor's shield, like a whale through water."

Braak made a questioning frown; his scaly brow turned his eyes to narrow slits. "What's a whale?"

"The biggest fish on Earth."

"What's a fish?"

"Things that swim in water," Zubkov said. But then he thought for a minute. "Like you."

"Ahh...now I understand. Actually, my thoughts had been running along those same lines. Yes, yes. We go right through the plasma, as easily as I can move about through my home-world."

233

"Exactly."

"I always knew Jherilon was powered by his own plasma generator, but I had no idea he could raise a plasma shield around the entire ship."

Zubkov shook his head. "Me either." Then he turned to Jack. "Did you?"

"No." Jack replied, with a low sigh. "Never really had a reason to raise shields. The only fight we were ever involved in, happened on Brashnor, but a plasma shield wouldn't have done much good against balls of plasma shot from a cannon."

"That's how Jherilon was able to destroy those other ships then," Ghan said. "Their own plasma shields couldn't protect them against plasma."

"And that's why Jherilon didn't bother to raise his own."

The door of the main deck slid open (with a soft hiss) just then, and in came Ford, stepping over the threshold onto the bridge. Behind her, Semhek towed close by, eyes darting all around, as if trying to find the slightest thing that looked out of place. "Did we jump here?" she asked, noticing how close they'd gotten to Idinor in such short space of time.

Semhek had noticed it too. A little while ago, Idinor was just a small red marble floating in space. Now they were close to entering its orbit. The giant shield resembled a pink membrane, covering unhatched larvae. A trillion veins of plasma pulsed and throbbed around the globe, like vessels flowing with life-giving blood. It was then he realized they must've been traveling at incredible amounts of speed the moment Morlaak's shuttle vanished through the wormhole. And even if the Seezhukans did arrive to investigate the shuttle's disappearance, Semhek would've never known, because Jherilon had taken them a quarter of a million miles by then. So graceful, so smoothly done, that he wasn't able to feel the slightest shift of movement under his feet.

"Yeah...sort of," the big Russian replied. "Not a big long quadrant jump. Just a little teeny one."

"I thought such things were mathematically impossible," Ford said, making her way to Zubkov's side.

"Apparently, it's not. At least not to him, anyway."

Semhek grew curious as to who Zubkov was actually referring to, because he didn't mention any names, nor did he point or look up at anyone else when he said it. But then the absence of the most trivial thing caught his eye, and when he looked toward the ship's port-side, he noticed Jherilon's holographic face was no longer there. At the helm, sat the all-too-familiar little box, nearly completely enshrined within the console——barely noticeable——as if it was actually designed to be there. A whole new web of circuitry had formed around it, like electronic tentacles reaching out from the box to connect with the ship's entire operating systems.

"What happened to Jherilon?" the little Tekwhaan asked.

"Some kind of fussion." Ford replied.

"That's not what I meant," Semhek said. "By looking at it, that much is already obvious. What I really want to know, is Jherilon still there?"

"I am," came that familiar voice from all around.

Instinctively, Semhek's gaze shifted port-side to see the ship's ghostly features. However, he found nothing but a broad window, where Jherilon's face should've been. He turned to his companions just then, searching their faces for some kind of explanation.

"This is our first real mission with Jherilon," Zubkov began. "We all decided that it's best for Jherilon to remain hidden while we approach Idinor. We don't want to be careless this early in the beginning stages. We have to be everything the Seezhukan's expects us to be."

"And that goes for us as well," said Jack, raising up from his chair. "We have to assume our disguises before we cross Idinor's shield. It's mostly maintenance droids down on the surface. But keep in mind that there are still a lot of Seezhukans down there on patrol. They can detect us in ways we have no idea of knowing, so the best thing for all of us is to avoid suspicion altogether."

"I'm disguised as an AIMC-1286," Jherilon said. "The latest model of Seezhukan Materials Carrier."

"Is this what you wanted me to see?" Semhek asked Ford. He didn't look too impressed. Nor did he share the other drones' enthusiasm to begin this mission. "A fusion?"

"Not just any fusion," Ford replied. "A reunion, between Jherilon and his master."

"You mean, his creator," said Ghan.

"That's not how Jherilon describes him," Ford shot back. "Jherilon always referred to the Technician, as his master. So that's what I call him."

"I think we're being hailed," Jherilon said, bringing a sudden change to everyone's mood on the bridge.

"Already?" said Ford, incredulously. "But we're on the far side of Idinor. Vermilion is still on opposite side of the moon."

"Doesn't matter," said Jack, swiping gently at his collar, so his armored helmet quickly draped over his face. "It was bound to happen sooner or later. For now, I want everyone to fall into disguise, before Jherilon opens up any channels with the surface below."

Jack reached for the armored screen implanted near his wrist and tapped in the commands that caused his form to change in an instant. Unlike any construction or maintenance worker on Earth, this droid did not come with any hard-hats, or long oily wrenches. It had a squared face, with no workable hinges to form a moving jaw. It didn't even have a mouth or a nose; just two coin-shaped eyes to scan its own environment. No more than two digits on each hand that opened and closed like pincers. No toes, no ankles, no soles, just two hydrolic stilts that pumped from one step to another.

By the time he looked up, all the other drones were already in their disguises. Even Semhek——the shortest of them all——had changed and was now standing shoulder to shoulder with Ghan. "Okay," Jack began, through some unseen vocalizer inside the droid's neck. "We all know what we have to do, so let's do it." He then turned to the console on the helm. "Open the channel."

"This is the realm's guardian of Vermilion," a rough, synthesized voice sputtered throughout the bridge. "What purpose do you have coming to Idinor, Materials Carrier?"

"A transport of six to Vermilion," Jherilon replied. "Replacement Units to continue service on the northeastern grid."

A brief moment went by before the guard came back on. "Proceed to the grid through the southern boundaries."

The ship moved forward without any further replied from Jherilon, nor did the guard come back on to verify if his instructions were heard, or being followed.

"Is tha——" Ford began, but then Jack quickly held up a pincered hand to silence her. He fixed a nervous gaze to toward the helm, silently urging Jherilon to say whether or not the coast was clear for them to speak. And that's when he got the answer behind the sudden silence. Right there, on the console's radar, nine warships had appeared in the Novid System, bearing down on them fast. He was almost grateful for Ford's inquiry, because at least he spotted the ships not too long after they arrived, and Jherilon was already on the move at full speed toward Idinor.

However, those warships belonged general Voch. They were all that remained of his fleet, after the Kraaglor Front's brazen invasion of the Oxloraan and Eridani Sectors. More than enough to destroy Jherilon before they reach the surface of Plagnor's moon.

The sudden silence was no coincidence, either. It was a weapon, used to disorient the enemy by blocking off all sound. Voch must've cut off all communication between Jherilon and Idinor. Then he used the weapon to cut off all sound altogether, because Jack couldn't even hear his self telling the drones to man their stations.

He rushed to the helm's main display screen, where he could see the radar up close and monitor Jherilon's course. He also wanted to communicate with the ship by manually typing written messages on the display, the same way Morlaak had done on the shuttle. There was also the problem of Idinor's force-shield, seeing that Jherilon was now shooting toward the moon at a much faster rate than he usually would. They were so close to the moon now, that it was all that could be seen from the window, and the shield appeared to be just outside the ship and in much finer detail.

Jack typed frantically into the display. "Raise your shield."

"I can't," came Jherilon's immediate reply. "If I do, then Voch can lock on to my location. But without my shield'd magnetic source, their cannons will have a much harder time locking on to their targets."

It made sense. Had the enemy use any other weapon besides the giant plasma shooting cannons on their warships, then Jherilon's plasma shield would've been the perfect defense against anything hurled at him. But it wouldn't be so this time. Plasma fire can go through any shield, and Voch's targeting systems were designed to lock onto a ship's electro-magnetics, since it was usually the enemy's first line of defense.

Jack remembered Jherilon's last encounter with Voch on Brashnore, and how difficult it was for those huge warships to shoot down the much smaller craft. He didn't understand it then as he did now, but still, something had to be done within the next few minutes or they were all going to die. "We have to raise shields now, or abandon the mission," he typed.

"Wait."

It was the only reply Jherilon made before Jack felt the ship lurch forward and they plunged right into Idinor's shield!

It all happened so fast. He didn't have time to react or brace for impact. As the ship banked sharply to the right and left; he lost his footing and went stumbling into the wall.

Moments later he saw the bright pink flashes of plasma fire as they went streaming past the ship, and down onto the surface below.

That was close!

Jherilon must've activated his shield a split second before entering Idinor's orbit, then deactivating it the instant the ship was clear. And even in that incredibly short space of time, Voch was still able to let off a short burst that could've easily pierced through Jherilon's hull.

The sound of his own footsteps seemed to help him regain his balance. "Close all channels," he quickly said, coming back over to the console. The fact that he could hear himself again––and everything else around him––made him hope that Voch had somehow given up on them and returned to the Plogg Sector. But things were never that easy for the drones. In fact, it appeared as if dozens of more warships had suddenly been added to Voch's forces. The center of the radar was now a cluster of blips.

"Two Seezhukan fleets have entered the system," Braak shouted from his station.

"Reinforcements?" Semhek asked.

"Our cover's blown then," said Ford. "That fool of a general just won't give up."

"Why would the Seezhukans help Voch?" Zubkov asked. "I hope the famed general of the United Order of The Kraaglor Front isn't asking an old enemy for back-up."

"I don't know if that's the case," Jack said, taking his seat back at the helm. Based on what he saw on the console's screen, another dogfight was sure to happen, and he didn't want to be bouncing about all over the bridge again. "But Idinor's planetary guard have definitely been alerted. There're about three fighter-squadrons heading our direction right now. In another four or five minutes we'll be intercepted."

"That's not for us," Jherilon said, in such a matter-of-factly way, it sounded as if he was stating the obvious.

"Not for us...?" A perplexed Jack began. "Then who are those fighters gunning for?"

"Voch's warships are being intercepted by the Seezhukans," Jherilon replied. "The planetary guards were summoned. But I don't think it'll do much good once they leave Idinor's atmospheric shield."

"And why's that?"

"Voch's disorientation weapons are still active and operational. But because of the plasma and electronic field surrounding the moon, his weapons have no effect down here; which is why the guards were able to receive the Seezhukans' call."

"And why we can still hear each other," Braak added insightfully.

"We should warn them," said Ford.

"I don't think that's wise," Ghan said. "If we warn the guard, we jeopardize our own mission."

"Aye," Zubkov reluctantly agreed. "Maintenance droids aren't programmed in matters of war. We'll only betray our disguises if we decide to warn them. Besides, the planetary guard, the Seezhukan, and general Voch are all our enemies. Let'em all destroy each other up there; less trouble for us down here."

Easily, they all came to a silent agreement on this point. For it seemed to be a universal code, that the enemy of one's own enemy, is also an ally.

And as if to confirm Jherilon's earlier statement, the three fighters of the planetary guard could now be seen shooting up through Idinor's horizon in the distance. Just three bright lights, streaming higher and higher, up towards space until plunging into the plasma shield and coming out through the other side. They were already out of view by the time Jherilon's nose dipped towards Idinor's most southern continent.

Jack followed their path on the radar. The three small blips making tiny hops across the screen toward the much larger shapes that represented the Seezhukan force. "I wonder if those fighters had their own plasma generators to get through the field?" he asked, remembering how smoothly Jherilon slipped into Idinor's air space. He knew if the fighters were equipped with their own generators, then they would surely be armed with their own kinds of plasma cannons. Which, in a sense, would make them equal to Jherilon.

"They do not have generators," came Jherilon's reply. "I scanned their system, and found only a dual polarized mechanism that would allow them to disrupt the field's continuity for a brief moment in time."

"And weapons?"

"The most advanced in this system. Magnetic shields, very powerful electron railguns, as well as hyperbombs. Quite effective against any other in the galaxy. But they're no match for Voch's defenses."

"Take me back to these...hyperbombs. What are they?"

"Old technology of the Regality. They're mainly explosive devices, sent through time and space to detonate within a ship's hull. Very effective against much larger vessels, but notoriously inaccurate when it comes to targeting smaller ships."

"I think I read about that weapon in the galactic archive," said Ghan. "Centuries ago, during the Pasian wars, in the Midatlan Sector; they're some kind of special weapon. Chronicled as the 'magical bomb', because they would magically appear on the bridges of Meeracnzion warships. It was said that the bombs were sent through very snort warp-tunnels that opened up within the ranks of the enemy's fleets. But the weapon had a main flaw; it's virtually impossible to lock onto a target through hyperspace, so they were basically launched from an estimated range. A lot of ships were damaged in that war; out most of those bombs appeared miles away from their targets and exploded harmlessly in empty space."

"They were taken out of service not too long after those wars," Jherilon said.

"Only to be stationed here, in the Novid," Ford concluded. "The Seezhukans better pray that those bombs are still operational after all these years. They have the best chance of inflicting some real damage on Voch's fleet. Considering the close range they have, and the size of those giant ships, it shouldn't be too difficult for them to hit their marks."

"Hyperbombs wouldn't work on Voch's ships," Jherilon said. "and that's mainly because the warp tunnels wouldn't be able to go through his shields. They'll simply be deflected away."

"But they can still get through, using those polarizing disrupter things," Jack blurted, as if the new idea had suddenly struck him.

"Considering they don't get destroyed in the process... yes, I think that's very possible."

"Is there a way we can get that message to them? Maybe use one of the Seezhukans own warships to relay it indirectly."

"No. There's no way the guard can receive our message without discovering the data's true origin."

Jack fumed under his breath while looking at the three tiny blips on the radar. He desperately wanted to give the guard a fighting chance against Voch's fleet. Strangely, the success of their mission now relied on whether or not the Seezhukans were strong enough to hold the general at bay. It was the only way he could use this new developing situation to his own advantage. "How far are we from Vermilion?"

"We've already crossed the Southern Boundaries," Jherilon replied. "We'll reach Vermilion in the Northeastern Grid in another fifteen minutes."

"Could you get us there in five?"

"There's no written speed limit laws for anyone flying above Idinor. But there are certain expectations on how fast, or slow, one should travel. The typical Materials Carrier usually travels at a normal cruising speed. If I exceed these expectations by too much, it would raise the suspicion of the planetary guard on the ground."

"What do you have planned?" Semhek asked suddenly.

"A huge battle is about to happen in space," Jack said. "Voch's about to destroy the Seezhukans and the planetary guard. Then he's gonna blow this moon apart, the same way he did to Apellon, in the Oxloran Sector. When that happens, we should be well on our way out of here." He turned back to the helm, even as Jherilon began to triple his acceleration toward Vermilion. "Open a channel," he said, causing the others to fix him with curious stares. "I want you to relay these specific instructions to the planetary guard on how to defeat Voch's warships."

'Should this be a direct message?" Jherilon asked.

"Yes," Jack replied.

"Are you crazy!?" Zubkov was the first to protest; probably because the others didn't understand the folly of Human recklessness the way he did. "At least give us some time to do what we have to do first. Let the Seezhukans deal with that mess up there. Alert the guard now, and they'll come after us too."

Jack took one glance at the console and began shaking his head. "I'm afraid time has run out for us down here."

"What?" A perplexed Zubkov rose up from his chair and walked over toward Jack. "What are you talking about?"

"Just take a look at what's happening on the radar," Jack said, as he made room for the big Russian to approach the helm. "The battle's already begun. And from the looks of it, the Seezhukans are losing."

One look at the radar and Zubkov could already see that what Jack had been saying was true. The larger blips that represented the Seezhukan forces were beginning to vanish from the screen. But at least the three tiny blips of the planetary guard were still there...for now. "Have you sent those instructions to the guard already?" he asked, in a new humbling tone.

"The message have already been sent," Jherilon replied.

"Close channels," Jack said. "I think the guard's gonna be having their hands full from this point on. No need to confuse things with frivolous questions."

The red Idinor landscape blew past the ship in a long streaky blur. Jherilon was flying so fast, it appeared as if the Southern Boundaries had all of a sudden just slipped into the background, to allow the jungle of tall metal spires in the Northeastern Grid to come into view. Only then did the ship reduce its own speed, and the buildings that rolled by outside looked like they had finally slowed down to catch up with them in real time.

"We're now entering Vermilion," Jherilon began, reminding Jack so much of a tour-guide back on Earth. "The red city of ice and steel."

"Okay now," said Jack, at the helm. "Keep it steady; use the quickest possible route. But in the mean time, I'd like to get a good look at the city's maps to see exactly where we're heading."

Like magic, three holographic cubes appeared in the middle of the bridge. One for each section of the city.

Jack walked over to the nearest cube, but paused at the one in center. The one of the Northeastern Grid; the one in which they were currently in. A slight wave of the hand caused the others to vanish, and the one before him to expand to the size of the entire bridge. Soon, he found himself walking in the midst of the holographic city, surrounded by red hazy towers and black metallic roads.

He would quickly discover that the red hazy towers weren't actual towers or buildings at all, but components and parts joined together that made up the entire machine responsible for the Dark Void. Like being in the midst of giant capacitors and resistors on a circuit the size of a football field. Even the black metallic roads turned out to be something else; they were more like conductors, snaking in and out of these huge components in multiple lanes. These roads, Jack figured, were what distributed the different levels of power throughout the entire city; they were like the electrical wiring on a mother-board. "Jherilon, I need you to show me the exact point of our destination."

Suddenly, the entire hologram of the city began to turn and shift until Jack found himself standing directly in the western region of Vermilion. There, stood the tallest structure, flashing bright yellow as it eased up toward Jack and came to a complete halt in front of him.

"Is this it?" he asked, studying the hologram and noticing they were almost the same height. "What is it?"

"It's the one thing the Seezhukans couldn't replicate," Jherilon replied. "A quantum reflector. With enough power, it can open up any dimensional portal in existence."

"So is this what Vermilion is then? One huge power source, strong enough to feed this reflector unlike anything else beyond measure?"

"That's one way to look at it. But yes, that is the city's main function. And that is why we couldn't just fly in and bomb everything we see. It would've been a wasted effort, because it'll all be rebuilt in a matter of days. But destroy this one reflector, and all of your troubles in Bhoolvyn will be over."

"And how much longer until we reach this reflector?"

"A few minutes more."

"Good." The hologram of Vermilion City suddenly withered away into nothing and the bridge reclaimed its normal look.

"We have incoming!" Ghan shouted from his station.

"What?" Jack rushed back over to the helm. "Everyone brace for impact!" He hollered over his shoulder, while strapping his self down in the pilot's chair. On the radar, he could see that most of the Seezhukan forces had been all but destroyed, and the three tiny blips of the planetary guard was no longer on the radar. However, one of Voch's warships was also missing, and that told him that at least the guards were able to destroy one of its targets completely. Something the Seezhukans wouldn't have been able to accomplish if they had ten whole fleets at their disposal.

"Hold on!" Jherilon banked sharply to the right to avoid a stream of fire from above.

Up ahead, a hail-storm of plasma could be seen riddling the Idinor landscape. Everything that stood on the ground were blown to bits, even the icy crags way off in the distance, crumbled under the barrage and sent huge chunks of ice erupting into the air. It seemed the whole city of Vermilion came under attack, as if Voch and his remaining fleet just fired their cannons rapidly at whatever moved down below.

From space, the swarm of plasma fire came silently, without the slightest peep of a sound, until they dove into Idinor's protective shield in droves, then out through the other side with a thunderous roar. Red rain was what it looked like! A sudden downpour from sparsed clouds, setting everything ablaze, even destroying a group of towers that stood miles away from their main target.

Nothing was safe.

Not even Jherilon, who continuously managed to dodge in and out of Voch's deadly rain of fire until two bolts of plasma went streaking through his rear engine. Another three ripped through his hull (at the stern) in rapid succession, blowing bits of metal out of his belly like the blood and guts of a wounded soldier. They began losing altitude after that...fast!

The ship did a lame roll to stabilize itself. It spun once, then twice, then a third final time before righting itself in the air. Black smoke trailed from the dead engine in the back and made a crooked descending line across the sky as Jherilon continued to go down.

At a height of three-thousand feet, the tallest structures on Idinor now stood in their path. The city of Vermilion was a jungle of towers, spires, and electric components. A seemingly perfect place to provide cover for the wounded ship. A sort of refuge, that is, until a dozen balls of plasma came bursting out of the walls of one of the tallest towers behind Jherilon, who made a limping bank around squat structure to avoid being hit, again. "I'm losing power!" He said, in his usual calm voice, depicting neither pain nor fear. "My generator's been damaged. It's leaking fuel."

And as if to bring his point home, the lights on the bridge kind of sputtered for about ten seconds before coming back on. The radar no longer worked, because there wasn't enough power in the ship to keep the console's display fully operational. Even the little box (the Technician) seemed to have sensed the end of things to come and had released the hold it had on the helm. It now jiggled freely within its own enclosure.

Perhaps sensing the same end, Jack took the box from out of its slot and held it tightly in both of his hands. Through the port-side window, he could see Voch's fleet were still raining all hell down on the city below. A sudden turn switched the view from collapsing spires, to the tallest tower in the western region: the quantum reflector. By some miracle, it remained unharmed in the midst of all the destruction happening all around it. He wondered if there was a reason for that; perhaps Voch knew of the tower's importance. That's why he would stop at nothing to prevent them from getting there.

The ship shuttered for what seemed like a long time, and Jack prayed they were just flying through a strong field of turbulence. But as the nose lurched downward and he could see the reddish ground speeding up toward them, he knew Jherilon had taken another hit. And this time, it seemed to be a crippling blow. "Pull up!" he commanded the ship.

"My rear engines have all been disabled," came Jherilon's flat response. "I can no longer fly, and I can't prevent us from going down. I barely have enough fuel for the base-thrusters; they're the only things left available that can at least slow us down before we crash."

They were the last words Jherilon said before Jack began to feel the comforting drag of the base-thrusters flaring up below the ship. The nose beginning to rise, however, they'd already fallen too far and the ground was already too close. The base-thrusters slowed the ship down just enough to prevent a fatal crash, but nothing else.

EXPEDITION TEN

CHAPTER
ONE

THE SHIP BROKE in half the instant it hit the ground. The frontal end of the fuselage bounced once, then went skipping across the surface, parting the red snow like a shark's fin through water.

On the bridge, complete darkness had taken over. With no power, and his generator fully depleted, Jherilon was dead. For a while, it seemed as if all was still. Silent. Jack was still hunched over in his chair, waiting for that final collision, which never came. Instead, the thunderous roar of dozens of plasma bolts falling toward them returned, along with his senses, frantically alerting him that it was time to move.

"Switch to night-vision!" He shouted, hoping the rest of his crew was still alive. In the mean time, he went to swipe at his collar, but stopped when his whole body suddenly froze.

'You can't take off your helmet, Jack,' Klidaan, his symbiot, advised. **'We have to stay in disguise.'**

'But I can't see, and we're still being fired upon. We have to get out of here.'

For the briefest of moments, Klidaan considered this bit of reasoning, then released his hold on Jack. **'I don't think it's wise, but under the current circumstances, there's no other choice but to break protocol.'**

'Protocol's been broken the second Voch entered this system,' Jack said, swiping at the collar to retract the maintenance droid's helmet. Instantly, his vision returned to a sea of the darkest red. So much so, that he thought blood had somehow gotten into his eyes.

'These droids weren't designed to have strong lenses to detract light in their optical receptors.' Klidaan quickly explained as he sensed Jack's mounting panic. **'They don't have use for eyes down here. All of their duties are pre-programmed for a specific task.'**

'Yeah, and I don't think we'll have much use for these disguises any longer, either.' Jack said. He moved to unstrap his self from the chair, when he finally realized that he no longer held the box in his hands. He had obviously dropped it during the crash. "I lost the Technician," he said out loud.

"I have him."

A quick look around the bridge, and Jack was relieved to find that all the crew had survived the crash. But it was Semhek, however, the only other drone who had totally abandoned his disguise, that held the box in his hand.

"Good," said Jack, hurrying over toward the main door. He was glad to know that someone, other than himself, was thinking along the same lines. "We're not safe, trapped inside this ship. The sooner we get out of here, the better for all of us."

"And our disguises?" Zubkov asked.

"Lose them," said Jack. "With the city under attack. I don't think anyone's gonna be paying much attention to us."

"These things go blind under the dimmest light," Braak said.

"Leave it up to the Stendaarans to choose the worst disguise for our missions," Ghan added, as he walked up to the main door. Under normal circumstances, it would've slid open upon his approach. But with no power, the door was just another part of wall.

Luckily, Ghan—the tallest and strongest of the drones—also had the longest, slimmest fingers to fit down in between the seams in the floor and manually hoist the door up over his head. A brighter, more intense red light, poured into the bridge from outside. Up high in the sky above, bolts of plasma still rained like embers from a forest fire. A subtle sign, that general Voch was still shooting blindly onto the surface of the moon; he didn't know that his target was down....

They used their grav-boots to jump off the jagged edge, where the ship was torn in half, and landed softly on the thick red snow. The only thing left for them to do now, was run! Run as fast as they could, away from the dead ship—Voch's main target. But then again, the entire city appeared to have been Voch's target. For even when they'd gotten a good distance from the ship, they were still in grave danger of being hit by any one of the countless bolts that came zipping down all around them.

Before his death, Jherilon was mindful enough to get them as close to the quantum reflector as he possibly could. And because of that, the drones had to run no more than 200 yards before they reached the tower. But it wouldn't be without another dramatic event taking place.

Way off in the distance, a huge fire-ball erupted and lit up the sky over the entire city of Vermilion. The explosion must've been heard for miles; and for a brief while, the

Red City of Ice and Steel, turned white from what must've been the brightest light in all the Universe. Too bright for the naked eye. The drones would've all went blind if they hadn't instinctively covered their faces up in time. A mild tremor caused some to lose their footing, but it was the shock-wave from the incredible blast that laid them all flat on the ground.

What lasted for no more than a few seconds, seemed to go on forever. The strong wind from the blast pelted and covered them with rock, snow, and scrap metal. Then it suddenly stopped, as if what had sent this great blinding ball of fury had spent the last bit of its energy on one big grand finale. The ground stopped shaking and the sky reclaimed that famous crimson glow over the red city. Even the deadly rain of plasma bolts gradually slowed to a drizzle until they ceased falling altogether. Either Voch's cannons had finally ran out of ammunition, or that huge explosion on Vermilion was seen from out in space, appearing as if the entire city had been destroyed.

"What the fuck was that?" Ford rose slowly to her feet, inspecting her own armor for any signs of damage.

"Some kind of explosion," said Braak, stating the obvious.

"Voch must've hit some kind of depot," said Zubkov, noticing the warships weren't firing down on them anymore.

"No," said Jack, looking up into the red sky, then down over to where the explosion began. "That was our own bomb that went off. The same bomb we were supposed to use on that thing there." He nodded up at the tower looming high above them.

"It must've taken a hit from one of those plasma bolts," said Ford. "That, mixed with the blast from Jherilon's own generator, would create quite the explosion."

"Good thing that part of the ship had broken off, all those miles from where we crashed," said Jack. "We wouldn't have survived."

"Jherilon's generator was the only thing that Voch could've gotten a clear reading on," Semhek said. "And once that was destroyed, he knew for sure that Jherilon was gone."

"So it's over then?" Ford asked. "That's the only reason why they aren't shooting at us anymore? I feel safer already. But what about the quantum reflector? We don't have a bomb. How the hell are we supposed to destroy that thing now?"

"With this," Semhek said, holding up the little box in his hand. "He said that he could shut it down from inside."

"And how do you know that?" asked Zubkov. "Did the Technician whisper that in your little ears?"

"He's communicating through my armor, directly to my implant."

"Hmm..." said Jack, thoughtfully. "I suppose he can do that, can he? Our suits are electronic after all."

"Yeah," Semhek replied. "And so's this reflector."

"Do it then," Jack said. "Let's get this over with."

It was just a dozen or so more yards before they reached the reflector, but as they continued to walk, Jack took the short time to survey all the destruction around them. And indeed, Voch's warships demonstrated their full power today. The entire city of Vermilion, it seemed, looked broken and on verge of total collapse at the slightest tremor. And yet, the Dark Void still covered the rims of the Bhoolvyn Sector.

He wondered what part of this lunar machine Vermilion served, then guessed not a very important one, after taking such an attack––most of its components blown to bits––and not even causing a glitch in the machine's main functions....

The quantum reflector itself, was a plain, but enormous tower. No steps, pathways, or walkways to direct one to an entrance. And speaking of entrances, there weren't any. No doors, windows, or gates to be seen anywhere on the whole tower. Just metal, the brownish kind, like dull brass, wrapping around the tower and making the whole thing appear more solid.

Jack thought it resembled one gigantic pill-bottle, at least fifty yards in diameter just jotting out of the red snow, with enough medication to treat the whole moon.

But all that changed the instant Semhek approached the reflector with the little box in his hand. Nanos, trillion and trillions of them, reacted and opened a cubic slot the instant Semhek pushed the Technician all the way inside. And the reaction was immediate. A strong surge of energy seemed to have been sucked up from the depths in the ground to go pulsing up through the length of the reflector. The tower glowed, like hot metal on the verge of melting. It was then Jack realized that the surface of the tower wasn't brass at all. Its true color must've been a metallic chrome that absorbed the scarlet hue all around it.

Heat began to radiate from the surface of the reflector. So much so, that the drones were all forced to back away. Even the red sky, where the plasma shield still surrounded the moon, began to shine brighter as if the red star itself allowed it to feast on its own power.

Something was happening!

That much was obvious.

However, all would remain dubious of the current events taking place on Idinor. And by the time Jack spotted the first (new) swarm of plasma bolts shooting down toward them, it was already too late. He barely had enough time to give them a full warning. "Everybody, look out!!!

———•———

From space, the explosions taking place all over Vermilion were like tiny bulbs flashing on and off. But there one explosion in particular, that flashed bigger and brighter than all the others. One that stayed on for a few seconds longer, then blew itself out, as if being extinguished by a sudden gust of wind. And it was this one explosion that general Voch was most interested in. The only thing that could've caused him to order his fleet to cease fire.

"Readings indicate significant amounts of plasma radiation as the source of the explosion," Sollack said, from where he stood at his station. He looked across the bridge of the Kraaglor warship and fixed his general with a meaningful stare. "It was Jherilon. He suffered a direct hit that destabilized his generator. Nothing would've been able to survive that kind of explosion for miles."

"And what of the Viceroy?" Voch asked.

A perplexed Sollack paused, wondering if the general had heard everything he'd just mentioned. Surely, Voch had every right to have even the smallest doubt. But the obvious conclusion should never be ignored, nor overlooked. The general himself had taught him that. However, the admiral thought it was wise not to remind him. "In this situation," he began, choosing his words very carefully. "With all things considered. The Viceroy had certainly perished, along with Jherilon."

Voch didn't respond right away; nor did it appear that he wished to make any comments on the recent information any time soon. For the hard truth was, the Plogg Sector had suffered a devastating loss, by losing the Viceroy. It was indeed, a time for mourning. A time for deciding Kraaglor's place in the uncertain future to come. A future without the Viceroy's leverage. A future, now more than ever, at risk of falling back into the hands of the Seezhukans.

"General," Sollack finally called, when Voch's long silence became too unbearable.

"Is there anywhere out of this place?" Voch asked. It was a question that came from elsewhere in his mind. A place that was eager to put the Viceroy's death behind them.

"There is," Sollack replied, with a reassuring nod. "Our computers have constructed a map of all the dimensional regions. It is a simple matter of going around, then re-entering the other side. But it will take years of travel. Perhaps decades, depending on the rate of speed these portals continue to grow. And if its a matter of speed, then a whole century might pass before we make it to the other side."

"But there is a way out," said Voch, with a new glimmer of hope in his voice.

"Aye sir," Sollack affirmed once more.

"Set the most appropriate course then. Let's hope we can out-run this thing and be back in Plogg before the next festival. I've had more than enough of all these different quadrants and dimensions for one lifetime. Alert the rest of the fleet that we're going home."

"Aye sir."

That all too familiar hum and vibration of the warship's engines coming to life began. They served to bring ease to the otherwise fatigued general's mind. This foresaken quest to retrieve that ungrateful Viceroy, was finally over. Besides, it was a mistake coming here. If Voch had known the Viceroy was willing to plunge himself into some bottomless void in the middle of space, he wouldn't have followed him there. He would've turned his fleet around and headed back to Plogg a long time ago. In fact, he might not even have bothered to leave the sector.

But now, however, he was here. Somewhat trapped in another dimension, with the Viceroy's remains scattered across the red surface of an icy moon. The main objective now, is returning to the Plogg, no matter how long it might take. With their built-in generators, he and his entire crew would see eons go by in a single blink of an eye. So a century in this dimension, would be no more than a second to Voch, in his own galaxy....

The ship's engines suddenly began winding down, and soon nothing stirred on the bridge, save for the periodic beep and click of the work-droids at their stations. It was enough to rouse Voch from his brief moment of rest. A sudden stillness, a most disturbing thing to any general, perhaps.

"What, is it?" He asked his admiral, who was now suddenly so busy at his own station.

"Something's happening on the surface of that moon," Sollack replied. "Our sensors just picked up a power-surge.

Something beyond measure, and its affecting the whole moon."

A bright flash came from Idinor's shield just then. A sudden glint, like a sparkling marble in a light's glare. So strong, that Voch could actually see the power through the bridge's starboard window. "Locate and identify the source, quickly!" He hoped it was anything but the Viceroy. However, he knew it was only wishful thinking.

"It's coming from a tower in the northeastern section of the southern continent. The same site we just destroyed."

"Well, destroy it again! All of it! Starting with that tower! All cannons target that tower. Now!!!"

Voch's entire fleet responded in an instant. All at once, the firing began, sending long bolts of plasma in the form of dozens of orange streaks back down onto the surface of Idinor. And this time, the firing looked to be more intense, as all twenty-one cannons focused all of their firing on one target. Dozens of deadly bolts, originating from a wide arching crest, then eventually converging together to form one single line of fire; or what appeared to be one solid beam of plasma.

From Voch's point of view, it looked as if his warships were attempting to drill a hole right through the moon in order to have that beam of plasma go bursting out through the other side of Idinor. And it would be all for the better, he thought. He would destroy all of Idinor, break it down to one hundred smaller pieces, the same he'd done to Apellon in the Oxloraan Sector.

The Viceroy was still down there...Voch knew this for certain. There was no going back now; the Viceroy had to destroyed. He now understood the purpose of coming here.

Why the Viceroy chose to flee to some hidden dimension. This moon. It was Idinor: a source of unlimited power.

The tiniest twinkle of light appeared directly to the north of the tower––Voch's target. But then it grew, like the headlight of an incoming train, bigger and brighter, until it shot out of Idinor's shield and destroyed one of Voch's ships with a single strike! So violent and powerful it seemed, it looked as if the ship had just been ripped apart by a cyclonic wind.

"It's the Viceroy," Sollack said, gawking over at the now weaponized moon. "He using the generator's own force shield as a weapon." Even as he said this, another one of their ships was being destroyed. "We don't have enough time to escape."

"Then dive!" said Voch, quickly rising to his feet and approaching the starboard window as if he could help guide what remained of his fleet from there. "It's the only way. Dive under the shield, then attack the generator from within Idinor's own atmosphere."

Understanding the general's intention, Sollack quickly turned to the nearest station. "Alert all ships! Evasive maneuvers now! We are to breach Idinor's atmosphere at once. Get below the shield's range of fire!"

Another ship suffered a direct hit before it had time to respond. But perhaps it had provided enough time for the neighboring vessel to evade a deadly blow as it used its own plasma to plunge down into Idinor's force shield.

It all appeared to be a success at first, until the nose of that warship suddenly crumbled and a huge beam of light went bursting out of the back of it. And it just sat there, for an instant, skewered by this beam of light, trapped between

Idinor's shield as if that thin film of plasma was the only thing holding it up. And then the whole thing just exploded!

It was then Voch realized that he'd made a grave error in his command. Or maybe his eyes played a fatal trick on his senses, for the Viceroy's weapon was riot Idinor's shield, but some other thing down on the surface of the moon. And Sollack, had been correct all along, there was no escaping the attack from this weapon. Voch had only succeeded in hastening the defeat of what remained of his fleet.

Another bright light came from Idinor; and this time, there was no other targets left remaining, except Voch's own warship. Alas! the general stood there, not feeling defeated as much as he felt out-witted. Thwarted by his own master! He wondered, then and there, how much of his own actions had been real and how much of it was pure folly. At what extent did the Viceroy go through to make Voch believe that he was in control? That he could actually keep his own creator imprisoned for all eternity. But alas! even as the entire bridge became smothered by that vicious, deadly light, Voch realized now that he'd never been in control of anything....

CHAPTER
TWO

THE BOLTS CAME all at once, like a heavy downpour from a cloud directly above them. There wasn't even enough time to think, yet alone react. And for that one brief moment, they all thought they were gonna die.

But then the bolts cane and the red snow hissed like frying butter in a pan. It melted the snow all around them, and soon, a small puddle of water began to form under their feet. By now, the drones should all have been sprawled out on the ground with those drops of plasma dissolving their dead bodies like rain on salt. But not one of them was harmed in the least; not even a brush-burn. In fact, the dense shower of bolts landed nowhere near the drones!

"It's going around us," Semhek (apparently the first to recover from that near-death experience) said.

And indeed the shower of bolts had formed a wide circle around the whole tower in which they were now enclosed. From inside, it appeared as if they were standing within an immense tube of fire that stretched all the way up to the heavens.

"What the hell's happening?" Jack was bewildered, and grateful, to be alive. The cylinder of plasma fire that surrounded them had blocked out all of the natural light from Idinor's red star, and for the first time since their arrival into the Novid solar system, they were seeing things within their encasement under a more accustomed spectrum of colors. The molten snow that formed a puddle under their feet, for instance, no longer appeared like a bloody pool, but clean and clear water. The tower nearby stood like a building made from the shiniest chrome, reflecting the rapid bolts of plasma in their natural golden hue.

"I think it's the Quantum Reflector," Semhek replied, pointing over toward the tower that now appeared to have the same metallic sheen as their armor. "It's deflecting the plasma."

"It's protecting us!" Ford exclaimed.

"No," said Ghan, shaking his head. "It's protecting itself. The tower must be emitting some kind of opposing force that's preventing the plasma from hitting it directly. And luckily for us, because of its sheer size, the plasma's being pushed far enough away so that it missed us completely as well."

"It's a good thing that we were still close enough to the tower when those bolts came down," said Zubkov. "If we'd walked just a few more meters in any direction, we'd all be dead."

"There must be some kind of protective bubble around this place then," Semhek said. "And it's definitely the reason why the whole city of Vermilion was destroyed, while this tower remained untouched. It makes sense now."

"I wonder how long those warships can keep firing down on us like this?" Jack said.

"With the size of their plasma generators," Semhek began, remembering his fierce battle with Kaypac, that had cost him his leg. "I think they can keep this up for a very long time. And by that, I mean indefinitely."

Jack released a heavy, burdensome sigh. "Well, let's all hope and pray that Voch and the rest of his fleet have better things to do then. With all this concentrated fire, he must surely recognize that he isn't hitting the target. Sooner or later, he's gonna have to——"

The were all interrupted by the sudden brightness that engulfed the whole sky just then. Bright enough to shine through the curtain of plasma surrounding the drones. But then it lessened in size and volume, sort of shrinking itself down to one single beam of light that stretched all the way up into the sky——into space and beyond!

But as quickly as this beam of light appeared, however, it vanished. Then another one popped up, a few miles to the west of them, and shot across the horizon before quickly shutting itself out of existence. Then another and another, all in rapid succession, until it became clear what these strange beams actually were.

"Giant Photon cannons!" Braak observed, pointing over at a stunning beam that had suddenly went bursting out of the face of a nearby mountain. "Most similar to the ones they have on Lanns. But these cannons are the biggest I've ever seen; the most powerful too. And they have to be, to pose a threat to any kind of warship that far out in space."

However, these extraordinary blasts of photon proved to be far beyond threatening to anything out in space that stood in its path. For with each beam that went zooming up into the sky, the wave of plasma bolts that shot down to the surface of Idinor, gradually decreased until there were no more than a few bolts coming down at a time.

At one point, the giant weaponized nose of one of Voch's warships plunged menacingly through Idinor's thin atmosphere, like the face of a curious god, eager to know the fate of its subjects on the ground. But again, an incinerating beam of photon-blast met that face head on, and appeared to go right through it. So clean, and so fatally abrupt, that the ship died before the beam vanished within its bowels. The ship didn't even explode! With no power to keep it loft, it just succumbed to the moon's gravity, falling and falling, then smashing into a mountain like a broken toy.

Three more beams went shooting up into space before the last and final bolt of plasma fell harmless into the snow, just twenty yards away from the tower. Then all became peacefully quiet, save for the humbling sound of running water around their feet. Even the soft crackling of burning structures in the distance, brought a warm and comforting effect to their ears, that their worst ordeal had finally ended.

"Is it over?" Ford was almost too afraid to ask.

With no more warships left remaining to continue the flow of plasma around the tower, Idinor's red sky had returned. And with it, came the cold. That bitter, icy frost, several degrees below zero——the only kind of cold that could remain on a frozen moon so far away from its own star. The shallow puddle that was so crystal-clear, now looked like diluted blood swishing about around their feet.

"It won't be too long before all this melted snow begin to freeze," said Zubkov noticing the thin sheets of ice that was already beginning to form in certain areas on the surface of the puddle. With a single command to his grav-boots, he gently rose above the pool that had been no more than four or five inches deep.

Seeing the big Russian's point, and not wanting their legs to freeze when the puddle turn back to ice (which was

268

happening very quickly), the drones all did the same and soon they were all levitating over the water.

"So now what?" asked Break, seeing that they were all safe, and their feet had finally dried. It seemed that there was nothing else left for them to do, but keep hovering above the frozen ice. Not one of them dare venture beyond the edge of the icy rink, lest a hail of plasma strike them outside the protective dome of the tower.

"I don't know," said Jack, shaking his head, because he too was unable to come up with anymore ideas on their next course of action. Jherilon was gone, and general Voch, apparently had been destroyed. The machine, the quantum reflector, wasn't dismantled––as originally planned––but appeared to have been neutralized. So that meant that the Dark Void was gone; the Bhoolvyn was free. The mission, to say the least, was over. They'd won!

"Maybe we should call Morlaak," Ford (all too eager to leave the strange world) said, "Get him to get us the hell out of here."

Jack seemed to agree––they all did––so he turned to the tall Lannsillian. "Is it safe to contact the 19th fleet this far behind enemy lines?"

Ghan shook his head. "No. Not without the Seezhukans trying to intercept our frequency. And if they do that, then they'll know we're here."

It was then Jack remembered they hadn't been in disguise the entire time they arrived on Idinor. However, there didn't appear to be a single maintenance droid for miles, nor any Seezhukans, or the planetary guard. Only destruction. The entire Vermilion, was under rubble. "Can you locate Morlaak?"

Ghan tapped on the implant behind his ear, listened for a few seconds, then shook his head again. "Can't get any readings past the moon's force shield; its creating too much of a disturbance. But——" He paused here, listening intently as if there were ghosts nearby. "There are six squadrons of planetary guards flying up from the Southern Boundaries. As well as maintenance units and Seezhukan patrol."

"How long till they get here?"

"No more than ten minutes. But they could arrive sooner."

"We should all try to stay out of sight then. In the mean time, we'll wear our disguises from now on. Maybe we could sneak on board one of those guard ships to fly past Idinor's shield."

"And how do you suppose we do that?" Ford asked.

"We'll ask to do it," Semhek suddenly said, pointing over toward the tower. "I think the Technician owe us a bit of gratitude for getting him all the way over here; not to mention a huge favor."

"Wouldn't hurt to at least try," said Zubkov, readily agreeing with the whole plan. As he hovered there, he watched all the drones transform into their Maintenance Droid disguises. What a strange-looking robot, he thought, before donning his own coppery outfit. He wondered what the planetary guard would think when they arrive to see them just floating there on hydrolic stilts.

Since it was Semhek's idea to summon the Technician, they all followed the furry little Tekwhaan as he drifted over towards the tower.

A bit muddled at first as to how to exactly proceed on getting the attention of the little box inside the machine, he did the basic thing by tapping gently onto the surface of the tower. But nothing happened.

"Try talking to him," Jack said. "The way how Morlaak did. He seem to respond better when confronted with the spoken word."

"Alright then," Semhek replied, then cleared his throat before he addressed the tower. "I think you should know that one of your own creation, as well as our own friend, Jherilon, was destroyed by Voch's forces."

"Yes," came the Technician's harsh response. The word sounded rough, and jagged, as if formed by a choir of buzz-saws. The source, however, wasn't too hard to locate since the tower didn't have a mouth or a synthetic vocalizer to form any words. So the Technician had to use the trillions of nano-bots that made up the machine, rubbing them together in a very sophisticated sequence of vibrations. The result, was not perfect, but very coherent tremulous words, as if spoken through the mouth of a bee. "Jherilon has perished. And so has general, Voch. They were both my creations...."

"Is the Dark Void, still in existence?"

"No. The void is no more. All portals have been closed. The outer rims of the Dasphealon and Seezhukan quadrants have returned."

"So that's it then," said Ford, sounding relieved. "We did it. We can go home."

And that brought Semhek back to their current situation, a rather concerning one at that. For regardless as to the outcome of their mission, whether or not they succeeded in destroying the machine and freeing the Bhoolvyn, the main horse that drove their wagon was the fact in knowing they always had a place to return to in the fourth quadrant. But now their only means of transport was gone, a part of this drive had diminished as well, and so did most of their hope.

Semhek knew it was a long shot, but he had to ask. "We need transport back to our quadrant."

There was a slight hesitation, as if the tower had a few things to consider, but it replied: "I will provide you a ship that will guarantee safe passage out of this quadrant. In a few minutes you'll be on your way."

The tower seemed to shut down after that. The nanos all stopped vibrating, and that continuous din beneath it all was heard no more.

Semhek was unsure what to do next, he moved to say something else, but decided against it. He felt weird, bombarding a giant tower with questions somehow. Perhaps he sensed they were in the presence of great wisdom, and didn't want to appear inferior by confronting it with trifling concerns.

However, he didn't have much time to contemplate in either case. About three miles south of the tower, Seezhukan ships began to appear on the horizon. In less than a few minutes, they swarmed over the entire city of Vermilion.

Efforts to repair the Northeastern grid began immediately. All kinds of ships, crafts, and vessels were in the area now, hauling supplies and lowering teams of maintenance droids on the ground. Floating cranes snatched up tons of debris and rubble with giant grappling claws; they drifted away in droves, only to return a short while later to get some more.

Soon, the sound of a whole city under construction began to hum. All at once, all around, the blinding sparks and the deafening grind of metal being welded and cut, had reached their peak levels. So loud, that the drones couldn't hear themselves speak, and they were forced to communicate through their com-links.

"If they continue at this rate," Zubkov said to Jack. "This whole city might be up and running again by the end of the week."

Jack gave a thoughtful nod in agreement. "I think that's what they're aiming for," he said. "These droids can go at any pace without stopping or making mistakes. When they're done with this place, no one will ever know that the whole thing had been knocked over and rebuilt in a matter of days."

Something caught the big Russian's eye and brought his attention to the only craft that wasn't taking part in the huge, mega construction, happening all around. It just cruised, it seemed, in one straight lane, only swerving to avoid the cranes and material-carrying ships that came in its path. It flew with purpose, bent on getting to one specific destination. "That ship looks familiar."

"Planetary Guard," Jack said. "Same as the ones that flew by us when they were trying to intercept general Voch."

"Well, one thing's for sure...they ain't here to work."

As the ship neared, the drones felt a new sense of admiration for the skill and craftsmanship of the Planetary Guard. Not many ships and flying vessels possessed wings and tails as they do on Earth. So it came as no surprise to see the wingless, cocoon-shaped Guard, come easing up over the tower to do a quick circle around the machine before landing effortlessly on the ice. Sleek curves formed its every shape and dimension. Under the crimson light of the Novid star, the ship was obviously red, with just a few orange patterns in certain places. Jack figured that it's true color——under normal lighting==would've been yellow. However, regardless of the ship's dull hue and pattern, it was still a beauty to behold. One of the few "precious rares" to be seen outside his own quadrant. With no mounted railguns or built-in cannons anywhere on the ship, it didn't appear to be the vicious battle-cruiser it had been so famed to be. In fact, a bulky, slow-moving materials-carrier filled with harmless maintenance droids, appeared more fearsome than the sleek, almost delicate-looking craft parked in front of them right now. But as far as looks go, that was as far as it went. For they all knew that a beauty, just like this one, single-handedly took out one of Voch's giant warships.

"I think it's time that we get going," Semhek said, as he was the first to begin floating over toward the ship.

"And what about him?" asked Ford, referring to the Technician, who was still sitting quietly somewhere inside the machine.

"He's not coming," Semhek replied from over his shoulder. It seemed like he is in a rush to leave; get back to his quadrant, sip some Shaapkrot and forget all about the Technician. "His place is here now. There's nowhere else for him to go. If we take him with us, more enemies, like Voch, will just keep Looking for him, attacking defenseless sectors——innocent civilians who've never once heard of the Plogg Sector."

None argued with the Tekwhaan, not even Jack. They all quietly followed Semhek to the ship, where some kind of passenger door suddenly opened up as they approached the Guard's port-side flank. He even went as far as to shed the ridiculous disguise of the Maintenance Droid as he stepped inside, knowing the ship would be absent of all crew and pilot.

It rose gently off the ground as the door swung itself shut behind the last drone to step inside. One final circle around the tower seemed to confirm Semhek's conclusion: that the Technician had at last found his new home. He didn't even bid them a "farewell", or "safe travel", as the Guard flew over the on-going construction of Vermilion, then went speeding up toward the horizon where it parted Idinor's force shield and entered the awaiting darkness of space.

It came as no surprise that there weren't any chairs or stations aboard the Guard. As an A.I., most Seezhukan ships flew unmanned. And as readily expected, the Guard was no different. The drones simply used their grav-boots to cling to the floor and held on to whatever piece of metal they could find protruding from the walls.

From out a port-hole window, where Braak was lucky enough to be standing next to, the destruction of two different fleets of warships——both Voch's and the Seezhukans——came into view. Tons and tons of debris seemed to clutter most of the space in the moon's orbit. Whole warships, once too huge in size for the mind to fathom, now broken and blown to bits, like so many of the towers that had been destroyed on Vermilion. Things just floated out there! Lifeless, drifting aimlessly, causing the Guard to dart and swerve out of the way in order to avoid colliding into the huge chunks of space metal.

Through the soles of their grav-boots, they could feel the strong vibration of the warp drive engines coming alive.

This was it! They were finally going home! In another minute or so, they would leave this strange realm of redness and return to their own quadrant. They would rest, then drink Shaapkrot, and celebrate!

But then something weird began to happen. The engines...it felt as if they were slowing down. And just the warp drive engines, but all of them! Soon, they began to feel nothing at all. No vibrations! Then all the lights went out inside the Guard. So they were now drifting aimlessly in space, in the pit of darkness, same as the debris, caused by all those broken ships out there....

What the hell happened? The Guard had suddenly lossed all power. Or, to put it another way, the Guard suddenly died out in space, with the drones trapped inside!

Deep resentment amounted inside of all of them; and perhaps a little bit of fear as well. Not because they all knew they were about to die, but because of the manner in which their deaths was about to be delivered. Not in a hail of fire, shot from dozens of cannons, but inside some dark tomb, left to live for as long as their symbiots can keep them alive. No one would ever find them in this much clutter, in this much debris. But perhaps they could be fortunate enough to be delivered from such a terrible fate. Perhaps the gods felt pity for their cause, and decided that it would be too harsh to allow them to suffer in such a long agonizing death. And that's probably why a huge chunk of a shattered warship drifted directly into their path. And with no power to steer clear; with no sensors for the dead Guard to detect their impending doom, they crashed violently into the jagged bowels of that spiteful wreckage....

CHAPTER
THREE

AND CRASH THEY did! Smashing everything in their path as they plunged deeper and deeper into the belly of the ship's wound.

For the drones, it was a complete nightmare in the pitch blackness as the dead Guard continued to spin and twirl out of control, literally tearing itself to pieces each time it bumped up against the jagged, scrapped metal protruding from the ship's inner hull. A most dizzy and disorienting experience. Jack's stomach rolled as the Guard spun. If it weren't for the fact that he hadn't eaten in over a year, he would've vomited several times over. If it weren't for the powerful magnetic soles of his grav-boots, keeping him firmly planted to the floor, he would already be dead.

But then something else happened. The Guard's wild and violent tumbling began to decrease and gradually slow down to a point where it took up to twenty seconds to complete a single revolution. Slow enough for the drones to regain their senses; shake off the dizzing hold that once churned their minds to madness. It no longer felt like they were on a deadly collision-course, where certain doom lurked at the end.

It felt as if they were drifting again, and maybe not so aimlessly this time. They could feel the dead Guard shifting slowly from side to side, as if avoiding things. On a few occasions, it felt as if they executed careful bends around corners, and at one time they even stopped and backtracked (as if missing a turn) before floating upward for more than a hundred feet.

They found themselves in an upside-down position when the Guard finally came to a stop and just plopped itself down on a flat, even surface. They could hear a dozen or so footsteps from all around, surrounding them. The side door was blasted open––with a loud explosion––and a flood of red hazy light poured in and filled up the cabin inside. They immediately began thinking that they'd somehow landed back on Idinor. However, when a squad of armed AIGD droids rushed inside, they finally realized where they were, and who had brought them there....

It was general Voch! And somehow both he, his droids, and the most vital section of his ship had managed to survive the attack from Idinor's mega photon cannons. From the looks of it, it appeared that the ship's plasma generator remained intact––virtually untouched––by the devastating weapon. That was obviously why there was still power on the ship. Enough to use some kind of weapon to disable the Guard the instant it left Idinor's orbit. Then he used the ship's tractor-magnetics to pull them all the way here: a huge docking area inside the ship.

Voch's droids used some kind of magnetic device to grab hold of the drones––despite their grav-boots––and haul them, single file, from the cabin of the dead Guard. Out of all the drones, Jack was the only one who had prior experience with the powerful device. A magnetic tool, in the shape of a long rod; the one that Kaypac had used to grab hold of him on Brashnor. It was the same now, the drones were all frozen stiff as one of the droids used the rod to carry them in the air as though walking across the deck, holding a bunch of balloons by a string....

Jack had been fortunate enough to be laying on his side as he floated through the air. Hundreds upon hundreds of fighter-crafts sat assembled on eastern side of the docking area. A herd of demolition droids stood poised in the next row, with one stalking down their ranks like a giant arachnid inspecting its own array of spiders. And yet, there was a humble, timid air about the place. As if each droid and bot had a duty of maintaining silence. The hum of the engines was barely heard, and even the lights were kept to their lowest, with just enough radiance to get an adequate visual of the environment.

Jack quickly realized that this low emission of power, and minimum range of operations, were being done intentionally. The plasma generator, and what remained of this broken ship, were the only two things keeping Voch and his crew alive. There was no doubt in Jack's mind that the generator was kept low enough to prevent detection by the Technician. If it wasn't, a second photon blast would've surely been fired on their precise location.

They continued walking past rows and rows of all kinds of fighter-crafts and different land-vehicles. The drones couldn't help but marvel at the sheer enormity of Voch's warship. Even at a fraction of the size it once was, the docking area lone appeared to cover an area of at least three square miles. At one point they came across an empty lot that was so vastly emmence, that it seemed to go on forever. It was here, that Jack spotted the ship that nearly caused his heart to nearly jump out of his chest. He thought he might've been seeing things at first. Hallucinating! But upon a second, third, and forth glance, he knew that his eyes weren't deceiving him.

It was Jherilon! Well...maybe not the same Jherilon that had been destroyed on Idinor. But an exact copy, nonetheless. In fact, as they walked further up the empty lot, they began seeing whole squadrons of "Jherilons", lined neatly together in eight rows. Each an exact make and copy of the other.

"So this was where he came from," he heard Zubkov saying, (to someone behind him).

"Probably ran away from this place," another drone (sounding like Braak) stated....

They came to a halt, not too long after walking past all those ships. And at last, they were finally made to stand on their own two feet. However, they were by no means free. The AIGDs quickly surrounded them, each aiming a rifle at their heads.

Suddenly, a bright doorway shimmered into existence, and out walked two hideous-looking creatures. The same kind of monsters, that the drones all witnessed walking the tetragons on the planet, Stong. The ones with the same ill-fitting, silicone skin, that hid their metallic bodies. One resembled a male version of Kaypac (perhaps because he was taller) with rough green skin, and two red coin-slots for eyes that shone intently. The other was a bit shorter, with two long horns on his head——each about a foot long. The same green skin appeared to sag on his robotic face, and made one eye look droopier than the other. A triangular, lipless mouth, took up most of its face (probably because he didn't have a nose) and seemed to make room for some kind of synthetic vocalizer that was clearly visible inside.

Despite the different statures in height and the obvious pair of pointy horns, there was still one other thing that distinguished these two creatures apart. And that was the different kinds of robes they wore, the one with the horns wore a tunic kind of dress––all black––that fell all the way down to his feet. Some kind of crested alien character was etched neatly across the chest of the smooth fabric. A symbol that belonged to the United Order of the Kraaglor Front; one that was etched on the surface of every ship and droid that belonged to that syndicate. But this one clearly distinguished the alien's rank, because the taller one wore a similar robe that was more kingly in stature. Neatly etched on the black fabric, was the same Kraaglor insignia; however, this one had three smaller alien characters on each side of it. There was also gold alien lettering running down the entire length of the robe, and more finer character-trimming around the cuffs on both sleeves.

Sollack, the droid with the horns, stepped forward. "Which one of you is the one called Puppycock?" he asked, in a grave tone of voice.

"That's me," Jack immediately replied. He moved to come forward, but was nearly clothes-lined when one of the droids stuck a rifled arm out in front of his face.

"There's far enough," Sollack said. "There's no need for any unwarranted movements here."

"Why're you taking us hostage?"

"Hostage?" Sollack seemed a bit taken aback by the comment, as if he was being persecuted. Falsely accused of a wrong-doing. "We aren't holding you as hostages. And in the event that we are, then there's no one in this realm that can pay for your ransoms, anyway."

"Then why bring us here? Why prevent us from leaving?"

"To save you," the taller droid (general Voch), suddenly said. A voice so deep and stunningly powerful, it seemed to reverberate and resound throughout the entire expanse of the bay.

By now, Jack (and perhaps all the other drones as well) had already surmised who these two droids were. Even though there was never any mentioning of Sollack, as they were being chased all across the four quadrants, he knew there was a big possibility they might be confronted by the infamous general Voch one day. And that day, considering the strange and unexpected circumstances, had come at long last.

Though Jack noted Sollack's mentioning of the term "realm", it hadn't yet occurred to him what the admiral actually meant. But then Voch made a similar comment; something running along those same lines that really got Jack wondering what this was all about. They could kill him! Even now, with all the drones standing here, surrounded by a dozen droids, all armed with plasma rifles. They could cut them all down in an instant. But they chose not to. Instead, they were being kept alive, for purposes Jack was all too eager to find out.

"Save us?" He began, hoping to play on the general's emotions (if Voch had any), "You and your entire fleet have been destroyed. You're stranded here, doomed to a repetitive orbit around Idinor for the rest of your days. And up until you kidnaped us, and brought us on this dead ship, it looked like you were the one who needed saving.... So, let me ask you a question, general...what exactly were you saving us from? Because it appears that you doomed us all."

"I was saving you from the Viceroy," Voch replied, flatly.

"The Viceroy?" Jack was genuinely puzzled. "I don't know of any Viceroy."

"I think he means the Technician," Semhek said.

"The Technician...?" said Jack. But then he thought for a second. "Ah...yes...I suppose the Technician would be the Viceroy of Plogg. It makes sense now. Or was he the Viceroy of Kraaglor? Doesn't matter; either way, I don't believe you. It was you who kidnaped your own Viceroy, and kept him hostage for all those centuries. Until we rescued him, and freed him. Brought him to our quadrant. The Technician, is now a Meerachzion ally. He fought along our side against the Seezhukans. Then he liberated the entire galaxy from the Dark Void.... So I can't see how you could've possibly saved us from——"

"You organic fool!!!" That was Sollack. Finally losing his temper. If it weren't for the fact that these six drones were their final and only hope for survival, he would've killed them all right there on the spot. But he didn't. He broke ranks instead, storming through the circle of his droids to get up close to Jack. So much so, his slimy silicone face came just a few inches from Jack's while he shouted. "There's no such thing as Novid. And you are in the Dark Void!!!"

CHAPTER
FOUR

OF COURSE SOLLACK'S shocking revelation worked to create a certain effect on the drones. Though not outward, at first, it definitely brought an immediate freeze to all of their minds. That icy chill that cause one to shiver––if only for a moment, as daunting realizations begin to form: death, the thought of being trapped; lost forever. Then, as quickly as it came, those fearful thoughts began to fade. A more reasonable, and perhaps logical, mind-set began to take over: doubt!

And why shouldn't it? The admiral was obviously desperate, and would say anything to manipulate the drones. For what other purpose would he and general Voch be holding them prisoner? The Dark Void, (while it was still in existence) was light-years away from their location. A forbidden zone, clearly highlighted on any archival map. It wasn't something that was hard to avoid. Like a star, or a black hole, it was something you made sure you stayed away from. And you definitely wouldn't be there without knowing it....

"The Dark Void?" Jack, as expected, was obviously not convinced. "We're nowhere near the Dark Void. You're mistaken. Maybe you have the wrong coordinates."

Sollack made a weird, coughing sound, that might've been a ridiculing laugh. "Do you believe, for one second, that we're capable of making such an error?"

"Yes," Jack said, matter-of-factly. "Before they died, neither Kaypac, nor Zhorg, had any prior knowledge of the Dark Void. They didn't even know it existed because those very coordinates had been erased from their internal data-maps. I don't see any reason why——"

"And do you know why, or how, such things came to be?" Sollack asked, cutting him off. "You came to the Plogg Sector, meddling in affairs you'll never understand. The Viceroy, is a criminal! A traitor! Loyal, not to us or the Seezhukans, but to his own cause. The only world that belong to our dimension is Idinor; which is how we was able to create his machine. The Seezhukans were the first to discover the Viceroy's plan, and despite all of their treachery, they alerted us before he had time to swallow up the whole sector, just outside the Bhoolvyn.

"We were the first ones to go into the Dark Void back then. But all those centuries ago, the Void was nothing but a small hole in space, not even a light-year across. It was easy for us to capture him and return, by simply going around the portals and coming out from the other side. But thanks to his legion of work-droids and planetary guard, his work continued over all these years. His machine has become incredibly powerful, spreading the Void across the rims of two quadrants. They even built weapons and force shields to protect the machine in the Viceroy's absence——the only things we failed to foresee all those centuries ago. We should've destroyed Idinor back then, but we didn't. And as for Kaypac and Zhorgh, they couldn't be trusted with knowledge of the Void's existence. They were still too loyal to the Viceroy. He would've tricked them, the same way he tricked you, into freeing him and bringing him back to his machine."

"So after all the destruction you caused in the Oxloraan and Eridani Sectors, you want us to believe that your Viceroy is the real enemy, responsible for all of our troubles?" asked Jack. "Even the Dark Void? So you say that he's the one that actually created the Dark Void? The Seezhukans had nothing to do with any of this?"

"That is exactly what I'm saying," Sollack growled back.

"But why? It doesn't make sense. Why swallow up the whole galaxy in another dimension, when he could simply remove himself from this one and go to another?"

That coughing sound came from Sollack again, and this time, Jack felt certain he was being laughed at. "I have to give it to him," Sollack said, almost to himself. "The Viceroy is clever, so I don't fault any of you for buying into his schemes."

"What schemes?"

"The Viceroy created this Void so he would have enough time and space to erect his own army. And when that happens, he would seek to destroy us all. He has no intentions of swallowing up the whole galaxy; for all we know, this might be as big as he would ever allow the Void to be. The only place that he could safely construct his own weapons––on this scale and magnitude––is in the privacy of another dimension. But in his absence, the Void became larger and larger, growing out of control for centuries. This is why things have become the way they are now.

Unfortunately, we had no way of knowing the Void was an ever-increasing portal."

"So you mistakenly flew into the Dark Void, to destroy the machine, knowing that you might never return to your own dimension?"

"No," Sollack said. "That was done intentionally. We had no other choice but to come here. And as far as us never returning to the Plogg, that is also a myth. It might take a few centuries for us to get around the portal, but most of us have already lived for a thousand years. You, on the other hand; an organic, won't last throughout the decade without a sufficient supply of replenishing nutrients from your symbiots. So you see, you're never gonna leave this dimension without our help. You and everyone you consider dear to you, is at the mercy of time now. You'll die slow here."

"I think he's right," Semhek said.

Jack turned to the Tekwhaan with an angry frown. "No one's dying here," he said. "We'll figure out a way. We always do."

"I wasn't talking about that," Semhek replied, shaking his head.

"Then what're you talking about?"

"The Technician tricked us. He tricked us into bringing him here to the Dark Void, knowing that we would never be able to return to our quadrant."

"We still don't know that for sure. Voch's fleet is gone. He's desperate. It could be he who's trying to trick us."

"I don't think it's a trick, Jack."

"How could you know that?"

"General Moraak."

"Morlaak?"

"Aye. I knew something was wrong, the instant his shuttle left this system. Usually, after a jump, especially this far into the enemy's quadrant, Seezhukan patrol always show up at the exact same location to investigate. But this time, when Moraak left, no one showed. At first, I thought that maybe the Seezhukans picked up on the Technician's signature, which was reasonable enough, since he got us this far into the system without much scrutiny from the enemy. But something was still off. I just couldn't get a good grip on what it was. Until now.... It makes sense, Jack. All of it. The Seezhukans didn't show up to investigate Morlaak's departure, because they couldn't. Not from outside this dimension. Our dimension. This could very well be the Dark Void, Jack. The Technician might've been manipulating us all along."

"If what you're saying is true, then that means that Morlaak––"

"Morlaak did not return home!" Semhek said, completing Jack's sentence. "He's still somewhere out there, in the midst of the Dark Void. Lost!"

"And you believe this?" He asked Semhek again, this time, gazing intently into the little Tekwhaan's face to know for sure if he wasn't mistaken..... "And how about you?" he said, turning to the other drones. "Do you all think we got played into coming to the Dark Void as well?"

"I gotta admit, Jack." Ford began. "I wasn't there when Morlaak's shuttle left, but I did find Semhek gazing out of the window after the general's departure. He looked pretty spooked at the time, so I know he wasn't lying about the

Seezhukans not showing up to investigate a hyper-jump footprint."

"So you think the reason why they didn't show up, was because we're in the Dark Void?"

Ford hesitated for a moment, then gave an uncertain shrug. "I'd say it's very plausible, Jack," she said. "A whole Seezhukan fleet, along with this one, was utterly destroyed. A massive debris of wreckage is now cluttering Idinor's orbit. Some kind of reinforcements should've been here by now. It's even expected that the Seezhukans should be arriving, but they're not. That in itself is strange."

"And what about you, Zubkov?"

The big Russian nodded. "I think we should look into it. If Voch wanted us dead, he could kill us right now. But he need us for something. And I doubt it's to help him fight a war. We should hear what he has to say: what does Voch want from us?"

Jack turned back to stare at Voch this time. "What do you want from us?"

"Only you can get into Idinor's shield and destroy the Viceroy's machine now." Sollack said, answering for his general. "He might not suspect too much malice from the six of you, once he read your signature."

"And how are we supposed to get back to Idinor?" Jack asked. "You killed the only ship we have that wore the signature of the planetary guard. And even if we do somehow manage to get past the shield, there's no way we can destroy that machine. There's some kind of protective force surrounding it, causing anything fired at it, to be repelled. And this, we witnessed for ourselves, when you reigned all hell down on Vermilion. You destroyed the city, you even killed Jherilon, but your fire came nowhere near that machine. Even when you concentrated all of your firepower on a single target, you only succeeded in melting the snow around the tower."

"Made a deep kind of moat around there, too," Ford added, not caring that she so rudely spoken out of turn.

The comment caused Sollack to cock his head curiously to the side. "What's moat?"

"Nothing too important in this matter," Jack said. "We need to come up with a plan. A much better one than we have right now."

As if to respond to their immediate concerns, a new planetary guard came floating up to the dock, past the old broken one that they arrived in. It eased itself up not too far from where they stood, and lowered one side of its main entry door. For a moment, it appeared as if a vicious squad of droids would come hopping out to do some aimless patrolling around the ship. But no such thing happened. The cabin in this new Guard was just as empty as that of the old one. All it needed now, was for the drones to go filing in. "We captured this one when it ripped a hole through our shields," Sollack began to explain. "But not before it managed to destroy one of our ships with a hyper-bomb."

A light immediately flashed into the minds of all the drones. The intent was so obviously apparent that new hope could be felt surging inside of them.

They could win!

They could destroy the tower.

And if Voch would allow...they could all go home!

"We know now that the Viceroy's machine can't be destroyed from the outside. But with precise calculation, we could put a hyper-bomb right at the heart of the tower. Destroy it from within."

"And what about Vermilion's photon cannons?" asked Jack. "Not to mention the dozens of other Guards now covering the area down there. If your Viceroy don't detect us, the planetary guard surely will. Then you're back to square one; but we, on the other hand, we'll be dead."

"We have squadrons of fighters to assist you in any event. But I don't think you'll have much problems with the Guard. We studied this one's personality very carefully and have uploaded its memory with an exact replica. You should be able to move around on the surface in relative ease."

"There's a convoy of Materials Carriers, Seezhukan builders, and a few other planetary guard vessels, in route to Idinor as we speak," said Voch all of a sudden. "You'll blend in perfectly with this convoy as one of their own. But you don't have much time. They've already entered Idinor's orbit. If we stand here, doing nothing, you could miss the best opportunity of re-entering Vermilion unnoticed."

"But I have one more question," Jack said, sensing the mounting urgency in both the admiral and his general. "We're trapped behind a portal, in another dimension, as you say. But if we destroy the machine, then we'll be trapped here, forever. The whole purpose of us bringing your Viceroy here, was so that he can reverse the portals, and those lost in the Dark Void can eventually find a way out. But with the machine gone, we make it impossible to leave."

"Dimensional portals don't work that way," Sollack said, grumpily, as if Jack had made a great error in saying this. "The portals that we are so accustomed to in our own quadrants are nothing but doors that exist at certain points between time and space. Within our own galaxy these doors can be found in millions of different locations all throughout the four quadrants. But there's only one door that can exist for a dimensional portal, because this door can only serve as the initial opening, or entry, into this dimension. And due to the amount of energy required to create a gap between two dimensions, there's a remaining force that exist to forever bind us to our own dimension."

"Like a tether," said Ford.

"No," Ghan said, to the contrary, letting Sollack know that he too, knew something about these kinds of dimensional rifts. "Not like a tether, because a tether will eventually prevent you from traveling beyond a certain point. The force that Voch is trying to describe, is more like a web of energy that covers the entire dimensional gap. It's what keeps the door open. It's also the same force that everyone must fly through, in order to reach this dimension. However, we never actually fly through the web, so as to come out on the other side. It's something that can never be broken, only stretched. And the amount of energy that was used to create this dimensional portal is so immensely vast and incredibly strong, we can travel all the way to the other end of this dimension and still be bound to our own."

"Okay," Ford began, with a bit more insight than she had before. "So it's like a infinitely strong web, that can stretch from here to infinity."

"That is precisely what it is," Ghan said. "One of the unexpected quirks of creating dimensional portals."

"So what happens when we destroy the machine?" she asked.

"The portal will collapse, and the opening will begin to dissipate," Sollack said. "And as the force recedes, we'll be pushed out of this dimension and back into our own."

"So the stretchy web will simply just snap back into place, slinging us all back out into the second quadrant?" Ford couldn't believe it was that fundamental.

"That is exactly what will happen," Ghan replied. "And it will happen so fast, that we will instantly be back in our own dimension before you could blink."

"I have one more question," Jack said, turning to Ghan. "If we're simply bound to our own dimension by some invisible web of energy, then why can't we just fly out of the Dark Void by retracing our steps?"

Ghan shook his head, regretfully. "Not sure if it will ever work out that way. Maybe if the web was less flexible and more rigid, maybe then we could've followed some kind of pattern that could lead us out of the Dark Void. But there's too many twists and turns to retrace, especially after jumping through hyperspace. Once you've traveled from one point to another, lightyears upon lightyears in distance, it is nearly impossible to relocate the exact route that was taken. Because our Universe is always in motion, the trail that was made through hyperspace is immediately erased."

"Like a submarine traveling under water," Ford said, letting everyone know that she was getting a hang of all this dimensional stuff being discussed. "Even though the sub's moving in a straight line through the ocean, the water itself is in a constant state of motion. There're all kinds of currents, tides, and waves; all rolling, squeezing, and bumping into each other. So instead of a straight line, the submarine's long trail, now becomes a jumbled, tangled up mess.... Is that what it's like, Ghan? Is that why we can't just jump back out of the Dark Void?"

The tall Lannsillian, for all of his dull expressions, seemed mildly impressed by Ford's explanation. "That's sort of what it's like...yes. That's one way of looking at it."

"Okay then," said Jack, finally feeling satisfied enough to move on to something else. "Just wanted to make sure we weren't so deeply invested in the immediate problem, that we overlook the more obvious, simpler solutions."

"As you already know," said Ghan. "The knowledge of space-travel is a specialty among the members of my race. We would never overlook something as trivial as that."

"And you've proven that very thoroughly just now, ghan," said Jack. He turned to Sollack, but then looked up at general Voch, as if something of more importance crossed his mind. "You say we don't have much time left before we miss the convoy heading back to Idinor. I think its best that you tell us everything we need to know so we can get moving."

"Join the convoy and destroy the machine," Voch instructed.

"Yeah, we already covered that. Is there anything else we need to know?"

"That is all."

"And what of my crew?"

"The remainder of your crew is to stay here, in case further commands are needed."

"Commands?" Jack began to inquire, but then his whole body suddenly froze. 'What are you doing?' He secretly asked his symbiot.

'**It's not me,**' Klidaan replied. '**I think he's using that magnetic weapon on us again.**'

As if to confirm Klidaan's statement, Jack began to feel that on-coming weightlessness when his body was lifted off the ground and floated toward the awaiting guard.

CHAPTER
FIVE

LONG BEFORE HIS meeting with the Whorganian back on Earth; long before he was implanted with his own symbiot to offer guidance and tell him secrets, Jack always relied on his natural instincts to navigate the world filled with treachery and deceit. That ole' gut-feeling, had never once steered him wrong. Even when they had him killed, drained his body of its natural sustenance then replaced it with an alien presence; somehow, that raw intuition remained.

It was what steered him now. The instant his frozen body was floated into the empty cabin of the planetary guard, he could feel that something was different. A different energy, or radiance perhaps. It felt cold and static-driven, filled with a familiar electrical flair. It felt like... Jherilon....

The lights flicked themselves on when the cabin's door closed. And immediately, Jack could feel the guard lifting off the ground.

"Wait," he said, not knowing exactly why he said it. Though he understood (all too well) the urgency of their plight, things were still moving too fast.

Surprisingly, the guard stopped at his command. He hurried over to the small confines of what could've been a bridge, or a cockpit. Like the guard, there was no place to sit––not even something for him to hold on to––so he used his mag-boots to plant himself firmly on the floor. Frantically, he scanned the whole area for any of the familiar knobs, buttons and screens, anything he could use to control the guard. But there was nothing! No windows, no console, no controls. The guard was strictly A.I.; it had no need for such things.

However, since the guard did obey his last command, maybe he might be able to control it that way. So he tried another oral command. "What's your primary objective?"

"To rendezvous with the incoming convoy, and destroy Idinor's quantum reflector," the guard replied, sounding exactly like Jherilon.

The resemblance nearly stunned Jack out of his wits at first, but he quickly recovered, becoming more relieved that he'd gotten some kind of response from the guard. "Jherilon...is that you?"

"We're all Jherilon."

"But how?"

The guard began moving again, as though mindful that they running out of time. "This particular guard attacked our fleet. But instead of destroying it, we decided to capture it by neutralizing its central operating core and replacing it with one of our own."

From spending so much time with Jherilon, Jack had already learned that the central operating core of any A.I. was its consciousness. It was what made it think, and feel... and speak. Then he remembered floating past all those squadrons of Jherilons, assembled in the docking bay; and finally understood whose central operating core was now controlling this ship, and why it so readily responded to his oral commands. But what he did not know, however, was that the central operating core——known as Jherilon—— worked as a single unit. The Jherilon that he once knew, was not just one ship operating on its own, it was actually a part of a whole——the same as the one controlling the guard right now.

"Are you capable of projecting any kind of synthetic imagery?" He asked.

"Yes," came the reply. "I can project a total visual replica of my immediate surroundings."

"Let's do it then," Jack said. "I need a complete visual of our environment in real time."

"Okay." The whole interior of the guard came to life after that. And not just the front of the cockpit, where some kind of rectangular window appeared to reveal what laid directly ahead of them, but it seemed as if the entire hull of the ship began to peel away, giving him a complete 360° view of his surroundings. Once again, it began to feel as if he floating in mid air, drifting through the lifeless debris, deep within the bowels of Voch's broken warship. The only difference now, was that he knew it to be an illusion. A simple trick of paneling imagery. There must be thousands of pin-sized cameras embedded just under the surface of the guard's outer hull to create such an overwhelming effect. However, as spectacular as it was, this kind of global panoramic visual proved to be more than was necessary to navigate the guard. Actually, it was more of a distraction than anything else.

"I need you to cut the environmental spectrum by 75%," Jack order. "Then give me the outer visual of both starboard and port side."

The gray floor under Jack's feet instantly returned, giving the illusion that he was now floating atop a gray metal platform. But then, the rear inner hull of the guard began to appear, inch by inch, like the unfolding of one huge blanket to cover the rest of the ship, stopping just at the nose, so that only the front of the cockpit was exposed.

The result offered a weird kind of visual, appearing as if the cockpit existed within its own transparent bubble on the nose of the guard. Not exactly what Jack had expected. However, seventy-five percent was seventy-five percent; he couldn't ask for anything better. Besides, it was all still an illusion, and even though he had a complete view of everything ahead of him, no one else could see him from the outside. The guard was still a solid-looking ship, with no windows. He would just have to get used to the uncanny visuals from the inside....and fast.

They were already emerging from the warship's fatal wound as the convoy prepared to approach Idinor's shield. From the looks of it, there appeared to be five other planetary guards that accompanied the convoy, along with over a dozen Materials Carriers, and what could've been a huge fleet of Seezhukan warships. The latter caused a bit of concern, because it meant that the Viceroy could be expecting another battle, soon.

"Give me a closer visual on that convoy," Jack said. "Focus in on the fleet, and I need a full read-out on their capabilities." Jack still wasn't sure if he giving the right commands to the guard, but to his delightful surprise, a live image of the convoy zoomed in up close, giving him a clear visual of the fleet from no more than a hundred yards. "I wonder why he's taking all these extra precautions?" He mused to himself. He half-expected some kind of response from the guard, but when he didn't get one, he thought it best not to linger on the subject. Voch's presence had obviously taken the Viceroy by surprise, so it made sense that he should call more reinforcements from Plagnor, chosing never to be caught off-guard again.

"Are there plasma generators on any of those ships?"

"No," the guard said. "the convoy will use the planetary guard to gain entrance through the shield. But the Seezhukan fleet will have to remain in orbit; the ships are not required to enter Idinor's atmosphere."

That's a relief, Jack thought. The mere presence of the fleet had brought many foreboding signs along with it. And he would hate to think of his predicament if the Seezhukans were initially joining the convoy on the surface.

It was a somewhat perilous trek, flying through the thick field of debris now cluttering Idinor's orbit. And on a few occasions, the guard was forced to make some evasive maneuvers in order to avoid being side-swiped; rammed in a head-on collision. But when they finally cleared the last piece of scrap-metal that went flitting across the face of the guard, miles and miles of free space had suddenly opened up to them....

Before they could travel a significant way toward Idinor's shield, the sound of loud crackling static erupted all throughout the cabin. At first, Jack thought it to be just routine noise coming from the guard (perhaps it was tweaking out some audio glitch in its circuits), but then the static grew louder and louder until it became almost unbearable. At one point, he plugged his ears with his fingers, fearing he might suffer some kind brain damage.

"What the hell was that?" He asked, when the torturous auditory assault ended.

"The Seezhukans," the guard replied, "they were inquiring my presence in the ruins."

"And what did you tell them?"

"Being as though this guard was among the original two to intercept general Voch's fleet, the Seezhukans would readily accept that I was simply returning from battle. And that is exactly what I told them."

"And all this was planned and foreseen by your general?"

"Yes...."

The guard sped up and joined the convoy just when the First Materials Carrier was going through the shield. "Do you know where to go from here?" Jack asked. "The Red City, I mean: Vermilion. Do you know how to get there?"

The hologram of a detailed map appeared before him just then. "The city of Vermilion is located in the northeastern grid, on Idinor's southern boundary."

Jack made an affirmative nod when he recognized the ruined city; tower and all. Then he noticed the broad mountain range behind it, remembering the destructive weapons they hid within, "and what about the photon cannons? Do you know where they're kept?"

The holographic city vanished, but the mountains remained, rotating slowly like a ferris wheel before coming to a sudden stop. The mountains's outer layers all began to dissolve, like thin ice in the sun, causing the surface of their crags to become transparent, revealing the huge long-nosed cannons buried inside. There were nine in all, scattered all throughout the range. Each pointing upward, as if waiting for the next threat to breech Idinor's orbit.

"We have to watch out for those things," Jack said. "The minute we destroy that tower, they'll be gunning for us."

They flew on in silence, following the convoy high up in the moon's atmosphere. And as Jack would soon find out, the Materials Carriers weren't fast-moving vessels by any means. And being their only armed escorts, the planetary guards couldn't just fly off and leave them behind, so they were all forced to move at the slower vessels's pace––at cruising speed––thus slowing down the mission.

He decided to use the brief gap in time by picking up where he and the guard left off. "So what happened to one of your fighters? The one named Jherilon?"

"We're all Jherilon," the guard replied, in that usual matter-of-factly tone.

"I know, I know," he said, with a bit of frustration. "I mean, the rogue fighter. The one that abandoned your fleet and and joined Kaypac and Zhorgan's cause."

"That one was indeed a member of our fleet, but it never abandoned us. Spagon, was once an ambassador of Kraaglor, and that was her personal fighter."

The name, Spagon, was somewhat familiar to Jack. He'd only heard it mentioned once before, when Jherilon used it describe Kaypac, which was only a code-term (like the Technician), devised by the Meerachzions. But Spagon was Kaypac's actual name. What everyone in the Plogg Sector knew her as. "But then she became leader of the Piilor Syndicate."

"Even while she ruled Piilor, she was still loyal to Kraaglor. We weren't aware of her betrayal until we arrived on Brashnor, and heard of the Viceroy's escape. By then, both she and Zhorgan were already dead."

"So the Viceroy was your prisoner, but not your leader?"

"Yes. But he was once our leader; he's one of the original founders of Plogg. Then at some point, his visions grew and grew until they finally exceeded all of our expectations of a peaceful future."

"What do you mean by visions? How could the Viceroy of Plogg, threaten the future of Plogg? I don't understand."

"As you already know, and witnessed for yourself, Plogg is one of the most peaceful sectors in the whole second quadrant. And most likely the most peaceful in the whole galaxy. It has always been that way; but then the Drofh came and we had to fight. And thanks to the Viceroy's supreme intelligence, we defended our worlds. By the time we won the war, the Plogg had become a divided sector. Generals, who once defended their realms against the Drofh invasion, became warlords, who turned their worlds into garrisons, controlled by syndicates.

"It was around this time that the Viceroy began talking about a 'New Plogg'. He wanted to leave the sector and find some place new. He said we needed to flee the Drofh, as we once fled the Seezhukans. And the only place where we'll ever be free of both, is in a whole other dimension, entirely."

"I don't see how that was such a bad idea," Jack said.

"How about exterminating whole civilizations?"

"He actually wanted to do that?" Jack found this hard to believe.

"In order to live peacefully here in this new dimension, we had to cleanse these old worlds of all their inhabitants. This is what the Viceroy wanted us to do. These were the kind of dark places his visions were beginning to take him to. And when he realized we would never assist, or follow him into these new worlds, he sought the aide of the Seezhukans. And with their own lust and thirst for absolute power, the Regality was all too happy to help."

"So that's how the Seezhukan's were able to intercept Voch when he first arrived near Idinor's orbit," Jack said. "He didn't call for reinforcements, they were already here. I wonder how many fleets are really out there?"

"When the Regality realized the true potential and possibilities of tapping into unlimited resources of new dimensional worlds, they offered the Viceroy complete command over the battalions that were still stationed in many areas around the Plogg. Among these forces were the planetary guard; five whole fleets of what remained of the old command."

"And that's when Voch decided to lock him up," Jack said, surmising the end result on his own. "Kaypac once said the Viceroy was aiding the phony empire. She was telling the truth…. But how could she not know that he was already captured and being confined?"

"We had to keep the news of the Viceroy's incapacitance a secret, and for obvious reasons."

"The Regality."

"If they knew the Viceroy was being hold prisoner, they would've sent all their forces to destroy Kraaglor, maybe the whole entire Plogg."

"And then we came to free him." Jack said this regretfully, as if knowing they'd made the biggest mistake in the history of the galaxy. "Let loose the very thing that could destroy us all."

"You couldn't have known."

Jack knew the guard was right, but still, it didn't stop his inquiring mind from racing through the events of the past, all the way back to the beginning––when they first came to the Plogg Sector. That Wizard, with his quirky assistant.... Considering everything that had happened so far, it could be very well likely that the robotic fortune-teller was on the side of the Seezhukans. After all, the whole plan of kidnaping the Viceroy was his idea. Or was he following the orders of another? And yet still, freeing the Viceroy, in order to locate and destroy the quantum reflector (along with the Viceroy) might have been all part of the plan, with the only unforeseeable event of having to actually fly into the Dark Void. And if Jack knew anything about visions, prophecies, and predictions, its the fact that they are notorious for leaving out all the important details....

He was left to muddle over these––as will as many other things––until the convoy flew across the Southern Boundaries and was now approaching the ruined city of Vermilion. Though very little had changed in the city's construction since he left the world just hours ago, there appeared to be a whole lot more traffic in the sky over the ruins. Many of them were floating cranes, just hovering. Some continued to haul debris away from the city. To the north and east, stood the Viceroy's tower, like a living pole, overseeing it all....

"Okay, so when are we going to target this thing?" He asked, not at all sure how a hyper-bomb is supposed to be deployed.

"When the Materials Carriers break off and head to their designated areas, the rest of the planetary guard will be re-routed to the outer boundaries of Vermilion. That will be the most suitable time for us to take the opportunity."

"And how soon will——" Jack stopped, feeling himself becoming too anxious to engage the Viceroy. However, his mounting excitement wasn't the sole reason for the abrupt pause in his speech. It was something else, attracting most of his focus and attention. A bright light in fact. A sudden white flash, way off in the distance beyond the tower. He barely had enough time to react. "Bank right, now!!! Bank right!!!"

It was unclear whether or not the guard saw the flash in time, or if it was simply following Jack's command at the drop of a dime. But it seemed it all became irrelevant once the guard made that sudden right turn as the tunnel-sized photon blast just vaporized the entire convoy in one push (Materials Carriers and all). The light from the swirling tunnel was enormous, shoving the natural crimson rays of Idinor back up into the atmosphere. It was an awesome sight to behold. And a most frightful one as well.

"Get a target on that tower, now!" Jack shouted, even as the rays from the photon blast diminished. Then, as an after-thought, he said. "And I need you to give me a 50% visual of our outer surroundings."

It appeared as if the two commands were being executed simultaneously as the green holographic targeting display materialized right before his face, while the outer hull of the ship receded to reveal a clear open sky directly above his head and below his feet. Not the most desirable field of vision for his enjoyment, but one that was most crucial to his survival now. Nor did it take too long to prove this bit of judgment true, for up on his left flank, another flash appeared from another distant crag, and just like before, Jack had no more than a second to react before another photon cannon fired off its incinerating tunnel of light to vaporize everything in its path.

He ordered the guard to dive just when the blast came beaming over the ship, causing a strong turbulence that shook him down to his knees. It was a close one! However, he didn't have time to experience any form of relief or gratitude, because another blinding flash appeared from the corner of his eyes. There was only one place left for them to go––and that was up. So the guard hopped back up into a climb while a huge laser (shot from a cannon) dug a long trench below them.

The beams were coming more frequently now, causing Jack to evade certain death every ten seconds or so, as well as getting a firm target on the tower, virtually impossible. So busy was he, that he almost failed to notice when one of the cannons began to flash, but then suddenly winked itself off. No vicious blast followed in its wake, but something else happened entirely. The cannon exploded!

CHAPTER
SIX

FORD WAS ALMOST afraid to ask the question of what's to become of them, once Jack flew off with the planetary guard, back down to Idinor. For a good moment they all stood on that same spot on the dock while being surrounded by Voch's droids. No one moved or said word until Sollack confirmed that Jack had made it past the Seezhukan warships and safely met up with the convoy.... It felt as if the admiral was afraid of jinxing the only bit of luck they had left.... He even took it upon himself to grab the metal pole from the nearest droid to freeze the drones once more. Then he lifted them in the air with no effort and rushed them all to the bay where the A.I.B.S-137 fighters (or Jherilons) were assembled. Only then did he release his hold and allowed them to float down to the floor on their mag-boots.

"We don't have much time," Sollack began. He waved a hand, and the nearest fighter's cargo-door began to slide open, as if by magic. "Your leader will soon need your assistance; he'll never get past those photon cannons once the Viceroy detects that the guard is actually one of our own."

"Photon cannons?" Zubkov wore a puzzled frown. "You knew that Jack could still be detected? Why didn't you warn him?"

"If he knew that he was flying into a trap, his judgment might've been clouded. And he might not have stood a chance against the Viceroy's attacks. He'll need his natural instincts."

"So you used him as bait?"

"Yes," the admiral replied, in a most affirmative tone, as if no moral boundaries existed in this cooked up plan to beat the Viceroy. "A necessary bait. One that'll depend on your precise moment of attack if we are to prevail in our mission."

"Precise moment?" asked Ford incredulously. "But you haven't debriefed us on anything. When is this precise moment supposed to happen? And what are we supposed to do in this precise moment?"

"Jherilon will explain," Sollack replied, sounding more urgent than before. "But it's very simple. You just have to destroy the photon cannons... and let's just hope that your leader is still alive when you do."

"These droids think different," Semhek began, as he walked to Ford's side so that he could face Sollack. "Their plans and strategies aren't as layered as ours, and yet, they make things work. They probably had this all figured out the moment they saw us leaving Idinor. There's no point in debating with this one. I think I have an idea of what they got in mind."

"We are running out of time," Sollack warned. "You must prepare to leave now, or be trapped in this dimension, forever."

If nothing else, those last few words seemed to strum a chord in all the drones' minds, for they all began to move toward the fighter––however reluctant.

"And what of you, and general Voch?" Semhek asked, out of sheer curiosity.

"We'll be watching," Sollack replied from behind, while rushing them faster toward the fighter. "Farewell...."

Semhek was the last to make it up the ramp into the fighter, and even as the cargo doors began to close, he looked back and saw that Sollack was already on his way back up through the dock. "This is incredible," he heard Ford say, from somewhere behind him. When he turned around, he too was amazed to see what they all marveled at.

"This is exactly what our ship looked like Zubby," Ford said, as they walked down the familiar hallway, checking all the corridors, aisles, and quarters, as if to prove to themselves that the fighter was an exact replica of Jherilon. Even as they entered the bridge, that same box-shaped face appeared on the broad window, eyeing them intently, but not saying a word. The captain's chair at the helm, sat directly at the center of the bridge, just as they all knew it to be on the old ship. And so were the stations and consoles; everything was arranged in exactly the same way as they remembered it.

"Are you Jherilon?" Zubkov asked, while taking a seat at his old (or new) station.

"We're all Jherilon," the ship replied, in that same friendly voice they were all so accustomed to.

"But how...?" A perplexed Ford inquired. "I mean... there're over two-dozen fighters in this bay. There isn't much of a surprise that you're built exactly alike. But what I've come to know and understand about the Seezhukans is that each droid, fighter, and ship, are all equipped with their own individual sense of self."

"I think this one's different," said Braak, as if suddenly becoming enlightened. "Jherilon's unique. He's a single consciousness uploaded into all the fighters. Maybe even the entire ship. That's why Voch could've located us no matter where we were in the galaxy."

"So this Jherilon's no different from the one that was destroyed on Idinor?"

"Technically, no. This is the same Jherilon. He knows everything about us, as well as our mission, and that's how Voch was able to track us down so easily."

"That is correct, Braak," Jherilon said. "We are all one and the same. I know you just as the old fighter did."

"But are you **our** Jherilon?" Ghan asked.

"You are Ghan, the Lannsillian, from the Ghoric Sector," Jherilon replied. But then the cubic face turned to Braak. "And you are the Taaslan, from Haleon Sector."

"Indeed, I am," said Braak, sounding impressed and becoming all too happy that he hadn't lost another friend after all. "And its good to know that you' re——"

"And what of this new mission?" Semhek asked (getting down to the more important matters) while taking his seat at the helm. Though he hadn't meant to cut Braak off in mid-sentence so abruptly, he began to feel the same sense of urgency as Sollack once did. He felt a need to know as much as possible, as soon as he could. "At what precise moment are we supposed to make our move? And more importantly; what is our next move?"

"We are to attack the Seezhukan warship the instant those photon cannons become operational on Idinor," Jherilon said, in a more serious tone. "It's the only way to get a head start on the Viceroy, before he could set his target on us."

"But there's not just one ship out there," Semhek said. "That's a whole fleet of warships!"

"They can't hurt us," said Jherilon, matter-of-factly. "They do not have the right equipment to penetrate our shields."

"That's right." said Braak. "Those ships have been trapped in this dimension for at least three centuries. There isn't a single plasma cannon on any of them. We could fly right in their faces, and they'll be powerless to stop us."

"And that is exactly what we intend to do." Jherilon said. "We only have to be concerned about the planetary guard; we have no defense against their hyper-bombs."

"But we out-number them," Semhek said.

"Just barely," Jherilon replied. "And that is way we have to strike at just the right moment, destroy the cannons, so that Jack can have a clear shot at the quantum reflector."

"If we decide to move, the Viceroy will detect us and have his cannons destroy what's left of us before we could even clear the dock," Semhek said, surmising what would happen if they were to make that fatal mistake by jumping the gun too soon.

"Yes," Jherilon said. "And that is why we have to give Jack a chance. Allow him to distract the Viceroy long enough so we can safely deploy combat divisions. Those cannons will have a hard time fixing a target on our fighters once we're out in space."

As eager as they all were to engage the enemy, and more importantly ––prevent the Viceroy from killing Jack on Idinor, there was no other options open to the drones.

Unfortunately, such a moment consisted of the possibility of Jack losing his life; however, they would all lose their lives if they reacted too soon. A reaction that would cause them to be trapped in the Dark Void, forever. A future in which they would certainly suffer a long and slow death.

The only good news awarded to them laid in the fact that they wouldn't have to wait too long for their moment to arrive. For as soon as they found their old posts and began to settle down on the bridge, their stations came alive in a show of lights and the jabbing sounds of all the fighters suddenly communicating with each other. They could feel Jherilon lifting off the floor in that instant, turning starboard until his nose faced the wide opening of the dock. It was there they saw all the other fighters hovering above their landing stilts; the ones up front were already flying out towards the Seezhukan fleet. And no sooner thereafter, they too began moving at a high speed that left Voch's broken ship miles behind them in a matter of seconds.

It all happened too fast for them to immediately recognize what was actually going on. And up until he spotted the first battle between their fighters and the Seezhukans, directly up ahead, Ghan was yet to pull up a full display on his console. "I need a complete read-out of all of our immediate targets," he said to Jherilon, as he felt most of wits returning to him. On the console's flat screen, the schematics of the first Seezhukan fighters began to appear, along with detailed diagrams of its nose, flank, and rear. An AICW-147, one of the old Seezhukan cruiser-wings: basic primary weapons, high intense laser cannon, and electron rail-guns. Nothing that would harm Jherilon without first penetrating the ship's plasma shield.

"It looks like the Seezhukans didn't bother to deploy their old fighters," Semhek said, from where he sat at the helm. "They immediately sent their planetary guard divisions instead."

"They must already know that their own weapons would be useless against Jherilon's shields," said Braak.

"Maybe the Viceroy instructed them prior to their arrival in Idinor's orbit," Zubkov concluded.

A slight twinge of resentment crawled through the Lannsillian as he realized that not only was he slow at properly manning his station, but he also the last one to assess their current situation. A reckoning that caused him to abandon the console (and schematic diagrams altogether) and approach his port-side window where he could survey the ensuing––and growing––dog fight in real time.

From the looks of it, Ghan could see that Jherilon's divisions were still superior in numbers, and more successful in destroying their targets. But this was only due to the Jherilons' rapid-firing cannons that made easy prey out of their enemy. However, the planetary guards' numbers were also growing, as whole squadrons of them continued to pour out from the Seezhukan battleships. And in the midst of all this chaos, Jherilon units were taking casualties, as hyper-bombs eventually found their way into the fighter's cabins to blow entire vessels in a shower of embers.

"We have to take out those warships," Ghan said to the little Tekwhaan, seated at the helm. "Target their main power supply and shut down their operations."

"The warships aren't the problem," Semhek said, shaking his head dismissively. "It's those hyper-bombs."

"I think Sollack might've underestimated the Seezhukans on this one," said Ghan. "There could be whole divisions of planetary guard inside those warships. If we aren't outnumbered by now, we soon will be. Then they'll over-run us before we even get the chance to breech Idinor's shield."

"Okay then," Semhek replied, quickly making sense out of the Lannsillian's suggestions. "Target all the power supply stations of the entire Seezhukan fleet. All fighters should be accompanied by at least one other escort. Cover each other's flanks, and try not to let guard fall on your tail."

"Understood," Jherilon replied, before Ghan could relay the order. Outside, in the battle taking place near Idinor's orbit, the scene was like a huge flock of migrating birds suddenly changing direction, where Jherilon's division reacted simultaneously to a single command. In unison, they all formed this massive swirl, causing a once violent dogfight to become a frantic chase as the fighters all jetted up toward the warships with the guards hot on their heels. Now it seemed more explosions were happening than ever before, for the guards were unable to get a steady lock on their fleeing targets. So in desperation, they simply warped their bombs into the evasive flock in a rash attempt to disrupt the incoming assault.

It was as if the Seezhukans knew what Jherilon had planned, and as soon as the first swarm of fighters came mounting up over the fleet, a barrage of missiles was immediately launched in their direction. Round after round they went, with each projectile scoring a direct hit, only to be vaporized the instant they collided into the fighters' plasma shield. A most violent display, but nothing more, causing as much harm to the fighters as a strong pocket of turbulence might; in which case they merely suffered a few shakes and tremors each time they were hit. Harmless fire. So much so that the fighters didn't even try to avoid, lest they brake ranks and flew off course.

But the guard on the other hand, wouldn't get off as easy. Friendly fire or not, they weren't equipped with the same shields, so they were forced to dodge the explosive projectiles the best way they could. Many managed to avoid the barrage, but a few still fell, succumbing to the stray missiles that blew their hulls to pieces. And those that did survive, had broken so far from their ranks, they gave some of the fighters enough time to swoop around their flanks and attack them from behind.... A good portion of the planetary guard were destroyed this way, as the fighters unloaded rapid bolts of plasma into the rear engines before they even knew what hit'em.

"The warships' power supply's located near their main thrusters," said Ford, from her station, while reading a detailed diagram on her console's screen. "And from the looks of it, I'd say they're one and the same."

"We'll start at their main thrusters then," Semhek said. "Alert all fighters to lock on to their targets and fire at will."

Once again, the battle was shifting as Jherilon's entire division loomed over the whole Seezhukan fleet. The planetary guard was still pouring out of the warship's docking bays in herds, and it took no more than a minute for the guard to replenish their numbers and make up for the ones they lossed, rejoining the digfight to outnumber them in one sudden swarm.

Plasma fanned out from the fighters' cannons to go ripping through the warships' hulls as easily as rocks hurled through spider webs. Nothing but big holes remained, with rims of molten metal glowing redder than the sector's own star. As they entered one of the ships' mainthrusters, they caused an explosion so grand that it can only be compared to that of a volcano's eruption, where hot gases and magma are spewed out from the bowels of the Earth. So too did the ship's main fuel tanks erupt and go bursting out of her side in a torrent of flames.... And this was just what was allowed to be jettisoned out into space. Most of the explosion was directed inward, where the real force of the blast swept through every floor, tier, and cabin of the ship until the whole tiling just popped! and blew itself to pieces....

All across the battlefield these explosions began, one warship after another, as the fighters all found their marks. Soon, the entire Seezhukan fleet was reduced to space-scrap and wayward and debris. The planetary guard, now slightly out-numbering Jherilon's division, was all that was left of the Viceroy's forces.

"We have to get to Idinor right away," Jherilon said, as they took out one of the last remaining warships. "We don't have much time left." As he said this, he began turning away from the scene of battle, accompanied by two other escorts, on their way down to Idinor.

"What about the other fighters?" Semhek asked, with a tinge of guilt. "They need our help. There's still a lot of fighting to do out there."

"There's only one fight that matters now...."

Right before they pierced Idinor's shield, about five guards neared their flanks, and might've succeeded in killing them all, if it wasn't for the guard slowing down before the force shield (in order to part the plasma barrier) while the three fighters just flew right through. It was as if Jherilon didn't even consider them as a threat at that point. And being equipped with more highly advanced, power engines, they left their pursuers behind them and was already approaching the northeastern grid by the time the guards finally cleared the shield.

So fast, it all happened in the blink of an eye. But Ghan was ready for the disorienting speed this time. He quickly pulled up a diagram of the photon cannons and located the nearest one. "They're blind on the top," he said to his crew. "If we attack from above, they'll never see us coming...."

CHAPTER
SEVEN

"JACK!" FORD'S VOICE was filled with excitement as it came through his intercom. "Jack, are you there?"

"Yeah," he replied, not wanting to engage in too long of a conversation, lest he become too distracted while scouring the distant hills for the slightest glint of light. "Where are you?"

"We're right above you, Jack."

"What? You're kidding."

"We're here to destroy the photon cannons," Semhek said. "They can't fire on us if we're right on top of them. And as you can see, they blow quite easily." As a show of testament to support the Tekwhaan's claim, two more explosions suddenly erupted to the south, and then to the east somewhere behind him.

"How'd you do that? Voch's ship is destroyed. It can't fire on anything."

"For starters we're not on Voch's ship. We're on Jherilon. And as it turns out, they're all Jherilon––"

"Hold on!" Jack yelled, as another flash sent a vaporizing beam in his direction. He made a sharp left to avoid the assault.

"How'd you do that?"

"Do what?"

319

"You just dodged that cannon blast."

"They're slow. Not designed to defeat the human eye."

"So that's how you survived this long."

"...Yeah...." Jack said, after dodging another blast. "How about finishing off the rest of those cannons, so I can destroy this tower."

"Not so fast."

"What? Why?"

"There's a squadron Seezhukan fighters heading your way. And it looks like half of a dozen planetary guard are trying to intercept you from the west."

"The same ones from Vermilion. They're trying to stop me."

"We're on our way."

———•———

"I need one other escort to engage the Seezhukans on Vermilion," said Semhek, to Jherilon. "And have the last remaining fighter locate and destroy the rest of those photon cannons. Then we'll need a dozen more fighters to reinforce us. The planetary guard are crawling all over this moon; it's only a matter of time till they get here."

"Message sent," said Jherilon. "Reinforcements are on the way."

"How're they doing up there, by the way?" Semhek asked.

"More than half of the planetary guard have been eliminated. Their defeat is inevitable."

"That's good to know.... Let's see if we can get behind those old fighters."

"Once we lower our latitude, we'll put ourselves in direct range of the photon cannons," Jherilon warned.

"But Jack said they're slow. Can you detect the precise moment before the cannons start firing?"

"I think I can. Their photon emissions are significantly high. If I recalibrate my sensors, I can most likely pick up on their initial charge before firing."

"Okay. Do that. But let's not waste anymore time."

"It's done," said Jherilon, as he redirected the two fighters down toward Vermilion city.

"We should start at the construction sites," Zubkov suggested. "Destroy everything."

"We have to deal with the Seezhukans first," Semhek replied. "Swoop down from the east and cut them off, before they could fire on Jack. His ship is not protected by the same impenetrable shield; one hit and he'll down."

Through the starboard window, an orange ball of flame erupted on an eastward mountain-top, and informed them that Jherilon's fighter was effectively doing his job. But not long after that however, they could feel their own ship lurching upward in the air as a huge photon laser went shooting by below them. The intensity of the beam filled the bridge with a bright light for a few seconds then faded.

"We're now within the photon cannons' range," Jherilon explained, before either of them could ask what the hell happened. "We'll be fired upon from time to time."

"Just don't take us too far off course," Semhek said. "We're approaching the Seezhukans now. Four fighters in all."

Before Semhek could give the command, Jherilon was force to dodge another blast by swerving left. But he quickly righted his course and fell right in behind the Seezhukans. Both Jherilons converged on the fighters, firing deadly plasma into the rear engines and climbing back up into the sky before getting vaporized by a beam that was shot a fraction of a second too late.

———●———

"The quantum reflect is now within range," Jherilon informed Jack.

He didn't need the calculations of a highly advanced robot to tell him that, however. He could see the tall tower coming up on them in plain sight. All he required now, was time. "Okay, get your targets on it. Let's see if we could destroy this thing in one shot."

"There're fighters approaching from behind."

"Let's see 'em on the radar."

Four holographic blips appeared in mid-air, and was closing in on them fast. The fighters were built for speed; more so then the planetary guard. He couldn't out-run them. "Shit! Do we have a lock on the reflector yet?"

"No. There's still too many structures in the way."

"Then bring us up higher. We're running out of time."

"The cannons will find us." Jherilon warned.

"Just do it."

The ship began to rise. "The quantum reflector was now in plain sight."

"The Seezhukans have a lock on us."

"Get a lock on the reflector and fire when ready," Jack knew it could be his only——and perhaps final——chance of destroying the Viceroy, even if it meant that he too might be killed in the process. It was a chance that he had to take.

But then one by one, the blips on the radar vanished. And for a brief moment, Jack thought it was a glitch.

"The Seezhukan fighters have been destroyed," Jherilon suddenly said.

"There's no one on your tail now, Jack," came Semhek's squeaky voice through his implant.

"Yeah," Jack began, half-jokingly. "It took you long enough. Better watch out for those cannons."

"Jherilon got it all covered. And I think he just might be quicker than your human eye."

"Not even close."

"Just hurry up and kill the Viceroy. This place is starting to wear me out."

"Soon as you get out of my head...." When Semhek didn't reply, he turned back to address Jherilon. "Are we locked?"

"Target's locked," Jherilon affirmed.

"Okay then, f——" Before he could get the word out, a flash caught his eye in the distance and he was forced to take cover. "Duck!"

The ship dipped just in time as the beam whooshed by overhead.

"Get us back on course."

The ship rose as another flash came. But this one was different. It was brighter. Brighter because the cannon had already fired its weapon. Not on Jack, but on the two fighters behind him. the two fighters who had more than likely jumped out of the way; he was just unfortunate enough to rise up into the crossfire. There was nothing left to do. It was late to do anything else. Too late to think. Too late to move out of the way. He only had time left for one more thing. "Fire! Fire! Fire!!!" He began shouting frantically, as the intense light from the cannon's vaporizing beam began to blind him.

———●———

Everything went black at some point. He couldn't remember exactly when, or how. But he do recall giving up. When he realized he couldn't avoid the photon blast. He just let it all go. Fuck it! At least he wouldn't have to suffer. Probably wouldn't stay awake to feel the first singe on his skin. It was a good way to die. Yeah. To die with no pain. Lights out! Just like that! Yeah. He was okay with that. He accepted it. He wanted it.... Why not?

Then the white light filled his eyes; covered his whole vision. Even when he blinked, everything was still white.

Then all sound faded; not even the sound of his own breath. Dead silence. White vision. Was he dead? No, He could still feel motion under his feet. Jherilon was still flying. The low vibration of his grav-boots clinging to the floor still thrummed through the soles of his feet. And that's probably when the whiteness in his eyes began to dissolve, like frost on a warm glass, giving way to complete and total darkness.

"What's happening?"

"We're crossing some kind of dimensional threshold," Jherilon replied.

"But didn't we cross a dimensional threshold to get to Idinor? The transition was so instantaneous, we weren't even aware that we had entered another dimension. Why the sudden change? Why's it so dark?"

"It has something to do with the quantum reflector. It was the only thing keeping the portals open, bridging the gap between the two dimensions. But when I destroyed the reflector, the portals collapsed and the gap returned. Our dimensional tethers are all that's pulling us back out of the Dark Void."

The mentioning of the quantum reflector's destruction (along with the Viceroy) brought some relief to Jack's mind. But not a whole lot. In truth, they did succeed in their mission, but now they were trapped in what appeared to be the **real** Dark Void. And the thought of starving to death for all eternity didn't sit too well with him at all. "So how long do you think we have to stay in this place?"

"It all depends."

"Depends on what?"

"On how fast we're traveling through the threshold. And that could be anytime between now and a thousand years."

Jack couldn't help but laugh at Jherilon's assessment. Between now and a thousand years: he said it so casual. As if a thousand years would go by over-night. He couldn't see the problem with traveling through the Dark Void for that long. And how could he? With a plasma generator to keep his lights burning for eons, a thousand years was nothing but a long night's sleep.

"That was one hell of a shot, by the way," Jack said, choosing to change the subject, instead of discussing the physics of interdimensional travel. He even sat down to lay his back flat on the floor. The rest felt good.

"Thank you, Jack."

"I thought we were dead for sure."

"We were locked with the target as I regained my former altitude. Unfortunately, we were also on a head-on collision with a photon blast."

"But you got it off in time, though."

"I did."

Jack thought he sensed a bit of pride in that last response, but he didn't bother to comment on it. And why should he? After all, it was he who gave that command. It meant nothing now, though. The quantum reflector was destroyed, the Bhoolvyn Sector (he hoped) was safe, and the Dark Void...well.. was still the Dark Void, considering all the thick darkness that surrounded them now.

But at least he felt good, laying there on the floor of his ship. Nothing but blackness and silence. Besides, he had Jherilon to keep his company for all eternity. It shouldn't be too bad....

He hadn't realized that the ship was still operating on a twenty-five percent outer visual, until he followed a thin streak of light whizzing over the hull. It's all in my head, he thought. Probably some left-over remnants from when the rays of photon that fried his retinas.

But then another streak went by. And another and another, until whole groups and clusters of stars began to streak by overhead.

Excited, he scrambled back up to his feet, and his heart jumped when he saw a distant planet directly ahead. A huge yellow star peaked out shyly from behind its north pole, giving the planet's ozone layer a murky blue haze. "Where are we?" he asked, looking all about to see if he could see any other ships in the area.

"On the outer rims of the 2nd quadrant, near the Bhoolvyn Sector. It's where the dimensional portal once stood."

"And what of the Bhoolvyn?"

"On the other side of the rim in 3rd quadrant."

"So we did it, then."

"We did."

Just then, one of Jherilon's fighters suddenly popped up on the radar. Then more, and more, until the whole division (or what was left of it) came flying into view.

"Jack!" came Semhek's shrill voice through Jack implant. Apparently, they must've experienced the same dark dilemma through the dimensional threshold. "Jack! Where are you?"

"I'm here."

Semhek sighed his relief. "We've made it back to our own dimension then."

"Yeah, I think so."

"Good. We should get back our quadrant immediately. We are behind enemy lines, and the Seezhukans will be showing up here at any time."

"I don't think so," Jack said.

"And why's that?"

"Because," Jack began, easing his self back down on the floor to feel that good rest and relaxation on his body again. "According to the signature of our ships, we are Seezhukan. And even if they do show up, I have a planetary guard that hasn't seen this dimension in centuries. I could probably destroy a whole fleet with these hyper-bombs...."

END.

Printed in the United States
by Baker & Taylor Publisher Services